VAMPIRES
of
EL NORTE

ALSO BY ISABEL CAÑAS

The Hacienda

VAMPIRES

of

EL NORTE

Isabel Cañas

Berkley
New York

BERKLEY
An imprint of Penguin Random House LLC
penguinrandomhouse.com

Copyright © 2023 by Isabel Cañas

Library of Congress Cataloging-in-Publication Data

Names: Cañas, Isabel, author.
Title: Vampires of El Norte / Isabel Cañas.
Description: New York: Berkley, [2023]
Identifiers: LCCN 2023013940 (print) | LCCN 2023013941 (ebook) |
ISBN 9780593436721 (hardcover) | ISBN 9780593436745 (ebook)
Subjects: LCSH: Vampires—Fiction. | Mexico—History—1821-1861—Fiction. |
LCGFT: Vampire fiction. | Gothic fiction. | Historical fiction. | Novels.
Classification: LCC PS3603.A533 V36 2023 (print) |
LCC PS3603.A533 (ebook) | DDC 813/.6—dc23/20230324
LC record available at https://lccn.loc.gov/2023013940
LC ebook record available at https://lccn.loc.gov/2023013941

Printed in the United States of America
1st Printing

Title page art: Desert sky © Charles T. Peden / Shutterstock
Book design by Alison Cnockaert

For my sisters, who taught me how to tell stories

Duérmete, niño,
Duérmete ya,
Que viene el Coco
Y te comerá

1

~~~

NENA

Octubre 1837

IT WAS OFTEN said that a strange kind of magic ran in the
waters of Rancho Los Ojuelos, the kind that made the Spanish ex-
plorer Cabeza de Vaca go mad, the kind that made mustangs swift
and the land rich. Nena knew, even as a child, that *magic* was a turn
of phrase. A way that adults talked about bounty and blessings:
with reverence, and perhaps a bit of fear, for when you had much,
you never knew how much of it could be lost.

She and Néstor were thirteen that year. She knew that magic,
in as many words, was not real. But as summer's heat stretched thin
and reached into fall, there was something she sensed whenever she
set her palms to the soil of the herb garden behind la casa mayor or
turned her face to the twilight-bruised sky. A strangeness. A ripple
of unease. An understanding, though timid at first, that perhaps
there was some truth to the stories of blood-hungry beasts and river
ghosts that the abuelas on the rancho spun to keep children close
to home after sunset. A sense that there was a reason to watch one's
back when shadows grew long.

Perhaps *magic* was the wrong word altogether.

For what Nena and Néstor found that night was monstrous.

FOR THE SECOND time that week, Nena slipped out from under her blankets, stone floor cool beneath her bare feet. She had waited for hours, sleepless, her mind racing as she counted the heavy breaths of her younger sister and cousins. At last it was time. The moon hung full outside the bedroom's single window, heavy as a bag of coins. By its light, she snatched an already dirty dress and slipped it over her head. It had a muddied hem; the plans she and Néstor had would make it dirtier still. He would already be waiting for her by the anacahuita trees, a shovel in hand. Ready to dig. Ready to test the last of the fireside stories that they still believed.

Of all of Néstor's abuela's stories, the tale of the Spanish count's buried silver paled in comparison to that of El Cuco, cloaked and carrying a child's severed head in the crook of his arm. When the children of the rancho settled around Abuela's feet in a crescent of devout supplicants, they begged for La Llorona's wails or the long talons of La Lechuza, not the tale of a well-heeled Spaniard perishing of exhaustion in the chaparral. Nena no longer feared boogeymen or ghosts snatching at her plaits when rain lashed the rancho and lightning fractured the broad, black sky. In the last year, Tejas had been ripped out of México, leaving a gaping wound in its wake. She had learned that there were real monsters to be mindful of now.

Which was why the tale of buried silver beckoned her. Its promise was a coin with two gleaming sides. The first: protection for the rancho at a time when its safety hung in the balance.

The second: a life of her choosing.

After the events of the last week, she knew she would not be at ease until she had both. Until she felt certainty about her future as firmly as cold metal in the palm of her hand.

When she pushed the bedroom door, it gave a mournful, arthritic creak. She froze, heart drumming in her ears. If Mamá woke and found her now, she would receive a sharp slap and be sent back to her room; the next morning would open with a lecture on how inappropriate it was for a young woman of her age to be sneaking into the night.

But no one stirred. Not in the girls' bedroom, nor in any of the other rooms of la casa mayor. Holding her breath, she crept across the great room to the door. Slipped on her boots with practiced silence, then tiptoed onto the patio.

Night slipped over her warm skin like stepping into cool water, sending a pleasant shudder over her shoulders. October days were hot, but when the sun set, autumn announced itself with a nip in the air, its smell piney and crisp with the promise of change.

Beyond the kitchen vegetable garden grew a copse of anacahuita trees. In the moonlight, their trunks gleamed silver with secrets. Néstor's slim shadow waited for her there, leaning casually against the trunk of the largest tree. The boy who had kept step with her, as close as her own shadow, since they first met five years ago.

Nena hiked up her skirts and ran toward him.

He straightened at her approach. "There you are."

His voice was like coming home. It loosened the unease that had curled in her chest all week.

"Sorry I'm late." The words hitched as she caught her breath.

"I heard about the Anglos," said Néstor softly.

She searched for his eyes in the dark. Had to tilt her chin up a bit more than usual to do so. It seemed as if every time he came back from three or four days in the chaparral with the other vaqueros, he was half a hand taller. His voice was changing too. Sometimes it was ragged like torn cloth; other times it shifted and creaked like an oak in a playful breeze. But its tone was as it always had been: a question. An invitation. A door she could either open or shut.

That was the way it was with Néstor. If she chose to barrel through the door and pour out her thoughts like a torrent, he would listen. If she kept the door shut, he would ask no further questions.

Three days ago, when Néstor was in the chaparral, bearded strangers had appeared on Rancho Los Ojuelos seeking its patrón. Vaqueros brought them to la casa mayor, the great central house of the rancho, to speak to Nena's papá, Don Feliciano Serrano Narváez. Nena had peered around the corner that separated la casa mayor's outdoor kitchen from the patio, where the family dined and Papá received guests. The strangers were lean men, road-hardened and parched as strips of beef left out to dry into acecina. When they removed their hats, they revealed high points of faces reddened by wind and sun and pale, hungry eyes.

Nena's mouth went dry when she realized they were Anglos. From the east, they said, their Spanish ripped and creased in all the wrong places. They had moved through Tejas and come farther south, seeking land. Did the patrón know of any for sale? Was he interested in selling any of his cattle?

It was like seeing El Cuco materialize before la casa mayor to ask after something as ordinary as horses for sale, one clawed hand caressing the severed head he always carried. These were the creatures of tall tales and nightmares come to life and walking in broad daylight.

Papá had kept the conversation brief, barely granting the strangers the courtesy of the shade of the patio. *No*, he said to all their questions. Firmly. Politely. No, and no again.

But as he watched their retreating backs, his black mustache twitched. Nena watched as he shifted his weight and clasped his hands behind his back, fidgeting with the signet ring he wore on his left hand. Apprehension circled over his shoulders like vultures. It spread to Nena. It spread to the rest of the rancho.

And so, the evening after the Anglos had appeared and left, she eavesdropped, ear pressed against her wooden bedroom door, straining to make out the irregular rise and fall of argumentative voices in la casa mayor. The women of the family had retreated from la sala as the men gathered: Papá; Nena's elder brother, Félix; and Mamá's own brothers, the three de León uncles who also lived on the rancho. Everyone had heard of increases in cattle theft. Of good men—rancheros, even—vanishing in the night, leaving widows and unguarded land in their wake. Stories slinked like snakes through the ranchos of las Villas del Norte, the five great towns that hugged the lazy bends of Río Bravo, rattling their warnings from house to house. Had not some of Papá's own vaqueros come to Los Ojuelos after fleeing the bloody seizure of the rancho where they used to live, the Dos Cruces land just south of San Antonio de Béxar?

Everyone knew the appearance of a few Anglos was the harbinger of worse to come.

Worse still, Nena thought, was the manner in which everyone agreed to protect Los Ojuelos.

"It's time for Félix to marry," an uncle's voice cut in. "Marriage is the surest way to an alliance with a strong hacienda."

Félix did not reply. She yearned to know what he was thinking. She would be horrified, or filled with rage, if Mamá's brothers talked about her future so callously.

"Exactly!" Another voice rang with agreement. "Family defends family. If I had daughters, I would give them gladly." That would be Tío Julián, who had no children. "What of Magdalena? Surely she's old enough now."

At the sound of her full name, Nena's heart dropped through her stomach.

When Félix raised his voice and pointed out that it would be six or seven years until it was appropriate for Nena to marry, the men began to argue about which rancho to marry her off to when the time came. Which had the most sons, or the ones who showed the most promise? Which had the strongest vaqueros, the most cattle, the most land?

Names slipped through the crack of light that lined the underside of the door, twining around Nena's ankles, ready to drag her away from Los Ojuelos and her family. Away from Néstor. She could not let that happen. She *would* not.

But if Papá insisted, if Papá shouted the way the tíos were shouting now . . . she would freeze like a rabbit spotted by hunters.

And what would happen then?

If she told Néstor about that night, he would listen. He was the only other speaker of their shared, silent language, the only person on the rancho who listened to more than her voice: he read her shifts in energy, her expression, the way she held her weight. She loved him fiercely for it.

Now, he sensed her unease. He reached into the dark and took her hand. "Was your mamá mad about something?"

His words touched a familiar ache, sore as a day-old bruise.

If Mamá was angry with Nena, it was going to be about Néstor.

She and Néstor had met when they were eight, when Néstor first came to Los Ojuelos with his family. Within days they were a matched set, inseparable as a pair of old boots as they fetched water, fed the chickens, and watched the sheep with the old shepherd Tío Macario in the chaparral. For years, no one noticed or cared—Nena losing herself in the pack of the rancho's children meant she was out of Mamá's hair as she cared for the baby, Javiera, and so Nena did as she pleased.

But lately, Néstor had grown taller. He began to work with the other vaqueros, heading into the chaparral for days at a time. As

Nena outgrew dresses and inherited some of Mamá's, the tías began to exchange whispers about her attachment to Néstor. Overnight, their time together was halved by his work, then halved again by Mamá and her obsession with propriety and honor. First, Mamá insisted that Nena was too old to be playing with the peones' children barefoot in the courtyard; then, when her first blood came last month, Mamá forbade her outright to be seen alone with a young man. Much less the son of a vaquero.

During the day, Nena obeyed. Mamá and Papá's love was a fragile thing. Lately, she felt that if she moved too quickly, it might snap.

She hated it. Growing older felt like holding water in cupped hands; the harder she pressed her fingers together to keep life with Néstor the way it used to be in her grasp, the faster it slipped away. So she held Néstor's hand tightly. With him, there was no Papá or Mamá, no work or tías casting sharp glances at how she behaved. There never had been. Tonight, the moon was high, the night cloudless; they were blissfully alone, their only company a corona of stars that winked like flint.

If they found Spanish silver, perhaps they could keep it that way forever. With that money, Papá could hire double the vaqueros he currently had. Los Ojuelos would be safe. There would be no reason to marry Nena away to a stronger rancho or hacienda, and she could live her life as she pleased. Marry whom she pleased.

But if they failed? Once Papá had decided which path was the best to ensure the safety of the rancho, there was no changing his mind. Félix was already engaged to the daughter of a powerful hacendado. Nena had no desire to think about what lay in her own future, nor did she want to talk with someone like Néstor about marrying a stranger.

"I'm fine," she said. "Let's go find some silver."

In the moonlight, Néstor's grin was like mother-of-pearl, bright and eager.

Nena knew the story from Abuela, but recently, Néstor had heard another version of the tale. It was one of his first nights in the chaparral, and the vaqueros gathered with a group of itinerant carreteros, merchants who left the distant capital and crisscrossed México with their ox carts to the ranchos north of Río Bravo. They came bearing cotton and silver and china, yes, but when vaqueros encountered them on their curving paths north to las Villas del Norte, stories were the currency of the chaparral.

Néstor had listened in reverent silence to the tales of a Spanish count who fled north with his wealth during the war against the crown, thinking he could make a new life for himself in El Norte. But he was not strong, not like the carreteros and vaqueros and the Indios who made the broad, arid wilds of the north their home. The burden of his silver was too great; unless he lightened his load, he knew he would stumble and become food for coyotes and vultures. He chose a secret place to bury his treasure, blessed it, and carried on. Legend said he died in the chaparral anyway.

That was where Abuela's version of the story ended. But the carreteros spun the story further: if you saw a winking orb of light deep in the chaparral at night, they said, it hovered over the place where the Spaniard buried his treasure.

When the vaqueros returned to the rancho, Néstor came rushing to meet Nena in the anacahuita grove before evening vespers, his eyes alight with a look she knew well: he had a secret, and he was dying to share it with her.

"There are lights by the springs at night," Néstor whispered. "I've seen them. Casimiro didn't believe me, but I swear I saw them before dawn."

"Mamá once said that my abuelo told stories of Spaniards passing through Los Ojuelos, years ago," Nena had said. "Maybe it was them."

So tonight, they passed the smaller, wooden jacal houses of the vaqueros and other workers and slipped through the gate of the high fence around the central grounds of the rancho. Néstor carried a shovel in one hand; Nena had left a second for herself near the springs during the siesta, when no one would notice.

"I wonder if those Anglos were here because they were looking for it," Nena mused.

"They'd better not be," Néstor said, voice dark.

Anglos were why Néstor, his uncle Bernabé, his cousin Casimiro, and his abuela had come to Los Ojuelos five years ago: they shot the ranchero for whom Néstor's papá worked to steal the land and the cattle. Over the course of long afternoons, while watching the sheep with Tío Macario, Néstor had told her what it was like to see his home in flames. It was as if the whole world—everything he had ever thought of as safe and permanent—were turning to ashes. How he saw his own father's body bleeding in the corral, shot by Anglos.

How in the midst of the chaos, Bernabé packed what few things he could carry, took Abuela and the boys, and fled. How every day since then, he had felt like a burden to his uncle. An outsider in his own family. This was why he wanted his own rancho, Nena knew: to belong. To never be powerless again.

"Did they say where they were going after your papá told them no?" Néstor asked. "They didn't mention the porción by the river, did they?"

"No," Nena said. When the Anglos left, she fixated on Papá, trying to gauge how severe the threat they posed was based on his reaction. If the Anglos spoke among themselves as they retreated, she did not hear them. She wouldn't have been able to understand them anyway. But why was Néstor asking after the unoccupied bit of land south of Los Ojuelos, farther along the river? "Why?"

They walked in silence for a few steps. "Because that's the land I want to buy," he said at last.

He had often mentioned wanting to become a ranchero, to build his own casa de sillar, but for some reason, Nena had never connected that with him no longer living on Los Ojuelos. Now that he said it aloud, it was painfully obvious. Was he planning to leave all this time?

"You'd leave me?" She felt the panicked pitch of her voice before she heard it.

"I won't. Never." He gave her hand a reassuring squeeze. "I'll still live on Los Ojuelos while I'm building the house. It'll take time, lots of time," he said. "Then when it's finished, you can visit every day. Maybe . . ." he added, then his words quickened, as if pausing meant what he intended to say would be swallowed by the night. "Maybe, if you wanted, you could even live there too. With me. We could get married. Or something like that."

Hand in hand with Néstor, she felt as if each step they took led them closer to a future that *she* wanted, one she caught in glimpses of color and smell like a half-remembered dream: cutting rosemary and lavender in her own garden like Néstor's abuela. Holding hands with Néstor unabashedly, with no Mamá watching her every move, her disciplining hand waiting to bend Nena to the strict ways of honorable womanhood. Life would be as simple as it was when they watched the sheep together with Tío Macario, dozing in the heat of the siesta. Life would be perfect.

Knowing that he wanted the same thing she did filled her chest with a pleasant, tingling warmth. It spread over her cheeks too, drawing gently at the corners of her mouth.

"Or something like that," she said, squeezing his hand back.

The slope of the path curved downward now as they followed the well-worn trail to the springs. It was the same trail Nena walked every morning with her cousins to collect water and bring it to la casa mayor. Habit guided her around every rock and root.

But something felt off.

The happy warmth in her chest faded as she scoured the rocky path before them, willing her eyes to peel away shadows. As they grew closer to the springs, the distant cheeps of bats and hooting of a screech owl faded away. It was as if even the crickets fell silent in anticipation, or fear; as if the breeze caught its voice in its throat, apprehensive of the way the night thickened.

One last turn of the path, and they reached the twin springs, the eyes that gave Los Ojuelos its name. Moonlight filtered through the laurel trees that curved over the water; doused by its silvery touch, the trees' roots plunged into the rippling water. They looked like curving, skeletal fingers gripping the edges of the pool and the stream that led south.

Her heart jumped as Néstor stopped them short. The whites of his eyes glinted with surprise as he gestured sharply with his chin before them. *Look.*

A wink of light reflected off the surface of the springs. Its color was not that of moonlight. It was like an orange from Reynosa— no, it was like a grapefruit, perfectly round as a full moon, heavy with a strange, warm light.

Néstor stepped forward.

Nena hesitated.

She had believed Néstor when he told her the carreteros' version of the legend, the lights in the night that marked the place where treasure had been buried. But she had not anticipated feeling so uneasy when they found it. The world felt twisted in the way of dreaming; needles skittered up her arms and down the back of her neck.

She wanted to tell him to stop. The air hummed with the prickling tension of a gathering storm, and like facing down a storm, she felt a powerful, overwhelming need to find shelter. To hide.

But from what? Nena knew this land like she knew every inch of the square rooms of la casa mayor or the lines of her siblings' faces. There shouldn't have been any reason to feel this uneasy, but she did. She felt as if the darkness were watching them, as if it had a mind and a will, as if it *wanted* them to draw closer.

She should have told him that she was frightened—silver or no, he would have stopped then. Or would he?

Néstor released her hand and walked forward, his jaw set. If he felt the same sudden unease she did, he gave no hint of it. He gripped the shovel with determined intention.

"I think . . ." *I think we should go back* was what rose to her lips, but at that moment, her words were cut off by Néstor's shovel striking the gravelly earth with a metallic sound.

The orange light vanished.

Nena let out a cry of surprise as darkness bloomed around them. Was it a trick of the night, or were the shadows lengthening?

No, it was a figure. It was a *creature*.

It darted forward, fast as a cougar, cutting between Néstor's turned back and Nena. Fear flushed her limbs as she stumbled backward, as the creature reared up on hind legs. It towered over her, as tall as Papá, perhaps taller, with limbs as long as a spider's.

She had to get away, but her limbs moved too slowly. She turned; her boot caught on a root, sending her sprawling. Her breath shattered out of her. She gasped, coughing, curling into a tight ball on the ground. Black spots pocked her vision, growing and darkening.

"Néstor!" she cried, grasping and failing to push herself up. He had to get to safety. *She* had to run. She could still get away, if she could only force herself upright.

A crunch of gravel by her right ear, then her left, as the creature's feet—or were those hands?—struck the ground on either side of her head. Its hot breath washed over her face as its head swung low, thick with the odor of carrion.

A flash of teeth in the darkness.

Fear was sour in her sweat, in her breath, in the pale, wordless ringing in her ears as teeth as sharp as knives sank into her neck.

2

⤜⤛⤚⤙

NÉSTOR

AT THE SOUND of Nena's sharp intake of breath, Néstor straightened. She only ever made that sound when she was hurt—was she all right? Was something wrong?

When he turned to ask her what was the matter, a dark form bolted forward from the thick brush alongside the stream.

Toward Nena.

He could not see if it had four legs, or two; now it lunged high, now it dived low on all fours. All he knew was that it was a threat to Nena, that it was racing toward her, and that he had to get between her and *it*. He wrenched his shovel out of the ground and adjusted his grip on it, so that he held it like a machete, and when he was about to run forward, he heard his name.

"Néstor!" Nena's cry was weak and breathless; it was followed by the sound of a body striking the earth. The dark form was upon her, holding her to the ground.

A wet sound, like the butchering of a hog, sent fear coursing through Néstor's gut.

Nena was his home. The one thing on earth more precious to him than his own life. Whatever that creature was, it did not matter— the only thing that mattered was getting it away from her.

He ran forward, shovel held aloft. When he was upon the dark form, he raised the shovel higher and threw his weight into bringing the shovel down.

The creature whirled on him.

This was not a trick of the darkness. This was a bent-legged beast the likes of which he had never seen before: its humanlike head was a mouth full of teeth; its face was wrinkled and hairless and mottled gray, gray like the rest of its hide. There were two slits where a nose might be. He couldn't see its eyes in the dark, but there was no doubt in his mind that it was *looking* at him as an aggressive hiss came from its lipless maw of teeth.

The hiss nearly froze him. It was sharper than a rattler's, as angry as a cougar's. A feral part of him, deep and black and curled at the back of his mind, knew that this was a predator, and he was prey.

Nena was its prey.

Nena was down and trapped beneath it. Every part of his being wanted to run, but he would not, not without her.

He raised the shovel again.

His world narrowed to a single purpose: get to Nena. Get to Nena and get away.

But first he had to draw the beast away from her. He could drive it back, or tempt and taunt it and somehow get between its fangs and Nena.

Through the dark, if he squinted, he could see Nena's form, prone on the ground, the beast's forelegs pinning her arms down.

If he did not act now, there might not be any Nena left to save.

He rushed forward, shovel held high, and brought it down against the back of the beast as hard as he could.

"Get back!" he roared, but his voice cracked with fear. It was thin—too thin—against the night, against the possibility that unless he fought harder, he might lose his home again. He raised the shovel and struck once more, pouring all of his fear into his arms. He had to get to Nena.

With a strangled cry, the beast rose. It lifted its forelegs off Nena and turned to Néstor.

Nena was free.

"Run!" he cried. His next words died in his throat, choked by the smell of rotting flesh. His gut clenched with nausea; he gripped his shovel harder as the monster bore down on him.

Perhaps his eyes had adjusted to the darkness; perhaps he had moved into a part of the clearing by the springs where the moonlight was stronger, but he could see the thing's face clearly now.

It had no eyes.

Skin stretched over its hollow eye sockets, thin as corn husk. Its bat nostrils flared; it bared its teeth at him, its mouth slick with something wet, something that shone black and oily. He had never seen a creature like this, not in his worst nightmares. Run, he had to *run*—

No. Nena had not risen. Nena needed more time.

He planted his feet and gripped the shovel tighter. He did not run, not even as the beast charged him like a bull, not even as the pounding of his pulse in his skull drowned out the sounds of claws scraping the pebbly earth.

Let your gut guide you, Casimiro always said. *When you're bringing down a bull, your gut knows you could die. Your gut wants to live. Shut up and listen to it.*

His world narrowed to that sightless, blood-slicked face. To the stench of carrion. To his hands gripping the shovel.

He waited a heartbeat longer than his head wanted to. Then he brought the shovel down toward the beast's neck with all his might.

It sank like a cleaver into meat, slicing sinew, crushing bone.

The beast fell, dragging the shovel down with it. Néstor fell to his knees, still holding the handle, bracing for a spray of foul, hot blood. He had seen cattle being butchered. He knew this had to be the same.

The monster twitched, and was still.

No blood came.

With a long, low hiss, the beast's body deflated like an empty waterskin; within moments, it had curled in on itself like kindling in a fire, and like kindling, was reduced to ash.

Néstor's shovel lay on the ground in a pile of soot.

He sucked in a long gulp of air. That was stranger than any nightmare, worse than any of Abuela's stories. What was it?

It didn't matter. What mattered was that it was dead, as far as he could tell, and could no longer harm Nena.

"Nena?" It came out strangled.

She was a heap of skirts and limbs, prone on the ground. He could not tell if she had moved after he drew the beast away. That was not good. Fear twined tight in his chest; he rose and scrambled forward to her side.

Her face was serene, as if she were sleeping, with wisps of her hair stuck to the sweat on her forehead and cheeks.

But her neck . . .

There was a place between her shoulder and neck where he used to rest his head during long summer siestas watching the sheep. There, strands of her hair and the neckline of her dress tickled his cheek as he rose and fell with her steady breath. There, he would smell *her*: soap and a tickle of kitchen smoke. Dried herbs. Sunshine. The impossibly sweet, impossibly soft scent of her skin, the one smell on earth he would drown in if he could.

That place was now a wound.

"Dios mío," he breathed.

Even in the dark, he could see it: a mauling, a butchering. When he gingerly brushed the wound's edge with his fingertips, they came away warm and wet. A metallic smell soured his mouth as he fumbled for his pocketknife and tore away strips of fabric from the bottom of his shirt. He pressed against the wound, his hands shaking.

"Nenita?"

He put one hand to her chest, below the neckline of her dress, where he would otherwise never have the courage or the shamelessness to touch. Should he feel a heartbeat? A pulse? How strong was a pulse supposed to be? He was too stupid to know what to do. Nena knew more than him. She was smarter than anyone he knew. What would she do, if their positions were reversed?

He tried to imagine her voice, tried to imagine her hale and breathing and alert.

We have to go back to the house, she would say. *Abuela will fix this.*

"You're right," he said, his voice cracking. "You're always right. That's why I love you."

He had never said that aloud before; he had never felt brave enough, especially not recently. Not when Doña Mercedes looked at him like he was manure on the sole of her boot, not when, with every passing day, Nena grew more beautiful and more like a lady of the rancho, more impossibly out of his reach.

His arms trembled as he arranged her limbs so that he could lift her. He had carried her before, but not in years; he grunted as he swung one arm over his shoulders and lifted her to her feet.

"You've gotta help me," he forced out. "On your feet."

But she was as limp as a lamb. Her feet would not catch her weight; her head lolled forward.

"Carajo." Néstor shifted his weight and reached his right arm under her knees, then lifted her like a baby. He swayed; caught his balance.

The air of the clearing by the springs had shifted. It grew less dense, even relaxed. One cricket cried out into the night, timidly at first, then others rose in chorus. The night had sensed that danger was gone.

But the farther Néstor walked, the closer he drew to la casa mayor, the more he grew tense with fear.

For Nena did not stir. Not when he told her how Abuela was going to fix everything, not when he told her how her mamá was going to be angry with him if she did not wake.

"Look at me," he whispered, voice catching on the uneven hitch of his breath. Then, louder: "Look at me."

The crickets sang on.

He had to force himself to keep moving, to grind through the pain of carrying her, to take sharp, raw breaths past the sob that was buried in his throat.

Because he knew that if he were to pause, if he were to listen to his gut, he would hear only one answer:

It was too late.

AT LAST HE was on the patio of la casa mayor, shaking with the effort of carrying Nena. He collapsed, cradling her head tenderly as his knees met the tipichil floor. Her wound had oozed blood over his shoulder, but the bleeding seemed to have slowed. *Please, let her be all right.* Perhaps he had always known how fragile a home she was. Perhaps he had grown complacent over the years. Now he knew better: one false move and he could lose her.

"Help." It was too weak, too soft. He lifted a hand and pounded on the door of la casa mayor. "Help!" He pounded again, until sounds of waking sleepers rose from inside. Confused voices; footsteps.

Don Feliciano filled the doorway, a candle held high in one hand, throwing his mustache and the lines of his face into sharp relief. Past him was Doña Mercedes in white, hovering like a ghost, and the shadow of Nena's brother, Félix, yanking a shirt over his head as he rushed into la sala.

For a moment, Don Feliciano peered into the dark, then his eyes fell to his feet, where Néstor and Nena were crumbled.

"Magdalena?" Néstor had never heard him speak so softly.

"Madre de Dios." Doña Mercedes was at his shoulder at the sound of their daughter's name. Her voice pitched high with surprise, with panic at the sight of Nena's prone form on the threshold.

She shoved Don Feliciano aside. Néstor stumbled back. He had never seen them act with so little composure; their fear threw oil on the fire of his.

A commotion of arms, of the candle being set down and others lit to fill the room with light. Nena was brought into the house and laid gently on the floor, Doña Mercedes kneeling at her side, repeating the Hail Mary with feverish urgency as she examined Nena's wound. Don Feliciano stood as if struck dumb; Félix kept lighting more candles.

They seemed to have forgotten Néstor was even there. He pushed himself up on aching legs and leaned against the doorway for support. As the son of a vaquero, he had never stepped foot inside la casa mayor. He would not now, not even as Félix brought the candles to Nena's side.

Her eyes were still closed. In the candlelight, her face was waxy. Still. Her lips were dark, almost blue.

Her wound glimmered red and raw. Blood streaked her chest and stained her dress. Red gleamed wet on the chain of her golden scapular.

Doña Mercedes leaned over her, ear pressed to her chest, still murmuring prayers.

Any moment now, Nena would open her eyes. She would look around, be surprised that she was home, be ashamed that she and Néstor had been caught. There would be punishment, yes. Don

Feliciano would surely come after him with a switch, and Doña Mercedes would scold Nena for her impropriety. They would lick their wounds and then, they would reunite beneath the anacahuita trees, another misadventure behind them.

But not *this*.

Not Don Feliciano standing dumb, the candle still in his fist, his face slack even as wax dripped onto the back of his hand. Not Félix growing increasingly agitated at Doña Mercedes's litanies.

"Is she breathing?" Félix asked. When Doña Mercedes did not respond, he reached out and held his fingertips over Nena's lips; then jerked his hand back as if he had been burned. "Mamá, say something."

Doña Mercedes did not lift her head. "My daughter is dead!"

Her wail was the wind on a cold winter night, pinning Néstor to the spot. He could not breathe. He was not a body leaning against the doorway anymore. He was a spirit looking down at Nena, at her blue lips, her blood-slicked scapular, her colorless face. He wanted her to rise, to move. He wanted to shake her until she cried out for him to stop.

But she was as still as a statue of a saint in a chapel. Still. Still.

This was his fault.

It had been his idea to look for silver tonight. His hand that drew them toward danger.

"Boy!" Don Feliciano's roar rose above Doña Mercedes's weeping.

Néstor jerked away from the doorframe, his exhausted body alight with fear. Don Feliciano's face had transformed, rage making it grotesque in the candlelight. Don Feliciano beat any boy who misbehaved on the rancho, Néstor included. Néstor knew that the patrón's anger was a blunt weapon, a thing to flinch away from. The full force of Don Feliciano faced him now: he pointed at Néstor with one powerful, trembling hand. In a moment, he would bear down on Néstor with all the rage of a charging bull. "*Boy.*"

Fear seized him and drove cold spurs into his side. He launched away from the doorframe, away from the flickering candlelight and the weeping, away from Nena, into the night.

He fled.

Away from la casa mayor, past all the jacales of the workers, past his own home. To the fence surrounding the rancho and through it. Arms pumping, legs flying, barely breathing, tears streaming from his eyes from the sheer force of his speed. From the burgeoning, dark guilt that built like a summer storm in his chest—swift and violent, all of a sudden too heavy for his body. Still he tore through the chaparral, thorns slashing his arms, stinging his cheeks, until its weight was too much. He fell forward on hands and knees, arms shaking, heaving, certain—for a fleeting second—that he would vomit, but no. It was weeping. It burst from him with the crack of a whip, then it was a torrent.

Nena.

Thoughts shattered and drifted through the storm.

This was his fault. The beast. The stench of carrion; the way it curled over Nena. The blood on its fangs and chin—Nena's blood. Nena's weight against him, limp and lifeless.

Nena.

DAWN. NÉSTOR LIFTED his head; a shard of pain drove through his skull. He winced. Every movement ached. Every limb was stiff.

He lifted his head.

He was in the chaparral. Clothes wrinkled, throat dry.

All he could see was Nena on the floor of la casa mayor, surrounded by flickering candles, wan and still. Blood gleaming raw in candlelight.

It was his fault.

Don Feliciano pointing at him, bellowing with rage.

He could not go back.

He rose on trembling limbs. The sun was still low on the horizon, and behind him.

He walked.

HE WALKED. WEST, for days. When he reached the river, north.

He never turned back.

NINE YEARS LATER

3

NÉSTOR

THESE DREAMS ALWAYS ended the same. Whatever had unspooled over the course of Néstor's sleep would tighten. Refocus. When the disorientation steadied, he was watching the sheep.

He lay on his back beneath the shade of the oaks, listening to crickets, the warmth of the siesta steeping the scene with softness. With the heavy, quiet certainty of dreaming, he knew he was not alone. He knew she was there.

If he was lucky, the warmth would keep his awareness dulled, and he would spend the rest of the night beneath the tree, until the horses' whinnies or the voices of other vaqueros roused him.

But if his awareness lifted, if he thought of *who* was with him, who lay next to him? If he focused his attention on that weight against his shoulder and how *real* it felt—or worse, if he tried to turn his head to look at her? That thought alone could wake him.

On worse nights, it poisoned the dream.

Tonight, as he looked up at the branches of the tree, tracing their splay against the blinding summer sky, awareness sent a ragged bolt of yearning through him.

She was there.

She was with him, as real as she had been in life. He wanted to see her. He wanted to see her face more than he wanted water on a hot afternoon, more than he wanted rest after weeks in the saddle.

He turned his head.

Before he saw her, the dream shifted. His movement drenched the dream with night, steering its course away from trees and sheep and crickets to a spring deep in the chaparral. To eerie, unnatural light glinting off the surface of the dark water and a shadowy form rising from four legs to two. To a voice screaming his name.

Néstor!

He sat up sharply, heart pounding the tender flesh of his throat, his eyes peeled open, his hands clutching thin sheets. Sheets. The texture of cotton against his clammy palms; the uneven firmness of a mattress. Air that tasted not of bare night but of being beneath a roof, of sleep and breathing caught within walls.

He pulled himself back from the terror of dreaming, hand over hand, winding the rope back to himself.

It was a dream. It was always a dream, when he heard that voice.

Néstor!

The coolness of morning wicked sweat away from his shoulders and brow. He shuddered.

Weight shifted on the mattress to his right. Celeste had her back to him. Thick black curls spilled over the pillow she curled into as she sighed and slept on.

Around the four-poster bed were furnishings finer than Néstor had seen anywhere but a few stolen glances inside la casa mayor of Los Ojuelos. He tallied them to ground himself. Silver candlesticks. A table of Nicaraguan cedar where Celeste cast expensive things carelessly: a hand mirror of polished silver; cosmetics; the black mantilla she had been wearing the afternoon before, on her way back from Mass to the Romero family's second house in the center of Laredo.

This was where Néstor generally stayed when cattle drives brought him south from El Paso del Norte. He had when Celeste's husband was alive too.

The shame in Néstor's gut pooled deeper. Perhaps because of the stray thought of Celeste's dead husband, perhaps because of how his habit of staying with Celeste continued without remorse. Perhaps because lately, and with unnerving frequency, he woke with terror alight in his skin.

Or perhaps it was because lately, whenever he slept next to a woman, he woke with someone else's voice in his ear.

Someone who was long dead.

He threw the sheet off. Planted feet on floorboards. He dressed with as much speed and silence as he could muster, keeping his eyes averted from the bed. He needed to be out of this house. Away from Celeste and the fine furnishings that reminded him so keenly of Los Ojuelos.

As a rule, he didn't vanish before Celeste woke as he might with other women. That was rude. It might imperil the possibility of future stays when he was next near Laredo or Rancho Buenavista, the land she had inherited from her late husband. Usually, he and Celeste slept late. They had coffee in bed. Néstor kept her talking about the business of running her rancho, learning all he could from her venting about finances, cattle rustlers, and her beef buyers in Cuba. If it was spring, there was branding to do, which brought Rancho Buenavista's herds close to Laredo and kept Néstor in the town's orbit for several weeks. It kept him in Celeste's bed for just as long.

Women took Néstor out of his own head. Celeste was more engaging to him than most—with her shrewd mind for business and interest in his questions about her rancho, it was not often when he was with her that he felt like conversations were hollow, that he was a shell.

But last night he did. Last night, awareness of his own emptiness writhed under his skin. He was a mask turned out to the world. A husk.

If Celeste noticed this change in him, it only made her conversation more animated, her kisses more determined. She was eager to rein him back to her. If she woke, this would continue, for she was not a woman accustomed to the word *no*.

But he could not stomach speaking to anyone. Not after waking like he had. Not after feeling so powerfully that *she* was there.

So he crept downstairs. He helped himself to some water and one of yesterday's breads from the open-air kitchen, then slipped away before any of the Romero household's servants woke.

Madrugada hung still and gray over the town. The moon was long set. The stars had paled, but the cool tinge of the sky said sunrise was an hour away yet. The air was spiced with dozens of kitchen fires. Somewhere in town, bakers were at work. After weeks of waking to the piney, cold sharpness of the chaparral, the smells of town were usually novel to him. Welcomed, even. Now, the sight of other buildings, tidily nestled next to one another like crows on a corral fence, made his skin itch.

His mare, Luna, had spent the night tethered with Celeste's favorites just to the side of the house. She raised her head in greeting, her velvety black ears pricked at the sound of Néstor's boots in the dirt. She shifted her weight. Let one cocked back hoof come to the earth with a stamp. When Néstor rubbed her forehead and murmured good morning, she exhaled in reply, her breath warm on his chest. A soft sound that was half greeting, half chastisement, as if to say *we're in town, why on earth are you awake this early?*

"Bad dreams, Lunita," he answered, planting a firm kiss on the sickle-shaped white star that gave the mare her name. Luna smelled like sleep and night and home. "You know how it is."

He curried and saddled her. Checked her hooves. Lost himself in the ritual of buckles and saddle blankets and packing his supplies. He kept his attention away from the house, from Celeste's expensive glass windows. He had grown too comfortable in Laredo lately, too comfortable with Celeste, and that was dangerous. He had been foolish enough to make his home another person once before. He would not do it again.

He mounted, put his back to town, and rode.

BY DAWN, HE found the outline of nine horses, the horns of their saddles like a small mountain range against the lightening horizon. A thread of smoke curled up from a fire; low, sleep-roughened voices rose as he approached. He had reached the encampment of Buenavista's vaqueros.

The pungent smell of the herds rode the breeze toward him; the cattle were not far. Good. That meant the caporal, the leader of this corrida of vaqueros, meant to leave today for Texian territory.

"Is that Duarte?" a voice called as Néstor dismounted.

"No," said another voice, the syllable long and incredulous. "I told him . . ." One figure rose, unfolding like a lean plume of smoke. Albert Fitz Cepeda—universally known as Beto Cepeda—cursed soundly as Néstor left Luna to gossip with the other horses. A chorus of the other vaqueros' laughter followed.

"Morning, Beto," Néstor said.

"The *fuck* are you doing here?" Beto held a tin mug of coffee; he glowered at Néstor over the rim as he took a long sip. "We're driving today."

"I know."

"I thought I told you to rest."

"I did."

Beto rolled his eyes. He alone among the other vaqueros—who were all Celeste's employees—knew where exactly Néstor stayed while he was in town.

"When you're as old as me you'll regret working the way you do," Beto grumbled. The so-called old man—twenty-seven to Néstor's twenty-two—smelled like his incurable tobacco habit. Mesquite wood smoke, cold night. A white curl of steam rose from the coffee as he offered the mug to Néstor. It was hot against his calluses.

For the first time that morning, Néstor felt like he had his feet on the ground. Like he was looking out his own eyes instead of being caught in cobwebs.

"And you'll regret the drinking. *God,*" Beto swore in English. "You still smell like it. Disgusting." Beto had taken Néstor under his wing six years ago after Néstor saved his life by roping a charging longhorn and bringing it to its knees in front of an unhorsed Beto. The vaqueros of the ranchos surrounding las Villas del Norte knew them as a matched working set, itinerant and as inseparable as brothers. They only rarely hired themselves out to separate drives, except when Beto was trying to teach Néstor the virtues of rest by planting him in a town and ordering him to stay at least a week. "Would it kill you to sleep in a bed for at least two nights in a row? By yourself, even?" he added in a lower voice.

Néstor shrugged, taking a sip of coffee as the other vaqueros broke camp, shoveling dirt on the fire and beginning to sing.

"Imagínalo," Beto continued his lecture. "Three square meals a day, fresh pan dulce every morning, meat that isn't salted leather? Maybe get your sinning ass to church, for once? Doesn't that sound appealing?"

Néstor handed the coffee back to Beto. "Not really."

"So are you with us or not, Duarte?" The caporal barked as he saddled his mare.

"With," Néstor called.

"Lord knows why," the caporal said dryly, casting Néstor a dubious look. "I will never understand why you would work yourself to death for a ranchero, chamaco."

"Because I'm going to be one of them soon," Néstor shot back, adding a wink as he said, "and if you're lucky, I'll *let* you work for me, old man."

Laughter rose from the vaqueros; Néstor's cockiness even drew a gruff laugh from the caporal.

Beto alone was unamused. He did not take the mug Néstor offered him. Under his breath, he asked, "You didn't quarrel with the widow, did you?"

Maybe if he let Beto think that were the case, he would stop asking. It was better to stop him now, before Beto got to the question he sometimes asked when he was trying to figure Néstor out. A question that reminded Néstor too much of places and people he only saw in dreams. It felt like a thumb pressed on a half-healed bruise, and he shied away from it.

What are you running from?

He wouldn't lie outright to Beto. He had tried in the past; it was never worth the effort. Beto saw right through him.

So instead, he said: "I need to work."

"Don't you always," Beto said. He slapped Néstor on the shoulder with a defeated sigh. "Come on, then. Won't hurt to have another English speaker on this drive. Finish that coffee and we ride."

DON'T YOU ALWAYS. This followed Néstor as the men mounted, as they followed the caporal's orders, divided into pairs, and began to collect the Buenavista herd.

Yes, he did. He needed to work hard, ride hard, sleep hard. It kept nightmares at bay. It kept a steady trickle of money flowing toward him, which he counted and saved with the sharp eye of a miser. Other vaqueros might laugh at him as he struggled to break the most aggressive mustangs, as he flew through the air and ended up with a mouthful of dirt. But he always brushed himself off and straightened his vest with a sharp, self-assured gesture. Spat out the dirt and set his hat back on his head with his chin held high. Let them laugh. *He* was the one whom wealthy rancheros paid lavishly for his trouble, for downing and castrating the most dangerous longhorns.

Don't you always. He did. Porque así fue la suerte. Nothing worth wanting came easy; nothing worth wanting was ever given to men of dust and sweat.

And Néstor *wanted*. He wanted land. But land was not simply granted to men like him, vaqueros who were sons of vaqueros, whose great-grandfathers came north from Tlaxcala and Puebla, lured by peninsulares' promises of work and horses and dignity. No. The Spanish crown gave men of noble blood pieces of paper inked with flourishes a hundred years ago, gifting land grants in the wild, windblown north of Nueva España. It was the pampered hidalgos who owned the land to this day, who barely broke a sweat as they hired servants to raise their houses of stone, lining their mantels with silver as their workers lived in dark jacales. It was their entitled sons who reaped the bounty of what had fallen into their laps by virtue of their noble names.

But Néstor?

If he wanted to stand on the patio of a casa mayor that was all his own, he had to work for it. It was easy to work hard, when he knew what he wanted.

He had ample time to envision this over the last nine years on long, slow drives, as he sat on watch during cricket-filled, hot siestas on the ride east to San Antonio. A house of rough sillar stone mined from his own quarry. The golden sweep of his own land at sunrise. Corrals of horses bearing his own brand. The intricate engraving of a silver-trimmed bridle, fit for a powerful ranchero, running under his fingertips as he slipped it over Luna's velvety ears.

That part was easy. If he told Beto that was what he was saving his money for—a porción of land with a spring and a quarry—Beto would understand.

Beto might also suggest marrying Celeste for her land. This made Néstor's skin itch with discomfort, not least because the widow was of a class so high above Néstor and Beto that even the suggestion was veiled in gentle mockery.

But because Beto might suggest *marrying*.

An empty house was incomplete. A husk. It needed family to fill it with noise and food and memories. Family Néstor had, if he ever built the courage to speak to them again, but what about children?

What of a woman?

When Néstor was brave or drunk enough to dream about this, he was met with blankness. An empty wall. The sweep of crinoline silk, the echo of a voice, but no face. The sensation of knowing someone was next to him. Of turning only to find the dream shattered, to realize he was utterly, achingly alone.

When he was a boy, he knew exactly who would stand on the patio of the dream house next to him. He knew her light footsteps and the shift of her skirts like his own heartbeat, the weight and silky texture of her plaits between his fingertips.

But the boy he used to be was long dead, along with many other precious things besides.

At last count, he had nearly saved enough to buy a small porción, some cattle, and a few horses. It was more than most vaqueros—bound to ranchos and forever indebted to their rancheros—could dream of achieving. It was time to begin. But he was dust clinging to a wind, too afraid to touch the earth, too afraid to meet the ground. He could dream of a house, but the next step paralyzed him.

Don't you always.

He did. Because without work and a distant goal, he did not know what else he was living for.

4

NENA

HUMID TENDRILS OF mist pawed at Nena's skirts as she crossed the central rancho, the bag of her curandera's supplies beating an urgent rhythm against one thigh. She strode through cold, dewy grass toward the vaquero Ignacio's jacal, her breath coming short from haste.

Yesterday, Abuela's hands clicked and curled inward from the damp. The promise of a storm stiffened her joints; her movements became slower than usual, restricted by pain. Nena put warm compresses on Abuela's hands and promised that she was capable of taking on any ailments that might strike the people of the rancho—God forbid—while Abuela rested.

So when a young vaquero pounded on the door of la casa mayor as madrugada lightened, asking for a curandera, Nena had risen and snatched the first work clothes she set eyes on. As she left the house, she made sure to meet eyes with Papá and give him a curt nod. Though his expression was bleary from being woken suddenly, she prayed that he recognized how important her task was: her presence was integral for the strength of the rancho. Necessary. Especially as Abuela grew older.

The rancho was a lively beast with many limbs; lately, she fretted about it. It was tired, stretched thin, its strength paled by sickness at the worst possible time. They could not afford weakness when Anglos breathed down their necks. So she would tend to it with every technique she knew, and would not rest until it was well again.

She reached the high walls that enclosed the rancho's most precious organs like curving wooden ribs and passed through the gate, leaving it to creak shut behind her.

Metal scraped over metal; the gate's latch clicked into place with a tone of finality.

Stillness hung with the mist over the rest of the rancho.

She should hear crickets. At this hour, she should hear the trill of birds.

Everything was as it should be on a March morning in the hours before dawn. Everything smelled as it always had.

But for some reason, she felt as if she were suspended in a pocket of silence between the central rancho and the jacales, silence broken only by the swish of her skirts in the chill, damp grass. The soft crush of the soles of her boots, now hesitant, on the earth.

Her own breathing.

The more she noticed this, the more her breath pulled raspy. The louder and farther it seemed to stretch through the mist. The faster she sought breath after breath.

She cast a glance over her shoulder.

Behind her: mist curled between her and the walls of the central rancho. To her left: a sea of fog sheathed the dark line of oak trees on the way to the springs.

A longing for a torch flared sudden and urgent in her breast.

That was odd for her, someone who happily snuck outside to her herb garden after moonset to be alone beneath the stars.

It was odd that she should feel as if something was observing her.

Along the dark line of trees, a shadow shifted.

She shied sideways, boots scuffing the dirt, nearly stumbling as she righted herself. Her heart leaped to a gallop. A hot, itchy prickling spread over the skin above her right collarbone, right over her scar.

She scanned the trees, rubbing a hand over the rippled skin at her neck. Her palm rolled over the chain of her scapular, grounding her. That must have been a deer. So where was it now?

She saw nothing.

And yet, a sensation lifted on the back of her neck, cloyingly soft as the legs of insects, that she was being watched.

That she should run.

But there was nothing there.

She inhaled sharply through her nose and set off toward the vaqueros' jacales at a brisk, determined pace, rubbing her scar to dismiss the prickling sensation. She ignored the creeping on the back of her neck. The messenger who pounded on the door of la casa mayor said Ignacio had suffered susto. Haste was of the essence. Now was not the time to let the mist play tricks on her.

The sloping roofs of jacales sharpened through the mist as she grew close to Ignacio's home. They slumbered like dogs curled around a fire, but not for long. Within a short time, before sunrise, vaqueros, pastores, and farmworkers would rise for the day's work. The rancho would twitch and stretch, yawning and rising to sniff out the news: was the young curandera successful at curing Ignacio or not?

But for now, the only sign of life stood on the patio of Ignacio's jacal. The dark hair of his wife, Elena, hung in sleep-loosened plaits over her shoulders. The closer Nena drew to the patio, the more evident the worry and grief on Elena's face was.

Elena was two years younger than her; they had known each other their whole lives on the rancho, listening to Abuela's ghost stories together around the fire at Nochebuena, feeding the chickens every morning until they were old and strong enough to help carry water from the springs to the house. Now, Elena was married and—judging from her recent and persistent requests for ginger to combat nausea—was with child. Worry weighed on the gentle slope of her shoulders as she looked past Nena.

"Where is Abuela?" she asked, voice high and strained with anxiety.

"She's ill," Nena replied. She nodded at the mist. "It's the damp. She will recover when the rain breaks and passes, but for now . . ."

A cloud passed over Elena's face. Nena knew that look well: it was a flicker of doubt about Nena. It struck like a stone flung against her shoulder, but she pushed the hurt aside. Whatever state Ignacio was in, she had to be able to heal him. She *had* to. Elena would never trust her as a curandera otherwise. Neither would anyone else.

"Come in," Elena said, and turned to the door.

Nena cast one final look over her shoulder at the mist, at the dark line of trees, then followed Elena into the jacal.

But behind Nena's turned back, something shifted through the fog. A dark shadow moved, fluid as spirit, from one tree to the next.

THE JACAL WAS one room, lit by candles and thin streams of gray light from its single high window and the door. Humble, sparse furnishings attested to how recently its inhabitants' life together began. Elena and Ignacio had been married less than a year ago, and their jacal completed not long after—a feat of speed and strength that few but a vaquero like Ignacio could accomplish. He was tall and fast and canny-eyed; his precision with the lasso and skill with breaking wild mesteños matched by only one other person Nena had ever met.

She pushed that thought from her mind before it had the courage to take the form of words. An old reflex, a hard-won habit. A necessary one, for the state Ignacio was in demanded her full attention.

The vaquero lay on a sleeping pallet at the back of the jacal, half covered in a blanket. Nena crossed the room and knelt by his side, Elena her shadow to her left.

His face was bloodless, slack. No spirit animated its grooves and creases. No breath lifted his naked chest.

Or so it seemed at first glance.

Yes, this was certainly susto. Madre Santa, why did Abuela have to be ill today of all days? Only she had ever cured a man of susto. Nena had watched.

"How long has it been?" she asked, keeping her voice crisp to mask her rising panic. She shrugged her bag off her shoulder and bent forward, placing her ear to the man's chest. His sweat reeked of fear and sickness; his skin was cool to the touch.

"Maybe half an hour?" Elena offered. "That's when his brother brought him here and ran for help."

Nena listened for a heartbeat. She waited. She closed her eyes, and in the darkness, in the silence broken only by Elena's jagged breathing, she waited.

There—just barely—she felt a soft beat.

She exhaled in relief.

"He's alive." She had suspected this, she had hoped this, but hearing his heartbeat shored up her shaky confidence.

Elena let out a soft whimper. When Nena straightened, she saw that the young woman's hands were twisting in her lap. Nena reached out and put her left hand on Elena's, willing calming energy to flow from her to Elena.

"It's going to be all right," she said softly. "I know what to do. I've seen this before."

It wasn't a lie, at least.

She reached for her bag and pawed through its contents, placing them on the floor to her right. She felt the weight of Elena's eyes on her hands as she removed a bundle of rosemary for limpias, a bag of herbs for tea.

Abuela did not know what caused these incidents of susto. But she had taught Nena what to do.

Nena reached for her bundle of rosemary. As her hand closed around the dried herbs, she thought of sinking her fingers into the earth as she grew the rosemary in the herb garden behind la casa mayor. Of watching it grow. Of Abuela next to her as she cut it one morning, the herb's cleansing fragrance rising from where leaves crushed against her palms as she cut stalks with a small knife.

Now, those herbs were bound together and ready. She inhaled deeply through her nose to steady herself, then ran the rosemary over Ignacio's prone body to perform a limpia. Head to foot, down his limbs.

If she closed her eyes, if she closed herself off to the sharp spikes of Elena's anxiety, she could sense the contours of Ignacio's aura. It was weak; porous. Wounded in a way that she had come to recognize through Abuela's instruction. She focused her limpia over his chest, where his aura was the darkest, the most wounded.

The cases of susto that had occurred in the young men on the rancho—even ones as seemingly impervious as Ignacio—all presented the same. They had experienced a violent shock that left a severe wound in the aura, that separated the soul from the body. Abuela had called three souls back; two, she had been unable to retrieve. Those graves were still fresh behind the chapel. She saw them every day.

"Regresa, Ignacio." *Please, come back.* She closed her eyes and thought of directing her energy into him to help heal that breach in his aura, to heal its wounds, to strengthen him as she called his soul back. She reached. She beckoned.

Nothing happened.

Panic rose in her throat.

Come back, she willed, curling her hands so tightly around the rosemary the aroma of crushed leaves rose to her nostrils. No, Abuela said she had to be relaxed in order to call a victim of susto back. She inhaled deeply and refocused. *It is safe now. We are waiting for you.*

"Regresa, Juan Ignacio Rubio Espinosa," she said. *Los Ojuelos needs you. Elena needs you. Come back, be whole.* "Regresa."

Elena gasped sharply; Nena's eyes flew open in surprise.

Ignacio's chest rose and fell—softly, at first, and then with more vigor. He coughed, and his eyes opened.

A sob rose in Nena's throat. She moved out of the way as Elena bent over Ignacio.

She had done it. Relief rushed through her shoulders like a cool breeze. She made the sign of the cross and sent a prayer to whomever was listening—God, la Virgen, whichever saint had lent her the energy to call Ignacio back.

"¡Querido!" Elena cried, her voice cracking. "Dios mío, I thought you were dead." A softness drew at the corners of Ignacio's mouth as Elena fussed over him, as he looked up at her and, in a creaky voice half mired in sleep, asked what on earth the matter was.

Nena turned her face away. To grant them a moment of privacy, she told herself. It was not because something in her heart twisted at the sight of such open affection. She was stronger than that. She cleared her throat and put the rosemary back in her bag.

Ignacio reached his right hand up to caress Elena's face. The motion caught Nena's eye, but what drew her attention was the glint of a wound beneath the man's underarm.

She turned sharply to examine it.

It oozed with blood.

"When did that happen? How?"

Elena and Ignacio turned to Nena in surprise, as if only just then remembering that she was there.

"What?" Confusion clouded Ignacio's face. Exhaustion hung over him like a soaked rebozo.

"You're bleeding." She immediately turned her bag out, searching for the strips of fabric she always kept there for bandages. She was an idiot. She had been so afraid of failing to cure Ignacio's susto that she had completely overlooked this. What if she had gone back to la casa mayor and left his wound to fester?

How could she ever tell Papá that she needed to stay on the rancho as Abuela's replacement if she was this careless? She was arrogant, she was stupid. She needed to be more diligent. She needed to work harder.

She pored over Ignacio's wound as she cleaned it. There could be no infection. It was a strange wound—it looked as if a snake had bitten the man's arm, if a snake had six fangs. If those fangs were several times the width of a snake's.

Very odd. She would tell Abuela about it as soon as she could. Ignacio was too exhausted to be asked questions about the wound— whether Nena liked it or not, it would have to remain a mystery for now.

When Ignacio's wound was clean and bandaged, Nena gave herbs to Elena with instructions on how to brew a strengthening tea for Ignacio. It was possible his recovery would be long—the vaqueros who were felled by similar bouts of susto still suffered from weakness, sensitivity to bright sunlight, and exhaustion. Abuela could not yet track a precise amount of time to their full recovery.

"Thank you so much," Elena said as they stepped onto the patio. "I should have never doubted you."

Nena kept her false smile firmly affixed as she stood on Elena's patio and said goodbye.

There was something that kept the people of the rancho from trusting her like they trusted Abuela. It didn't seem to matter how hard she studied Abuela's practices, never mind how early she rose to help young mothers with colicky babies or how many broken bones she successfully set.

Abuela had her theories. She had poked a gentle finger in Nena's upper arm as they hung laundry to dry one recent afternoon.

"It's your aura," she said. "It's wounded."

Nena looked up at her in surprise, her pride stinging.

"People can't see it as I do," Abuela continued. Her voice was tender, almost pitying. "I know where this wound comes from. You do too. You must find a way to heal yourself from it, or you will never be able to live your full self. Can't you sense how it confines you? The sick can. That's why they hesitate."

This, Nena knew, was nonsense. The reason people did not yet fully trust her was because she was young. The only thing that gave them pause was her lack of white braids and the gravitas that came with Abuela's age.

She was untested. That was all. Every morning she woke before dawn to cross the rancho and demonstrate her skills was a step closer to proving she could be trusted. Even mornings like this one, where she stepped from Elena and Ignacio's patio feeling a familiar, bruising loneliness well beneath her heart.

The mist had thinned. Soon, it would burn away entirely. The eastern edges of the rancho, over the roofs of the jacales and la casa mayor, brightened with the promise of dawn. Crickets hummed a steady melody. The trill of birds waking filled the air; from the chicken coop came the bright, bold crow of a rooster.

Then why did the hairs on her forearms stand on end as she reached for the latch of the gate? What drew her eye over her shoulder toward the line of trees?

It was nothing. It had to be nothing.

Nena gave her shoulders a brusque shake and slipped through the gate.

But she was still grateful for the click of the latch behind her.

5

～✦～

NENA

LATE MORNING FOUND Nena sewing on the patio of la casa mayor. Stitches blurred before her eyes as she counted them, replaced in her mind's eye by the wound in Ignacio's arm. It was unlike any other animal bite she had seen. What would it look like when it healed? Would it scar?

She reached absentmindedly for her neck. The necklines of her dresses were unfashionably high. Every time she inherited a dress from Mamá or one of the tías, Mamá ensured that it was altered so as to cover the scar that puckered the skin of her lower neck, above her collarbone.

Part of her insisted that it was not the same kind of wound as Ignacio's. It couldn't be.

But it *was*.

The night she received the scar, she had stepped into the dark, yearning for the comfort of Néstor's company, intent on finding Spanish silver to protect the rancho from Anglos, and then . . . she lay in bed, the sun that streamed through the window midmorning yellow, her throat parched. Abuela was at her side, holding her hand, whispering her full name like an incantation. Mamá hovered just behind her, face drawn, her fingers tripping over the coral beads of her rosary.

Everything in between was a sinkhole of darkness.

Mamá never spoke of that night. Yes, she watched Nena hawkishly in the weeks that followed, as she regained her strength. Yes, she fussed over altering necklines, claiming that such modesty was becoming, that it would certainly endear Nena to suitors in the future.

Neither did Abuela. She monitored Nena's recovery closely and asked a few questions about what had happened, but did not pry. Months passed. Years covered the night, burying it firmly.

Of the many unspoken dicta that ruled life on the rancho, one of the most important was this: if tragedy struck and you escaped unscathed, it was unlucky to call attention to your fortune by talking about it. Even if you emerged with scrapes and bruises, it was simply not prudent to talk about it. You survived, and that was what mattered. Nothing could be gained from lingering on the past.

But now Nena wondered.

There was one person who had been there. One person who knew what had happened.

But he was long gone.

She swept this thought away with twice the force she normally would.

Her stitches had gone askance, loosened by her distraction. Wonderful. Now she had to painstakingly undo them.

"Then the witch removed her skin and left it in a heap on the patio." Abuela's voice drifted over to her from the far side of the patio, where she sat in a spacious rocking chair next to the bushes of jasmine and oreja de ratón that grew on the shady side of the house. While she had said that her hands still ached, she was still able to keep watch over the rancho's many children. A circle of them—young cousins of Nena's and vaqueros' offspring alike—fanned around Abuela's feet like supplicants at a saint's shrine. Their eyes were all fixed on Abuela, wide and greedy as moons, as she spoke.

"She was nothing but a skeleton!" Nena returned her focus to rethreading her needle. She knew exactly which theatrical gestures Abuela was making at that moment, her gnarled hands spread wide, her threadbare brows reaching for her white hairline. "Her husband was terrified and trembled in his hiding place as she rose into the air and flew away into the darkness. When she was gone, he took salt from the kitchen and spread it over her skin. The skin began to hiss!"

The group of children gasped in unison. A smile twitched at the corner of Nena's mouth. Even now, it was difficult not to think of herself at Abuela's feet, listening to those same stories with Néstor's shoulder pressing into hers. He always swore he wasn't afraid, and she always knew he was lying. The memory flitted through her with the ache of an old, familiar bruise, then was swiftly engulfed by the commotion, voices, and smells of women at work in the kitchen.

"It began to shrivel!" Abuela continued. "And then, when the skeleton returned—"

"Come here, Javiera." Mamá's voice layered over Abuela's as she brought Nena's younger sister to the patio table, her arms full of a pile of mending. "If you have questions, your sister will help you."

Javiera settled onto the bench next to Nena, shooting the pile of mending before her a baleful look. Resigned reluctance was Javiera's response when presented with chores. At fourteen, she was the baby of the family, and was left to play with the rancho's children and her runt yellow dog, Pollo, for several years longer than Nena and their cousins had been. The familiar click of the dog's claws on the tipichil patio announced his presence; soon he would be curled beneath the table at Javiera's feet.

"Nena," Mamá began.

"Don't worry, Mamá, I'll handle it." Nena set her sewing down and selected a piece of mending from the pile: one of Félix's shirts, ripped neatly along the seam beneath one arm from lassoing. An easy fix. "Start with this one," she said to Javiera.

Dark eyes woeful, Javiera accepted the shirt.

"It's not that," Mamá said. "Would it be possible to tame your hair? Sometime in the next hour? It looks as if you were thrown from a horse."

Nena's needle hovered above the next stitch as her stomach dropped in dark, unwelcome surprise.

"Why," she said flatly. It was more a statement than a question—she knew why.

"You remember Don Hortensio's son Don Felipe," Mamá began. "You met him at Nochebuena. The handsome one with the bay mare."

Nena stabbed her needle into the next stitch. Don Hortensio was the patriarch of Rancho Las Palmas, situated northwest of Los Ojuelos along the curves of Río Bravo. *Rancho* was perhaps a misnomer for the lush acres granted to Don Hortensio's family in a royal land grant nearly a hundred years ago—it was large enough to be considered an hacienda, with thousands of head of cattle and vaqueros aplenty. Don Hortensio was exactly the kind of person Papá would want to be allied with.

"Of course I remember," Nena replied. "Beautiful mare. Well proportioned. Intelligent face. Why, is she for sale?"

Mamá released a long sigh, the kind she gave when she wanted anyone listening to know exactly how much she was suffering.

At twenty-two, Nena was no spinster. Her parents had only begun asking her to consider this ranchero's son or that one two years ago. Yet here she was, being asked to make herself presentable for a stranger for the umpteenth time. Ever since she was old enough to bleed, she became something to be sent away. Something to be bartered like meat or salt in exchange for a powerful relationship, in exchange for more cattle or land or vaqueros.

Every morning, she rose early and spoke to Papá's peones, soothing their colicky babies and upset stomachs and headaches and monthly pains. She shadowed Abuela's visits to pregnant women and was an extra pair of blood-soaked hands at births. She mended dislocated shoulders and applied poultices to injuries caused by bull or beast in the chaparral.

Then why, after so many years, couldn't her parents see that she benefitted the rancho already? That she was worth more than a means to an end?

Nena set her mending down with more force than was necessary. Javiera jumped.

"Thread your needle and get started," she said sharply.

"Will you do this, for me?" Mamá's voice was pleading. "Your papá says—"

"Yes, Mamá. I will." Everyone on the rancho was a prisoner of Papá's moods, especially his anger; it was not fair to punish Mamá for carrying out his will. So Nena would brush and plait her hair, made frizzy by the heat of the morning, and pin it back up off her neck. She would wash away the soil that always traveled to her cheeks and nose from her herb garden. She would transform into the wealthy ranchero's daughter she was meant to be when she met these suitors: obliging, ornamental, obedient.

It all made her want to shed her skin like the witch in Abuela's story, let everything that made her a woman fall to the ground to be salted and ruined as she flew into the night, her bones bare and cold in the starlight.

"But first I'm going to check on my rosemary," she said. Mamá's face gave no indication that she realized how pointed Nena intended this reference to the herbs she used for limpias to be. Of course she didn't. She was relieved that Nena would oblige and meet this Don Felipe, this new addition to a yearslong string of empty-headed hidalgos who droned on about stallions and cattle and business and trouble with the Texians without any input.

"That should be finished by the time I'm back," Nena said to Javiera, pointing at the mending in her sister's hands.

"Yes, Nena."

Nena stepped off the patio into the brilliant March sunshine.

After this Don Felipe had come and gone, she would have to find her brother at lunch to dissuade the suitor. Whatever excuse she could spin against the match—and there were always many—would be enough if it came to Papá's ear in the voice of a man.

Nena and Félix could repeat the exact same sentence, yet Mamá and Papá would always listen to Félix. He was gentle, a peacekeeper always ready to do what was best for the rancho, whatever his true feelings might be. Even when he had to marry a stranger, he had done so without complaint—for after all, he told Nena, what was marriage to a woman when it was Los Ojuelos to whom he had really pledged his life?

Mamá and Papá relented to his calm demeanor and level way of speaking, even when it was blindingly obvious he was advocating for Nena because she had badgered him to. But if Nena tried to speak up for herself? She could shout until her voice was raw and it would be as if she were not even there.

Sun beat on her shoulders as she bent to examine the long sprigs of rosemary she laid out on a cloth earlier that morning. Their fragrance wafted up to her, soothing her. One word from Félix was all it would take, and all would be as it was.

There was a time when the idea of marriage was not such an affront to her. When whimsy and romantic notions about someone in particular on the rancho spun childish fantasies in her mind.

She had been young and stupid, her dreams as weak as autumn

frost: as soon as morning broke, as soon as reality dawned and that person was gone, they melted away.

She thrust the thought of Néstor from her mind. She hated how memories hung around her like kitchen smoke, clinging to her hair and clothing. How witnessing the tenderness between Elena and Ignacio or the dark-haired children clustered shoulder to shoulder at Abuela's feet stung like lime on a cut.

She straightened from examining her herbs, a bead of sweat rolling down her lower back. As she turned to la casa mayor, motion from the wall surrounding the central rancho caught the corner of her eye.

The gate was thrown open; a horse and rider thundered through, racing for the main house with the urgency of a messenger.

But even at first glance, Nena knew the rider was no ordinary messenger. Her steps back to the house quickened as she held up a hand to shield her eyes from the sun. She squinted at the broad, clean hat, the finely engraved saddle, and the silver that gleamed beneath sweaty froth on the mount's bridle.

That was no vaquero, no peón, no common messenger with urgent news. A ranchero slowed to a canter before la casa mayor, flinging himself from the saddle and passing the reins to one of the boys who leaped up from Abuela's feet to assist him.

"Don Severo!" Mamá cried, coming forward from the open-air kitchen. "Please, come sit! Whatever is the meaning of this?"

Something was wrong.

The Serranos' neighbor Don Severo owned Hacienda del Sol, a rancho nearly twice the size of Los Ojuelos. Even with vaqueros in the chaparral during the day, he had dozens of peones to call upon to carry a message to Los Ojuelos for him.

Nena lifted her skirts and broke into a run.

"I had to come," Don Severo was saying as he removed his fine hat and wiped sweat from his brow. Javiera was ushered off the patio with the mending and Nena urged to get refreshments from the kitchen in the same brusque gesture from Mamá. Nena obeyed, but kept one ear turned to the patio as her cousins helped her prepare a tray of cool water and fruits and coffee and breads for the unexpected guest.

"I must speak with Don Feliciano immediately," Don Severo said. "It is of the utmost urgency."

"He will already be on his way," Mamá assured the ranchero. "Look, there he is now!"

Taking a heavy tray of refreshments in her arms, Nena turned to see Papá and Félix striding up to la casa mayor from the corral.

"Don Severo!" Papá boomed, his voice filling the patio a few steps before his presence did. "A hundred men at your command and you could not send a messenger?"

Nena brought the tray to the table on the patio and served refreshments to the men, settling her face into a docile, innocent expression. She moved her hands at a deliberate pace as she poured cold water into cups and set them down, purposefully lingering to hear Don Severo's news.

"It's the Yanquis," Don Severo said.

Nena paused as she set the pitcher back on the tray, anxiety prickling in her chest. News of Yanquis was never good. News that brought a ranchero racing to speak to Papá instead of sending a messenger? It had to be urgent. It could even be dangerous. She could not go back to the kitchen until she knew what was wrong.

"They're saying everything from the Nueces to Río Bravo is theirs," Don Severo added.

Papá snorted, dismissing this with a sharp wave of the hand. "Let them talk!" he said.

"It's not talk. They took Puerto Isabel." Don Severo leaned forward, eyes bulging as he brought his hand flat against the tabletop for emphasis. Nena started at the sound. Don Severo's face was still darkened and sweaty from the midmorning ride to Los Ojuelos, giving him a desperate look. "They're building a fort across the river from Matamoros," he said. "Don Hortensio's vaqueros saw it with their own eyes, te lo juro. There are already thousands of soldiers, and more arrive daily. They mean to take the land by force."

A hush fell over the table. Not even Papá spoke. All Nena could hear was the crackle of the kitchen fire, the faraway whinny of a horse. It was as if even the chickens and the crickets fell silent.

The chapel bell tolled. An hour to noon. A group of children poured from the shadowy interior of the chapel as they did every morning, freed from their lessons. Their laughter was hollow and tinny when it reached Nena, as if it were carried on a wind from far away. In her mind's eye, she saw a whiplike, dark boy running among them, his black hair falling into his eyes, his hand-me-down, too-large trousers bunched where they were belted around his slim waist.

I still dream about that day, Nena, Néstor once whispered to her, many years ago. *I wake up certain they're coming.*

All her life, Yanquis circled overhead like vultures. First, they tore off pieces at the edges of her world. Néstor and his family fled from San Antonio, bringing nightmarish tales with them. Then came news that Anglos had declared Tejas independent of México, its own nation. Now that they were a part of the United States and set their eye further south . . . Would they sink their talons into Los Ojuelos next?

She took the tray, gripping it hard, hard enough that she knew the wood would leave pale indentations in her palms. She would never forget the men who, long ago, came to speak to Papá in their broken Spanish, asking after land for sale. How shifty their pale eyes were. How untrustworthy. Loathing stretched and grew under her skin, flushing her cheeks with heat.

This was *her* home.

She knew every tree that grew between la casa mayor and the

spring: the oaks, the anacahuitas, the laurels. She knew which ones grew over her grandparents and infant siblings' graves and which ones protected the carefully buried afterbirth of her siblings and cousins.

She hated the presumption that her home could be bought and paid for. They could no more take it than they could take the bones from her body. They would have to kill her before she let them get close to la casa mayor.

A cool realization unfolded in her mind.

They might.

I didn't see them shoot him, Néstor had said the afternoon he told her how his father died. They sat in the shade, far from la casa mayor, watching the sheep. Néstor lay with his head in her lap, looking up at the sky. Branches and clouds were reflected in his eyes, in irises so dark and liquid they were almost black. The weight of his head pressed her thighs against the earth; his warmth was right there, but she had never seen him so distant. It made her want to find where his mind wandered and snatch it back, to cradle it safely in her arms. *But I saw him in the corral. You know how pigs are when they're butchered? People bleed like that too.*

Anger lifted in her chest like an October storm: with wind like the lick of a whip, with crackling, with the promise of thunder.

"But this is *our* land," she spat. "They can't take it. We live here!"

Don Severo looked startled to see her standing there, even though she had been placing food and drink before him since he arrived. "Indeed, señorita," he agreed.

From the corner of her eye, Nena caught the edge of a severe look from Papá.

"That is enough, Magdalena," he said. "Leave us." His tone was a stinging dismissal—if she ignored it, she risked kindling his temper, and nothing good could come of that.

Her outburst was inappropriate; she should not be listening to the men's conversation, much less interrupting it. Mamá would be mortified that Papá had had to raise his voice at her before a guest.

For once, she found she didn't care. How could she not react as she did? She retreated to the kitchen as Papá began to volley question after question at Don Severo about the news. Instead of setting the tray down where it belonged, she slammed it with a resounding clatter, causing the tías to startle and scold.

They mean to take the land by force.

Through the lazy smoke of the kitchen fire, the rancho moved as if a wildfire had struck. It bucked and crawled with the news, as if a thousand ants swarmed forth from their hill, stirred to agitation by a malevolent child's stick.

For years, the vultures had circled, carried high on a hot updraft.

Now, they were close enough for her to hear the rustle of feathers, the click of talons. Close enough to feel their fetid breath on the back of her neck.

"Nena?" Javiera's voice broke through the agitated humming in her chest. Mending was still clutched to her chest. She had been frozen in the kitchen ever since Don Severo arrived with the news, her eyes wide as a deer's. "Nena, are we in danger?"

"No." She took the mending from Javiera and planted a firm kiss on the side of her younger sister's head. She was not sure if this was true, but the coals that burned in her chest brought the words to her lips all the same. "Not as long as we fight, we're not."

TWO AFTERNOONS LATER, Don Severo returned to Rancho Los Ojuelos at merienda. He did not come alone. A group of six rancheros accompanied him, their bridles and spurs glinting in the morning sun as they dismounted and joined Papá on the patio.

Mamá and Nena served them sweet breads and coffee. Oddly,

Mamá did not scold Nena when she spied her eavesdropping from the corner of the kitchen. A few moments later, she joined Nena, hovering just behind her shoulder, her focus also trained on the men seated around the table on the patio.

The men's conclusion was final: each would muster as many vaqueros from their peones as they could spare. They needed the fastest, the hardiest, the best shots from among their men. Their militia would be a formidable addition to the government's cavalry.

"Provided we don't lose any more vaqueros to susto," Don Severo's voice added darkly. Rumors whispered that Los Ojuelos was not the only rancho to fall victim to the strange sickness. Some even said it infected portions of the Mexican army stationed along las Villas del Norte. "We need every man we can get."

The men rose with murmured, solemn agreement, taking their conversation with them as their footsteps carried them off the patio.

The mention of susto was like kindling dropped on embers. A plan licked to life in Nena's head. It was dangerous, it was improbable, and with Félix's help, it just might work.

Nena stuck her head around the corner of the kitchen and spied Félix, the last among them, placing his hat on his head and moving toward the corral.

"Félix," she whispered. "*Félix.*"

But he did not hear her. He was already striding behind the other men. Nena gathered her skirts and darted out onto the patio, ignoring Mamá's hissed scolding that she stop.

She ran after Félix's turned back, her skirts swishing through the grass, her boots crushing pebbles as she caught up with him and the other men.

She loved this land as fiercely as any of the men, from the sun and heat that brought sweat to her brow as she drew level with Papá to the dirt beneath her boots. She, too, could defend it.

And this was her chance to prove it.

"Papá," she began softly.

He cast her a sharp look down his nose. "Go back to the house. Your mother is calling you."

Indeed, Mamá was. Nena ignored her.

"Papá, the squadron will need curanderos," she said. "With so many men ill from susto, you need to keep the healthy ones well. To prevent them from falling ill. To set broken bones, to stitch up wounds. To stop infections from turning to fever and killing the few men you have."

"Magdalena, I said go back to the house."

Nena turned her head to Félix, who walked just behind Papá. She ignored the curious looks of the other rancheros, some of whom glowered at her for so openly disobeying Papá's blunt commands.

Help me, she mouthed at her brother.

"Casimiro Duarte would have never walked again, much less ridden, if it were not for Magdalena," Félix said slowly.

"War is not the concern of young ladies," Don Feliciano snapped.

"Of course it is my concern," Nena said. "This is my home, too."

"Your daughter is right," said a voice behind Nena.

She nearly tripped over her skirts at its support of her plea.

Don Antonio Canales, the voice—if her eavesdropping served her correctly—of the ranchero from whom the idea for the squadron originated.

"We need all the help we can get to keep these vampires from sucking our land dry," Don Antonio added. "We need every man in good health."

"Vampires?" Don Severo snorted as they approached the shady corral where the rancheros' horses were tethered. "Now you sound like Cheno Cortina."

"A lot of people sound like Cortina these days," Don Antonio said. To Papá, he added: "We need every man in good health. Can she ride?"

Nena bit her tongue and cast Félix a meaningful look. *Answer,* she prayed.

"As fast as any vaquero," Félix said.

Papá cast Nena a sideways look. Beneath the shade of the brim of his hat, she could not parse its meaning.

Asking him this in front of all of the other men was a gamble. A risk. It was possible that none of them saw the sense in her idea, even when it was supported by Félix. It was possible that she could have embarrassed Papá in front of all of the men he held in the highest esteem, which would earn her his ire behind closed doors.

Perhaps she had. Perhaps she had already sealed her fate.

But now Don Antonio was asking her if she knew how to stitch up bullet wounds and cure snakebite, and she was nodding with affected humility, hope unfurling timid and new in her chest as the praise from this other ranchero slowly began to erode Papá's sternness.

He had to let her come. He must.

"Señorita Magdalena will join us," Papá announced.

Don Antonio clapped a hand on Papá's shoulder. "Good man," he said. "She will be an asset to our cause."

Nena's heartbeat thrummed in her ears as the rancheros turned to their horses and began to mount. The prospect of a battlefield was but a distant fog in her mind.

She had won. With Félix's help, she had convinced Don Antonio of her worth. Now, all she had to do was show Papá in front of all of his peers what she could do.

A hand fell heavy on her shoulder.

The unsmiling look on Papá's face quelled her burgeoning optimism, freezing it like a monarca killed by early frost.

"You can have this on one condition, mija," he said sternly.

"When we return, you will marry immediately. You have caused your mother more than enough grief and disappointment with your stubbornness. If she is to suffer watching her daughter ride with me to war, then she will be rewarded when it is over. Is that clear?"

Nena's hand closed around dice in her mind, sweaty and firm as she prepared to cast her second gamble of the morning. If Papá allowed her to ride to Matamoros with the squadron, her life on Los Ojuelos as she knew it was forfeit the moment they returned.

Unless . . .

In the course of her time with the squadron, she could prove to Papá that she had worth beyond bartering. That she was as vital a part of this rancho as he was. That she would not leave it any more than he would, that she was of more use and value to him on Los Ojuelos than being haggled away to an hacienda with more cattle than theirs.

She inhaled through her nose to steady herself. There was no choice in this gamble. She was already playing.

"I understand, Papá," she said. "You have my word."

6

NÉSTOR

Abril 1846
LAREDO

WHEN THEY RETURNED to Laredo five weeks later, Rancho Buenavista's vaqueros went back to their mistress's property. Néstor did not follow. Though he was happy to work with Buenavista's herds and had stayed at the rancho in the past, passing Celeste's house in town on the way to the post office left him with an odd feeling of emptiness.

If pressed, he would not have been able to explain why, nor how the feeling arose. Nor if it had something to do with the last morning he woke up in her sheets, bolt upright with fear.

Néstor stepped beneath the shade of the post office patio and removed his hat. The single room swarmed as if someone had kicked a beehive; the well-heeled men of town and silver-spurred rancheros traded grim news of the fall of Puerto Isabel, voices rumbling as steadily as the movement of a herd as they pocketed their mail.

Néstor's chin lowered out of habit. He was keenly aware of the dust on his chivarras and boots as he made his way forward to the counter to speak to the postmaster. The man recognized him and held a finger up for him to wait while he spoke with an agitated ranchero.

Néstor hung back. He fidgeted with a loose thread in the brim of his hat. He was, to his knowledge, one of few vaqueros who ever stepped into this room. Most were illiterate. News among vaqueros traveled from mouth to mouth, rancho to rancho; if letters were necessary, they went from ranchero to ranchero on behalf of the workers.

Néstor eavesdropped on the ranchero ahead of him, the man's wealth evident from his finely embroidered blue jacket to his polished boots. The man sought letters from Durango on behalf of one of his peones. Though it had been nine years since Néstor left Rancho Los Ojuelos, he could not picture hard-eyed Don Feliciano asking after letters for his peones. As if the man would go out of his way for anyone, much less someone he considered so beneath him.

It was Don Félix to whom Néstor's uncle, Bernabé, dictated his rare letters. Since leaving Los Ojuelos, guilt drove Néstor to write to his family a few times a year, posting the letters from Durango and from El Paso del Norte. Once, he even wrote from as far as Santa Fe. He did not envy the task he gave Don Félix when the ranchero's son had to decide where to send Bernabé's reply. Often, Don Félix defaulted to the closest town to Los Ojuelos that Néstor frequented: Laredo.

When at last he had a letter in his hands, Néstor retreated to a corner where there were shelves hammered into the wall to serve as surfaces for people to read their letters and reply. Most did not, and Néstor stood alone; he curled his shoulders inward for privacy all the same as he opened the letter.

The date in Don Félix's firm, confident hand was recent; it must have arrived a week ago at most.

Esteemed Señor Duarte, the letter began.

Néstor frowned. When dictating, Bernabé began with *mi hijo.*
His eyes skipped to the bottom of the page, to the signature, where
his suspicion was confirmed: Don Félix had written him directly.
He shifted his weight, taken slightly aback, and began to read.

The letter was only a few lines, and judging from a smudge or
two, dashed off quickly:

> *I trust that you are well and I pray you receive this letter
> quickly. I am sure you have heard rumors of the North
> American army moving through Tejas toward Matamoros;
> I have seen them with my own eyes.*

Cold swept through Néstor. Gunshots rang in the dark shadows of his memories; a sweep of blood, violently bright, pooled beneath his father's hand, laying limp in the corral. Néstor was
yanked from his feet and placed in a saddle in front of Abuela, the
pommel digging into his stomach. Thundering hooves and Bernabé's shouting filled his skull; acrid smoke stung his eyes as they
fled south, away from Rancho Dos Cruces and all he knew.

> *My father has joined with other rancheros of las Villas del
> Norte to support the Mexican army's defense of Matamoros by
> forming an auxiliary cavalry squadron. All the families of
> Rancho Los Ojuelos must provide as many men as they can
> spare. Señor Casimiro has bid me write to you with a request:
> that you return to Los Ojuelos to dissuade Señor Bernabé from
> joining the squadron by going in his stead.*
> *I am certain your professional ties span far and perhaps
> your loyalties now lie with another rancho, but I ask in earnest
> when I request that you return and join us. Encourage as many*

vaqueros as you can to do the same, either to defend Los Ojuelos—where they will be paid handsomely for their trouble—or to join el Escuadrón Auxiliares de las Villas del Norte.

   Vaya con Dios.

                    Sinceramente,
                    José Feliciano Serrano Segundo

Néstor's heartbeat had quickened, his posture stiffened. He turned the letter over, searching his shirt pocket for the one pencil he kept there. Patted his other pocket for his knife. A reply began to swirl into place as he sharpened the pencil. *Thank you for relaying the news,* he would write. *Please inform Señor Casimiro that I am on the road.*

He set the pencil to paper and scribbled the date. *Esteemed Don Félix,* he wrote, *I will return—*

There, the scrape of the pencil stopped. The sound of rancheros and townspeople talking around him, the click of bootheels and spurs—all of it faded.

No, hold it like this.

Nena's hand was over his, hers summer brown over his dark one, both small, both dappled by the shade of anacahuita trees. Her fingers were warm as she adjusted his hold on the stick they were pretending was a pencil. Her dark brown hair always worked its way loose from its plaits over the course of the day; now, mid-siesta, it tickled Néstor's face. Birds crooned sleepily overhead. The hum of crickets was a steady lullaby, cocooning them in the afternoon's warmth.

I'll help you, Nena said, and guided his hand over the patch of dirt they were using to practice letters. They were eight and determined to get Nena's mother, Doña Mercedes, to allow Néstor into the schoolhouse. He was not allowed if he could not already write, Doña Mercedes and Nena's aunts had concurred; he would only slow down the other children.

Néstor had lowered his head, humiliated. He knew he was too slow for the other children. Besides, he told Nena—what need was there for the son of a vaquero to read?

He had underestimated her. The tilt of her chin accepted her mother's challenge, and every siesta since that day, they met behind la casa mayor to practice.

Now, she leaned close enough to him that he could almost taste the bite of woodsmoke in her hair that lingered from a morning helping in the kitchen, how it layered over the soapy, wildflower smell that rose from her sun-warmed dress.

Together, they wrote his name in the dirt. *Néstor.*

There, she said. *Now you only need one more letter to make my name.*

She moved Néstor's hand below the letters, then released it and traced her own name in the dirt with an index finger. *You can do it on your own.*

Her name was easier than his. He never had to lift the stick. He followed the flow of the sounds. He followed his own heartbeat. *Nena.*

He looked up. In the siesta light, everything seemed suspended in honey: an amber halo around her brown hair, the smile that lit her face. The proud glint in her dark eyes. The dimple nestled deeply to the right of her mouth.

Perfect, she said. *You wrote it perfectly.*

An argument erupted like a gunshot behind Néstor. It was a splash of cold water to the face, yanking him into the present. Rancheros lingered on the patio of the post office, quarreling loudly about whether México would go to war against los Yanquis. The postmaster raised his voice to be heard as he wrangled new patrons into line. The sun cut harshly through the building's one window.

Everything was suddenly too sharp against his ears, his skin.

He put the pencil down.

He forced his hands to fold the letter, ignoring how they shook. He shoved paper and pencil into his shirt pocket. He snatched his hat and left the post office, the ringing in his ears broken only by the click of his spurs.

BETO FOUND HIM at the bar they haunted, elbows on the counter, head in his hands. The aguardiente in front of him untouched. He had been sitting there for an hour at least, without moving.

Néstor left Los Ojuelos for a reason. He could not even think the words, shape them in his mind like so many letters traced in the dirt.

Visions flashed behind his eyes instead. The eerie glimmer of orange light. The flash of teeth in the dark. Nena screaming. Visceral sensations: the weight of Nena's body against his as he carried her back to la casa mayor. Falling; curling around her to protect her, the sharpness of rocks digging into his shoulders.

How still she was.

How cold.

My daughter is dead.

His neck stiffened; the back of his throat clenched against his will, no matter how hard he tried to relax it.

Beto's greeting was effusive as he clapped Néstor on the back.

Néstor did not move.

Perhaps he would be frozen here forever, roped tight between two unbreakable truths.

The first: he could not return to Los Ojuelos. Nena's death was his fault. Her whole family knew that.

The second: he feared Anglos. He knew what they had done

and what they might do. He would do anything to protect his family from them.

To Beto's credit, when he saw Néstor's rigid shoulders and the untouched glass before him, he didn't press him with questions. He didn't click his tongue with sympathy or ask after the widow Celeste. He sat. Ordered a drink. Music rose around them; violins and singing. Laughter cut through clouds of blue cigarillo smoke. The aguardiente came; Beto drank. He waited.

Beto was like this: patient as a shepherd. He could outlast any of Néstor's silences. It was the reason Beto was Néstor's closest—perhaps only—friend. One of the many reasons Néstor didn't deserve him.

At long last, the rope that pulled taut in Néstor's chest snapped.

He spoke the words before he believed them. "I'm going back."

"Back where?"

"To Los Ojuelos."

Beto coughed. Néstor lifted his head to see the other vaquero wiping his mouth. His proclamation had made Beto nearly choke on his drink.

"Something's wrong, isn't it." Beto stated this more than he asked, his voice low.

"Los Yanquis . . ." Néstor began. He straightened, took the letter from his pocket and handed it to Beto. It was easier than explaining.

Beto skimmed the letter quickly. Like Néstor, he had been educated in his youth: the son of a pastor from Massachusetts who settled west of the Sabina and took a Mexican wife, he learned his letters in English and Spanish before fleeing his alcoholic father's beatings. Like Néstor, he had found his way in the world alone. He did not know why Néstor had left Los Ojuelos, but he understood something about ghosts.

Beto refolded the letter and returned it. He then reached into his own pocket for a piece of corn husk and tobacco and began to roll a cigarillo. He did not speak until it was finished and lit.

"My mother's family lives south of Matamoros," he said. "If Zacarias Taylor is headed that way, they'll need all the help they can get protecting the ranchito. Mind if I ride with you as far as Mier?"

A flush of relief spread in Néstor's chest. Of gratitude for the promise of company, for the way Beto gingerly stepped around the tangled roots of conversations Néstor did not want to have. Sometimes, he thought Beto was the only one who sensed why he might work or drink himself into an early grave.

He sometimes wondered, on the cusp of sleep under the stars, if that would be so bad. He deserved it, for failing Nena. But whatever was in the beyond—darkness, dust, or some sort of gilded God flanked by angels—he would be able to find Nena there, wouldn't he?

"Come all the way to Los Ojuelos," he said, perhaps slightly louder than was necessary. He cleared his throat; straightened the taut muscles of his shoulders. "We'll keep you. Let you rest for a few nights before we ride to Matamoros."

He took his half-forgotten aguardiente and dashed it back. His lips tingled; his throat burned. Let it scald the storm that built at the back of his throat at the thought of facing Don Feliciano. He raised his hand to catch the attention of the cantinero, then tapped the rim of his empty glass. One more, to try in vain to burn away what was painted on the backs of his eyelids:

Don Feliciano, candle in hand, pointing at him, his face a mask of rage.

Doña Mercedes, weeping like La Llorona. *Mi niña está muerta, mi niña está muerta.*

Nena. Her hair sticking to her pale, clammy cheek. The lurid wink of blood on her golden scapular.

One more drink, but no more than that. It would be a waste of money. Even if he drank himself into a stupor, there would be no respite in that restless, sweaty black.

Not now, when the memories were awake.

They flexed their bright claws and flashed their teeth and sank them into him with greedy victory.

There would be no sleep tonight.

7

NÉSTOR

NÉSTOR AND BETO rode the last two miles to Los Ojuelos in silence. Luna's ears were pricked; one flicked back toward him every few steps. The mare sensed his dread, but could not tell what was wrong. She shied at shadows, alert for danger.

The only danger that lay at the end of this familiar road was toward Néstor. Anxiety twisted his chest as they passed onto Serrano land. There were no markers, no ugly fences that Texians so loved. He knew when he crossed onto Rancho Los Ojuelos from the dip of the road, the familiar ridge of the horizon over a creek. Trees that he recognized, that drew him off the main road to a shortcut he had forgotten about until he nearly stumbled upon it. He gestured for Beto to follow him.

They would approach the broad walls of the rancho from the south and dismount at the comisaria in the earlier hours of the siesta—this would keep them out of sight of la casa mayor and out of sight of the Serranos.

Yes, Don Félix asked for him to return. But he could not imagine that Don Feliciano and Doña Mercedes would be happy to see the person who caused their daughter's death.

Beto spoke; his words floated right past Néstor. He barely clocked them. He hadn't heard—nor answered—many things Beto had said over the last hour. Not his singing, not his speculation about the weather, not the few questions flung his way about what his family was like. Beto carried on anyway. Even when Néstor's dread was so thick jokes couldn't crack it, he liked to fill the silence of the chaparral with his voice. It had a pleasant, resonant ring—a preacher's voice, Beto often said. The only thing he did not mind inheriting from his father.

But one word caught Néstor's attention. "Plague?"

"Yeah," Beto repeated. His tone hinted at surprise that Néstor had finally answered something he said. "You never know with rumors, but I've heard there's some kind of plague of susto around here, on the ranchos near Mier. Haven't you heard about it?"

"No." Any letter Néstor received from Los Ojuelos was painfully succinct. He could almost hear Bernabé's self-conscious awareness that he was taking up Don Félix's valuable time as he dictated. Letters were filled of news of Casimiro and Abuela and nothing more. He knew beneath the surface were Abuela's long, meandering tales, full of ghosts and innumerable cousins, and Casimiro's raucous jokes, but the lines themselves were brisk and blunt. They contained no news of the rest of the rancho.

Whenever any member of any cattle drive brought up news from Mier—or God forbid, from Los Ojuelos itself—Néstor stood, put his back to the fire, and walked away. He had learned the hard way that idle gossip and the swapping of news between strangers could spark things he did not want to feel. A fresh hit of loss, like a horse kicking him in the gut. A tingle of fear racing over his skin. If he was not vigilant in avoiding all news from Mier or Los

Ojuelos, he could be caught off guard by the sensation of a ghostly presence, a too-heavy weight slung over his shoulder. It could take hours to shake it off, if not days.

No, it was not surprising that Néstor had not heard news from Mier.

THE CHAPARRAL CLEARED. Néstor could scarcely breathe as the line of the comisaria's roof appeared, then the building itself and new jacales around it. Everything was so much smaller than he remembered, except the wooden protective walls surrounding la casa mayor and other, older jacales, including his family's home. Several figures with rifles lounged in the shade near the gates. That was new to him, but not surprising. Sharp images of Don Feliciano's blustering anger toward the government's disinterest in protecting las Villas del Norte and the ranchos that surrounded them still lingered in his memory. He could, with surprising sharpness after so many years, picture the patrón praying over the midday meal, served to the whole rancho before the siesta. He could see Don Feliciano sitting at a table with his family and visitors from neighboring ranchos, his mustache following the angry set of his mouth as he cursed the government's requests for volunteer soldiers and more donations of horses.

Not when the army ransacks good, honorable ciudadanos and stays in their homes without paying, he would say, his gestures sharp and animated, to the concurring cries of other rancheros. *Not when we have already given so many horses. The Anglos can take Tejas for all I care, so long as the damn army leaves us in peace.*

The Anglos did take Tejas. And thanks to the newspapers and the rumors that licked through the countryside like wildfire, Néstor knew that they lay claim to the horizon that stretched before him, all the way to the glimmering banks of Río Bravo.

The smell of the trees and the sight of the comisaria sparked a flinty lash of protective anger in his chest.

He was here to protect it from guns and greed. He would place himself between the Yanquis and this place, the soil over which he and Nena raced barefoot as children, the trees that cast their welcome shade over the closest thing to heaven he had ever known.

So he could swallow his fear and face Don Feliciano. He could. He *must*.

He turned his attention to the comisaria. Two well-dressed young women, their features obscured by hats shading their faces, dipped inside the building as Néstor and Beto approached. Four men lounged in the shade of the building's patio, smoking and talking.

One spotted Néstor and Beto; stood up suddenly. Crossed to the edge of the patio in two strides.

That movement alone shook recognition loose.

It was Casimiro.

"Oye," Casimiro called. "Duarte?" His voice had the lift of a question, a shade of disbelief.

Néstor lifted his hat in greeting. He nudged Luna to a trot to cross the final distance to the comisaria.

"*Jesucristo*, it's Néstor!" Casimiro cried, and let out a feral whoop. The men on the patio were on their feet in an instant, one shoving the others aside to get to Casimiro at the edge of the patio. He shaded his eyes and took the cigarillo from his mouth, then seized his hat.

Bernabé.

Casimiro seized him by the arm and started slapping his back in excitement as Néstor and Beto approached. It was Bernabé with a gray mustache and deeper lines in his face, but Bernabé all the same.

"That can't be him," Bernabé cried as Néstor dismounted. "That *can't* be him, that's a man! ¡Qué hombre!"

They were at Néstor's side before his boots even hit the dirt. Bernabé seized him in a backbreaking embrace. He smelled like leather and tobacco and Abuela's kitchen and so much like everything that was right in the world that a knot formed in Néstor's throat.

Bernabé released him and kissed both his cheeks.

"Mijo," he said, his voice raspy with emotion. "You look just like your father."

Néstor, as a rule, did not cry. If he hid his weakness from the world, then the world could not hit him where it hurt the most. It became habit to blink away any stinging sensation from his eyes, to lower his voice and push it gruffly past any emotion.

He knew now that if he spoke, he would break.

"I can't believe you're *here!*" Casimiro cried joyfully. His face was exactly the same, albeit more weather-beaten. His broad smile and the crinkle of amusement that always lived at the corners of his eyes were unchanged by time. "Look at you! You actually grew in the end, didn't you?"

"And you brought some Anglo?" Bernabé added, a shade of wariness in his eyes as he glanced over Néstor's shoulder at Beto.

People never know whether to call me gringo or greaser, Beto often told Néstor dryly. *Based on years of observation, I'd say their choice depends on the weather.* Today's weather dictated gringo, it seemed, so Néstor inhaled sharply to steady himself and began to explain that Beto was a vaquero, that he was a friend, and—

Shouts of "Néstor, Néstor" from the vaqueros behind Casimiro and Bernabé drowned out any attempt he made to introduce Beto. He could barely string words together. Luna tossed her head as one of Casimiro's friends took her reins and led her and Beto's horse away to be cooled down and watered. Néstor was taken by the arm and brought to the shade of the comisaria patio just as the two young women exited the building. Bernabé and Casimiro touched the brims of their hats in respect; Néstor did the same. Their dress, hats, and way of walking indicated that they belonged to the family of la casa mayor, but he did not immediately recognize them.

The young women exchanged a conspiratorial look, linked arms, and walked at a quick clip toward the walls surrounding the inner heart of the rancho. A trill of suppressed laughter rose from one of them.

Cold rushed through his veins, swift as poison. That couldn't have been Nena's cousin Didi . . . could it?

Didi knew he was here. She was going back to the house, to tell them all. What would she say? That the boy who caused Nena's death was shameless enough to show his face on Serrano land?

"So tell us everything," Casimiro demanded. Néstor was forced down into a chair, a jug of water and a plate food placed before him on the table. "Where the hell have you been?"

He reached for words, found none. His mouth was dry as sand. A parched riverbank.

"A bit of everywhere," he mumbled at last, helping himself to water.

"Well, when I found him it was in Durango." Beto jumped in. "Six years ago I fished this whelp out of a silver mine and gave him a job. He saved my life a week later, so I'd say it was a good investment."

"Durango?" Casimiro repeated, incredulous.

"A silver mine?" Bernabé said.

Beto met Néstor's eyes briefly before launching into one of his many stories. *I've got your back*, that said.

There was so much Beto didn't know, but he understood this: Néstor could not face Los Ojuelos alone. Beto kept the conversation moving at a quick clip, shielding Néstor from too many questions. Inevitably, talk turned to war, and Beto mentioned how he planned to join his family in Matamoros.

Bernabé's forehead creased with concern. "It's not wise to ride that way alone," he said. "Is your family in town?"

"Outside of it, señor," Beto said. "They have land south of town."

"Do they have young men to protect them?"

"Many, señor."

"I wonder if they can spare you a short while longer," Casimiro said, stroking his chin thoughtfully. "The army conscripted many of our men last year and we are short on the number of vaqueros the patrón promised to supply to the squadron. He's not happy. If you ride with us . . ."

"But enough grim talk," Bernabé said. "You"—here he pointed at Néstor—"need to see your abuela."

Casimiro and Bernabé brought Néstor and Beto through the gates into the heart of the rancho. Néstor kept his eyes trained on the ground before him as they passed la casa mayor; kept his back to it as they approached the Duarte home. Abuela was sitting on the porch mending, her needle catching the afternoon light as it flicked back and forth like the swishing tail of a bull. She rose from her chair, mouth wide in surprise, when she spied the men approaching.

"Abuela, it's Néstor!" Casimiro said, giving Néstor a gentle push forward. "We asked Don Félix to bring him back, and here he is!"

"Madre de Dios," she said, drawing each syllable to twice its length, shading her eyes from the sun as Néstor caught his balance.

"Buenas tardes, Abuela," he said.

His grandmother raised her sewing and smacked his shoulder with it. He flung up his arms, belatedly, in surprise.

"When Jesus Christ told the story of the prodigal son, He says the father forgave the boy," Abuela cried. When Néstor left, he was a hair taller than her; in the nine years that passed, he had grown to add a head and shoulders to that height difference. Perhaps she had shrunk as well, but that did not prevent how she still towered over him. "But did He talk about the boy's grandmother? No!" Another smack. "Because she was angry and that would ruin a pretty fable!"

From behind his back, Néstor heard Casimiro chuckle. "I knew she would do this," his cousin said slyly to Beto. "Watch, I bet he's gotten slow."

"Abuela—" Néstor ducked away from another whack of the sewing; it caught him stinging on the upper arm. "I missed you."

"Cruel boy!" she cried, and at last, flung her arms open to embrace him. Her cheek was soft when he kissed it and smelled like the rosemary of her limpias. "I missed nine years of seeing you grow. And for what! Why?" Abuela demanded, punctuating her declarations with firm kisses on his cheeks.

"It's a long story," Néstor murmured.

"Well I'm running out of years to hear it, so talk fast, mijo," Abuela said, releasing him. Her arms were smaller and weaker than he remembered. Everything was smaller. The house, the patio.

The only thing that remained the same size was la casa mayor looming behind him. Its presence hovered over his shoulder with the unwelcome intimacy of a lover, whispering in his ear. *I am here,* it hummed. *Remember me?*

He did. Too clearly.

He had never been inside, but still he knew every place from which Nena had slipped out in to the night. He knew just how high her bedroom window was from the ground; if he returned from the chaparral too late to say hello, he would leave her little gifts on the wide, stone sill. The girls often left the shutters cracked at night, just enough for a breeze to cool the room, and there he put a few inches of ribbon he bought from the comisaria. Fruta guadalupana, just ripe enough to crack open for the ruby seeds inside. A note written on a scrap torn from one of Don Feliciano's old newspapers.

He knew that twenty steps behind the window of the girls' bedroom was the Serrano and de León family graveyard. The crosses and stones there marked the resting places of the first settlers on Los Ojuelos. A chill crept up the flesh of his back at the thought of what new stones might be there.

"Later, please." He cleared his throat and introduced Beto, explaining that he would stay with them for a few nights.

"Then rest and get cleaned up, chamaquito," she said, patting the side of Néstor's face affectionately. "You can't go before the patrón like this. Besides, this cheek is too scratchy to kiss."

Néstor's heart stopped. Bernabé had told him that he and Beto arrived just in time for a gathering of rancheros and their vaqueros from the surrounding ranchos to discuss the organization of the squadron and how they would travel to join the Mexican forces gathering at Matamoros. He had decided immediately that he would not attend. He knew he would have to be in the vicinity of Don Feliciano as the squadron rode to Matamoros, but he had hoped to avoid the full force of the patrón's attention for at least a few days. If not weeks. If not the whole experience, however long it lasted. He rubbed a hand over his jaw self-consciously. "I don't think . . ."

"You must come to the assembly," Bernabé said. "It is a show of force for the other rancheros. They need to see that Don Feliciano's finest are ready to defend this land. Besides," he added, "it'll be good for you to see people. You've been missed."

These last words bore a weight that made Néstor think Bernabé meant something else; panic hampered his ability to parse them. What family would want to see the person who caused Nena's death on their very threshold? What would Don Feliciano say if he saw him? *When* he saw him?

But Bernabé made it clear he didn't have a choice. Néstor and Beto slept for the rest of the siesta, and when he woke, he washed in freezing water. Shaved for the first time since leaving Laredo. Let Casimiro elbow him out of the way to the one piece of polished copper they used as a mirror on the one side of the patio that caught sunset's light best. When it was his turn, he squinted at himself for the first time in several weeks.

His thirteen-year-old face stared back, wide-eyed and bloodless. He blinked, and the vision vanished.

Nausea shifted in his chest.

He seized a comb and attacked his hair. For nine years, he had pushed these memories down. He pretended they had never happened. He was just another anonymous vaquero on the road, another man with secrets that—if ever they bled—were buried deeper than silver. Unless they were jolted out of him by a bad dream, the memories never happened. They were never real.

He was hard. He could keep the past pushed down, even when he was here.

But every time he turned his head, every time he felt the breeze shift or smelled the heat that rose off the soil, something reminded him of a life that used to be.

The life that he ruined.

The comb fell to the floor. "*Shit.*" He picked it up. Only then did he notice his hands were shaking.

"Aren't you done yet?" Beto called.

"Give it up, you'll never be as beautiful as me," Casimiro said.

One last run of the comb through his hair. It would do. He would be fine. He had years of practicing being hard and cool-headed. Nothing could shake him now.

He shoved his hands into his pockets as they set off toward la casa mayor with Bernabé, toward the sound of dozens of voices and the smells of food. He focused on putting one foot in front of the other. Keeping his shoulders squared.

"I've never seen you this clean in my life." Beto fell into step beside him and gave him a friendly pat on the shoulder. "Relax, compadre. Why are you so nervous?"

He had never said it aloud before. There was no way in hell he would try now. He shrugged; made a noncommittal noise. "The whole rancho will know that I'm back by now. They're all going to look at me."

Beto scoffed, deeply amused by this answer. "Don't be so conceited. It'll be fine."

They arrived at the entrance of la casa mayor's courtyard. The music swelled; grew louder as they passed through the stucco arch and entered the party. Torches lined the walls, illuminating the courtyard and the dozens of men who had already arrived. He had never seen the courtyard so packed, not even at Nochebuena. There were at least six rancheros and nearly a hundred vaqueros gathered, their voices thickening the air like the weight of a storm before it broke.

And yet. How strange it was how the gravity of attention in a crowd so large could shift so nimbly. It gathered and spilled toward the entrance like water, toward the Duartes.

Toward Néstor.

Strange, how conversation could carry on uproariously and an uncanny quiet could fall at the same time, like the dropping of a thin sheet over a bed. For the length of a breath, Néstor could hear nothing but his own heartbeat. The silence settled. Shifted; lifted. Conversation collected itself and reeled on, underscored by whispers spinning like a top from one corner of the courtyard to the next.

Beto let out a low whistle.

"Well I'll be damned," he drawled. "Everyone *is* looking at you."

"Thank you for the observation," Néstor murmured. He stepped forward, a measure behind Bernabé and Casimiro. His heart was lodged somewhere in his throat, but he could breathe past it. He could still his shaking hands and scan the room just as he would at any other gathering, be it a group of men outside church on Sunday or a fandango hall in Laredo. He swiftly listed the rancheros present; among them were the most important owners of ranchos and haciendas between Guerrero and Mier. Three were gathered near a familiar figure near the back of the courtyard.

His palms went slick as he recognized Don Feliciano and, to the patrón's left, Doña Mercedes. The patrón's wife was seated and engaged in conversation with a young, well-dressed woman. Through gaps in the crowd, Néstor noticed that the young woman was decidedly distracted; in fact, she was staring directly at Néstor.

Their eyes locked.

It wasn't that his heart stopped beating, no—it hurt too much to have simply stopped. It buckled in surprise. It collapsed in on itself. It pinned him to where he stood, for he was certain—deliriously certain—that he looked into the face of a ghost.

Her brown hair was braided and coiled around her head like a crown; a delicate white scarf wound around her shoulders and the high neck of her dress, though the night was not yet cold. Her lips were pink, bare of rouge; they parted slightly, as if in surprise.

She rose like the first coil of smoke from kindling: slowly at first, then all at once.

If he looked away, would she vanish? He could not look away. He could not move, not even as she took a hesitant step forward.

Doña Mercedes's sharp voice shattered the spell.

"Magdalena," she said.

The woman turned her head toward her. Quickly, smoothly. A reflex.

"Magdalena, it's time for us to leave."

The young woman turned her back on Néstor as Doña Mercedes took her by the elbow.

Magdalena.

It thrummed in step with the pulse in his head.

Magdalena.

An eerie orange light filled his vision, winking over the spring.

From the darkness a monster thundered forth, pinning Nena to the ground and sinking its fangs into her neck.

Now here she was.

She was standing there, her back to him, not ten strides away. Alive, grown, beautiful. Carrying on a conversation with Doña Mercedes and Don Félix, her head bobbing affirmatively at something Félix said. A gesture so familiar it sent a shard of bone through Néstor's ribs.

This could not be real.

He saw her on the floor of la casa mayor in the candlelight, pale and bleeding. So small beneath the concerned shapes of her family curled over her like mournful trees. So fragile. *Dead.*

Because of him.

Néstor turned on his heel and strode back through the courtyard entrance.

"Hey!" Beto was right behind him. "Where are you going?"

He didn't know. His feet were carrying him; all he could process was the realization, with chill certainty, that he was going to be sick. A ringing rose in his ears, drowning out Beto asking what was wrong with him, drowning out the noise of the assembly as it faded behind him, as he walked as quickly away from la casa mayor as he could.

He focused on the thump of his boots on dirt. He walked until he came to the patio of his childhood home. He walked two steps farther. Put his hand on the side of the wall, fell to his knees, and vomited.

He felt as if he were throwing up his lungs. Though his eyes were shut, there were shadows rippling through the black; Nena's screaming drummed against the back of his skull.

Beto seized him by the arm and yanked him, coughing, to his feet.

"What the fuck," Beto hissed. "You aren't drunk, are you?"

He wasn't. Not even remotely. He leaned away from Beto, spat, and straightened.

"You go back," he said hoarsely. "I'm fine."

"What, you're not coming?" Beto said. Néstor did not reply. "I don't know anyone there without you. You should come."

Before he could stop himself, Néstor spoke the truth. "It's too much." Shame flushed his neck with heat when he realized what he had said. It *was* all too much. He was weak to feel that way, weak to admit it. "Find Casimiro."

Beto hesitated. Néstor could almost hear the calculations whirring through his head: Néstor was obviously in distress, but the smell of the food the Serranos had prepared for those attending the assembly was rich on the night.

Shame turned to embarrassment, burning hot in Néstor's face. He was a man; he could handle himself without Beto fussing over him like a mother hen. He gave his friend a half-hearted shove.

"Go on," he said. "I need to be alone."

Beto gave him one last long look. "All right," he said. "Just don't do anything crazy, like run off or something."

"I'm not going to run off," Néstor snapped. There was more venom in those words than he intended. He couldn't see Beto's expression in the dark, but could sense his friend was taken aback.

"Fine, fine," Beto said. "See you."

He returned to the assembly.

Néstor stood, hand against the wall of the house, for a long moment. Echoes of voices traveled through the night to him. His heartbeat had not slowed.

Nena was alive.

She was alive.

Which meant that for the last nine years, *nine goddamned years,* every step he had taken since he left Los Ojuelos, every day spent driving cattle under the burning sun, running farther and farther from home, every night he had stared at the sky, begging for sleep to bring the one dream that eased the ache in his chest . . .

The fundamental truth on which he had built every one of those years was *wrong*.

8

※⁓∾⁓⁓

NENA

LATER THAT NIGHT, Nena sewed in la sala while Javiera, her cousins Didi and Alejandra, and Félix played a parlor game. The familiar sounds of her family needled her as she mended: Didi's occasional squeals of delight grated; Javiera's insistence that someone was cheating pitched too close to whining. Félix hushing the others because Mamá had gone to bed already brought no relief.

She thrust the needle through the skirt she was mending and pulled the thread through so sharply that it snapped.

"Madre Santa," she hissed under her breath, rethreading the needle.

It was impossible to focus. Against her wishes, her mind kept looping back to the assembly, like a moth obsessed with a flame. To the moment a group of Los Ojuelos vaqueros had stepped into the warm light of the party, scrubbed and decked in their Sunday best, their mood restless as a group of stallions.

The purpose of bringing them all together in the same court-yard, to listen to the rancheros all at once, was of a logistical as well as a more political nature. They would be discussing the number of wagons and cattle to bring, as well as the best route to join with the Mexican army at Matamoros. But of the ten or so rancheros who had agreed to join the squadron, many had rivalries with one another. They were neighbors with long histories that were not always harmonious. Even now, as the final ranchero arrived with his vaqueros and the group shifted and settled with anticipation, Papá's voice pitched in agitation as he spoke with Don Antonio Canales. Papá and Don Antonio were not arguing outright; perhaps the other rancheros kept the conversation at a civil keel. But they were close to it, and continued speaking heatedly even as the conversation beyond Nena and Mamá shifted in surprise. Out of curiosity, her eye followed the attention of the assembly as it swooped like swallows to the courtyard entrance.

The Los Ojuelos vaqueros were among the final arrivals to the assembly. As de facto leaders of the rancho's vaqueros, Bernabé and Casimiro arrived first, a matched set with dark hair and nearly identical features, polished and gleaming like bright coins.

Behind them was a third.

Nena's eye passed over the figure for a moment, caught by the presence of a man who looked like an Anglo among the vaqueros, then her attention tripped over itself in belated surprise. *Wait*, it cried. *There.* She looked back.

She knew him.

Over the years, on the rare occasions that she let her guard down and allowed thoughts of him to slip under her skin and bruise, she wondered how he had grown. If he would resemble Casimiro, or if he would be so changed that he was a stranger to her. If he ever walked into her life again, would she recognize him?

Néstor Duarte walked slowly into the courtyard and paused, a beat behind his family, sweeping the room with dark eyes.

The answer was yes.

Undoubtedly, undeniably *yes*.

Recognition struck her like a pail of freezing water. It was one thing to imagine how he might have changed as she hovered on the cusp of sleep. It was another entirely to see him. To take in polished boots, dark trousers, and shirt fitted to his compact, muscular body. To see the angle of his shoulders, the black hair combed away from his face, a strand or two of it already falling loose onto his forehead, as it always did by the middle of Mass on a hot Sunday morning.

His face was both familiar and remade by age: the distinctive cut of the Duarte jaw was more pronounced now, the slope of his cheekbones so like his cousin's they looked like full blood brothers. But if Bernabé and Casimiro were drawn in broad, rustic strokes, Néstor was a sharp, precise carving. A reflection in a mirror that had been polished harshly bright. His expression was even, almost stern, giving him a look like serious Bernabé. But the set of his mouth still had a hint of playful wickedness, a glimmer so familiar she would know it in any face. Even if it was the face of someone she had not seen in nine years. A man who was as good as a stranger to her.

His sweep of the courtyard slowed. Stopped.

On her.

Their eyes locked.

Mamá was speaking, but her words were a distant hum, a hive of bees falling further and further away. Nena was standing. She was moving around the table, past Mamá and Félix.

Néstor was here. It was impossible. She felt a powerful urge to touch him. To know that he was real. To know that he was no longer a memory, the dull ache of a thorn long buried in her side, but a boy of flesh and blood.

No longer a boy—a man. Taller than he once was, his shoulders and ribs filled out, weathered but confident.

"Magdalena." Mamá's tone sliced into her, demanding her

attention. The voice came from farther behind her than she expected; she had begun to cross the courtyard. She hesitated.

He was still watching her.

"*Magdalena*." Mamá seized her by the elbow. "I said, we must return to la casa mayor. These conversations do not concern young women."

Nena faced Mamá. She had to stay, not least because of what hung on the success of her going with the squadron to Matamoros.

"But I am going with them," she said. "Of course it is appropriate for me to stay. Félix," she called, drawing her brother away from Don Severo with the insistence in her voice. "Félix, tell Mamá that I need to stay to listen to plans being discussed. I need to know."

"Mamá, Nena is right," Félix began gently. "It is important for her to hear the logistics being discussed." Mamá's posture and expression shifted at his level, reasoned tone. Her hold on Nena's elbow loosened.

Nena was both relieved and fought the urge to scowl. Thank goodness Félix had been present. If Papá was going to take her bargain with him seriously, then she needed to be present in moments where the men spoke. Félix's role in this did not sour her victory at all, for such was the way of the world. Such was the way she fought each battle and won.

When Mamá retreated, turning her focus to instead search for Javiera, Nena whirled to where the Los Ojuelos vaqueros had entered. Where Néstor had appeared.

She scanned the crowd of men as they shifted and settled around Papá and the other rancheros, her eyes skipping from face to face.

He was gone.

Was it a mirage she saw? No, he was there. He was *there*. The courtyard was suddenly too full of people, too noisy; though it was not yet twilight, it was too bright.

He was back. After nine years, Néstor Duarte returned to Rancho Los Ojuelos.

But not for her.

She was a stone sinking to the bottom of the spring as Félix led her to a bench to sit while Papá and the rancheros spoke. Memories washed over her in thick, cloying waves.

She was fourteen, cleaning dishes very badly as she waited for Félix to return from the comisaria. When he did, he walked in the direction of the Duarte house. The comisaria meant mail. Walking to the Duartes' meant . . . that meant news of Néstor. It *had* to.

She had slipped out of the kitchen, quietly so as not to draw attention, and dashed after Félix. She came abreast of him just before he reached the Duartes'. Abuela was on the patio; she lifted a hand and waved. Nena lifted her hand in return greeting, fighting to catch her breath.

"Is it from him?" she said to Félix, in between sharp breaths. "Is it Néstor? Where is he? Is he coming back?"

Félix was looking down at her, then looked over her head at the Duartes' house. Bernabé stepped onto the patio, wiping his hands after cleaning saddles.

"You need to stop asking, Nena," Félix said sharply. "He's gone. There's no news."

Nena looked over her shoulder. Bernabé looked expectant, his face shifting toward hope as he watched Félix and Nena.

"And now I have to tell Bernabé there's no news, no letter, just a request from Papá to come speak to him," Félix snapped. "Can't you see your acting like this just causes him more grief?"

He's gone. You need to stop asking.

She didn't. Not then.

Not when Abuela told her that sometimes, young men needed to stretch their legs like colts. They needed to dash off and see the world. Not when Abuela refused to add Nena's desperate pleas that Néstor return into their letters. They were in the kitchen garden, removing weeds that snarled around the herbs and vegetables, the early-afternoon activity of the rancho settling around them.

Abuela gave her a sharp look. "You are the patrón's daughter," she scolded. "You should know better than to ask something of a man that would anger his patrón. That would be inappropriate for Bernabé to say in a letter."

Nena bit her lip and curled her fingers into the dirt, the arches of her fingers blurring as her eyes welled with hot liquid. Félix had refused to post her letter for fear of angering their parents. Mamá had scolded her for obsessing over one missing peón, for she was the patrón's daughter and should not care.

How could she not care? She was a tree with its roots yanked violently from the soil. She was a bird without its flock, a colt cut off from the herd and lost to the chaparral. The world could not make sense without heaven overhead and earth beneath; so, too, did the world make no sense without Néstor. How could it be that everyone seemed to have forgotten about him? How *dare* they expect her to do the same?

"It is best for you to let go," Abuela said, her voice softer. "We cannot know his mind. We can only pray that God cares for him and brings him back to us one day."

Praying was not enough. Praying every Sunday in the chapel, every evening at vespers, and every night into a pillow wet with tears had not brought him back. It had been months. It had been nearly a year.

"But why did he go?" Nena's voice cracked, bringing her a lurching step toward shattering altogether. "Why won't he come back?"

Abuela sat back on her heels and gave Nena a long, solemn look. Nena's pride snapped its head back, awakened and restless. That was the look Abuela gave the ill or the suffering. When she was peering deeper than their surface, seeking what lay beneath flesh and bone. That was a look that didn't just reveal Nena's aura, it assessed it.

And it was pitying.

Nena stood abruptly, dirt falling from her skirts.

She could endure scolding from Mamá and impatience from Félix. But she would not be pitied.

From that day on, as she turned her back on the kitchen garden and Abuela, she swore she would never think of Néstor again.

She failed. Daily. Memories of him circled her footsteps like hungry curs. Every shift of the trees whispered his name, every turn of the wind carried his voice.

Hurt hardened her bones. Thickened her skin against the infrequent but searing shock of news that a rare letter had reached the Duarte jacal from a distant town.

She grew accustomed to it. She grew older. Sometimes, she found herself forgetting about him for days at a time. Perhaps in a few years, he would have faded entirely from her life, a childhood bruise too distant to be thought of with anything but resigned, genial forgiveness.

But then she saw Néstor tonight.

She was caught by surprise. She felt the earth tilt under her feet. The skies turned themselves inside out and shook shattered starlight over his head, illuminating him like a saint.

Then the shock faded. The dust settled.

Now, as she sewed in la sala, Nena could see that nothing about her life had changed. Yanquis still threatened her home. She would be riding to a battlefield and had much to prepare: herbs for limpias and poultices, bandages and needles and thread for wounds.

It did not matter that Néstor was back.

There was nothing that would distract her from her task of convincing Papá that she was worth more to this rancho on it than sent away from it. That she was Abuela's successor and was valuable in ways that could not be quantified like salt to be bartered or horses to be sold.

It did not matter that Néstor was back.

She wound these thoughts tighter and tighter around her spine as the parlor game continued around her. As a set of footsteps approached the house, as a figure stepped onto the patio and went to the door. If she had lifted her head and looked out the window, perhaps she would have seen him. Perhaps she would have not been surprised at the knock at the door.

Félix stood, taking a candle for light. The door opened inward; she could not see whom Félix greeted, but she should have recognized something in the way her cousins' faces changed, swift as the turning of pages, from disinterest to rapt curiosity.

She froze, needle suspended, as Néstor Duarte asked Félix if he could have a word with Señorita Magdalena.

Like a herd of deer lifting their heads at the appearance of a rider, every face in the room turned to Nena. Didi's and Alejandra's eyes were wide with delight; Javiera watched her intensely, brow creased. Félix looked at her from the held-open door, expectant. Waiting.

She lowered her gaze to her embroidery. Her needle was still suspended, gleaming silver in the candlelight.

She stabbed it into the next stitch.

"Tell him I've gone to bed already," she said archly.

A long-suffering look, eerily reminiscent of one of Mamá's, crossed Félix's face. "Nena, he can hear you."

A soft titter escaped Didi, though she clamped a hand over her mouth.

Heat flushed up Nena's neck to her cheeks.

Everyone was still looking at her. Every expression was an echo of another from the past: Félix looking down on her when she begged to know if he had picked up the mail at the comisaria; Didi creeping to her bedside in the dark to find her crying into her pillow; Javiera watching her, hawk-sharp, as her mind wandered while she chopped vegetables.

She was not weak, not anymore. She had not been for a long time.

She set her embroidery down. Stood. Smoothed her skirt with hands that shook. Her feet carried her across la sala to Félix as if they were someone else's, her heels crisp on the flagstones.

Félix handed her the candle and stepped back. Nena rested her hand on the open door and stepped into the spot where Félix had been.

She looked up at Néstor.

For a long moment, nothing but a soft chorus of crickets disturbed the silence. No one inside spoke. Neither did Nena.

Néstor's hands were folded before him respectfully, his black hair pushed back from his face and looking messier than it had been before. He was serious, perhaps even determined, but candlelight softened some of his sharp edges. This close, she could see a small white scar beneath his lower lip. She had forgotten that scar.

When they were eleven, he was thrown from a half-broken mustang. She was at the corral that day, watching as the colt bucked and flung Néstor into the air like a slingshot. She remembered screaming as he struck dirt; she slung herself through the rungs of the fence only to be seized by the arm and yanked back by his cousin Casimiro.

"He's fine," Casimiro said when she struggled to be let go and run to see if Néstor was hurt. "See?"

Even before another vaquero had reached him, Néstor had sprung to his feet. His face was bloodied, but he was grinning.

That day was the first her heart had beat so hard in fear for him that it physically hurt.

It was not the last.

But years passed; she grew tired of hurting. She built up calluses to it. She had bled and had her own scars now.

He was looking directly into her eyes. It was too familiar. Too intimate.

"Buenas," he said softly.

Without breaking eye contact, she shut the door in his face.

9

NÉSTOR

NÉSTOR PACED BACK and forth before the patio of his family's jacal. Voices old and recent waged a duel in his skull.

My daughter is dead.

Magdalena, come here.

Nena lived. He saw her. She met his eyes and stood. At that moment, time shuddered and slowed beneath his feet, hooves skidding on uneven ground.

But it couldn't be. He had held her cold body. He had carried her for God knew how long through the dark, willing her to breathe, willing her heart to beat. In vain.

From where he paced, he saw figures in skirts returning to la casa mayor from the assembly: Doña Mercedes and a tall, lean girl who might be Javiera. A few of Nena's aunts; her cousins Didi and Alejandra.

He kept pacing.

Don Félix and another figure approached la casa mayor. A figure with full skirts and hair braided around her head like a crown.

A figure whose gait he recognized even after not having seen her for nine years.

They disappeared into la casa mayor.

My daughter is dead.

Yet now she lived.

These two truths faced each other, pistols drawn and trembling. One had to win over the other. One had to be the victor. But neither would draw the trigger.

He had to speak to her. He *had* to.

Night settled around the rancho with all its sounds. Don Feliciano was still in the courtyard. There was no reason to be afraid to walk up to the patio. To retrace the path he had once carried Nena down.

Perhaps it took an hour. It felt like no time. It felt like three hours. He inhaled sharply, bracing himself, and let his feet carry him through the grass.

He went to the door of la casa mayor. Lifted his hand. Knocked. The sound rattled the breath between his ribs. He was thirteen, he was falling to his knees on rough tipichil floor, Nena's weight impossibly heavy against him. He shook his head to clear it. He cleared his throat.

Don Félix opened the door.

Then, before he knew what he would say, *she* was in the doorway.

Nena stood before him. So close that if he lifted his hand, he could have touched her cheek. Felt its living warmth.

For nine years, she was dead.

She was a ghost haunting his nights and his days; her mist thickened and faded with the setting and rising of the sun, but it never left. No matter how hard or far he rode, she clung to his skin like the smell of sleep. His soul bore her brand, the wound deep and blackened and scarred over. From the day he left Los Ojuelos, a part of him knew that his life was now a game of second bests. Of good-enoughs. A meager harvest grown in the long shadow of her absence.

None of that was true anymore.

For now here she was, candlestick in hand. Looking at him.

He should have sensed she was not happy to see him. He should have done or said something to begin on the right foot, but he was struck dumb. To him, the crickets fell silent. The noise of the assembly in the courtyard faded; the moon ceased to glow. The night had no mistress but her.

Silent, reverent, he watched the glimmer of the flame reflected in her dark, liquid eyes. Candlelight gilded the tips of her eyelashes and danced along her hairline, caressing the brown hair swept elegantly away from her face. She was a woman now, and more beautiful than he ever could have dreamed.

Nothing mattered but this: a bolt of yearning as wide as the sky. A certainty so brilliant it shattered every vision he once had of the future.

This was what he wanted.

His mind was on another patio, one he had dreamed of for years, one that he built with his own hands on his own land. In dreams he had turned and found no one next to him; now, he saw.

Nena.

He drank in her face, so changed and exactly the same, with slim, even brows, round cheeks, pointed chin. Full mouth. He should have noticed it was set in a firm line. He should have known his time was short. That he had but one chance.

"Buenas," he breathed.

Determination flickered across her features as she shifted back a step.

Then she slammed the door in his face.

✦ ✦ ✦

"¿*MIJO?*"

Néstor whirled. Abuela took him in from the doorway, her dark eyes scrutinizing. He had returned to pacing before the family's jacal, his chest heaving as if he had been running, his hair likely ruined from the number of times he had run his hand through it.

She raised a brow. "Is something the matter?"

His life was shattered underfoot, further crushed by every aimless step he took. He had no direction. He had nothing but these two pistols drawn at each other: Nena was dead. Nena lived. Nothing but that and a dark awareness in his gut, growing and spreading with a shameful heat, that he had done something very, very wrong. Something that could never be undone.

He said none of this. Instead, he said: "Nena."

Abuela's face softened with understanding. "I thought so," she said. "Was she angry to see you?"

So Abuela did not know either. Neither Casimiro nor Bernabé nor anyone at the assembly was shocked to see Nena. Nor her father or her mother. Doña Mercedes, whom Néstor had last seen wailing *my daughter is dead*, took Nena by the elbow and spoke to her as if nothing had happened.

It could not be.

At last, the pistols fired at each other.

"She died." He stopped pacing and faced Abuela head-on. She had sat at the table on the patio and patted the seat next to her on the bench. He ignored the gesture. "That night. I carried her back to la casa mayor. She was dead. Everyone said so. And I . . ."

His voice snagged on sharp breath. His feet were carrying him again, flattening the grass before the patio. Memories crushed beneath the soles of his boots. The weight of her in his arms, stiff and lifeless. Her cheek cold against his. A yearning for her to breathe, a need so desperate it became an ache in the hollow of his throat.

"Mijo." Abuela gestured for him to come sit by her. "You don't understand."

"It is *true*." The words stung the air like a whip.

"Néstor." This had the resonance of a command. Néstor's body responded before his thoughts could catch up: he stopped pacing and turned to her. "Breathe," she instructed. "Sit."

He stepped onto the patio and obeyed, taking a seat next to her on the bench at the table.

"One night, I was called to la casa mayor by Doña Mercedes," Abuela said. "It was Nena. She looked . . . as if she had been mauled by a beast. But that was not all. She was sickened by its venom."

Néstor braced his elbows on the table and placed his head in his hands. He focused on the knots and gnarls in the wood of the table before him, the familiar swirls he had traced with his fingertips dozens of times as a child, but all he could see was Nena bleeding on the floor. Doña Mercedes wailing over her.

"You know what happened," Abuela said softly.

It was all his fault.

He braced for the surge of grief, the nauseating darkness to pull him under. But for once, it didn't. Abuela's hand was on Néstor's upper arm, its weight comforting. Soothing.

But not soothing enough that he could bend nightmares into words.

"You assume I was there." He was deflecting. He knew that, and he knew it was stupid. Abuela always knew.

"I know my grandson," she said. "What happened to her?"

Néstor squeezed his eyes shut. Long, machete-like claws carved through the black; Nena's screams reverberated against the back of his skull.

"It was awful." The words were barely above a whisper.

"What was it?"

"I . . . I don't know." That was the truth. "It was dark." That was a lie: the weak moonlight illuminated gray skin, a nose flat against a skull like a bat's. And teeth, so many teeth, dark and dripping with Nena's blood.

"I couldn't see," he said. He inhaled deeply and opened his eyes. He spoke the words as quickly as he could, in one long, breathless phrase directed down at the table: "When it was gone, Nena was hurt. I carried her to la casa mayor. Doña Mercedes was there, and Don Félix, and the patrón, and they said she was dead. The patrón was shouting, and I . . . it was all my fault."

There his voice died. He had no more words.

"So you ran," Abuela said.

His silence stretched through the twilight, broken only when Abuela sighed deeply.

"And now I understand why I was robbed of you for so long." Her words were heavy with sadness. She patted his arm and rested her hand there, as if she never wanted him out of reach again. "You've heard of the sickness that has been plaguing the vaqueros, haven't you, mijo?"

Néstor lifted his head from his hands, taken aback by this sudden shift in subject. "Beto heard something about susto." Susto was one of the spiritual illnesses Abuela spoke of. When he was a child, her practices were the laws of his world; to this day, he never surprised anyone from sleep, for Abuela said doing so risked the wandering, dreaming soul being separated from the waking body. He did not know if he believed it. He only knew that if Abuela believed in something, it was usually in his best interest to follow suit.

"Many have been stricken on Los Ojuelos. It is a venom that stuns rather than kills—like a scorpion. Nena was poisoned that night," Abuela said. "But she also suffered a shock to her spirit. Two shocks, I believe. The first I healed her from, that night when Doña Mercedes summoned me to la casa mayor." She shook her head, her white braids seeming brighter as the light died and the night deepened. "But the second is one she has never recovered from."

Néstor lowered his hands from his face, waiting for Abuela to continue. This was a pause he knew from a thousand stories around the fire; he fell into the rhythm of her speaking as if he had never left.

"Losing you," she said, her dark eyes searching his face. "To you, Nena died. To her, you left. Those are two very different griefs."

Nine years he ran, and she was here. Alone.

He had *left* her.

Dread unspooled in his chest. It felt at once full of nausea and horribly, impossibly empty as he realized that yes, he had made a mistake. One that could never be undone.

Voices and footsteps approached; it was Beto and Casimiro, returning from the assembly. A lift in the breeze carried the rich smells of cabrito and beans toward the patio.

Néstor lifted his head. His stomach curled into an eager fist. He had forgotten to eat; now, presented with the smells of grilled onions and peppers and cumin and hot tortillas, he could think of little else.

"Brought you something, hermanito," Casimiro announced, setting a plate before Néstor on the table. Beto placed a second before Abuela.

"Brought you two somethings, actually," Casimiro added. He swung his legs over the bench and sat as Néstor tucked into the food. Beto sat as well, reaching into his shirt pocket for corn husk and tobacco. "A job."

"Oh?" Néstor asked as he raised a tortilla stuffed with cabrito to his mouth. Juices dripped over his fingers as he bit into soft tortilla and tender meat. Madre Santa, nothing he had ever eaten in the last nine years compared to Los Ojuelos's kitchens. There had to be something magical in the mesquite woodsmoke, or in the pans, or the way the maíz was ground. *Something.* Nothing could compare.

"The patrón's daughter is coming with the squadron to Matamoros," Casimiro said. "I don't know if you remember Señorita Magdalena," he added, voice lifting wryly.

"*What?*" Néstor coughed, nearly choking on his taco. "Why? That's not safe."

Beto pursed his lips as he rolled his cigarillo, brows lifted in interest at Néstor's reaction.

Néstor cleared his throat, wiping his mouth with the back of his hand. He couldn't let Beto see what Nena was to him. That would invite questions. Questions would require evading or explaining, and he was in no state to do either.

"The patrón says we need curanderos," Casimiro continued. He stole a roasted pepper from Néstor's plate and popped it in his mouth, then nodded at Abuela. "I guess you could call her Abuela's apprentice. Anyway, Don Félix wants her to be well protected on the road. He's enlisted us to trade watches, keeping an eye on her day and night. You can handle the extra work, verdad?"

Keeping watch over Nena would mean riding beside her, or at least near her. Standing watch outside her tent as she slept. Seeing her every day. His heartbeat quickened with anticipation at the thought.

It would provide opportunities to talk to her. He could say . . .

What would he say?

He had been speechless tonight, and she slammed the door in his face.

Those are two very different griefs, Abuela had said.

His grief had taken root in his legs and kept them running. Nena's, it seemed, walked hand in hand with anger.

"¿Verdad?" Casimiro asked again, drawing the syllables long.

"Of course," Néstor said quickly. As Casimiro and Beto began relating the other matters that had been discussed at the assembly, he looked past them at la casa mayor, at the candlelight that shone through the windows.

Over the course of an evening, his world had spun and flung him to the ground like a half-broken mustang. He had stumbled as he righted himself, but now, an unexpected calm swept through him. His feet were firm on the earth; his gaze was fixed on the horizon, on the one thing worth fighting for.

Nena lived.

Yes, he had made an unfathomable mistake. Yes, Nena did not want to speak with him—perhaps she wanted nothing to do with him. He could spend the rest of his life regretting it, or he could take this imperfect, broken miracle that fate had dropped in his lap and *do* something with it.

I will fix this, he swore, his eyes on the windows of la casa mayor. Though he had no idea what that might look like, nor how long it would take, it was an oath. A prayer. *I promise.*

10

~~~~~

NENA

BY THE TIME the bedroom candles were blown out hours later, no one had asked Nena about Néstor. She stared at the ceiling as her cousins' and Javiera's breathing softened the darkness with sleep. Javiera's dog, Pollo, paced the room three times, his claws clicking rhythmically on the stone floor, until he, too, settled at the foot of Javiera's bed.

Sleep flitted mockingly over the crown of Nena's head, close enough that she could almost touch it. It would remain there, both close and maddeningly distant, so long as thoughts circled her mind like a yearling in a training corral, hooves packing the dirt harder and harder.

How dare Néstor come to speak to her. How dare he interrupt her on one of the few peaceful nights she had left with her family before the squadron departed on the dangerous road to Matamoros. And to say what, after nine years of silence?

An irritated hum rose in her chest, fatally soft as a snake's rattle, at the memory of his face illuminated by the candlelight in her doorway. The way the glow from within the house caught the sharp lines of his features and gentled them.

How *dare* he stand there, as if he genuinely believed he was entitled to speak to her after so many years away. After no word. After nearly a decade of silence.

She owed him nothing. Not the courtesy of conversation, not the time it took for words to fall from his mouth.

As the girls undressed for bed earlier, Nena had been certain she caught Didi whispering *I told you so* to her sister Alejandra. She lifted her head and cast them an imperious look over her shoulder as she closed the latch on the room's single window.

"What did you say?" she snapped.

Her cousins shot each other twin guilty glances. Alejandra confessed immediately.

"We saw Néstor Duarte arrive at the comisaria this afternoon," she said, words crowding together as she grew flustered. "We could have told you, or maybe we should have, but . . ."

"But we knew you'd be angry," Didi cut in, her features turning sheepish as she ducked away from Nena's glower.

So Nena could have had a warning. Anger simmered in her chest when she thought of how someone could have told her that Néstor was about to walk into the courtyard. Instead, surprise made her a fool.

She didn't need him. She had learned to live without him and would continue to. In two days, the squadron would be leaving. The rancho would forget that Néstor Duarte had ever appeared.

She turned abruptly onto her stomach, casting thoughts aside like a too-heavy blanket. She shut her eyes.

Sleep eventually took her. Its embrace was ill-fitting, itchy as wool, never settling with ease.

She dreamed of Néstor.

She watched him thrown to the dirt by the bucking mustang,

once, then twice, and she was running toward him. Her legs were too heavy; it was as if she were running through wet sand as Casimiro reached for her. Darkness swept over both vaqueros, distorting their voices, swallowing them. The dream rippled and slipped forward; suddenly, thousands of arms were reaching for her, grasping at her in the black. She pumped her legs, desperate to flee, her heart throbbing frantically in her throat. She could not see behind her and she dared not try to look, for she knew the arms reaching for her were long and clawed. She knew they belonged to something terrible, something a hair's breadth behind her. *They* were just behind her: a thousand eyes, a thousand awarenesses descending on her like bats, blinding her. They were upon her. She was falling, falling—

She tried to scream.

Sleep swallowed the sound whole; when she woke, flinging herself forward into a seated position in tangled sheets, it was nothing but a strangled, fleshy cry. She gasped, uneven and harsh, taking in the room: the crucifix on the wall, Didi and Alejandra's sleeping forms, the small altar to la Virgen, the vanity covered with combs and jewelry and ribbons by the window. Everything was as it was.

Except—

Javiera was sitting upright in bed, her shriek splitting the night. *That* was what had woken her. The whites of Javiera's eyes were shockingly bright in the moonlight that spilled into the room.

Nena flung herself from her bed, tripping over Pollo and stumbling to Javiera's side. The dog was barking without cease, barely drawing breath, his voice rasping and angry.

Plaintive cries rose from Didi's and Alejandra's beds as they were disturbed from sleep and began to ask what the matter was. Nena ignored them. She sat on Javiera's bed and took her younger sister into her arms.

"Hush, hush, I'm here." Javiera trembled violently, but at Nena's touch, her screaming broke and crumbled into heaving sobs. Nena pressed her head into her shoulder. "Come back to me, Javiera. Breathe. It was just a dream."

The dog was still barking. Sounds rose from the rest of the house. Voices stirred, disgruntled; despite Didi and Alejandra's commands, the dog kept barking, his nose pointed at the window, his hackles raised, his legs splayed and braced, his tail held high and alert.

Javiera inhaled sharply. "That face," she whispered into Nena's shoulder. "In my dream. It had *no eyes*. And teeth, so many teeth . . ."

A light breeze struck Nena's back. Its cool, cloying fingers played over the soft sweat of sleep that sheathed the back of her neck.

The hairs on her arms lifted.

She tightened her arms around Javiera and looked over her shoulder.

Moonlight spilled onto the floor of the room, thick and slow as a pool of blood. The window was open. The latch was undone, the wooden shutters flung wide open to the cloudless night sky beyond.

In the center of the pool of moonlight stood Pollo. The dog's nose was pointed directly at the window, and he would not stop barking.

11

NENA

THE SQUADRON MOVED toward Matamoros like an un-
gainly, adolescent beast with too many limbs to be built for speed.
In addition to the rancheros and their horses, Nena counted at least
two spares per ranchero on the string. Then there were the vaqueros and their mounts, the livestock, and rancho cooks on lumbering
carts who would make sure the squadron was fed. Papá told Nena
as they rode that it was still considered a lean, fast-moving oper-
ation, compared to an infantry division—they would reach Matamoros in nine days, God willing, and there she would see the sprawl
of a proper army.

How Papá could speak so authoritatively of such things was not
clear to Nena—hadn't he spent his whole life north of Río Bravo,
in the rugged outposts of El Norte, oft forgotten by the rest of
México? But she bit her tongue. Nodded along as he and other
rancheros criticized General Arista's strategy or speculated about
how many Yanqui battalions had arrived north of Río Bravo to the
fortress they were building that they called Fuerte Brown. Eager to

remain in Papá's good graces, she obeyed quickly when he asked things of her and kept her head down and her focus on her tasks as a curandera and a woman in the camp.

The men's anxiety was palpable. Nena knew from eavesdropping that many did not want to be there—forced to leave behind wives and children and aging parents, they were present because their rancheros ordered them to be. Rumors of susto snaked through them like fingers of smoke, morphing with every twist of the breeze. Texians, it was said, eager to further expand their territory, had poisoned the streams—that had to be why men fell unconscious. Some claimed that the Yanquis had trained ferocious dogs and set them loose on the ranchos after they took Puerto Isabel—that was why some men had been mauled, not only among the vaqueros, but also among the Mexican infantry. Others still swore on their grandfathers' graves that the Yanquis had a new weapon, that it could maul and poison in equal measure.

That was the one rumor that slipped under Nena's skin like a huisache thorn and festered, calling to mind Ignacio's sickness and his strange wound. It kept her watching her back when she collected water and carried out camp chores, jumping whenever she heard a rustle in the trees. More often than not, the rustle turned out to be nothing more threatening than cockroaches in the palm leaves of a stout sabal by the riverbank, or the gossipy chittering of a gleaming black zanate in the mesquites.

Or her guards.

Papá had given Félix the responsibility of choosing the men who would protect her over the course of the journey. She thought nothing of it until she saw the cut of a familiar silhouette speaking with Félix during the siesta; caught voices and the bright flash of pistols being cleaned in the sunlight.

Papá did not have favorites among the vaqueros. Félix did. He respected Bernabé Duarte like an equal, turning to the older man for advice as often as he turned to the uncles or even Papá.

"The younger Duarte in particular is an excellent shot," Félix informed Papá that first night.

A strange feeling washed over her when she overheard this. A dash of dread, a dose of anger.

When one of the other rancheros offered his rancho's own vaqueros to join the guard watching over Nena, Papá swatted the idea away with a brusque gesture, as if he were brushing a fly away from his meal. "They have the manners of caballeros, Bernabé's boys. I trust them with my life."

Nena did not trust Néstor Duarte any farther than she could throw him.

She grew accustomed to the other two who took turns either outside her tent or shadowing her as she walked to get water from the river with the few other women who accompanied the squadron—some cooks, some servants, some vaqueros' wives. It was strange enough being apart from the familiar rhythms of the rancho; the disruption made it easy to take the addition of a bodyguard in stride. Casimiro was distant and polite, as usual. Years ago, Néstor had told her that Bernabé was incredibly strict with him and Casimiro about how to behave respectfully around the women of the rancho.

The other was the vaquero Beto. Though his appearance suggested Anglo parentage, with blue eyes and a reddish tinge to his light hair, he was indiscernible from the other vaqueros. He was a creature of the chaparral like them, all bowlegged from a life spent in the saddle and with the corners of his eyes lined from squinting into the sun. Unlike Casimiro's silence, Beto made pleasant small talk that, more often than not, spun into long, amusing stories of his years on the road, a cigarillo never far from his lips. Sometimes, if Nena woke in the night in the darkness of her tent, she could hear him singing to himself softly as he kept watch. She began to associate the smell of tobacco with comfort. She slept well those nights.

Casimiro and Beto were unfailingly polite in her presence. This was profoundly at odds with how they behaved around the campfire with the other vaqueros. She heard them from a distance at times, while helping other women stoke the cooking fire or in passing as she headed to different parts of camp to check on men recovering from minor injuries sustained on the road.

Beto in particular loved to hold a court of raucous laughter among the vaqueros, weaving yarns about Néstor. Néstor finding a cursed conquistador's helmet in the silver mines in Durango. Néstor downing bloodthirsty longhorns and branding them. Néstor breaking wild mesteño stallions that no one else could even approach. Néstor bedding the wives and widows of wealthy rancheros.

Nena's cheeks smarted hot as she overheard one of these last tales. She couldn't help but glance over her shoulder, agitated, to seek Beto's face and use it to gauge his tone better. Was it a joke? A brutal exaggeration?

"With all these stories you would think he's Pedro de Urdemañas!" one vaquero cried. There—that was someone who smelled the exaggeration of a vaquero tall tale. Comparing anyone to that trickster hero of folklore was as good as claiming falsehood outright.

"No, Pedro de Urdemañas had to rely on trickery to get out of Hell," Casimiro said. He had noticed Nena; caught her eye and held it for a minute. Casimiro had been all tipped brims of hats and genteel *buenas tardes* to her over the years, but now, something wickedly amused sparked in his eyes with the firelight. He looked away, refocusing on his listeners. But he had to know that she was listening too. "Néstor Duarte would charm the Devil senseless and walk out whistling."

Their words buzzed around her, as insistent and irritating as the mosquitoes that nipped at the squadron as it moved south. She should know better than to believe them. A vaquero tale was only ever half-truth at best, but they chafed at her like straw during the hours Néstor was on watch.

THEY WERE A day out from Matamoros. Anxiety knit around the men like thick threads of mist; their horses, tasting change in the air, grew restless, stamping their hooves and whinnying even as they settled into the siesta. Unease lay over Nena's skin like the constant sweat that lingered throughout each humid day. Papá and Don Antonio Canales had ridden ahead to meet with the general and had not yet returned as twilight reddened in the west. To make matters worse, Néstor was on watch.

She ignored him studiously as she left camp to fetch water, her long riding skirt dragging softly over the trampled grass of the path. The grasses grew unusually high among the ebony trees along the banks of the river. The air clung to the afternoon's heat; it hung in a thick veil over the riverbanks. Even the distant cry of raucous chachalacas was smothered by it.

The only sound was Néstor's footsteps, falling in time behind hers at a respectful distance. Unlike other times he had shadowed her in the last week, when he tried and failed to strike up smooth small talk, he said nothing.

Good.

She did not have the patience to brush him aside, not today. She had not forgiven him for having the nerve to show up at the door of la casa mayor with nothing but *buenas* to explain himself. For every morning or afternoon on the road he nonchalantly tried to chat about the weather or horses or the other vaqueros, or God forbid, asked polite questions about what curanderismo she had learned from Abuela in his absence.

For that absence always went unspoken. Their entire time on

the road, he acted as if striking up a conversation with her were the most normal thing in the world.

As she lay in her tent at night, slapping away mosquitoes and longing for the comforting breathing of her sister and cousins nearby, she reached a conclusion that made her eyes sting with unshed tears.

The boy she knew and missed was dead. The man who had returned in his place was a fraud who bore his name. Beneath his attempted charming veneer was an unfeeling stranger. He did not care how years of absence had affected her, for they certainly did not affect him.

She did not care to know him. In fact, she refused to.

She quickened her pace through the grass to the river, hoisting the water jug on her hip. The sooner she washed her face and collected water, the sooner she could get away from him. She could always tell when he was watching her. She felt it like a physical weight, like a soft hand on her arm, a whispered *I'm here.*

But where had he been for nine years? Why had he left? Why hadn't he sent her any word? These thoughts drove her forward as steer move at the whip; she was so wrapped up in them it took until she was halfway to the riverbank to notice how eerie the silence of the twilight was, broken only by a soft buzzing.

How the feeling of being watched was perhaps more than Néstor's presence as she scanned the unusually high grasses on either side of the path. How it hugged the back of her neck with a predatory intimacy.

She turned the last bend in the path and nearly tripped into the carcass of a bull blocking the path to the river.

Her gasp of surprise was almost a cry.

"Nena." A hand on her arm; it drew her back gently, catching her and keeping her balanced. Any other time she would have bristled at the touch, at the familiarity of her nickname. But she barely noted these, nor Néstor's sharp, hissing intake of breath.

The soft, claylike soil of the riverbank was roughened and mud-died by pawing hooves; the bull had been taken down in a struggle. It lay on its side, head at a sharp angle pointed toward Nena, eyes glassy and still untouched by vultures. Flies thickened its nostrils and a long wound at its throat.

The carcass was fresh.

Its face had the harsh, starved look of beasts in famine; its hide was pulled taut over protruding chest bones and hips, hugging each rib tightly over a strangely hollow belly. It was desiccated, like a lime left to dry out in the sun, like salted meat smoked for weeks, as if every drop of liquid had been sucked from it, leaving nothing but a husk in its wake.

An Hacienda del Sol brand blackened the bull's shoulder. This was no feral steer left to fend for itself, that might sicken and die with no one noticing. This was one of the healthy cattle that had been brought along with the squadron.

"What on earth?" she breathed.

The hand fell from her arm. Néstor stepped forward, moving gingerly around the carcass's head and crouching in the disturbed earth to get a closer look. Nena hovered a step behind him, holding the water jug tight to her hip.

The wound at the cow's neck was that of a predator: rough, un-even, ripped. Mauled. The dryness of the cow's hide emphasized needlelike punctures around the wound.

"I have never seen anything like this," Nena said softly, half to herself.

Even as the words fell from her mouth, she wondered if they were a lie. Something in the uneven edging of the wound called to mind the strange, snakelike punctures she had seen on the inside of the vaquero Ignacio's arm.

Néstor's hat shaded his eyes and hid most of his expression, but she could see the grim set of his mouth.

"I have," he said.

"What did this?" Nena asked. It didn't look like the work of a cougar, nor a coyote—there were no paw prints to be seen, no claw marks. Only the desperate pawing of cloven hooves.

"Well . . ." Néstor rose slowly. One hand rose thoughtfully to his jaw; the gesture sent a pang of familiarity through her chest. He was here. The strangeness that hung around them like a physical weight on the air made her raw, made the pang strike deeper. He was *here*, and she still missed him. "An old vaquero once told me it was the work of spirits."

His voice in her memories was that of an adolescent, crackling like frost underfoot. Now it was like worn leather: supple and dark, well-fit as an old saddle. She hated how natural it sounded. She hated how it felt like a draft of cool water. She hated how much she wanted him to keep speaking.

The sensation of being watched had not broken; if anything, it built, like a branding iron slowly reddening in the fire as the twilight deepened. Speaking would keep it at bay.

"What does that mean?" she asked.

"I don't know. The man was a bit, ah, strange. You know?" He whistled softly and made a looping gesture with one hand around his ear. He said *strange*, he meant *loco*. "Beto and I drove with him years ago, north of Presidio de San Vicente."

It was only a few sentences, but it was more than enough to damn him. The familiar gestures, the throwaway reference to a life lived away from Los Ojuelos. How casually he said *years ago*, as if that time slipped comfortably by, as if those were not long months Nena sat staring out the window, waiting for Félix to come from the comisaria with the post. Waiting in vain for any news.

You need to stop asking, Nena. He's gone.

Nine years. For nine years she wondered where he was, if he was safe, if he was coming back. She grew. The landscape of her life changed irreparably. She became more and more tightly bound by the ropes of womanhood; he roamed free, unburdened by responsibilities.

"Let's see if someone at camp has a better explanation," he said, lifting a hand to his lips. He let out a high, sharp whistle: two notes, repeated twice, a message clear as day to anyone who grew up on Los Ojuelos. *Come here, come see,* without the third, higher note indicating *help.*

"Here, come this way," Néstor said. He stepped back from the carcass and waved for her to follow him a few paces back. "We should wait for others to arrive, but then we'll go to the river."

She stepped toward him, then paused. Following him was a long-dead habit; she hated how easily it resurrected itself. How easily she fell into it.

She was caught off guard by the sudden, hot presence of a sob growing thick and fast and difficult to breathe around. Perhaps it was exhaustion. Perhaps it was something else. She quashed it either way. She lifted her chin haughtily, readjusted the jug on her hip, and stalked right past him down the path in the direction of the river.

"Nena?"

She didn't want to hear another word from him, not another syllable softened by his voice's light, rural twang that sounded so much like home.

"Wait, please." Footsteps behind her. "I said I wouldn't leave you."

Nena scoffed. "Bold words." She could taste the acidity in the words before they struck the air. "You shouldn't go making the kinds of promises to my father that you have a history of breaking. He's bound to lose his temper with you." She squinted. The river had appeared around a bend; its slow-moving surface reflected the reddening twilight.

The footsteps behind her hesitated. Continued. "What the hell are you talking about? Nena—"

"Don't call me that," she shot over her shoulder. "Strangers address me as Magdalena. Vaqueros may call me señorita, or better yet, say nothing to me at all. Understood?"

She heard a sharp intake of breath through the nose. Her barb struck him. Good. He deserved it. She wished she could turn around and pierce him with a thousand more, with every hurtful thing she had to say. To make this insultingly carefree man feel a fraction of what she felt.

"Madre Santa," he drawled, dry and mocking. "Casimiro should have warned me that you became such a brat."

Nena whirled to face him.

He touched the brim of his hat in an exaggerated gesture. "Señorita," he added belatedly.

She adjusted the jug haughtily and met his eyes. They faced each other down like duelers, pistols drawn and cocked and gleaming.

An unfamiliar feeling lifted its head in her chest: a rough, feral desire to brawl. A sudden need to fight him and win, to leave him defeated in the dust like he deserved.

"And what kind of treatment did you expect? You *left* me." She had never said the words aloud. Unleashing their weight rushed to her head like a goblet of wine—it left her breathless, heated, burning. It left her wanting more. She had never raised her voice at a man like this before, but now that she had begun, she found she could not stop. "You should be grateful I'm even speaking to you now. It won't happen again, trust me."

She expected him to fire back in kind. Instead, his shoulders slackened. He dropped his gaze.

"I'm sorry," he said.

"You think *sorry* is sufficient?" It wasn't. It changed nothing. It was a thin coat of paint over a rotting, broken house.

"I couldn't come back," he said.

"I woke up one morning and my best friend was gone without a trace," she snapped. "Without a word. For *nine years*."

His hands rose to his face as she was speaking; now his fingertips pressed against his temples. "Nena, I . . ."

She cut him off. "Don't call me Nena."

He kept speaking, voice gravelly with emotion: "You *died* that night."

Nena's retort died on her lips. She expected another half-hearted *sorry*. This tripped her and sent her sprawling in the dust.

"I couldn't come back," Néstor said. He gestured to his chest with both hands, every motion woven with earnestness, as his voice wavered close to cracking. He shut his eyes, as if bracing himself against something painful. "I couldn't face it."

He spoke with such conviction that she could not help but pause for a moment. She only held pieces of that night in her cupped palms; the more she squinted at them, the more they slipped through her fingers like water. Abuela told her she suffered from susto, but that did not explain the scar on her neck.

But it was not an excuse.

"Basta," she snapped. Her skin prickled with irritation, with the heat; beneath the neckline of her dress, her scar felt as if it had been stung by nettles. "You're full of shit. I'm not dead, am I?"

His eyes flew open. "Would I lie about something like this?" he said, as breathlessly as if she had struck him.

"I don't know. I don't know you anymore," she said. "Because you left."

He opened his mouth to reply, then stilled, head cocked as if he were listening to some faraway sound.

"Did you hear that?"

If Néstor's whistle had summoned other vaqueros, they should have replied in kind. Their footsteps would have been determined and noisy. But there was nothing to hear. The eerie silence that thickened the air since they discovered the carcass had not lifted; if anything, it thickened like heat the longer they were in the presence of the bull carcass, threatening to smother her.

Yet she could not rid herself of the sensation that something drew near. Something that lifted her heartbeat in fear as she realized how dark it had grown as they argued. She was acutely aware that they had no torch to light the path; she was seized by a fierce desire for one.

A metallic click brought Nena's heart to her throat. Néstor had turned and stepped close to her, his left arm outstretched as if ready to defend her. In his right he held a pistol.

"Is it Rinches?" Nena whispered, inching closer to his back. She rubbed her scar to ease the irritation. "Yanquis?"

His stance was tense as he searched the twilight, scanning the grasses on either side of them and the river behind them. "I . . . I don't know."

Then, she felt it: a humming, like that of insects, like the whir of chicharras' wings. But it did not touch her ears. She felt it on her skin, on her arms and cheeks, on the soft flesh of her neck as it rose through the grass. It felt like the smell of rotting meat, acrid and repulsive and *wrong*.

Néstor lifted the pistol. Nena gripped the water jug, ready to throw it away and flee.

Though neither of them moved, a footstep broke the silence.

12

NÉSTOR

NÉSTOR TOOK A slow step back, his grip on the gun tightening. A feeling crawled over his skin, soft as the legs of roaches: something was watching them. Something was crouching low, ready to spring.

He clicked the safety off.

Nena was just behind him, so close he could feel her breath on his neck, low and quick as a hunted rabbit's. His own pulse thrummed in his ears. Humming tightened the air. Twilight seemed to slip into full night between one heartbeat and the next; darkness fell around them in a cloying, intimate embrace.

"Jesucristo!"

He jumped, keeping his finger loose on the trigger. He lowered the gun immediately. That was Casimiro's voice. His whistle had successfully summoned other vaqueros.

The humming that closed in around him and Nena lowered to a soft buzz, then faded altogether. The darkness seemed to draw back, retreating into the river grasses.

The spell broke. It was twilight again, the air around them so light and normal that Néstor wondered if he had imagined the darkness. If he had imagined everything.

He inhaled deeply to steady himself and slipped his gun back into its holster.

"What the hell happened here?" another voice chimed in, crying out in surprise.

Nena brushed past him as she stepped forward toward the voices, readjusting the jug on her hip. He followed close behind.

Both Casimiro and Beto had answered his whistle and were next to the desiccated bull. Casimiro was crouched near the carcass's throat, shaking his head in bewilderment as he examined it.

"Beto," Nena called. The vaquero looked up at his name, his eyes skipping from Nena over her shoulder to Néstor and back again.

Beto knew. Beto always saw right through him.

Their second day on the road, Beto had begun without ceremony.

"So . . . this Magdalena. You have history," he said. They were saddling their horses and Casimiro's as camp broke around them, the morning still new and pale.

Néstor kept his eyes on adjusting Luna's girth. "What makes you say that?"

"I've heard you say *Nena* in your sleep," Beto said.

Néstor's heart dropped. His hand slipped; he nearly lost grip of the girth. He cleared his throat. "Could be anyone."

He made the mistake of glancing over his shoulder. Beto had the eerie, colored eyes some Anglos had; even in the gray of new dawn, they were so blue they were almost translucent. Néstor shoved his hat low over his own eyes to avoid them.

"What?" he challenged.

"Remember when we were driving out near Presidio de San Vicente?" Beto began, his slow drawl innocent. "Three years ago, working for Álvarez."

Néstor pulled the left stirrup down over Luna's adjusted girth. He made a noncommittal sound in reply.

He did.

They were in Coahuila, making camp in the mountains north of the river, when he thought he saw something move in the darkness of the chaparral. A shadow rising from four legs to two, standing as tall as a man in the darkness.

Then it vanished as soon as it appeared.

His heart began to race. His breath fought to keep up; his chest was so tight it hurt. Darkness gnawed at the corners of his eyes, threatening to drown him. He could not control his breathing. He paced the camp, agitated, long after the figure vanished, eyes ripped wide in fear as they searched the night for danger.

There was nothing but chaparral clothed in night. Nothing but the black silhouette of the mountains, looming silent on the horizon. Nothing but the glimmer of the fire, though its dancing shadows set him on edge.

By the time Beto grabbed him by the arm and asked what was wrong with him, fear had begun to fray at the edges. Awareness of the other vaqueros watching him warily sank in; thorns of humiliation prickled over his skin.

"You got wasted and started crying about a girl," Beto was saying. "You kept saying *Nena, Nena*. That's what they call her, isn't it?"

Néstor stared at the stirrup before him, scratching away an imaginary bit of dried saddle soap foam with his thumbnail. "I don't cry."

"You did."

"Don't remember it." He shoved his hat lower, then mounted Luna.

Beto had followed in suit. "Look, I'm not going to tell you what to do," he said. "All I'm saying is that whenever I'm having trouble with someone, I find the best approach is to be honest. To say things out loud. ¿Me entiendes?"

Beto's advice was solid. It always was. So he had tried, but he had stumbled spectacularly. The evidence of his failure was clear: the air around Nena crackled with irritation as she gestured for Beto.

"Come with me to the river, please," Nena said to Beto. "Then escort me back to camp."

"Of course, señorita," Beto said. "But wasn't Duarte—"

"Señor Duarte no longer has the privilege of my company," Nena said archly.

Néstor flinched.

His strategy at broaching the gulf between him and Nena thus far had reaped little harvest. He had learned to charm women, to flirt and coax smiles from the sternest face, but would not resort to such tactics. This was not any woman. This was Nena. At a loss for how to talk to her, he tried to warm the chill she shrouded herself in as Beto might—begin with the weather, comment on the horses. Lull her defenses with quiet, quotidian conversation until they lowered.

She rebuked him.

He told himself as he held watch over her tent at night that he could accept this. Nena lived. She moved through the world with the same determined tilt to her shoulders and flint in her eyes that drew him to her when he was a boy, a moth to her blazing light. Was she not miraculously resurrected? To see her was enough. To hear her laugh again, even if it was at one of Beto's long, meandering jokes and not his, was enough.

He could survive on the scraps from her table—had he not spent the last nine years starving? Anything she gave him now was a bounty. It would be fine.

"I respect your wishes, señorita," Beto said slowly, choosing his words with care, "but your brother instructed us to protect you, and given this"—here he gestured at the carcass of the bull—"there might be a cougar nearby. Or . . . worse." He paused, as if wondering what worse could mean. "I'll fetch the water, if you don't mind. I think it's best if you go back to camp."

"I'll say," Casimiro said, standing. "It's not safe out here." He set his hands on his hips and gave the dead steer one final look before turning to Nena and Néstor. "I think Beto's right. Shall we go back to camp, señorita?"

Nena hesitated. Was she weighing how much she wanted him out of her sight?

"Fine," she said at last. She shifted her weight and held the jug out to Beto, who took it with a genteel touch of the brim of his hat.

"Better safe than sorry, señorita," he said, and headed off to the river. As he passed Néstor, he murmured in English: "You're welcome."

Néstor bit his tongue. He could not see Nena's expression, not with her back turned to him as she stepped haughtily forward to walk beside Casimiro, but he imagined she would not take kindly to being whispered about behind her back in English.

Beto's whistle rose through the grasses, growing fainter, as they parted ways in the deepening gloom. The fires of the camp were just visible through the high grasses; by their light, Néstor saw Casimiro set a hand lightly on his holster and cast a meaningful look over his shoulder. It was a silent message, perhaps so as not to alarm Nena, but it was clear as if he had spoken it aloud. *Be ready.*

For what?

He told Nena the truth when he said he had seen something like that before, near Presidio de San Vicente. The same evening Beto claimed Néstor wept about Nena, he and two other vaqueros had come across an enormous longhorn bull downed in the chaparral. There were signs of a struggle: scratches on the bull's hide from thorns, the dirt stirred to madness beneath where it lay. But there were no other tracks around it. No sign that a cougar—the only predator big enough to down a steer of that size—had attacked. Even if it had been a cougar, it made no sense for the animal to abandon its kill out in the open.

Much less to leave it so desiccated.

Néstor drew back in disgust, a sour taste slicking his mouth. He had seen hundreds of dead cattle in his life. He had even butchered many. He had never seen something like *this*: its eye sockets empty and blackened with flies, but that was the only normal thing about it. It looked like a sack of bones, as if it had been left out to dry for weeks. Bones protruded like sharp roots breaking through earth; Néstor could count every single one of the bull's ribs, make out the ridges of its spine. As if it had been starved in a drought, though the entirety of the herd they were driving was healthy and hale. The levels of decay and lack of scavenging meant the kill was recent. Perhaps only a day old.

There was but one wound. Just beneath the curve of the bull's cheek, the soft flesh of the throat had been punctured by incisors . . . if those fangs had been situated in an enormous set of jaws.

And that was it.

It made no sense.

"Híjole." One of the vaqueros with Néstor that day was an older man they called Old Juan, a stranger whom no one had driven with before. Old Juan kept to himself throughout the drive; though he shared his tobacco, he never shared conversation or stories over the campfire. Néstor and Beto thought him strange—how could they not, when he left lines of salt around his sleeping bag and drew curious marks in the dirt around the horses? Everyone thought the man was a bit cracked, and cut him a wide berth.

Old Juan crouched near the bull's ravaged throat, then stood and crossed himself quickly. When he spoke, it was the most words Néstor had ever heard him string together in his ragged, shout-roughened voice. "No animal did this," he said to Néstor and the other vaqueros. "This is the work of spirits."

The brassy, mocking laughter of the other vaqueros shattered the eerie silence that hung over the bull carcass.

But later that night, after Néstor panicked about seeing humanlike shapes in the gloom, Old Juan approached and sat next to him. The older man rolled a cigarillo in silence, the campfire carving the lines of his face deep.

"I know that look. You've seen them," he said. His voice was like gravel underfoot. Néstor did not reply. Old Juan did not seem to care, for he continued without prompting. "I was born in Guadalajara, you know. Came north looking for silver, long ago. El Norte is different. Maybe you don't see it because you're from here—something strange lives in this land." He stamped earth under the heel of his boot for emphasis. The glow of his cigarillo being lit was like an ember, burning brighter as he inhaled, then released a thin, blue stream of smoke. "If you live cheek to jowl with danger your whole life, you're bound to be blind to it. But I'm telling you. There are no monsters in Guadalajara. Not like here."

Aguardiente blurred the edges of that night, but Néstor's mind clung to one sharp corner of the memory: that night, Old Juan took a small bag of salt and poured it on the ground in a circle around his mare and the place where he would sleep, his head on his saddle as a pillow.

A ring of salt. Perhaps, drunk though he was, his mind seized this detail because of how it echoed Abuela's stories of witches and monsters. Perhaps it was simply too strange not to notice.

Camp unfolded before them, a small field of tents and horses. Fires reddened the deepening night. Being back in their glow loosened something in Néstor's shoulders. As if he had been bracing against something when his back was exposed in the high grasses.

A guttural scream split the peace of camp.

Néstor, Casimiro, and Nena froze like deer. It carried for a long moment, pitching agonizingly sharp. Then snapped off as suddenly as it had begun.

The following silence pressed on his ears with a grim, dark weight.

The scream came from the riverbank.

Beto.

He had to go back. Now. Beto was in danger.

He ushered Nena forward into the camp's circle of light.

"Stay here. With Casimiro." His voice was not his own. Nena took a step back, closer to the fire. Her dark eyes were wide with fear. "Please," he added, panic fraying the syllables.

"A torch!" Casimiro bellowed, and when one was offered to him, he passed it to Néstor. "Be careful."

Néstor and a handful of other vaqueros turned and plunged back down the path. Metallic clicks rose around him as guns were readied. Sweat beaded at his hairline from the torch's heat; he felt the light it cast barely break the darkness as they surged forward. They dived around the desiccated carcass.

When they reached the riverbank, Néstor swore he saw a humanlike form bent over a body. Then, as he and the torch grew closer, it was gone—vanished like mist across the slick surface of the river.

The torchlight fell on reddish hair. A pale, stricken face.

"Shit. *Shit.*" Néstor passed the torch to the vaquero closest to him and ran the last steps between him and Beto, his boots slipping against the pebbles of the riverbank. "Beto."

The shirt of one arm was torn open; wet, sticky liquid oozed thickly from a wound on his upper arm. It needed to be bound to prevent him from bleeding out. Néstor tore the kerchief from his neck and frantically began to tie it around Beto's upper arm.

His hands shook violently. He fumbled; the kerchief slipped. Blood stained his fingers as he tried again to staunch the wound.

Beto's face was frozen in a mask of horror, his eyelids peeled wide. Torchlight reflected red in his pale irises.

His chest did not rise and fall.

Every time Beto fell, he sprang back to his feet. Even the day they met, when Beto was thrown from his horse in the path of a charging bull, he hauled himself upright and gripped his lasso, buckling ankle be damned.

Beto was so still. His eyes were glazed over like the eyes of the bull carcass.

Darkness curled intrusively around the edges of Néstor's vision. Beto was the rope that tethered him to this world. Beto was his brother in all but name. He was frozen, strung like a slaughtered lamb between one reality and another, where the smell of water was not Río Bravo but the springs at Los Ojuelos, where it was not Beto's chest that would not rise, no matter how hard he willed it to, but Nena's.

The other vaqueros exchanged curses over his head. They were speaking; scattered fragments fell on Néstor's ears, chaining in an order that made no sense.

"Susto," said a voice. "Poison."

"Like Ignacio," said another.

"Señorita Magdalena."

"Ándale, let's carry him."

An order he could follow. He slipped his arms under Beto's armpits, one of his hands slipping over blood as it grasped for purchase. Another vaquero took Beto's legs; a third led the way back to camp with a torch and Beto's muddied hat in hand.

Néstor's vision swam. Torchlight danced off the grasses ahead of him. Darkness curled into humanlike shapes in the back corners of his vision, nearly out of sight. Curling, humped backs; long, thin arms ending in claws like machetes. Beto smelled of the sweat of fear, metallic and acrid as gunpowder. He smelled of blood. Beto's head lolled against Néstor's shoulder; his crown cracked squarely against Néstor's jaw.

Néstor's teeth slammed together at the impact. *"Hijo de—"*

"Just a bit farther, compadre," one of the vaqueros called to him.

His back ached. His thighs burned from the effort of carrying Beto forward.

But this time, he was not alone. Other men cursed alongside him. Other men who did not say Beto was dead, nor seemed as panicked as he was.

They made the final turn through the high grasses. The low red glow of camp unfolded before them like a ribbon.

"¡Curandera!" the vaquero with the torch cried. "Quickly!"

A few more steps. Néstor's chest heaved with the effort as they brought Beto to the edge of the fire and lay him on the ground.

Néstor caught Beto's head and lay it down as gently as he could.

A female voice was barking orders. Shadows moved around him.

Beto's eyes would not stop staring overhead. Glassy, unblinking, so wide that their strange, pale irises were ringed with bloodshot white.

Nena knelt at Beto's side. She set two stones on the ground next to her with a harsh clatter; dried and fresh herbs emerged from a cloth bag. Lavender. Rosemary.

Abuela smells. A curandera's smells.

"I said, either get out of the way or help," Nena snapped. When he stared dumbly back, she made an annoyed sound and thrust the stones at him. Next came a fistful of herbs that he could not tell apart. "Grind these."

He obeyed. It forced him to tear his eyes away from Beto's blank stare. The aromas that rose from the crushed herbs eased the nausea that crept up the back of his throat at the sight of Nena untying his haphazard kerchief tourniquet, her fingers taking on the wet, red sheen of blood. A knife glinted as she cut away Beto's sleeve and lay his arm away from his side, exposing the wound on the inside of his arm.

The wound was round and puckered; it looked as if a beast had sunk its jaws into the pale flesh of Beto's inner arm.

Nena took a small pail of water and rinsed the wound. Néstor averted his gaze, focusing on his task.

"Now hand them back," Nena barked at Néstor, then took the crushed herbs. She added water to them and mixed it into a poultice, then scooped the mixture out with her fingertips.

She smeared it directly on Beto's wound, ensuring the entire area was covered. Her brows creased with concentration as she worked, bent over Beto's body. Then she rocked back on her heels and reached to the side for something.

"What is his full name?" she asked.

"What?"

"Beto's full name," Nena repeated. In one hand she held a bundle of dried rosemary. "I need it."

"Albert Fitz," Néstor said. "But he hates it. He uses his mother's name."

"Which is?" Nena prompted, impatience sharpening her tone.

"Cepeda."

With light hands, she ran the rosemary over his body, from forehead to chest, then over his limbs. Her movements mirrored Abuela's, smooth and confident.

"Regresa, Albert Cepeda," she murmured as she worked. "Regresa. Beto Cepeda, regresa."

Perhaps Néstor was imagining it. Perhaps Nena's repeated *regresa* lulled him into a trance, like a lullaby, like a spell, softening the edges of his reality, but as she spoke, he felt as if the air around them grew clearer. Gentler.

Beto's eyes fluttered shut.

13

NENA

BETO INHALED DEEPLY through his nose. His chest rose, then fell. Twice. A third time. A rhythm.

His eyes did not open.

Why wouldn't he wake? Surely the poultice had drawn enough venom from his wound for him to recover. Nena rocked forward and put her ear to his chest.

His heart beat. Steady and slow. But he did not stir to consciousness.

She would need to try again. Somewhere where she was not surrounded by people watching her, interfering with her focus. Somewhere where it was quiet.

The panic that the attack had caused still thrummed through her own body. Now that they had no occupation, a tremor shook her hands. If Beto had not insisted she come back to camp, whatever attacked him would have harmed *her*.

She straightened, sending a silent prayer into the night that she would not fail. That when she tried the limpia again, in quiet, Beto would wake and be whole again. She had only met Beto a day before coming on this journey, but it was impossible not to be fond of his long, roaming stories and steady presence. The Los Ojuelos men's morale would be devastated if he fell the night before joining the Mexican army. She would be devastated.

Though perhaps not as devastated as Néstor.

He still knelt in the dust near Beto's head. The firelight snuck under the brim of his hat and played over his expression: drawn, fearful. He had returned to the rancho at Beto's side. The most colorful stories Beto told, as much as she resented them, were about Néstor. For a moment, pity tugged at her heart.

"What's going on over here?" Papá's voice announced his approach. He and Félix were walking toward the group of vaqueros hovering around her and Beto. They took in the scene: Beto, bloodied but breathing, and Nena with her curandera's materials.

Papá almost never saw her working, but now he could see with his own eyes that she was already proving her worth. Through the worry that hung over her, thick as the humidity, a spark of hope flared. This was what she wanted. This was exactly what she wanted Papá to see.

"There was an attack by the river," she said, lifting her chin and forcing confidence into her voice. "He has susto. But he will be all right. I have healed this before." Louder, to the vaqueros who had gathered around them, she added: "Beto needs to be taken to a tent to rest."

"You heard her," Papá barked at the vaqueros who hovered around Nena. "Be quick."

He nodded curtly to her—his usual stoic sign of approval—and turned on his heel.

A flush of victory warmed her chest as she watched Papá's retreating back.

She stood, brushing dust from her skirt and collecting her bag of herbs. Néstor had taken the herbs as he stood and handed it to her. As she took them to place in her bag, he grasped her wrist gently.

"That's what happened to you," he said, voice ragged.

She cast him an accusing look. He pointed down at Beto, whose face was now so peaceful he could have been sleeping.

"*That* is what happened to you," Néstor said. "They all said you were dead."

For a moment, she had forgotten she was angry at him. He helped her without question, grinding herbs just as Abuela had taught them both how, the movements of their hands around each other like a pair of faithful swallows, always aware of where the other was.

But the familiarity of this touch, the very assumption that he had access to that kind of intimacy, sent a flash of resentment through her. She snatched her hand back.

But she had waited a moment too long. The movement was too conspicuous. Félix had not left with Papá; now, she could feel him watching her. The last thing she needed was for him to question whether Papá had been right to bring her, if she could be trusted to behave appropriately while with the squadron. If not, she proved Mamá right and sealed her fate before she had a chance to convince Papá otherwise. He would tell Papá, and she would be put under lock and key until she could be sent home to await whatever marriage her parents insisted upon.

Damn Néstor.

"Don't touch me," she snapped.

"You have to understand," he barreled on. Casimiro was looking at him strangely, as was Félix, especially when he pointed at Nena's brother. "He was there," he said, voice cracking. "He saw what I saw. They said you were dead and it was *all my fault.*"

Néstor was spinning a vaquero tale, embellishing a pathetic

excuse for his nine years of absence. Worse, he was doing it in front of her brother and a half dozen vaqueros. He was entirely without shame or a sense of propriety.

In a sharp movement, she turned her back on him.

"I need Beto in a quiet place, alone," she said, directing the words at Casimiro. "I will need fresh water and a fire to be made nearby so that I can work." She then jerked her chin over her shoulder, a sharp gesture at Néstor. "I do not want to see him and I do not want to speak to him."

"You have to listen—"

"Sí, señorita," Casimiro said quickly, cutting Néstor off and taking him by the arm. "Whatever you say. Néstor, get out of the way. *Néstor.*"

She adjusted her bag on her shoulder as men lifted Beto and carried him away. Before she followed them, she cast a quick glance at Néstor. She hoped he would be angry at her, that he would look ready to draw knives and fight as he had earlier, when he called her a brat and goaded her into a brawl.

But that was not what she saw at all.

He had pushed his hat back to run a hand over his face. For a fleeting moment, there was something etched there, in the solemn, grief-deepened crescents on either side of his mouth, that made her think he was about to cry.

THE VAQUEROS LAY Beto in a tent far from the main fires, in a part of camp where it was quiet. As one vaquero made a small fire, Nena pinned back the flap of the tent so that Beto would be illuminated. Kindling caught and crackled behind her, emitting the distinctive smell of mesquite.

She sat back on her heels. She could ask for someone to bring her more of her things from across camp: incense, perhaps. Abuela often lit incense for limpias that she knew would be more difficult than most.

But that would only waste time.

Whatever had attacked Beto gave him the same susto and the same wound as Ignacio had. His aura was bruised with the same darkness. Ignacio could not remember what had happened to him, but at least half an hour had passed between when he was attacked and when Nena revived him. What if that time spent unconscious was what prevented victims of susto from remembering what had happened to them?

Beto had been unconscious for mere minutes.

The sooner she called him back, the sooner she would be able to ask what had attacked him. The sooner she would know what plagued the rancho. What had left its mark on her as well.

When she appeared at Ignacio's jacal, Elena had looked over her shoulder, searching for Abuela. She didn't trust her.

But she had healed Ignacio. She could heal Beto as well.

She edged closer to him, taking the rosemary in her right hand. She put her left on Beto's shoulder, resting it lightly there.

She closed her eyes and began to envision his aura, began to rid it of bad energy with her limpia. Clearing the way for his soul to return.

"Regresa, Beto," she murmured. "Regresa."

The aroma of rosemary filled the tent; she clutched her bundle of herbs tightly as she brushed it over his chest, over his arms, down his legs. She returned to where his wound was and directed her energy into him.

Sweat broke out along her hairline and rolled down the small of her back.

Still nothing happened.

"Regresa." Her jaw was tight from clenching. "Beto Cepeda, regresa."

She was failing. She had done everything right, yet it was not working.

Could Abuela be right? Was she spiritually blocked, unable to heal others, because her own aura was wounded? That couldn't be so. She was able to heal Ignacio only weeks ago.

But then Néstor came back.

He disrupted everything. Reopened old wounds and poured handfuls of salt on them.

Say Abuela was right. Say her aura was wounded, that she could not be the full self that curing others demanded of her. What of it? Being wounded had never made her less strong in the past. It had not prevented her from healing Ignacio. She would not let it—nor Néstor and all he stood for—hold her back now, not when so much was at stake.

She reached deep into herself, calling forth every bit of her energy—wounded or not—and channeled it into calling Beto back.

"Regresa, Beto," she called. "Regresa."

A gasp.

Nena's eyes flew open at the sound, at the feeling of Beto's chest rising under her hand.

The man's eyes fluttered open. He searched until his eyes fell on Nena; he frowned as if he were trying to square her presence with their surroundings.

"Buenas, Señorita Magdalena," Beto said weakly. "To what do I owe the pleasure?"

A laugh burst from Nena, high and breathy and spurred by sheer relief. Stars speckled the edges of her vision; she set a hand down on the ground to brace herself against a rush of light-headedness.

Beto made to sit up, but she clicked her tongue.

"Easy," she said, waving him down. "You're wounded. Lie still."

He obeyed. A thin sheen of sweat veiled his brow and darkened his hair; his shirt stuck to his chest.

She placed her hand on his brow. It was warm to the touch—much too warm.

A fever was fine. A fever she could fix. She had ample herbs for that. Stars fading from her vision, she reached for her bag and began to sift through it.

She cast a look over her shoulder. A few of the vaqueros who had accompanied her carrying Beto lingered a few paces away, whispering as they watched her.

"Could someone bring me hot water, please?" she called.

"I'm burning up, aren't I?" Beto asked.

"It is good," Nena said. Her voice shook with relief. He was conscious, he was speaking, he was making sense. Those were far better signs than the fever. "Your body is fighting hard to burn away any remaining venom."

"Venom," Beto repeated slowly. For a moment, there was no sound in the tent but the crush of stone against herbs as she worked to make another poultice. "Was it a rattler?" he asked at last.

She stopped. Even in the shadows, confusion was evident on his face. "Do you not remember what happened?" she asked.

"I remember seeing the steer," he said. His gaze drifted toward the top of the tent. He frowned. "I remember seeing you and Duarte. Seeing that you were angry with Duarte." A smile crept sly across his otherwise wan face at the memory. Nena's face heated with a rush of embarrassment. "You know, I've never met a better man, but he can't express himself for shit. You ask him how he feels and it's like he never learned how to speak." He laughed softly. "One time, years ago, we had to stay in Laredo because he cracked a rib or two breaking a mesteño for some spoiled, silver-heeled hidalgo. Duarte charges through the nose for breaking, but for that beast? I swear it was not enough. That horse had the Devil in her eyes . . ."

This was the part of a patient's recovery where Abuela would meet Nena's eyes with a knowing look. Exhaustion and fever left them either silent and weak or loosened their tongues, making them prone to chatter. It was evident that Beto fell into the latter class. As she cleaned the wound on his arm, Nena listened to his rambling, grateful that he soon left tales of Néstor behind and wandered into a story about the Devil riding through the chaparral on horseback until he cursed the blistering heat of Tejas and returned to Hell for respite.

"Do you remember anything else about tonight?" Nena asked as she bandaged his arm with clean cloth. "You took the water jug from me and walked to the riverbank."

"I did?" Beto's face creased with concentration. "Ay, chihuahua." It came out on the same breath as a frustrated sigh. "I don't. I . . . can't. I saw you and Duarte, and the next thing I knew I was here, feeling like I have the worst hangover of my life." He lifted his uninjured arm and ran a hand over his face. "There was only darkness, señorita. Just darkness."

CASIMIRO ESCORTED HER back to her tent to stand guard; she nodded her good night and slipped into the tent. She lay in the stuffy dark for what felt like hours. She shifted her body from one side to the other as she listened to the sounds of camp and Casimiro carving something small to pass the time as he stood watch.

There was only darkness, señorita. Beto's words clung like thorns.

She forced herself to try to remember what happened the night when Néstor disappeared. She had slipped out of the house, desperate to see Néstor. He waited for her with the shovel gleaming like the silver they sought in the moonlight. They walked hand in hand toward the spring . . .

Then she was in her own bed, Abuela's white braids brushing her arm as the old woman ran rosemary over her body and called her back, her voice soft and rhythmic as an incantation. *Regresa, Magdalena Serrano de León. Regresa.*

The voice of Ignacio's wife, Elena, wove through her memory alongside Abuela's: *Dios mío, I thought you were dead.*

Wasn't that what this strange sickness looked like to the untrained eye? The body stiff and unmoving, frozen by venom?

Abuela thought it was a venomous bat whose bite stunned its prey like the sting of certain scorpions. For did the attacks not all happen at twilight or in the depths of night?

For months, Nena believed it.

But that did not explain the bull, and the bull had to be connected to what happened to Beto. She knew it in her gut.

Long past midnight, as the rest of the camp wound down into unsettled sleep, as exhaustion finally began to tug at her consciousness, footsteps approached her tent. She heard a crunch of gravel as Casimiro rose; a soft exchange of greetings. One voice in particular caught her ear.

Néstor.

She felt a swift prick of shame at how sharply she had spoken to him. Perhaps she was too harsh. His friend was wounded, after all—he was bound to be upset.

That is what happened to you. It was all my fault.

She rolled onto her back, her fingertips lifting to brush the scar at her neck.

As Casimiro's footsteps retreated, she heard Néstor sit and settle into his watch. Only a thin flap of fabric separated her from him; he was so close that she could hear his steady breathing.

Without her noticing, the rhythm of her inhales slowed to match his. Soon, it slowed further, and further still, until sleep finally claimed her.

14

❧

NÉSTOR

MATAMOROS, ESTADO DE TAMAULIPAS

SMOKE FROM THE army camp on the plain of Palo Alto rose high into the night, the light from hundreds of fires dyeing the sky red as a sunset. The Escuadrón Auxiliares de las Villas del Norte had joined General Arista's forces there with the Mexican infantry and the Morelia and Puebla battalions. A taste of brine rode the breeze from the gulf; it carried with it the smells of an army gathering. Smoke. Gunpowder. Sweat. These soured Néstor's mouth as he cleaned saddles, lingering even as he spat in the dirt to rid his mouth of the taste.

His forearms ached. Beto was still weak from loss of blood and the shock of the previous night's attack. He was barely able to ride his own horse the two hours it took them to join General Arista's forces, much less help Néstor. No matter. Néstor needed movement to still the anxiety humming in his bones like a swarm of mosquitoes. It did little good. Nothing—no matter how hard he worked, how little he slept—could stop Nena's angry words from looping through his head. The way she whirled at him with spark and flint almost made him wish for the first part of the journey to Matamoros, where she brushed him off coldly. At least then she was not calling him a liar. At least then he had some hope of being able to speak with her and make amends.

It was only as the words fell from his lips that he realized he should have planned it better, he should have anticipated how ridiculous it would sound to say *you died* to someone who stood right before him, her lovely cheeks reddened with anger, her chest rising and falling as she breathed. As alive and beautiful as anything on God's green earth.

But he had been caught off guard. He hadn't expected to have that conversation then. His mind was still on the cattle carcass.

And then Beto screamed.

Uneasiness thrummed an unwelcome beat down Néstor's spine as he checked the shoes of the horses and curried them until sweat dripped down his back.

Something was not right. The sensation that curled around him and Nena as they argued—that *silence*—reminded him too much of another night, long ago, when the two of them were alone in the dark.

He was so absorbed in his work he did not notice Don Félix approach until the patrón's son was standing over him.

"Buenas," Don Félix said.

When Néstor returned the greeting, Don Félix clasped his hands behind his back and lifted his chin slightly. Nearly nine years had passed since Néstor last worked with Don Félix, but his mannerisms had not changed a bit. That was the look he got when he knew he had to give orders that he did not like to the vaqueros, when he was trying to deliver his father's commands without seeming like an ass. Néstor readied himself. Whatever Don Félix meant to ask him, he was sure it would mean less rest before the battle tomorrow. As if he would be able to sleep anyway, with thoughts of Nena within reach of Yanqui soldiers haunting his nightmares.

"I am glad you volunteered to come with us and are tolerant of my father's demands that someone watch Magdalena at all times," Don Félix said. "I know it adds to your work and I am grateful for your service."

An unvoiced *however* hung at the end of the sentence, swinging open like a corral gate, waiting for the next part of what Don Félix had to say. But Néstor was impatient. This opened like a man-to-man conversation; he seized it and drove it forward like one.

"Doña Mercedes said she was dead," he said. After all these years, even with the knowledge that Nena was alive and well and angry at him, the words still made the ghost of a sob rise to the back of his throat. "That night when she was wounded, when she was attacked—"

The reaction in Don Félix was immediate. His brows snapped together, bristling, the expression an eerie echo of his father.

"Enough, Duarte," he snapped. "I know you were close as children, but *enough* with this fixation. Mind your boundaries." Metallic finality punctuated each word, dissonant as a farrier's hammer.

As far as the patrón's son was concerned, this conversation was over.

It put Néstor's teeth on edge. Protective anger rose in his chest, forming a barrier between Félix and the memories he guarded like silver. *I know you were close.* Close didn't even begin to describe what Nena meant to him. Don Félix didn't know the half of it.

But perhaps he sensed it.

"I'm afraid I don't understand, Don Félix," he said, dragging the words slow over coal, letting them burn and blacken. Let Don Félix hear the anger curling the edges of what he said like kindling about to catch flame. Let him remember that Néstor was not a peón of Rancho Los Ojuelos, not anymore. He had returned because Don Félix asked him a favor and he saw fit to grant it. He owed the Serranos no debt, no respect, not an hour of his time nor a lick of work.

It was their privilege to ride beside him, and one day, they would know it. Even Don Feliciano. All the vaqueros knew that the patrón was self-absorbed; many things that troubled the peones of his rancho escaped his notice.

Don Félix was another matter. Based on what Bernabé and Casimiro said, Félix would be a better patrón than Don Feliciano ever was. He possessed an inborn nobility that was often mistaken for aloofness; this was not a sin, for unlike many rancheros' sons, this meant he left the women of the peones untouched. He was generous with his time and his money. He was canny. He was observant.

Perhaps too observant.

"I think you understand me perfectly," Don Félix said. "Consider this your only warning: any man who says or does anything that might touch her reputation has more than my father to face. And as for me—I will not allow her to be hurt again."

A flash of shame seared Néstor's skin, hot beneath his neck kerchief. Yes, he knew he was guilty of hurting Nena. Whatever God or unseen hand that made the world had granted him a fragile, perfect thing, and through a foul stroke of luck, a flash of cowardice, he shattered it.

That was his shame to bear. It had no place on Don Félix's lips.

"I swear she'll never be hurt again, not if I have anything to do with it," he said hotly.

"Then we agree," Félix said, leaning closer. Each syllable he spoke next was slow, stressed, deliberate, a threat shadowing each word. "Keep your distance."

It was a patrón's command if there ever was one.

At this point, arguing would only inflame Don Félix's ire. If any word of this reached Don Feliciano, or if Don Félix changed his mind about who to have guard Nena, Néstor might be cut off from her entirely.

He bit his tongue.

He did not allow his hands to curl into fists until Félix had turned his back and walked away, his silver spurs catching the firelight and winking mockingly at Néstor.

No, he was no longer a peón of Los Ojuelos. But here he was.

This was one of the many reasons he had not wanted to return to Los Ojuelos.

One principle ruled Néstor's childhood on the rancho: the patrón's word was law. The patrón held the whip. He owned the land. He gave the vaqueros and other workers the opportunity to serve him. To make their living in the harsh world of El Norte under his benevolent rule. The patrón's word gave shape to the world and kept it tightly in his fist.

Néstor's leaving changed that. He chose for whom he worked and for how long. If he was mistreated or disrespected, he left. Unlike Bernabé or the other workers on Los Ojuelos or any other rancho, he was not financially indebted to any one ranchero. He bound himself to no master. If he wished to drive for Celeste's vaqueros and the Buenavista herd, he joined them for a short while, then took his money and his leave. Made no promises. He was the one who decided his fortunes. He determined his life's path. Yes, that freedom meant living hard, sleeping hard. It meant loneliness.

But once he had tasted that freedom, hollow though it sometimes was, he chafed at the heavy yoke of the patrón and his son.

He was always crisply aware of who rode with silver on their bridles and who did not. Whose hats and horses were new and whose were worn with age. He was a man of dust who served men of silver: it was impossible not to know his place in the world. Especially when he had worked for years to claw his way out of the dust and build himself a house of stone.

It was one thing to know that mending what lay between him

and Nena was an uphill battle. It was another to be reminded that, as far as many were concerned, there were no battles to be fought at all.

Vaqueros may call me señorita, or better yet, say nothing to me at all.

If he was honest with himself, he was afraid that Nena found him repulsive. Their differences never slipped between them in the past; what did it matter that she was the daughter of the ranchero and he the orphaned son of a lowly vaquero when they were watching the sheep together? Hand in hand in the chaparral, they were the kings of El Norte, no rule over them but the brutal, azure sweep of the sky, no law but the setting of the sun.

But the past was long gone. Long dead. Unlike Nena, it would have no miraculous resurrection. He was a man of dust and sweat; she was Don Feliciano's eldest daughter. There could be no friendship between them. Good manners forbade it. The very structure of their world forbade it.

Don Félix had explicitly forbade it.

But Beto's advice hooked into him like a burr.

She had shouted at him that afternoon, but now she knew the truth. She knew he had made a terrible mistake by leaving, but perhaps, after having seen Beto, she might one day deem it a forgivable one.

He had to keep trying.

For it was not enough to be her shadow, to stand between her and danger as much as he could. How could it be, when all he had to do was close his eyes and see siestas in the shade beneath the huisaches, listening to her breathe in time with him as they fell asleep? He had kept every one of her secrets like they were precious jewels. For years, he feared the pain such memories could cause, how they poured salt on his wounds.

But now, with Nena alive and before him, they overtook him

like heatstroke. Even when she was shouting at him, he could not help but think of how she had once stood close to him in the late afternoon shade of the anacahuita grove, safely hidden from the house. How she had said that one of her older cousins told her that some people kissed badly. This filled her with dread that she, too, might be a bad kisser unless she had practice. Was Néstor in?

He was thirteen. Of course he agreed enthusiastically. But when she took his hands in hers, when their faces were so close he could admire the dusting of freckles over her nose and the perfect curve of her lips, he was overcome by a wave of shyness.

"You're really bad at this," she whispered. Her eyes were like a doe's, big and dark and immensely trusting—but there was an amused glint there. She was laughing at him.

"I haven't even started!"

"That's what I mean, tonto."

"You could start too." He was deflecting. Buying time. His palms had begun to sweat. He hoped to God she could not feel it.

"The boy is supposed to," she said authoritatively. Her freckles were like constellations. He wanted to stare at them until they made him dizzy.

"Says who?" he said.

"I don't know. Aren't those the rules?"

This gave him pause. "There aren't rules. Are there?" What if there were? Was there some secret vault of knowledge Casimiro was hiding from him, some locked door that stood between him and manhood?

Nena shrugged lightly. "Fine, if you're going to be a coward . . ."

She leaned forward. Before Néstor could process this, her lips were on his. For a moment, his world was her dark lashes, the curve of her nose, her cheek. Loose wisps of her hair tickling his skin. Then he shut his eyes. Her lips were impossibly soft. Her skin smelled like sunshine, like her, like home.

She pulled away.

"There," she said with a tone of finality. Her cheeks were flushed as if she had been running.

A soft ribbon of desire unraveled against his spine. *I want this,* it hummed. *I want more of this.*

"That wasn't that hard," she said. She loosened her hold on his hands, as if she meant to unlace their fingers and step away; he resisted. She paused. He was certain that if either one of them looked down, they would see his heart beating out of his chest like a rabbit's.

"Wait," he said. "Can I try going first?" His voice felt unlike his own. He cleared his throat quickly. "For practice," he clarified.

"That's fair," Nena agreed brightly. She pulled her shoulders back and closed her eyes. "Go ahead."

He inhaled through his nose; held his breath. Brought his face close to hers. He lingered there, just for a moment, a hair's breadth from her lips, from her honey skin, to memorize every part of her.

He pressed his lips to hers.

When he pulled away, her eyes were open, her gaze liquid and intense.

A new understanding cracked open in his chest: they both knew that was not practice.

That was real.

"Nena!" A woman's voice rose from the direction of la casa mayor. "Nena, where are you?"

Nena's quick intake of breath was almost a gasp. "That's Mamá," she said. She stepped back; Néstor released her hands immediately. "She'll murder me if she finds out about this. Don't say a word. Promise?"

"Promise." He watched as she raced back to the house, her braids bouncing against her back, the sun cradling a bronze halo around her head.

✦   ✦   ✦

IT WAS NOT enough to be fine. It was not enough to keep his distance. Not when that was what he once had.

He would keep trying, no matter how many barbs she flung at him, no matter if she shouted or cried.

When the sun rose, the squadron would cross the river and ride with the Mexican cavalry. Let the army of the Mexicans rise or fall, let the Yanquis burn.

Nearly a decade of grief shaped his understanding of the world. He knew, with the acute awareness of a much older man, that there were some things too precious to lose. That so many things—his dignity, his work, his very world—meant nothing.

Not when Nena lived.

The only purpose of tomorrow was to survive it and to reach her on the other side.

And nothing—not Don Félix, not Don Feliciano, not his own cowardice—would stand in his way.

15

NENA

THEY HAD CROSSED Río Bravo early that morning on a broad, flat ferry. It was as unsteady on the river's slow waters as a drunk; Nena feared it would tip over at any moment. They marched to Palo Alto, where Arista's plan was to cut off the Americanos' supply shipments from Puerto Isabel.

The thunder of cannons split Nena's skull. She ducked with a cry, clamping her hands over her ears. Smoke and humidity lay thick over the low ground in a suffocating blanket, choking her with the taste of gunpowder. With the metallic smell of blood.

It was now two hours past noon. The sun beat mercilessly on her hair, and her clothes stuck to her sweat-sheathed skin.

"Bandages, Magdalena."

The camp women of the squadron fell under the command of a no-nonsense woman called Susana. She was a curandera from one of the ranchos outside of Reynosa and had long gray braids that fell over a chest as broad as a bull's. She boasted a voice to match.

Nena's boots squelched through marshy earth as she stumbled

toward Susana with arms full of bandages. She refused to speculate about how much of the mud was caused by water from the nearby resacas and how much from blood.

Wounded men lay in rows around her, some groaning, some trying to sit up as they waited for the curanderas.

Many were already dead. She could not look at their faces, at the peeled-back eyelids and vacant stares.

Thus far, the fallen were all strangers clothed in the regular uniforms of the Mexican infantry and cavalry.

But that would not be the case for long.

The Escuadrón Auxiliares de las Villas del Norte had been separated into two sections and stationed west of the center of the battlefield. Papá and the men from Los Ojuelos and the other ranchos surrounding Mier were positioned behind the regular cavalry, who had charged onto the prairie battlefield, straight at the line of Yanqui bayonets and cannons.

Nena and some women of the squadron, including other curanderas, created a makeshift healing area nearby to tend to the wounded. There had been some conversation about whether the curanderas who came with the squadron would go to the hospital behind the back of Arista's army. In the end, the rancheros decided to keep their women close.

Félix hovered nearby on horseback, pacing the quiet area between the mounted squadron and the space where the healers worked. His hat cast a dark shadow over his face, but beneath it, his mouth was grim as he kept watch. The wounded were already being carried in—and dragged in, mud mixing with blood on their uniforms—but Nena's attention was on the squadron.

Félix had told her that General Arista said that the rancheros, as auxiliary forces, might not see battle at all today.

Now that was not the case.

After she handed bandages to Susana, Nena shielded her eyes

from the sun with a hand, searching for faces she knew through the smoky haze. Mosquitoes hummed at her ears; she swatted them away. She caught sight of Papá and Don Severo, their horses prancing with anticipation and fear. In the line in front of Papá, she glimpsed a vaquero on a black mare. The white star on the horse's forehead—curved and perfect as a waning crescent moon—told her exactly who the vaquero was. The next moment, he was gone. Lost in the sea of vaquero hats and horses tossing their heads.

Worry for him stirred in her chest. The vaqueros would ride before the rancheros and the generals; the first to face the gaping maws of black cannons and Yanqui bayonets were not the landowners. There was a hierarchy on the battlefield just as there was on the rancho. It meant there was less of a risk of Papá being wounded, and for that, she should be grateful.

She wasn't.

The moment the black mare was lost in the crowd and the squadron joined the greater mass of the Mexican cavalry, a shard of fear buried itself in her chest.

The men raised their guns and voices, shouting *viva México*. All the horses of the squadron sprang into a canter, then lengthened their strides, whinnying and tossing heads. Formation remained tight as they drove forward into the smoke from the cannons.

Nena could feel the earth shake with hoofbeats as the squadron rode into battle. As they charged down the plain, some of the cavalry riders in the front broke into a gallop, surging forward, sabers raised. Vaqueros and rancheros behind them spilled forward at full gallop, guns at the ready. As soon as it hit the fray, the formation was cleaved in two; screams split the air as horses barreled over Yanqui soldiers and were swallowed by the chaos of the battlefield.

Clouds of smoke obscured the distance between them and the Yanqui line.

They were gone.

How many of them would return?

"Magdalena." Susana called Nena's attention harshly back to earth.

Susana crouched at a fallen soldier's side.

"I need you to tie a tourniquet around his leg," the older woman barked. "Hurry."

Behind Susana was another man. He wore the blue uniform of the Mexican infantry, but it was soiled with mud and a dark, wet patch over his stomach. The edges of his aura wavered, weak and dark. A foul smell crept up Nena's nostrils—the stench of a soiling of a different kind. Even if she hadn't seen the blood across his stomach, she knew he was going to die.

Nena glanced down as she walked.

Her heart collapsed on itself.

It was Néstor.

"*No*," she breathed.

No, it could not be him.

In between one moment and the next, the vision slipped; the cheekbones softened and widened. A mustache appeared where Néstor had none.

Nausea slicked her mouth. No, it was not him. It was a trick of the gloom.

She forced herself to walk forward to Susana, making the sign of the cross. She had to keep her wits about her to help the men who had a chance at living.

But fear for Néstor lingered at the base of her throat, persistent and sour and grasping.

Please, God, she thought as she knelt opposite Susana and began to tie bandages tightly around the soldier's leg to slow his bleeding. Her hands shook as she worked; too often they slipped as she used her knife to cut away clothing or bandages. Her knife shone with blood. The stench rising from the churned mud was like that of carrion. *Please keep him safe. Don't let him be hurt. Not like this.*

The tumult of galloping and screaming horses was shattered by a cannon impact. Nena's ears split with whistling overhead; she ducked, her back curling and shoulders folding forward over the man she tended. As if that could protect either of them. A ferocious tremor seized the earth, vibrating up through her knees; she envisioned horses being thrown to their knees, their riders sailing over their ears into the fray.

She peered up, certain she would see a cannonball directly overhead. Black smoke obscured the sky. Dark figures swarmed through the haze around the healing area.

"Get out of here! Run!"

That was Félix's voice. Nena wrenched herself upward, ears ringing. She clutched her knife. Sporadic gunfire pocked the air overhead; the screams of horses set her teeth on edge.

Félix was no longer quietly patrolling the healing area. He charged forward, his pistol held high.

Anglos on horseback charged toward the wounded and the women, their hats pushed low over their faces and chaps billowing like bat wings. Guns gleamed in their hands. *Rinches.* Texas Rangers.

A sharp movement caught her eye. Susana jerked backward abruptly, as if someone had put hands on her shoulders and shoved her back, away from the dying man. Red bloomed over her chest.

Nena screamed. It was half surprise, half horror.

Susana fell backward into the muck, staring blankly up at the smoke.

Her aura was gone, broken. She was dead.

The Rinches cut a rough path through the wounded, not caring if they trampled them. Nena dodged out of the way, effectively cut off from the other women like a steer from the herd.

Someone seized her by the hair; her head snapped backward, sending a white bolt of pain up her neck. She shrieked as she was yanked backward, her boots dragging through the mud. Hoofbeats thundered directly to her left; her cheek was pressed to someone's chivarras. The edge of a stirrup dug into her shoulder.

Pain seared her scalp. She was going to be trampled. Or the horse would stumble and her neck would snap, as fragile as a chicken's.

But she still had her knife.

With all her might, she gripped the knife and brought it into the leg of the Rinche.

A scream; her hair was abruptly released. Her heart flew to her throat as she was dropped to the earth.

She yanked her arms into her chest as she rolled in the reeking mud, then she forced herself up immediately. Her head spun, but the memory of hooves crunching over the wounded was too fresh in her mind. The ground meant death. She had to be on her feet.

When she steadied herself, ears ringing, she could not tell which way she was facing. East? Or west and away from the battle? Smoke hung over the battlefield like a fog, stinging her eyes and nostrils; no matter where she looked, she could see no landmarks to lead her out of the fray.

Her body shook uncontrollably; the skin beneath the scar on her neck prickled and itched as if she had been ravaged by mosquitoes. Her mind observed this in a detached fashion, sweeping the perimeter around her. Fallen bodies were scattered haphazardly around her, some blown open and dismembered by cannon fire. Garish, flayed flesh rippled with crawling horseflies; their hum hung on the air like the cannon smoke, thick and persistent. A vaquero's hat trampled into the mud. A kerchief, blue as a summer sky, darkened and sticking to a chest wet with blood.

The smell of sulfur snaked into her nose draping over her tongue and scalding the roof of her mouth. Gunmetal gray skies and swampy earth soaked with blood. For a moment, she could have sworn she saw figures appearing like phantoms through the gloom—figures that were long-limbed, bent on all fours, and loping like coyotes.

Then they vanished. It was a trick of the eye, a trick of the light.

Was Hell like this? Not a burning inferno but humid and cloying, the air thick with the tastes of sulfur and gunpowder, the clammy fingertips of the dead grasping at her, seeking her soul and dragging her down, down, down . . .

A sharp, metallic whinny wrenched Nena to her senses. A horse shied nearby. It was riderless.

And it was close.

"Tranquila," she cooed, praying this calmed the beast. "Easy."

The horse was backing up, eyes wide—it was ready to whirl and bolt. She lunged for the reins. Seized them. Dug her heels into the slippery mud.

"Come on," she muttered, focusing her will on the frightened animal. "If you want to live, you have to be calm. Whoa, tranquila."

The horse stopped backing up. Its nostrils flared; its legs trembled.

"Whoa," she repeated. She breathed it over and over, like a prayer, as much to steady herself as the horse as she edged closer through the squelching, blood-soaked earth. A few more steps and she could reach the stirrup. A few more steps and they would be on their way out of the fray.

From behind her came the crack of a gunshot. She ducked from sheer fear, hands flying to her ears. The reins ripped from her palms, leaving a searing burn in their wake. The horse reared; a flash of red streaked its hindquarters. A bullet had clipped it, flying just feet past Nena's ear.

The horse bolted.

"No!" she screamed. "No, stop!"

She was alone.

Shouting behind her. It wasn't Spanish.

Two Yanqui soldiers rode toward her. One raised a saber; its blade gleamed red and wet. The other leveled a gun at her.

There was nowhere to take cover.

Boots struck earth to her right. Out of the corner of her eye, Nena saw a vaquero's hat. Someone seized her by the upper arm and pulled her back. The flash of a pistol.

Bang. Bang.

The smell of fresh gunpowder bloomed before her. Two more bodies fell to the earth. Two more horses freed of their riders bolted into the smoke.

Néstor put her between his body and his mare Luna, shielding her from the battle. The front of his shirt was dark—but it was with sweat, not blood. Blood—his or not?—darkened one of his filthy shirtsleeves. But he was safe. He was standing. Thank God. His eyes swept her from head to foot, searching her—as she had searched him—for any sign of injury.

"You need to get out of here," he said, shouting to be heard over the fray. "Come."

He thrust his gun into its holster and, with a hurried tug of her upper arm, turned her around to face his black mare.

A leg up, and she was in the saddle. The stirrups were too long for her feet to reach, but there was no time to fix them. She gathered the reins and looked down at Néstor, who still stood at her knee, one hand on the mare's shoulder. He was murmuring soft things to the horse; she couldn't see his face because of his hat until he looked up at her. It was streaked with sweat and dust.

"Ride west," he said, raising his voice to be heard over the din. "Don't take the ferries—there's a retreat. People keep crowding them and drowning. West, the river is shallow—I heard the Yanquis say they sent spies to cross there."

But smoke hung over the battlefield like a fog, impenetrably thick. There were no landmarks that would guide her the ten miles to the river. Not even the sun.

"I'm not leaving without you," she said. "I can't."

She couldn't. He was unarmed, defenseless. She would not leave him to be lost among the bloodshed, to be shot or trampled or worse.

"Come with me," she said. "Can you ride behind me?"

His mouth opened softly; if he was going to reply, he never did. He turned on his heel and began running away from her.

"Néstor?" she called, panic rising in her voice as she gathered the reins. The mare, too, raised her head in alarm. She couldn't lose him. She would not leave him.

Néstor leaped over a fallen body and kept running. Nena looked beyond him: a horse with no rider in its Mexican-style saddle was cantering right toward him. Néstor whistled, then, as the horse pricked its ears and slowed, he ran toward the horse and vaulted into its saddle. He collected the loose reins and thrust his heels down in the stirrups to gain control and turn his horse in a new direction.

"This way!" he called to Nena.

They took off at a canter. The mare was as eager to follow Néstor as Nena was—though she shied from cannon fire, she seemed to trust that they were on their way out of danger. Néstor rode directly beside them, so close he could reach out and grab the mare's bridle if he needed to as they dodged Yanqui soldiers. The fray began to thin as they rode; soon, the bodies littering the ground in haphazard piles outnumbered those still fighting. Beyond, a wide resaca gleamed among tree trunks.

"What the hell?" Néstor said, softly enough that Nena almost didn't hear it.

Directly ahead of them, a trio of slim forms crouched over fallen

Mexican soldiers, cradling them tenderly. For a split second, Nena assumed the figures meant to carry the soldiers away, perhaps to a field infirmary.

Cantering closer revealed that she was dead wrong.

One of the crouched figures raised its head.

The humanlike figure wore no clothes. It was gray, its head hairless and mottled; its chin was slicked with fresh blood, which dripped down its neck and over a band of metal that lay like a collar around its throat. At its side lay corpses that were shriveled and dry, desiccated as if they had been under the desert sun for weeks.

The figure dropped the soldier it was holding. The corpse hit the ground with a sickening thud; its head fell back, revealing a bright, wet wound at the throat.

A second monster raised its gore-slicked head from its prey. It had no eyes, but she *knew* it was looking at them as it rose to its full height. Spider-thin limbs, bloated belly, thin chest. Face gray as the smoke and long, vulturelike claws slick with gore.

She needed to scream. She couldn't. Her mouth was too dry, her throat tight with terror as her mare shied away from the monsters, ears flat against her head and whites of her eyes flashing. Néstor's mount shied away as well.

"Madre de Dios," he gasped.

He reached forward, seized Nena's mare's bridle, and spurred his own horse forward. Their canter quickened, then broke into a gallop. Shock followed Nena even as they left the monsters behind.

It couldn't be real. It had to be a hallucination.

Hooves squelched in softer earth; they slowed to a canter.

The zacahuistle grass around the resaca was thick; their canter shortened and slowed to a trot. Néstor released the bridle of Nena's mare and rode slightly ahead of her, though he glanced over his shoulder at her every few strides, as if to check that she was still there.

Néstor stood in his stirrups to see through the trees. Then he sat quickly, one hand flying to his pistols. "Carajo."

"What?" Nena asked.

"When I say go, we cut through the shallows and keep galloping. Do *not* stop. You hear me?"

Nena's heart quickened. "What?"

"Go."

He spurred his horse forward, lurching into a dead gallop. Nena followed; she leaned forward in the saddle, knees and thighs tightening to hold her seat, as they burst through the last of the river grasses.

Shouting in English rang in her ears.

Bang. Bang.

A bullet zipped past Nena's head. A brutal, guttural sound that was someone crying out in pain. Néstor fired back at a pair of Yanquis. Judging from the fleeting glimpse she had of their uniforms as they fell backward into the mud, they were Rinches.

Then she and Néstor were charging into the marshy resaca. Water rose swiftly around them, as high as Nena's stirrups, then rushed into her boots. The water rose to her knees. Her mare raised her head to keep it above water as they moved forward.

"I hate this." Nena's voice pitched sharp; panic rose to her lips as a sob. "I hate this."

"Me too." Néstor turned in his saddle to look at her. He was just ahead of her to the right. "It's going to be all right. Keep moving."

Cannon fire thrummed in the distance. Nena looked down at the murky water. She imagined it coming up to her chest, her neck, over her face, choking her . . .

A fierce desire to turn around overcame her. She needed to get out of the water. She needed out.

"Don't look down," Néstor called. "Look at me."

She forced her chin up. He kept looking ahead of them then turning his face back to hers. "We're almost there."

They weren't. They were in the middle of the resaca. Water was dark and cold around her knees as the mare lifted her head further. A sick lurch; Nena grasped the pommel. The horses were swimming.

"Look at me," Néstor repeated.

Nena's breathing came harsh and staccato, but it was drowned by the thunder of cannons behind them. For a few ragged breaths, they were suspended in the middle of the resaca as the horses swam.

She risked a glance up. Néstor's eyes burned desperately in his dirt-streaked face.

He would not let her drown.

"Stay with me," he cried.

Then came the metallic clicks of shod hooves on stone; Nena's mare swayed forward as she found purchase among the weeds. Nena leaned forward to use her weight to help the mare move forward. One of her hooves must have slipped; the mare stumbled precariously.

"No!" Néstor cried.

Nena's heart leaped to her throat. She thrust her weight in the opposite direction to help the mare right herself.

"Stay with me," Néstor shouted. Their horses moved forward, necks straining as they laboriously pushed out of the water. Néstor leaned forward in the saddle and seized the bridle of Nena's horse with his left hand. "*Stay with me.*"

She knew then that she would.

Whatever awaited them, she would stay with him.

16

NENA

NEARLY AN HOUR later, their ride west through the thick chaparral finally slowed. Nena's legs ached from exhaustion; her hands were sore and lined from how tightly she had been gripping the reins. Neither she nor Néstor spoke as they rode. They kept out of sight of well-trod paths, with Néstor breaking chaparral with a machete that had been attached to his saddle. Cannons still thundered in the distance. A haze hung overhead, darkening the horizon and dyeing it red. Though the heat of the afternoon had worsened as the sun crept west, it was so humid that her clothes and saddle were still wet from the resaca crossing. Her skirt chafed the insides of her thighs and hung heavy over her legs.

When they reached a clearing, Néstor brought his horse to standing.

"We can rest here, if you want," he said, voice raw and tired. He dismounted and cast a broad, searching look at their surroundings. Here, it was quiet. For the first time all afternoon, the air tasted clear. "I think it's safe."

She released the reins with stiff, aching hands and came out of the saddle gracelessly. When her boots hit the ground with a thump, her legs shook violently, as if bracing for cannon tremors. She swayed on her feet.

Néstor was already behind her, placing a steadying hand on her upper back.

"Whoa there," he said. "Are you all right?"

How was it that after all these years, it still felt like second nature to turn into him and slip her arms around him, to bury her face in his chest? He responded in kind, tightening his arms around her back. She inhaled the smells of worn leather and sweat, the metallic tinge of drying blood, the warmth of his neck. A shadow fell over her as he rested his cheek on her hair—the brim of his hat was blocking out the sun.

"You're safe," he murmured. She felt his voice more than she heard it, rising from a soft rumble in his chest.

But Félix wasn't. Nor was Papá. Were they still alive? Were they hurt? What of the vaqueros from Los Ojuelos, like Casimiro? Fear bloomed in her chest for them.

Unbidden, the image of Susana staring up at the sky flashed behind her eyelids. The cracking of bones and wet, thick splitting of flesh as wounded men were trampled beneath the hooves of the Rinches' mounts.

A sob wrenched free of her chest, raw and dry. Within another breath, she was crying uncontrollably. She was aware that her body was shaking, yet could do nothing to steady it. Without his arms holding her upright, she might have collapsed where she stood.

Néstor said nothing. He simply held her, his feet planted wide to support them both, his breathing steady.

Finally, her sobs softened, then stopped altogether. Awareness uncurled in her chest: the afternoon around them was still, quiet.

There was no sound but for Néstor's heartbeat, his breathing. That awareness blossomed into a prick of embarrassment: she was in a man's arms, but not just any man's.

Néstor's.

She stiffened; Néstor loosened his arms and released her.

"I'm probably getting blood on you," she murmured and took a step back from him. Her forearms were still sticky with it. Its metallic aroma bit her tongue, still surprisingly fresh. She suppressed a shudder.

"Are you hurt?" he asked.

She shook her head. "And you?"

"No."

Her heartbeat was steadying. Here, miles away from Palo Alto, it was as if the battle didn't exist. The heat of the late afternoon rose as it always had, as it always would. Chachalacas squawked from the direction of the river; cheeping and the flutter of wings punctuated the trees overhead as Néstor led her to the shade. He unstrapped a water flask from his saddle and handed it to her.

She curled her fingers around the worn leather of the flask, still warm from the sun. The clicking hum of chicharras rose and fell in steady pulses as Néstor turned his attention to the horses. He led them into the shade and began to loosen girths and curry mud away from their coats. Presently, she noticed he was singing to himself under his breath.

Panic ebbed away from her body, leaving it shaking and weak. She sank to the hard earth and sat among the roots of the trees, pulling her knees up to her chest. Her skirt was still heavy and wet, its weight suffocating as it absorbed the afternoon heat.

The water in the flask was warm and stale on her tongue, but she drank it anyway, staring into space as Néstor found a branch around which to loop the horses' reins. The shift of leather grew closer; spurs clicked as he lowered himself to the earth and sat next to her with a heavy thump. He sighed deeply, but said nothing, not even as she handed the water flask to him.

In the distance, a cannon boomed.

She flinched. Her ears were still ringing. Perhaps they would never stop ringing.

"Are you sure none of that is yours?" Néstor asked softly. She followed the path of his gaze to her blood-streaked hands and arms. The blood had darkened and cracked like dried earth in the heat. It was beginning to itch; she scratched off flakes of it.

She had failed to save the nameless men whose blood this was. Out on the battlefield, she was next to useless. What help could she have possibly been, with her eyes stinging with smoke and gunpowder and body after body being dragged toward her and the other healers? What could she have done, in the face of such slaughter?

She was a fool to think she could have helped. A fool to think that she could have proven her worth as a curandera to Papá this way.

"I should wash it off," she murmured.

"We can find a place to do that," Néstor said. "But we'll go together. I don't want either of us to be alone with . . . *those* things out there." He had pushed his hat back from his forehead and ran a hand over his face. His expression had a distant, haunted look.

All Nena could think of was that gray, sightless face as it lifted from the bodies of fallen Mexican soldiers, gore slick on its chin, to stare at her. It had no eyes, but she knew with a cold certainty in the pit of her stomach that it was *staring* at her.

A shudder raced over her skin at the memory.

"What were those things?" she asked.

"You saw them too," Néstor said. It wasn't a question—it was firm, as if he were confirming that he was not mad. "They looked like they were feeding on . . ." His voice trailed off.

"Sucking blood," Nena said. "That's what they were doing."

She had seen it with her own eyes. She was on horseback and meters away, but there was no mistaking it. The long, spindly arms cradling the fallen bodies, bringing throats and arms up to their mouths. To their long, red-soaked teeth.

"Like bats?" Néstor said.

She thought of saying yes. Then, from the back of her mind, she heard an echo of Don Antonio Canales's voice. When he was on the rancho speaking to Papá about mustering a squadron, he had quoted some guerrilla when he called the Yanquis—

"Vampires," Nena said flatly. "Like vampires."

A long silence followed. The hum of the chicharras in the branches overhead had none of the warmth it usually did. It only served to remind her how alone they were, out in the chaparral. Their backs were to the trunks of trees, but otherwise, they were exposed. Vulnerable.

Duérmete niño, duérmete ya . . .

How often Abuela's voice had lulled her to sleep in the heat of the siesta when she was a child, the morbid rhyme shutting her eyelids with tender fingertips.

"Or El Cuco," Nena added. "Whichever makes you feel better."

She glanced at Néstor out of the corner of her eye; he was chewing his bottom lip, staring warily at the path that led them to this clearing.

"That's not much of a choice, if I'm being honest," he said dryly.

A laugh cracked out of Nena like the lick of a whip. It fell dissonant on her ears, unhinged, like the laugh of a madwoman. She certainly felt that way. She stretched her legs out in front of her, trying to release the tension in her back and neck from clutching her knees tight to her chest.

"Who knew Abuela's stories were real?" she said.

"I did," Néstor said quietly.

Nena's laughter died as quickly as it had erupted.

"Since that night," he added, his eyes still on the line of high grass. His gaze was no longer watchful; it was distant, as if he were purposefully avoiding her. He opened his mouth; hesitated. "I didn't want to believe it, trust me. That night . . . do you remember we wanted to find Spanish silver?" His words had none of the well-worn corners of a vaquero tall tale. He faltered and retraced his steps. He was speaking his way through a secret, untangling it for someone else for the first time. "One of those . . . monsters attacked you. It appeared, and the next thing I knew, it was upon you—"

"They're what's causing the susto," Nena cut him off abruptly. Whatever Néstor had to say about what happened to her that night, she could not hear it now. Not when the visions of those monstrous beings still seared her mind. Not when they were so alone and exposed, the tree at their back their only protection in the broad, open countryside. "There must be some sort of venom in their bite. At least that is what Abuela has concluded—how else would they leave their prey unconscious?"

Like Beto. He had wounds like those of the men on Los Ojuelos; he was weak as if he had been bleeding for hours. Yes, he was unconscious, felled by what Abuela believed was venom. But he had lost so much blood.

The monsters—the *vampires*—were after blood. *They* were what had attacked Beto. They were what sucked the blood from the desiccated steer carcass that she and Néstor had stumbled across.

If men were falling ill from susto and dying on Los Ojuelos, that meant that these monsters *were there.* That Javiera and the others woke in the dark of the night screaming because of that feeling of being watched, that feeling that they were prey.

Because they were.

These things harmed people on the rancho. They could harm her family.

And Nena had left them.

Now that she knew what was causing the illness, she could not stay here, far from her home and her family. Not when predators circled Los Ojuelos like wolves, waiting to snatch her sister from her bed and sink their sharp teeth into her flesh . . .

She had to go back.

She had wanted to prove to Papá that she strengthened the rancho, that she was essential to its thriving. But in trying to do so, had she not acted selfishly?

What the rancho needed was someone who could help Abuela cure susto, someone who knew what caused it and could learn how to prevent it. And here she was, days away from home, sitting beneath a tree covered in dead men's blood. Because she had been so certain that by curing those who defended México on a glorious battlefield, she would win Papá's approval.

How stupid she had been. Shame prickled uncomfortably under her skin, growing and sinking into her like thorns. She had been so determined that *this* was the solution, that by seizing this opportunity she could secure a future where she never left Los Ojuelos, where her parents were proud of her curanderismo, even if she remained unmarried.

But in doing so, she had left the rancho vulnerable. The very people she claimed to serve—she had abandoned them.

She had to return.

Perhaps if she returned to camp, she could redeem herself. She could still prove her worth to Papá the way she had originally planned. By continuing to care for Beto and any other men who fell victim to susto, it was inevitable that the other rancheros or Félix would speak of her actions to Papá, thus validating her in Papá's eyes.

But she could not. Not when she knew what prowled the chaparral so close to home. What might have caused Javiera to wake screaming in the night.

She had to go home.

And when she did, her bargain with Papá was complete. She would face the consequences of her failed gamble. He had allowed her to accompany the squadron to Matamoros, and in return, she would marry whichever son of a wealthy hacendado he chose.

A sour realization bloomed in her throat. Perhaps it was for the best. Perhaps Mamá and Papá were right, after all.

The sight—and horrific sounds—of the Rinches galloping through the smoke to attack the healers would forever haunt her. There were so many of them, so determined to harm the unarmed. The wounded, the women.

That was what they were up against. *That* was what Los Ojuelos needed to be strengthened against. It could buy that strength with money, with more men. With connections and reputations that money could not buy, but that the gift of a daughter could.

"So do you believe me?" Néstor's words were cautious. Probing. Testing the waters, waiting to see if—or how—she would react. "About that night?"

Néstor had pulled his knees up to his chest protectively and held the brim of his hat in front of his shins. His hair was sweaty, his cheeks and shirt streaked with dirt.

He was a man who wore the scraps of a boy she once knew, a stranger she did not yet know if she could forgive. Still, her heart caught at the tender hope in his eyes.

It shouldn't hurt. Not after what they had just survived. Not after he rescued her from danger. She should be grateful to him that she was safe, that they were *both* safe, even though there was no way to know what had become of Félix and Papá and Casimiro.

But some wounds ran too close to the bone. Some afflictions had sunk their claws in too deep and had poisoned the blood for years. They would not release their hold without a fight.

She left the question hanging on the air and turned her face away from him, out at the clearing.

"I have to go back," she said.

"To camp?" he asked, a shade of surprise in his voice.

"No," she said. She had to bring the knowledge of the vampires and how they caused the susto back to Abuela, to defend the rancho from monsters. She would also have to face the consequences of her failed bargain. But in doing both, she would be doing what was best for the rancho. This knowledge would have to fortify her, no matter what lay ahead. "To Los Ojuelos."

17

⌁⌁⌁

NÉSTOR

"*ABUELA CAN HEAL* the susto, but she doesn't know the true cause. She doesn't know . . ." Nena's voice had been shaky before, but it grew firmer. More confident. "About them. There is no one to help her. I'm going back."

"The patrón will worry that you are missing," Néstor said. "And Don Félix."

"You can go back and tell them," she said.

"And leave you alone?" Disbelief shot the pitch of his voice upward. How could she suggest such a thing? There was not a chance. "Hell no."

"Then I'll send a message to Papá as soon as I can," Nena said. "But this can't wait. I'm going back."

"*We're* going back," he corrected.

"What if I want to be alone?" Nena's tone was arch. Her moment of softness was retreating behind hard walls, too quickly for him to catch. Like smoke passing through his fingertips. She had not said she believed him, nor forgave him—perhaps she would not. He buried the thought as quickly as he could, before it could burn him.

He focused on the immediate danger: Nena could not travel alone. Not in a world where the gray forms that stalked his nightmares appeared on the battlefield. A visceral fear uncurled at the base of his skull at the memory of them among the bodies. They were not a mirage, not a shard of terror that slipped from unconscious memory into daylight among the horror of the battlefield.

They were real.

The sun was dull on their leathery gray backs, their sightless faces streaked with dark liquid. Curled over corpses already bloating and reeking from the heat, their ribs pulsing with each greedy draft.

"Then I'll follow at a respectful distance," he said.

"Like a dog?"

"A loyal one," he offered.

She scoffed softly. "Bold words from someone who left."

This dug into the softness beneath his ribs like a dagger, catching him off guard.

"I . . ." he began.

"Are you going to defend yourself?" Nena asked.

"Yes," he said, speaking so quickly he tripped over the word.

"Then go ahead. Talk." She was brusque. Impatient. Her face was turned away from him, its expression shuttered—she had no interest in anything he had to say. She might never. "We have nothing better to do."

For a long moment, silence hung between them. He could hear the breeze in the leaves above them, the distant sounds of the river. His own pulse beneath his jaw. The creak of his fate, bending and shifting.

"I couldn't come back," he said.

Even her scowl was lovely. He looked up at the sound of skirts shifting. She was rearranging the muddy fabric around her knees, making to stand.

Embarrassed heat crept up his neck. He had envisioned many reconciliations with her, sleepless night after night. None of them had featured him so tongue-tied.

But here he was. And here she was—not ten feet away, distant and unapproachable as a saint in a chapel. Not snapping at him to not call her Nena, or worse, insisting that he not speak to her at all. Had she not been in his arms just moments ago, warm and real and clinging to him as if he were the one thing keeping the ground beneath their feet and the sky overhead?

She was *with* him. It was all he wanted to do to keep her there with him.

"This whole time, if I had come back . . ." He would have seen what a fool he was. What a coward he had been.

Every sleepless night spent composing speeches to her lifted its wings and rose, flying from his mind with the synchronized grace of a dozen herons. Every clever, passionate word he had committed to memory as he rode behind her and Don Feliciano melted away. He had nothing. He was empty-handed.

"I'm sorry," he said.

It was all he had. That and his shame.

A cannon boomed. Its closeness sent them startling upright in the same movement, elbows and knees bumping into one another as they scrambled for balance.

But it was not a cannon. The crack was followed by a throaty rumble sounding high overhead. Néstor lifted his chin to the skies: in the east, dark clouds mingled with the smoke over Matamoros. Within hours, it would rain.

"We should go," Nena said softly.

They should. The echo of thunder jolted him into reality like a bucket of cold water to the face: aside from what he carried in his saddle, they had no supplies, no money, no shelter. A nightmare at their back. How were they going to get to Los Ojuelos?

He did not have answers. Instead of planning, he had been sitting beneath a tree, trying and failing to speak. Like a weakling. Shame unfurled in his chest. He could not be weak anymore. He cleared his throat.

"When we were riding to Matamoros, I noticed a few abandoned jacales," he said. "There was one probably a few hours' ride northwest of here. I think it would make a safe enough place to spend the night. In case, God forbid . . ."

He let the sentence trail off. God had nothing to do with it. Any belief in God that hid in Néstor's breast was a fragile, translucent thing, a cloth so worn and weak that if you held it up to the sun, light would shine through it. The events of the day had all but shredded it. *In case we have company* was what he meant, but saying it aloud felt unlucky on his tongue at best. At worst, it tasted like a prophecy.

"In case of the worst," Nena said, her eyes fixed on the skies—perhaps searching them, as Abuela often did, for hints of what the future's weather held in store. "And because the rain will follow us."

"Then let's hurry," Néstor said. The sooner they put more distance between them and what stalked the battlefield the better. He could think on the road. There would be settlements, small ranchos where he could offer to work and win them shelter and sustenance in return. He had done it before and would do it again, if it got Nena home safely. If they rode hard, and if Nena could ride hard, they could make the return journey in less than half the time the squadron took to reach Matamoros. "How fast can you ride?"

"As fast as you," Nena said, tone sharpened by defensiveness. "But I . . ." She looked down at her muddy skirts, still wet from crossing the resaca. "Not like this. The saddle sores alone . . ." She shook her head.

"Do you have . . ." Néstor let the phrase trail off, biting his lip when he realized how stupid the question was. Of course Nena did not have a change of clothes better suited to riding. All of her belongings were back at camp. And there was no turning back to get anything—it was too dangerous.

"Do *you* have anything I could wear?" Nena echoed his question pointedly. "Vaqueros travel with their lives in their saddle, don't they?"

They did. He had a shirt, at least. No chivarras other than those he wore, but he had a spare pair of trousers. He crossed the space between them and the horses. Luna's ears pricked at his approach, and he rubbed her neck with an absentminded hand before reaching for his saddlebags and his clothes.

His fingers brushed over something hard.

He frowned, fingers searching. He withdrew a small bottle, its glass dark and warped, its front etched with a rustic cross. It looked like one of Abuela's bottles for holy water, but was filled with something white. He removed its small stopper and peered inside.

Salt.

The bottle was filled with salt.

The night before he left Los Ojuelos with the squadron, he remembered seeing Abuela near the saddles that the Duarte men left perched on the railing of the porch. Had she snuck this into his saddle?

Why salt?

He slipped it back into the saddlebag and took out his spare clothes instead.

Nena was just behind him when he turned. He hadn't heard her approach. It made him uneasy—in a good way, a way that sent his heart to his throat—to be so close to her.

"You won't have chivarras, but it should be better than nothing," he said, holding out the clothes to her.

She took them, her bloodstained hands brushing his. "Thank you."

A long silence filled the space between them. Nena gave him a chastising look.

"Oh." He cleared his throat. "I . . . I'll turn around, of course." He did this immediately, the heels of his boots carving divots in the dirt, he turned so sharply. He focused on Luna's saddle. He occupied himself with tightening her girth, rubbing river silt from the stirrups. The smell of wet leather made him dread the discomfort of the ride ahead. He would have to scrub the whole saddle clean during their next siesta.

Despite how he tried to remain focused on anything else, he heard a shift of fabric behind him, followed by the undeniable deflated sigh of skirts hitting the ground around ankles.

His hands moved to Luna's mane. He focused on untangling knots there, focused on the dirt on his knuckles and the mare's coarse black hair.

"I'm dressed," Nena said behind him.

He would not turn quickly. He would not. As casually as he could muster, he shifted his weight and looked over his shoulder.

He had never seen a woman wearing trousers before. They were obviously too big—Nena had to hold them up. And yet. His eye fell on how the trousers accentuated the slenderness of her waist, how the cloth of his shirt—a shirt he had mended with his own hands over a dozen times—draped over her breasts.

He averted his gaze quickly. Why was his mouth so dry? He cleared his throat. Should he say she looked nice? Should he say nothing at all?

"You don't have a belt, do you." Nena's words, delivered humorlessly, were more a statement than a question.

No, he did not. He did have rope, however. He reached for it, eager for something to do with his hands. He brought it to Nena, holding it out as if he were going to measure around her waist.

She snatched it from him, fumbling to keep the trousers up at the same time. "I've got it." She slipped it through the belt loops of the trousers, then tied it in a firm knot. "Could you cut it?"

He reached for his knife, stepping closer to her as he took the extra length of rope in his hand. Her body leaned pliantly toward him as he drew it taut. Heat flushed his neck and cheeks. The rope was in his hands. If he wanted, he could pull her closer, close enough that he could smell her hair, bend his face to the sweet curve of her neck that was no longer covered by her dress and press his lips to her skin . . .

Then he noticed that the skin along one side of her lower neck, beneath her scapular, where it curved elegantly over the collarbone to meet her right shoulder, was dappled with a long scar.

He nearly dropped the knife in surprise.

"My God," he breathed. "Is that . . ."

"Just cut the rope," Nena snapped. When he obeyed, she ordered: "Let's go."

She cut past him to the horse he had ridden from the battlefield and began to tighten the mare's girth. Her movements were sharp, irritated. As if she were uncomfortable in the clothes or uncomfortable with his question. Or both.

Néstor watched her. For a moment, all he could hear was her screaming his name in the dark. The wet, nightmarish sound of a monster sinking its teeth into her flesh.

He wore pistols on either hip. Always had since the moment he could afford the second. He reached for the holster on his right hip and unbuckled it.

"Here," he said, folding the leather straps beneath the gun and handing it to her. "Let's hope you don't need this."

❖   ❖   ❖

HEAT HOVERED THICK on the afternoon, shimmering like a glaze, as they saddled the horses. Their backs were turned to each other; each was absorbed in their own thoughts as they mounted and set out. The clouds beat a steady march west across the sky, their color shifting deeper and deeper as thunder rumbled its threats in the distance. The smell of the storm nipped at their heels; humidity built until it was close to breaking, heavy and rank on their skin as the breath of a predator.

But it did not break. Not yet.

Perhaps one of them should have been keeping watch as they rode. Perhaps one of them should have cast looks over their shoulders as they rejoined the road closer to the river.

Perhaps then they might have noticed a lone figure along the riverbank, not far from where they had crossed. Rising from among the reeds, observing in silence, and slowly retreating.

But it did not retreat far.

Not far at all.

THEY RODE TO the river, washed off dried blood as quickly and as best they could, then carried on. Would they be able to cover the ground between them and the jacal Néstor had seen before nightfall? They risked the main road to save time, but moved off it if they heard riders approaching. Encountering strangers posed three potential problems that he sorely wished to avoid.

The first: if members of the Mexican military saw them and thought they were deserting the army, Néstor at least would be apprehended and forced to return, leaving Nena to return to Los Ojuelos without protection.

The second: it would be noted that Nena, an unmarried young

woman, traveled alone with a vaquero. If it were discovered that she was a ranchero's daughter, it would be easy to claim that Néstor had kidnapped her for himself, an offense punishable by the patrón of a rancho by whipping or death.

This seemed a trifle in comparison to the third: encountering Yanquis. He would not easily forget the sight of them at dawn, eastern sunlight glinting white off their bayonets. The sound of those bayonets thrusting through the stomachs of Mexican soldiers made him feel nauseous. He staved off the feeling and his hunger by slowing their horses to a walk and eating provisions of acecina—strips of dried, salted beef—wrapped in tortillas in the saddle as they rode.

Food was another concern that followed Néstor along with the storm clouds. Aside from the acecina and tortillas from camp kitchens, they had very little. In the dead man's saddle in which Nena rode he had found provisions for making pan de campo, but with the impending rain, he would not be able to make any when they rested tonight. Instead, he made sure they took the time to collect and eat a juicy, bright cluster of tuna fruits and cut provisions of nopal cactus while washing by the river. But until tomorrow, that, dry tortillas, and acecina were all they had.

Nena held the reins of conversation in a tight fist. Long periods passed where she would not respond to a cautious question. He could have left her in silence. But hadn't Beto often succeeded in teasing him out of his own brooding silences?

When he leaned over to offer her more acecina, he spoke.

"You look just like a vaquero," he said. "Eating in the saddle. You might have a future among us after all." He kept his voice carefully light, almost teasing, as he referred to a childhood desire of hers to become a vaquero like him. As if none of the events of the past two days had happened at all, and he was still trying to charm her out of her cold silence on the road to Matamoros.

Perhaps he wanted to break the eeriness that crept from the east, the silence that followed at their heels. The rumbles of thunder that ended in his chest, promising that if they didn't pick up the pace soon, there was no outrunning the storm. Even from his own horse, he could see that tension drew Nena's shoulders taut.

"You have a lot of work to do, though," he said.

"Oh?" she asked.

"You've changed," he said. "You're not nearly bad enough. You used to be defiant. Remember when Félix said you weren't allowed to ride that stallion he bought from Hacienda del Sol? The big-boned gray. He threw you into a prickly pear."

A smile flickered across her face.

"I swear you still have the scar on your cheek," he added.

"I do not." Was it his imagination, or was her tone warmer? Was that a hint of her dimple, to the corner of her mouth? "Mamá would certainly remind me if I did."

"Ah, Doña Mercedes." Néstor sighed theatrically, conjuring the overbearing villain of their childhood to mind. "She's made you so prim. I can't help but wonder if you've forgotten how to misbehave."

"Ha," she said flatly. "Perhaps you're right."

He imagined their voices casting a veil of safety around them. If they kept speaking, they may as well be only a few miles from Los Ojuelos. They may as well be riding from one rancho to another after a visit, with no worry of being followed.

He had no reason to believe they were being followed now. But a creeping sensation up the back of his neck twisted his imagination in sour directions, knitting his throat tight with anxiety.

"Then you need to relearn how to be bad in order to be a decent vaquero," he said, taking a bite of acecina and rolling the tough, salty meat over his tongue. "Fortunately, you happen to be riding with an expert."

She shot him a sideways look. "So I've heard," she said archly. "Your gringo friend sows stories like wildflowers."

Néstor's heart stumbled darkly, as if it were a horse who had lost its footing over pocked earth. Beto had promised to be unerringly polite when he kept guard over Nena. He had sworn he would be.

But other vaqueros talked. Hadn't they all been surrounded by vaqueros on the road to Matamoros? It was not impossible that Nena had heard about the bar fights, the wagers, the rumors of his relationship with Celeste Romero of Rancho Buenavista. Had she heard about Celeste? What *if* she had? What would she think of him?

He had never cared what women or other vaqueros thought of him in the past. He was happy to play the part of a wealthy woman's plaything. It got him what he wanted: better wages, better jobs. A precious look into what running a rancho could be like.

Nena was not the same.

His fears shifted beneath his skin; new ones rose and grew thorns. He did not know what he meant to her. *Vaqueros may call me señorita, or better yet, say nothing to me at all.* He feared that he was nothing to her. That if he offered her his heart, she would take it and drop it in the dust to bleed whenever her father called.

That alone meant Nena could shatter him, mind and soul.

The realization left him unhorsed, defenseless, vulnerable.

And he *hated* that feeling.

He threw up defenses, swift as a reflex.

"Then you can trust my expertise," he said, putting on the flirtatious mask that had won him the admiration of Celeste and so many others. "Imagínalo: I'll take you to a big town, somewhere where no one knows who you are, and I'll teach you to be bad." He left acecina between his teeth like a cigarillo and spoke around it as he counted off on his fingers. "First, we'll go to a bar. I'll teach you how to do shots. Then, we'll play cards."

A scene unfolded in his mind as he waited for her reply: the two of them at a bar in a dark room, surrounded by laughter, the clink of glasses, and curls of blue tobacco smoke. Him standing close to her, facing her, dressed in his finest as he had been the night he returned to Los Ojuelos. Rings on his fingers and spurs of silver on his heels. As good as any hidalgo from a land grant family. Good enough for a woman like her. The sounds of the room around them fading as he met her eyes. Her taking the small glass of pale liquid that he offered her and clinking it with his.

"Can I wear a red dress?" she asked.

"As red as fruta guadalupana," he said. The image in his mind shifted, dressing her in a frock as bright as the fruit's glistening, ruby seeds.

"I want it to be bloodred," Nena said firmly. "And cut so low the tías talk about it for weeks."

This alteration to the reverie sent a bolt of longing through his chest. He cleared his throat and refocused his gaze up ahead, on the horizon. "I'll buy the fabric myself," he said.

Out of the corner of his eye, he swore he saw a smile twitch at one side of her mouth.

"It's a deal," she said. "What then?"

It was intoxicating, how much he wanted her to trust him. To relax around him. To smile as she used to, when they were children. Broad and unguarded and sweetly dimpled, her teeth flashing like a loaded pistol in the sun. He would happily be shot dead by it any day of the week.

"I'll teach you how to cheat, and then I'll teach you how to shoot," he said, "in case you get into a fight after you've swindled a man."

This drew a laugh from her, a laugh so golden it pushed back at the dark clouds hovering at their backs. It created a halo of safety around them, a brilliant torch against the deepening shadows.

"Here's another idea," he said, egged on by her response. "In Laredo I've been to a brothel that has a bar *and* gambling inside, so we can do multiple bad things at once if we went—"

"You've been to brothels?" Nena asked, voice razor-sharp. Her good mood had vanished like the slam of a door.

Shit. He scrambled for purchase.

"I'm being honest with you," he said. He gestured to his chest, miming wicked self-assurance: "I'm a bad man."

"Then really be honest with me, *bad man*," Nena snapped, echoing the epithet with a dose of venom. "How many women have you slept with?"

He paused. Let the silence stretch long. If he lied, he did not doubt he would be caught in it eventually, the falsehood tightening around his neck like a noose. If he told the truth?

He cast his dice.

"Eighteen, I think? Twenty?"

"You *think?*"

"There was usually a lot of alcohol involved," Néstor offered with a light shrug. He could regain his footing. He could play it off by reminding her how bad he was. This was what Celeste and others liked, after all: he was the allure of vice in their otherwise tight-laced lives. He was their rebellion.

This did not help: Nena gave him a cold look, then scoffed. She nudged her horse to a trot.

"Nena—"

She held up a hand to silence him. "Don't talk to me until we pass that maguey," she said over her shoulder. Streaks of dusky purple loomed on the western horizon; the sky above it was a muted, faraway slate. She pointed vaguely up ahead.

"What maguey?" Néstor called.

"Exactly."

18

NENA

NIGHT DEEPENED TO full darkness around them as they rode, thickening the silence between them. Made them more prone to swiveling their heads toward small noises in the chaparral. The calls of birds fell silent, but no song of insects filled the husk of their wake.

Occasional forks of lightning split the sky behind them, wicked and grasping. The air pressed against her skin, heavy with the promise of rain.

"There," Néstor said at last, pointing into the dark.

Nena squinted at the jacal that emerged through the gloom. Overgrown huisaches engulfed half the patio, making its roof sag on one side; the doorway looked like a tall, toothless mouth. There was no door, no sign that anyone had been there for months, if not years. It was no fortress, but it was shelter. It was a wall to have at their backs through the long night. It was enough.

It would have to be enough.

Over the last hour, she could not rid herself of a feeling skittering over the back of her neck, down her spine. They had not seen a single soul on the road; this, she decided, was good, even if the isolation gave an eerie taste to the night. Even if she could not shake the feeling of being watched. Once the sun set, she even admitted to herself it was good Néstor was behind her, a pistol at his side. A machete for clearing chaparral attached to his saddle and bullets slung across his chest in a bandolier.

Still, she had not spoken to him for hours. She kept her silence as they dismounted near the jacal. She made to step onto the patio; he held up a hand and drew his pistol. He released the safety with a soft click.

"Stay with the horses," he said, handing her his mare's reins. "I'll check it out first."

He was light on his feet on the patio until he reached the doorway; then, staying to the side of the rotted opening, he stamped one boot loudly. Peered inside, pistol at the ready.

Silence.

"It's empty," he said, slipping his pistol back into its holster. She brought the horses onto the patio and returned his mare's reins to him.

"We should never assume we're the only ones looking for shelter out here," he said by way of explanation.

"That's clever," she said.

"I should tell you about the time I nearly got mauled by an ocelot in a cave," he said dryly. "Then you won't think I'm clever."

It was too dark to read his expression. There were times when he looked so much like the boy she had known that she felt a pang in her gut akin to a physical blow. This was not one of those times.

This man was a stranger.

"If you make the fire, I'll unsaddle your horse," he said. "Deal?"

"Deal."

Her spurs clinked as she stepped into the clearing around the jacal. A chorus of crickets rose around her, chirruping rhythmically.

Prickles rose along her neck, clustering around where her scar lay.

She shrugged her shoulders to loosen their tightness. There was nothing to fear. All she had to do was collect firewood and get back to the jacal. Then, she could start a fire, and there would be light. Blessed, leaping light licking up to the roof of the shelter.

She made quick work of gathering kindling, of finding branches from mesquites that were dry and thick enough to burn.

Néstor's smile flashed through her mind, wicked and sharp. *Eighteen, I think?* She stomped on a branch to crack it in two. It snapped easily beneath the force of the blow. She collected it with sharp motions.

Eighteen, or so he thought. The Néstor she loved had no eyes for any girl on the rancho but her. *This* Néstor was a stranger to her. She had no desire to learn anything more about him, not when every single thing he said upset her more.

She pictured herself sitting beneath the anacahuita trees behind the house, waiting for Félix to return from the comisaria with the mail. Looking—as a tía had once commented—like the lost half of a pair of shoes.

And where was Néstor? Off in bars and brothels, apparently, with no intention of coming home.

A cool brush of reason twined into her anger. *Think of why,* that voice said.

If what he said was true—that he had seen her attacked by one of those monsters, and that was the cause of the susto she remembered Abuela calling her back from—then it made sense for him to think that she was dead. They were children. How could he have known better?

A more coolheaded woman would understand why he never returned. A more rational woman would forgive him. She was neither, and had no desire to ever be. Not when it came to *him*, at least.

Her arms were full of wood when she stopped mid-step.

She was being watched.

She felt it like a brush of fingertips running down her spine, raising every hair on her body along the way. Discomfort prickled beneath her scar.

Until that moment, she had not realized how the twilight had thickened and vanished, how low the night sky swung overhead, heavy and dark with pregnant clouds. Nor how far she had drawn from the jacal. Now she felt the distance between her and the safety of the building like a phantom limb—long, exposed, and naked.

Néstor whistled as he curried the horses; each note rose and twisted in the night, stretching thin and eerie.

She was too far from the jacal.

She looked over one shoulder. Spun around to face the chaparral, heart pounding against the armfuls of wood she clutched to her chest. She searched the night, eyes wide and unblinking.

There was nothing.

No long-limbed, eyeless figures in the darkness. No glint of Yanqui bayonets.

She retreated as quickly as she dared to the jacal, jerking her chin over her shoulder to mark her surroundings until she reached the patio. The sound of the horses breathing soothed her. She could hear Néstor's whistling properly now, its melody commonplace and safe. She imagined it forming a barrier around the small hut, around the patio, keeping what was clearly her overactive imagination at bay.

But her heart was still hammering as she brought the wood into the darkness of the jacal, to the fireplace that reeked of mildew and rot. Néstor had brought in the machete from his mount's saddle;

she used it to chop larger pieces of wood down to size, forbidding her mind from wondering who the machete, the saddle, and the horse Néstor fled the battlefield riding had once belonged to.

Flint sparked; kindling caught. She focused on coaxing the flame brighter. Focused on filling the hut with its golden light and the smoky aroma of smoldering mesquite.

"That was quick."

Nena looked up. Néstor took in her progress from the doorway as he scraped the brush he had used to curry the horses clean.

"I had a decent teacher," she said begrudgingly, keeping her eyes on the smoking boughs of wood as she prodded them with a green branch into a better position. Of course it was Néstor who taught her how to make a fire, on cold winter mornings with the sheep in the chaparral.

She heard him say something, but didn't quite catch it. He had just stepped out of sight of the doorway.

"What did you say?" she said. She wanted him to keep talking. Voices could dispel her tenseness, her feeling of being exposed. She put one more branch on the crackling fire and followed him to the patio to collect her pack. Every bone in her body ached. There was nopal strapped to her saddle that she could cook over the strengthening fire, but she was too tired to be hungry. She thought she had gotten accustomed to travel, but the hours on the road today were much longer than when they traveled with an unwieldy squadron of five hundred men.

"I said, I knew you'd make a decent vaquero," he said, repositioning his saddle on the half-rotten table on one side of the patio. The horses were tethered on long ropes and grazed on the far side of the house, clean and content.

Nena frowned. There was something in the way he didn't meet her eyes as he tossed her a pack that made her think he had said something else. She caught the pack against her chest with a thump.

"If only I could be as useful as a vaquero," she said. Bitterness scraped a jagged edge over her words—it took her aback for a moment, to hear it so clearly. It made her voice sound unlike her own. "Perhaps then Papá wouldn't be so preoccupied with marrying me off to the highest bidder."

He did not reply immediately as he collected the second pack. His question, when it came at last, was tentative. Careful. "Is he really?"

She tightened her arms around her pack. "I don't want to talk about it."

Just like when they were children, it was as if she had closed a door. He left it closed. He gestured for her to step into the jacal.

Inside, she put her pack down and returned to tending the fire. Behind her, she heard Néstor lower himself to the floor with a long, exhausted exhale. The low, metallic clink of bullets as he rested his bandolier on the floor.

For a long moment, there was nothing but the contented crackle of the fire. She watched splinters smoke and curl before bursting into flames.

"I'm so tired of it," she admitted to the fire.

"Of what?" His voice was soft.

"Ever since you left, I've been the perfect daughter," she said softly. Perhaps *because* he left. Mamá and Papá's love was a fragile, fickle thing; Néstor was the one person she had trusted to never stop loving her. To never leave her. With him gone, scarcity seized her life in a brute fist, squeezing her dry: if she disobeyed her parents, if she stepped a toe out of line, she could lose everything they gave. Couldn't she? "I *have* changed, and I'm tired of it. I'm tired of being good. Of being *nice*."

Néstor released a soft, amused exhale. A half laugh she knew so well her heart turned over itself. If she didn't look at him, she could picture him as he once was, as vividly as if it were yesterday: gangly limbs, the thin arms Casimiro teased him for. The belt with extra holes punched in it to keep the too-large trousers inherited from a much broader cousin at his hips. His thick black hair as wavy and messy as always, no matter how much he pushed it back, no matter how much Abuela fought it into place before evening vespers. His eyes wide and innocent, his expression open and wholly hers.

She did glance over her shoulder, eventually. And there he was, his clothes dusty from the road, his hat on the ground next to him, his head leaned back against the wall of the jacal. Her eyes traced the line of his throat, from hollow to Adam's apple to his chin, then lingered on his mouth.

"So be bad, once in a while," he said, tiredness lengthening his syllables to a drawl. "Be mean."

She hated the effect his voice had on her. It was like fingertips drawn lightly over skin, awakening every nerve in their wake. "I don't think I know how."

"Ha," he said flatly. "On the contrary, you're quite good at it."

She shot him a sharp look. Was he serious? No—there was a glint of amusement in his eye.

"Don't believe me? Go on, see how easy it is to say something cruel to me," he goaded. "I can take it."

He was being serious. Well, serious about teasing her into a game. *You used to be defiant.* That had pierced her like the spines of the nopal they cut that afternoon. Some spines lingered under the pads of her fingertips, a constant irritation. So, too, had his words.

She paused, searching for words. "I don't like you."

"Awful," he declared. A playful smile drew across his face, sharp as a knife. "Try again."

"I think . . ." Nena averted her eyes to the fire. "I think you're ugly."

"I know for a fact you don't believe that." She could hear in Néstor's voice that his smile had curled into a smirk.

Nena's mouth dropped open, her cheeks catching flame like kindling. How *dare* he? She glared at him brazenly.

"Fuck you." The words came easier than she expected.

Néstor winked at her. Touched an imaginary brim of the hat. "A sus órdenes, señorita."

The pitch of his voice sent a sensation down her sternum like the gentle tap of fingertips. Like footsteps aimed, sure and true toward a doorway.

"Stop being like that," she hissed.

"Like what?"

He mimed ignorance, but his voice was smug—he knew exactly what he was doing. He should. Hadn't he weaseled his way into the beds of rancheros' wives and widows? Hadn't he weaseled his way under her own skin? She wanted to smack the self-satisfied look off his face.

"Like . . . don't *flirt* with me," she said hotly. "I don't want it."

Néstor groaned theatrically, a hand flying to his heart as if he had been shot. His eyes fluttered shut as he mimed pain. "Madre Santa, that one hurts!"

"I'm serious," she snapped. She didn't want the flirtation that won him favors among strangers. No winks or sharp smiles would suffice. She swore it to herself there and then: his whole soul was her price.

"¡Órale! Now we're getting somewhere," Néstor said, leaning forward eagerly. His eyes crackled as merrily as the fire. He held his hands loosely before his chest, as if ready for a fist fight. "Hit me again."

What was the cruelest thing she could say to Néstor?

If life had taught her anything, it was that nothing could wound as swiftly as the truth.

She turned her face to the fire. "Don Feliciano Serrano would sooner shoot a man than allow a vaquero to woo his daughter."

The silence that fell on the jacal was so complete, so thick, that she swore if she had dropped a needle, it would hover before touching the floor.

"Why would you say that?" he asked, voice soft.

"You said to hit you," Nena said flatly. "I did. I thought you could take it. It's your game, after all."

The shift of leather. The sound of heeled boots crossing the wooden floor of the jacal behind her. When Nena looked up from the fire, Néstor was in the doorway. He leaned there, facing the night, his back turned to her.

"This isn't a game, Nena." The words were directed out into the dark. "You and me."

Except there was no *you and me*. She felt the flush of anger like a ringing in her ears. There hadn't been a *you and me* since the day he left.

"I spoke the truth," she said. "You don't like it? Then leave again. There's nothing stopping you."

Néstor turned to face her, expression creased with hurt. What was he thinking? "Maybe I will."

The words were delivered slowly, deliberately, without an ounce of anger or venom.

That made them hurt so much more.

"I knew you wouldn't stay," she snapped. "Not a steadfast bone in your body. Go and be grateful that you're a man. Not all of us have the freedom to get up and leave everyone who loves us whenever we please."

"That's not fair," Néstor said, his voice low, rough like cart wheels over gravel.

"It's true," Nena challenged.

"You have that freedom too," Néstor said, his voice rising. "Look at you now!" He pointed at her trousers, her boots. "Boots, horse, open road. You could leave if you wanted, anytime you wanted. You are your own master. You just lack the spine to say no to anything your father asks."

She was on her feet, alight with the need to brawl. "Don't you *dare* say anything about my father," she said, pointing a finger at him.

"I'll say whatever I want," Néstor said. "He's an asshole who treats men like dogs."

"How *dare* you," she cried. Her hands balled into fists so tight her knuckles ached. Heat flushed her neck, prickling like a rash. "You don't understand what it's like to be responsible for a community. Papá does. *I* do. You don't understand responsibility at all. You only care about yourself."

"That's not true," Néstor said hotly.

Nena squinted, her night eyesight hobbled by the brightness of the fire. A shadow rose behind Néstor; he kept speaking, entirely unaware of how it coalesced, of how it drew close to his turned back.

Someone was there.

Every sinew of her body told her it meant harm.

"Get back," she snapped. "*Get back.*"

Néstor must have seen the panic in her eyes; he stopped talking and whirled to face whatever was behind him. He backed up a step, holding one hand out to signify *stop.*

Now that Néstor was out of the doorway, Nena saw that the shadow was a man.

A Yanqui.

Worse—a Rinche.

He seemed vaguely familiar—was this one of the men who had attacked the healers during the battle? One of the ones that Néstor shot during their harrowing flight? Firelight played off his blood-stained uniform; there was a bullet wound on one side of his chest, the blood from it black and dried with time.

Néstor began speaking English, his tone carefully neutral, even concerned, as he gestured at the wound on the man's chest. With each word, he shifted slightly to the right, slowly positioning himself between the door and Nena. With no hat under which to hide her braids, it was abundantly clear she was a woman.

Her mouth was bone-dry. With the man in the doorway, there was no other way out of the jacal. They were trapped. Néstor's gun was still at her hip; she slowly moved one hand over it, heart pounding in her throat. Rinches never rode alone, Félix had once said. The question was how many were at this man's back, waiting in the dark.

The man did not respond to anything Néstor was saying. His face was strangely neutral, even blank—something in his eyes kept them from focusing. They swept over Néstor, slipping over his features, sliding over the bare, dark walls of the jacal.

To Nena by the fire.

There they stayed. Fixed, intent.

Something in his eyes froze her blood. There was something wrong behind them. Something unholy, something that gleamed akin to light on dark water.

Néstor was trying to get the man to back up, it seemed; he wouldn't move. He was fixed on Nena like a cat on a bird, unmoving, utterly unblinking.

"Something's wrong," Nena whispered. She barely got the words out. Her heart was in her throat, choking her as it hammered soft flesh with an insistent command: *run, run, run.* The man took a step forward.

A click; a shout of warning.

Another step.

A gunshot.

Nena's hands flew to her ears. Her pulse throbbed in the silence.

Néstor's gun was in his hand, barrel smoking. Nena's eyes and nose burned with gunpowder.

He had shot the man at point-blank range. Directly in the chest. Right next to the other bullet wound. Right through the heart.

The man did not fall.

His neck went stiff, cocked backward, chin thrust in the air. Then, with a crack of bone that stole a gasp from Nena's chest, his neck bent further back. His neck split at the throat, sliced open from within by a long, clawed hand.

A monster clawed its way forth from within the man's body, slick with viscera, wet as a birth, its long teeth bared. The crack of bones and snap of sinew echoed against the walls of the jacal as its head and shoulders emerged from the chest. Soon the monster would claw itself free from the body it had followed them in, shedding its cage with butchery, shattering a protective egg of bone and gore.

"Fuck," Néstor breathed.

The fire was at their back. A small pile of firewood, broken branches. They had two guns. Néstor's ammunition lay in a pile against the back wall.

They were trapped.

19

$\sim\!\!\!\backslash\!\!\!\vee\!\!\!/\!\!\!\sim$

NENA

NENA CLOSED NÉSTOR'S fingers over the handle of the second gun. They trembled against her palm.

"Shoot," she hissed in his ear. "Shoot *now*."

His arm lifted. She braced against his back, hands over her ears. There was no missing at this range; the bang was followed by an unearthly, hair-raising howl. The horses tethered behind the jacal raised their voices in fear at the sound of the shot.

The vampire stumbled backward, out of sight of the doorway, and fell. It wrenched and spasmed like a beetle on its back, clawing at the meaty cage that bound it. Dark wounds were torn open through its chest, at its throat. But still it fought to be free.

"Bullets," Néstor rasped. "Back wall."

She stumbled back and sprang to snatch the bandolier from the floor. She pivoted on her heel and thrust it at him.

With a brutal, wet cry, the vampire shucked off the last of its meaty bindings and lurched forward onto all fours. As it rose to its full height, Néstor shoved a bullet and gunpowder into the first pistol, then the second. Bullets found their marks in the vampire's chest and neck; each blow sent shudders through its body, but still it loomed over them, a full head taller than Néstor. Blood slicked its hairless skull and the metal band around its throat, gleaming in firelight.

But it would not fall.

The only way to kill El Cuco is to cut off its head. Abuela's fireside tales were ghost stories. Nothing more.

Or were they?

Nena spared a quick glance at the fire for anything she could use as a weapon. Branches burned hot and white in the hearth. There was a pile of unused firewood; among the unburned branches was one long, green branch, one that she planned to use as a poker to nudge embers as the fire burned low.

Even better: next to the firewood lay the machete. Firelight reflected against scratched metal, winking up at her.

Néstor's attention was solely on shooting the vampire, on driving it back onto the patio.

Nena scrambled toward the fire. She seized the machete in her right hand and a smoldering stick from the fire with her left. Then she whirled to face the door as a cry—a human cry—split the night.

Néstor was ducking out of the way of the vampire's viscera-wet claws. Firelight from inside the jacal caught them like the edges of knives. Néstor was being driven down the patio by the monster, back to the rotten table and the thicket of huisaches, where he would be trapped.

But then the vampire turned, swinging its low head back toward the doorway. Back toward Nena. Perhaps it saw her as easier prey, trapped as she was in the close walls of the jacal. It filled the doorway, its attention wholly on her as it raised its long, spidery right arm, reaching to seize her.

With a feral cry and a blur of movement, Néstor appeared on

the back of the vampire. A flash of metal in his hand; he was bringing his knife down into the side of the monster's neck with all his strength.

The vampire released a strangled howl, half rage, half pain, its teeth bared like weapons in the firelight. It stumbled back a step, then, in a swift movement, seized Néstor by one arm and flung him across the patio as if he weighed no more than a wet rag.

A sickening pop cracked through the air. There was no cry, no scream; only a strangled whimper and the sound of a body falling. The clatter of a knife hitting the stony tipichil floor of the patio rang through the night.

Néstor.

She needed to get between the vampire and Néstor. He had no defenses. She crossed to the doorway in three steps and was enveloped by night.

Before her was the gray, leathery spine of the vampire. It curved over a prone body on the ground, in front of the half-rotten table that their saddles rested on, curled on one side like a sleeper.

Néstor.

The vampire lifted its clawed right arm high.

Nena thrust the smoldering branch into its exposed underarm as hard as she could. A sickening sizzle; the sudden smell of burning flesh. With a strangled howl, the monster whirled on her. Nena dropped the wood. Instead of falling back, she barreled forward, determined as a bull, dodging under the arm and claws of the monster. She clambered onto the rotting table, clutching the machete with both hands.

The vampire looked up at her. Though it had no eyes, and the sockets where eyes *ought* to be were slicked wet with gore, gooseflesh erupted over her arms: she could tell it was holding her gaze.

Santa Madre, help me, she thought. *Or whatever saint knows about these. Please.*

There was a wound in its throat where Néstor had stabbed it, just beneath the metal band around its neck.

She tensed.

When it stepped closer, she swung the machete as if she were hacking at the trunk of a tree, aiming just above the metal collar.

It struck like the sound of a pig being butchered.

Whether the machete was too dull or her strength was not enough, the blade did not sever the neck cleanly; it was deeply buried in viscera and flesh when the monster fell, dragging Nena down with it.

There was no cry. No shriek, no gush of blood spraying her.

She thought she heard the hollow sound of metal striking stone; then she hit the ground and rolled, grazing her cheeks and arms. She hit the wall of the jacal. Sparks filled her vision as she hauled herself upright, scrambling for the machete. She braced against the wall and held it out, heart pounding, breath coming in severe gasps.

But the vampire was gone.

All that remained was a coating of gray dust on the ground before her, sticking to the puddles of the Rinche's dark blood like ash from a kitchen fire.

Amid the dust and the blood lay the metal band.

But the vampire was gone. Madre Santa, it was gone.

"Néstor?"

He had not moved. He was still curled into the ground, cradling his left arm to his chest.

He gave a soft grunt. "Move inside," he said. His voice was mangled by pain.

She dropped the machete by the doorway. It fell with a clatter as she took in the blood that wet Néstor's shirt, how it was shredded as if it had been grabbed by a clawed hand. She crouched at his side. "Can you stand?"

He grunted again, pushing himself upright, still cradling his left arm. It hung at an angle from his body that she could only register as *wrong*.

She moved to his right side and pulled his good arm over her shoulders, bracing, her thighs burning from the effort it took to bring him upright.

Somehow, they made it back inside the jacal, ignoring the ruined body of the Rinche just past the door. They stumbled to the ground before the fire. He slid down as if to lie on his back, then, with an animallike yelp, shot upright. The sound tore her like cloth ripped in two.

He could not lie back on his shoulder.

"Let me see," she said. "Relax your left arm." Her voice sounded strange, distant to her ears. Like she was apart from herself watching this scene unfold before her. Néstor, his shoulder at a wrong angle and shredded by claws before the fire. His face pallid and beading with sweat as he obeyed, laying his left arm at his side. The smell of fear still thick on the air.

His arm dropped, the shoulder hollow beneath his flesh, sagging where it ought to cut the sharp silhouette that made her breath catch.

His arm was dislocated.

20

NÉSTOR

THE CEILING OF the jacal spun. Through the ringing in his ears, he caught Nena releasing a soft, sympathetic hiss. She knelt next to him, her attention focused on his shoulder.

"Are there more?" He could force out speech if he tried, but reaching for the words was like trying to grasp a fish in water. Slippery. He ended up with empty hands more often than not.

He tried to move his left arm and gasped from the pain. A soft tingling swept over his body; sweat sprang forth and lay clammy on his face, on his neck and chest. His mind spun off-kilter, like a wheel separated from a wagon in a collision. He had been shooting. The vampire loomed over him, then turned toward Nena.

He would never let a monster touch her again. He had seized his knife and acted.

He knew the slice of his own flesh when he heard it; a pop that made his stomach turn. Since then, he could only sense the world through a thick, brutal throbbing.

"It's gone," Nena was saying. "There aren't others, I don't think."

Nena was here. The nightmare was over. She was safe. He could rest. He could close his eyes and rest at last, couldn't he?

"Néstor." Her voice cracked like a whip. His eyes flew open. "Look at me."

He did. He loved looking at her. He wanted her to be the last thing he ever saw, the first thing he ever saw, his heavens and his earth. Her brown hair was a messy halo around her face, but her loveliness had no sweetness now: it was set and determined, the line of her mouth hard. "Sit up as straight as you can and look at me."

She reached for his shirt to lift it. This seized his attention and held it. His heart leaped to his throat at the brush of her hands on his skin. For a blessed, mad moment, pain was forgotten—*Nena was taking off his clothes.*

Madre Santa, who could think of pain when anticipation raced over his skin like a burning shot of aguardiente?

But she was lifting his shirt over his head, shifting his left arm in the process. His breathless reverie shattered at the surge of white pain. Stars burned around the edges of his vision.

"I'll be fine," he said through gritted teeth.

"Hush," she commanded. She tossed his shirt aside, then her hands were on his skin, exploring the left side of his body. The warmth of her palms was on his chest, his ribs, skating up to his collarbone. The gentle weight of her fingers. The brush of her breath on his shoulder as she leaned into him.

"Your shoulder is dislocated," she murmured. "I have to put it back into place."

She knelt so close that he could smell her hair: sweat, gunpowder, and precious lingering traces of wildflower soap. He wanted to bury his face in it and fall asleep engulfed by the scent of her. To slip into drunken oblivion and forget the jacal and all that had happened.

Distantly, he registered that she had spoken.

"Yeah," he said belatedly. "Yeah, all right."

The words came out breathier than he thought they might. They sounded as distracted as he was, as intoxicated as he was. Could she feel how his heart skipped every other beat, racing to keep up with his pulse? Could she see the gooseflesh that danced over his skin in the wake of her fingertips?

Nena shot him a suspicious look. He marked the sweep of her eyelashes, the appearance of a crease between her brows.

"This will hurt," she said flatly, as if having to clarify something that she believed was exceedingly clear.

"I can handle it," he said in a way he hoped sounded casual. He wasn't sure if this was true. Pain drummed a dull, throbbing rhythm in his left arm. As shock melted away from him like ice in the sun, different parts of his body began to ache. His back, from where he had been thrown on the stone floor of the patio. His good knee, which had struck first and broken his fall. There were smudges of bright blood on Nena's hand; dimly, he recognized that he must be bleeding.

But if Nena's hands on him were a spirit, he would drink until it made him sick.

Something shifted in her posture, in her breathing.

"I know you can," she said. She shifted her weight and leaned into him, bringing her cheek so close to his that he could feel the brush of her voice fall on his ear as well as hear it. "You're a bad man, aren't you? You can handle a little pain."

His breath caught.

The weight of her hands became seeking. More confident. One drew gently up his rib cage, the other up his breast.

All he had to do was turn his head to the left, and his nose would brush hers. She was so close that hair that had fallen loose from her plaits tickled his cheek.

He dropped his eyes to her mouth. The space between his lips and hers was candescent with promise. One short movement was all it would take to steal a kiss, to lose himself in her.

Somewhere in the back of his mind, a distant call went up.

He was too focused on the woman in front of him and not on the severity of the situation around him: they were far from civilization, with scant weapons and fewer supplies, their only defense against the night and its monsters the flimsy walls of this jacal. He was injured, and severely so.

But all he saw was her.

"Do you know the kind of trouble I would get into for being this close to a man? Alone, no less?" Her voice lowered, husky against his ear. Was her breathing as rough as his? As shallow? "But no one's here," she whispered. "And I like being alone with you."

Her hands were settling. One rested lightly on his left bicep, the other high on his chest. He wanted them running over his ribs. Pain be damned, he wanted them lower.

"Do you?" he breathed.

A dim alarm rose in the back of his mind as her grip tightened on his bicep. A faint warning whistle that was carried away by a swift wind as she turned her face to his. The tip of her nose brushed against his cheekbone. Nena. She was *his* Nena, lovely and perfect and real and *here*.

She lowered her dark eyelashes bashfully. "Yeah," she said. "It gives me ideas."

His heart pounded brassy and bold. If only she knew the kind of ideas being around her put in his mind. How watching her saunter ahead of him drove him to distraction as they packed up camp because of how trousers accentuated the shapeliness of her legs and ass. Even hours later on the road, he couldn't stop thinking about how they were *his* trousers, fabric that he had worn a thousand times brushing against her skin, lying against the softness of her inner thighs as she rode.

"What . . ." he began. He meant to ask *what kind of ideas*, but was cut off when Nena braced against him and wrenched his left arm.

A bolt of pain sang through his arm. A cry cracked out from him.

A *pop* in his shoulder.

A flash of nausea up his throat.

"Hijo de *puta*," he howled. "What was that?"

Nena rocked back on her heels, a self-satisfied smile playing across her lips.

She had taken his dislocated arm and thrust it back into place.

"That works better if you don't know what's coming. Fortunately," she added, with more than a hint of smugness, "you are very easy to distract."

She stood and went out to the patio, carefully stepping around the body of the dead Rinche. She returned within moments with Néstor's knife, then walked to the back of the jacal, to the saddlebags, and came back with her dirtied dress in her other hand. She dropped to sitting cross-legged next to him and immediately set to cutting broad strips of fabric from the skirt of the dress. She ripped another strip of fabric, examined it, and, satisfied, tied it to the first. Gone was the temptress who whispered into his ear, replaced by a workmanlike and focused curandera making what appeared to be a sling.

Heat flushed Néstor's face as she moved closer to him. He hissed as she touched his elbow, encouraging him to bend his arm over his stomach. This time, when she touched him, his vision was crisp, his mind sharpened by pain as she moved around him to tie the sling over his right shoulder.

He should feel sheepish by how easy it was for her to seduce him, how even in a moment like that she could drug him into compliance with nothing but her hands and her voice. He should even feel frightened by it. Never had a woman shown she had so much power over him with so little effort.

He wasn't frightened.

Instead, specters of what she could do to him if she were acting in earnest danced through his mind; wicked, perfect mirages that flickered just out of reach . . . and there they would remain. It made him want to groan in agony.

Her fingertips brushed over his back and upper left arm. His flesh throbbed tenderly in response to her touch as she examined something he couldn't see.

"Do you have alcohol?" she murmured.

"For the pain?" he said. What he wouldn't give for a tub of aguardiente to drown the events of the day.

She hesitated. "Yes," she said.

He told her where in the saddlebags to find the flask he had filled alongside Casimiro that morning. They mimed clinking the flasks like glasses, taking a solemn sip each before they turned to saddle their horses for battle. He shut his eyes. When visions of cavalry stallions impaled on Yanqui bayonets were all he saw, he forced them open and watched the shadows Nena cast as she crossed the room and came back.

A fresh pain, this time searing and stinging hot, ripped over his arm. Nena had dampened a rag torn from her dress with aguardiente and dabbed it on his bleeding cuts.

"¡Jesucristo, Nena!" he swore.

"No infections on my watch," she said. "Here," she then added, somewhat apologetically, as she passed him the flask.

He hissed as she moved onto the next cut, then took a sip of the aguardiente, savoring its harsh bite. Growing up under Abuela's wing meant he knew alcohol could help stave off infection in the immediate future. He should have made the connection sooner. But *shit*, it hurt.

"I don't have . . . I have nothing," Nena continued. "No herbs, nothing. All of my things are back at the camp." Her voice wavered as she moved and sat before him, brow creased, jaw set. "You're going to be fine."

She said this firmly, as if to convince herself of this fact.

"I've never been better," he said.

She searched his face, narrow eyed and suspicious. There was something in the way she looked at him that made him feel as if she were *really* looking at him, the way Abuela did when she was assessing someone's aura. It was a look that felt loving. A look that he wanted to keep so badly that it hurt with a sweet, tender ache.

"Really," he said softly. "I won't lie, it fucking hurts. But I'm fine."

She must have learned enough from that and her long look, for she made a small, satisfied noise. She straightened. "I should check to see if we still have horses," she said darkly.

Luna. Flashes of the desiccated bull snaked around the corners of Néstor's vision. What if she were hurt?

"I'm coming," he said.

"Absolutely not," Nena snapped. "Stay put." Her tone and the flash of pain that snaked over his left shoulder as he bent his weight forward stilled him. "You want to be useful? See if you can put your shirt on and reload your guns one-handed. *Carefully,*" she added firmly. She stepped toward the doorway, and, casting the gory body of the Rinche that was still splayed near the doorway a disgusted look, retrieved the machete she had beheaded the vampire with.

"You be careful too," he said.

On his deathbed, he would remember this image: Nena's long plaits gleaming in the firelight and shifting over the back of her sweat-stained white shirt—*his* shirt, and his trousers—as she turned to shoot him a look over her shoulder. Though he feared the claws of the darkness beyond the jacal, there was a boldness in her stance and in her firm grip on the machete. She would protect him. She was just as capable of watching his back as he was hers.

There was no woman on earth like this one.

She stepped into the darkness of the patio.

He listened to her footsteps until they hit gravel, then grass. He listened as he did what she ordered, grabbing his shirt and slowly slipping his good arm into it.

He would much rather she help him put it back on the way she had taken it off. For a fleeting second, an exceptionally stupid part of his brain wondered if he should have said that out loud to her.

Jesucristo, was he an idiot. Either the effect she had on him had not yet fully ebbed or the pain in his shoulder had fully robbed him of sense. He grunted as he pulled the shirt over his arm in the sling and clumsily undid buttons to let his left hand free.

On the contrary, the pain was keeping him remarkably sober. Nena's words from before the vampire appeared wound through his head like a loud drunk unsteady on his feet.

Don Feliciano Serrano would sooner shoot a man than allow a vaquero to woo his daughter.

Boy, Don Feliciano shouted as he had pointed at him. He was never anything but *chamaco* or *you* to the patrón. As if his existence were not notable enough to warrant a name. To Don Feliciano, he was no more important than the dogs on the rancho.

To hell with Don Feliciano. There were greater threats to Néstor's happiness and his dream of standing on the patio of his own home with Nena than the patrón.

Such as vampires, for example. The fact that he was down an arm and bleeding energy like a butchered steer. The fact that he needed to reload his pistols.

He stood, swayed, and lowered himself to the floor by the back wall of the jacal where his bullets were. He grimaced, fingers shaking as he reloaded. He couldn't help but think that Nena and Luna were out there in the dark. He couldn't protect them until at least this gun was loaded. The second was missing. Had he dropped it?

Why were his fingers so damn sweaty and slipping over the bullets? Why hadn't Nena returned yet?

"You good out there?" he called.

A muffled *all good* carried around the corner of the jacal. It did not soothe his fear, not for a minute, not until she was in the doorway. Her shirt was damp with rain; now that she was back and the buzzing worry cleared from his head, he heard the tentative, first sounds of rain on the roof of the jacal.

"They're shaken, but unharmed. And still there," she said, with a half-hearted, breathy laugh, as if she could not believe this fact. "I would be halfway back to Los Ojuelos if I were them. Here."

She lay his second pistol at his side. He nodded his thanks, too focused on reloading the first to speak.

Something in her other hand caught the firelight. Before he could ask what it was, she was back in the doorway, crouching as she uncorked a small bottle. She poured a thin line of what looked like sand across the threshold.

It was the salt from his saddlebag.

"What are you doing?" he asked.

"You remember Abuela's stories," she said, corking the salt and slipping the bottle into her pocket. She gave a defeated shrug. Exhaustion drew at the corners of her mouth. "Anything to help."

"Speaking of," Néstor said. He turned the loaded gun around so the handle faced Nena and handed it to her.

She took it hesitantly. Held it as if she were weighing its utility against the threats they faced. "I don't know how to shoot this."

"Then I'll teach you tomorrow," he said. "So you can defend yourself after I've taught you how to cheat at cards," he added. But his voice was a hollow imitation of what it had been that afternoon. Neither of them laughed.

Nena put the pistol in the holster at her hip and turned to the hearth.

"How do you feel?" she asked as she crouched before the fire and began to stoke it. It crackled and spat, filling the jacal with the comforting smell of mesquite.

"Honestly?" he said. He leaned his head back against the wall. The pressure of the wall on the cuts on his back made them throb. His shoulder throbbed. His whole body ached from having been flung on the patio. He knew from having been thrown to the dirt by half-broken mustangs that the latter would mend with a good night's sleep, but what was the likelihood of that? When all that lay between them and the night was a thin line of salt?

He let loose a deep sigh. Let that serve as his answer.

"I know," she said. Firelight flickered over her face, illuminating the weariness that weighed on its lines and angles.

She put two more branches on the fire, waited until they caught flame, then moved to where he sat against the wall. She sat with a heavy thump to his right.

The jacal had once seemed like a refuge. Now its walls felt flimsy against the night. It was so small. So easily surrounded. So poorly defended. Both he and Nena were beaten and bloodied and utterly spent.

"You should sleep," she said quietly, her eyes on the fire. "As much as you can."

God only knew how he was going to be able to sleep with the throbbing in his left shoulder. With the knowledge that beyond the thin walls of the jacal, the figures that haunted his dreams were real and living. Nothing protecting him from them but a thin line of salt and fragile belief in a folktale.

But Nena was safe on his right, her machete close by. A loaded pistol to his left. The fire was warm, but not uncomfortably so. If he imagined its glow as a ring of safety, if he tricked himself into believing it, perhaps he could shut his eyes. Let exhaustion lead him into oblivion.

"You too," he said.

"Fine," she said, reaching up to tug one of her plaits forward onto her chest. She fidgeted with its end. "But first watch is mine."

With that he could not argue. "Fair," he said, voice roughened by fatigue.

But her shoulder was pressed against his. He leaned his head to the side and touched it gently to hers. For a moment, she did not move; then, with a light sigh, she leaned her head against him. They sat in silence. Her hair smelled of the rain that now drummed rhythmically on the roof. The fire gave contented pops and crackles, oblivious to the dangers of the night beyond. If Néstor closed his eyes, if he listened to the rain and Nena's breathing, perhaps he, too, could trick himself into forgetting what lay beyond the jacal.

"I said horrible things earlier," she said, voice barely above a whisper. "I didn't mean them. I'm . . . I'm sorry. Please don't leave."

If the vampire returned and wrenched his arm back out of its socket, it would hurt less than hearing the break in her voice.

"I won't," he said.

He lifted his right hand, his fingers brushing Nena's as he took the end of her plait from her and ran his thumb over it. Its weight and silkiness against his calluses were just as he remembered. Toying with it was as natural as it had always been. Back when their world was still close and sacred, before they were burdened by the tyranny of adulthood and all of its expectations. When they watched the sheep together, the heavy heat of the siesta softening Tío Macario's shepherd songs to whistling snores. When he played with her hair as they lay shoulder to shoulder on an old rebozo, watching the branches of the huisaches lift on a breeze.

"You know, I dream about you," he said. If he spoke softly enough, the reverie would never break. The memory would wrap around them like a rebozo and keep them safe from the night. "Ever since I left." The only sound was the crackle of the fire, the softness of their breathing. "I dream of us watching the sheep. Falling asleep beneath the trees."

"That sounds so peaceful," she whispered.

"It is." He ran his thumb over her plait again, memorizing the braid's ridges and the tickle of loose hairs. "Until I wake, and I'm alone." How many mornings had he woken cold in the chaparral to the knowledge that Nena was dead? How many mornings had she opened her eyes and wanted him near? Did she dream of him too? Did she feel the absence of him in her life as much as he felt her lack? Perhaps it was exhaustion loosening his tongue, or pain, or the sensation of her shoulder against his, her smell, the weight of her plait between his fingers. It found the truth hidden behind his heart and drew it to the surface. Gave it words to be spoken, wings to fly.

"Your mother said you were dead, that night," he said. "Félix knew it. Your father knew it. They said you were *dead.*"

A bead of sweat, then two, rolled down his face. Dripped from his jaw. He dropped her plait to wipe it away. He paused mid-gesture—his cheeks were wet, but it was not sweat.

It was tears.

Shame washed over him in a hot, nauseous wave. "I couldn't face it," he said. "A world without you. I am not brave enough."

His breath came in shards, but he could not stop it. He could not catch it, no more than he could slow a bolting horse, no more than he could stop rain when it had begun to pour. He squeezed his eyes shut. A pitiful attempt to hide.

A touch on his thigh. Her hand rested there gingerly, light as a bird. He knew that if he moved, she would shy away. He was as still as he could be. As still as his shuddering chest permitted.

If he didn't open his eyes, nothing had ever gone wrong. Nothing had ever been taken from him. He had never run.

Her voice was soft. "You don't have to cry."

How long had it been since he wept for her? Years? He kept his feelings close to his chest, where they were safe from the harsh light of day. Not anymore. There was no rebuilding his walls, not now.

"No, I do," he said. "I think I really do."

He wept. Her hand stayed on his leg until he caught his breath.

"The way the breathing slows . . ." She let the thought trail off softly. "It looks like death. You are not the only one to think so."

She reached up and took his hand.

Nine years divided them, but time meant nothing to hands: her fingers interlaced with his as naturally as if they were eight years old, or ten, or thirteen. Palm to palm, thumb over thumb. A bridge between them. She drew their clasped hands down to rest on his thigh.

This journey felt as if they were crawling through a nightmare together, a dream that tricked the helpless dreamer into thinking it had ended, only to twist in a new direction and gallop away. His purpose, now, was to survive it. To ensure that Nena emerged from its clutches unharmed.

He had never felt more powerfully that there was something worth living and fighting for. If they made it back to Los Ojuelos in one piece, if they survived this next twist of the nightmare together, new challenges would rise. They glimmered with threatening promise on the horizon, oily as a mirage.

But whatever they were, he would not face them alone. She was here. And when he woke, she would still be here.

"Sleep," she murmured.

He did.

21

NENA

THEY TRADED WATCHES through the night. When Nena slept, it was fitfully. Dreams felt like waking: she was running across a battlefield, tripping across bodies that wore the grotesque faces of people she knew. Vaqueros she had healed back at Los Ojuelos. Papá. Félix. Each vision tumbled into the next without respite, and when she woke to Néstor's hand on her shoulder sometime before dawn, she knew she would not be sleeping again.

She positioned herself between Néstor and the door and listened to his breathing settle and slow. She wondered where Papá and Félix were now, if they were alive, if they were unharmed. She let the fire burn low. She did not wake Néstor for the next watch.

It was not until the night beyond the jacal's doorway grayed that she noticed something different on the patio.

Her breath caught in her throat.

Slowly, so as not to wake Néstor, she rose. Even after nine years apart, she still knew the pattern of his breathing. Still knew when his sleep was deepest, when she could rise and step carefully away without waking him.

The line of salt she put across the doorway hours ago was exactly as she had left it, tidy and straight as the seam of a shirt.

But beyond it, the body of the Rinche was gone.

As far as she could tell, squinting into the gloom, there were no drag marks through the puddles of blood that darkened the patio floor. No indication that someone had taken it away. It simply vanished.

But when?

Gooseflesh rippled over her arms, lifting the hairs to stand on end.

Néstor would have seen something. Néstor would have defended the jacal from anything monstrous, injured though he was, and that would have woken her.

Then the body must have disappeared during her watch.

She retreated from the doorway. There was a gun at her hip, but she had seen how ineffective that was. She reached for the machete and gripped it tightly. She stood just behind the line of salt and did not move for the rest of her watch.

"*I* HATE *FEELING* this useless."

Siesta's heat hung heavy over Nena's shoulders. They had set out at dawn and ridden for hours, until the sun was high in the sky and Néstor's face was gray with pain. He was unable to saddle and unsaddle the horses without help, but he curried the horses vigorously with one hand, swearing to himself periodically. He was far from useless: even with his injury, his movements had the rhythm of habit. He was in his element the way Mamá ruled a kitchen or commanded the schoolhouse. Still, there were things he could not do, so Nena followed his instructions and set a snare for something, *anything* to eat alongside their anemic supply of acecina, stale torti-llas, and nopal. Néstor had said the day before he planned to make pan de campo, but now he was injured. Her mouth watered as she waited by her trap, distracted by reveries of her tías' cooking and what she might do if they caught a jackrabbit. Or maybe a thick javelina, cut off from its herd by coincidence or injury. How its fat would crackle over the fire; how its juices would soften the stale tortillas and drip over her hands as she ate.

No javelina would be had; a quail that had seen better days be-came their afternoon meal.

After they ate, Nena bathed in the river. She inhaled deeply the smell of water as she scrubbed off blood and dust and sweat, relish-ing the silence that closed over her when she submerged herself in the water. Soothing coolness swept over her hundreds of mosquito bites. She dried off as best she could and dressed quickly, spurred by the knowledge that Néstor was not far away at their camp up the bank, and that he could be sneaking looks at her through the trunks of mesquites and sabales.

But every glance she shot over her shoulder was met with an innocent sight: him cleaning up their meal, whistling to himself, or currying the horses. Never looking at her. Not once. Of course he didn't. He shouldn't, and he knew that.

So why did she feel her mood dip when he didn't? *Why* should she want him to see her combing her wet hair, half dressed? It was a stupid thought. She ought to banish it immediately. Mamá and Papá would already be shocked to hear that she had spent so much time alone with a man unaccompanied. They would come to under-stand that it was preferable to her riding alone with Rinches and worse prowling the chaparral, but Mamá would wring her hands until they were bloodless and pale over Nena's honor all the same.

Thus far, however, Mamá's imaginary future hand-wringing was over nothing. Néstor was behaving as he should. He might tease and flirt, but otherwise, he gave her space and averted eyes when modesty required it.

It was Nena who had toed the line.

She could tell herself it was in the service of mending his dislocated arm, but was that the whole story?

She lay on her back with a thump in the shade of the trees, humidity and ill humor weighing on her like a too-hot blanket. She swatted away a mosquito and listened to the click of bridle buckles and Néstor's increasingly inventive curses as he checked the tack for damage and cleaned it. Finally, he stood, took off his leather vest, and then, with a soft grunt of discomfort, pulled his shirt over his head.

Nena's mouth dropped open in surprise. She propped herself up on her elbows.

"What are you doing." The sentence came out flat, as if it were not a question but an accusation.

Néstor shrugged. "You had a chance to clean up," he said, gesturing at her plaits, which were still damp enough to leave dark shadows on her shirt. "This," he said, balling the shirt in one hand, "will never be rid of blood unless I wash it soon. Then we'll pack up and ride just before twilight."

He turned and walked toward the riverbank. Sunlight licked over his hair and back, gilding them.

"If you're going to watch, you may as well sit closer," he said over his shoulder. He gestured for her to follow. "Better view from over here."

"Very funny," she shot back.

But she was glad that he did not turn around to look at her. He would have seen that her face was aflame.

She rested by the dying embers of the fire over which they had cooked their meal, half drowsing. Lazily watched a horned lizard skitter over rocks in the sun, lulled by the hum of chicharras and the sounds of the horses eating grass. She didn't realize she had fallen fully asleep until she was woken by the sound of footsteps and a click of the tongue, as if to urge a horse to hurry up. Néstor stood beyond the shade line, his hair wet and slicked back from his face. His chest was still bare—beyond him, toward the river, Nena caught a glimpse of a white shirt spread across a short, gnarled mesquite to dry in the sun, bright as a flag of surrender.

"When you wake up, could you do me a favor?" Néstor asked.

"I wasn't asleep," she murmured.

Amusement tweaked one corner of his mouth. "Of course," he said. In one hand he held the small tin bowl she had used to clean the saddle; in his other hand, still in the sling, he held a polished metal circle. "Would you hold up my mirror as I shave? *If* I can shave," he amended, with a touch of annoyance.

"All right," Nena said. She moved into the sun and rearranged her legs to mirror his as he sat cross-legged and took the mirror. It was nothing more than a polished piece of tin, warped and imperfect, but bright enough for Néstor to see his reflection as he covered his jaw in suds of Los Ojuelos soap. She had seen Papá and Félix shave dozens of times over the course of her life, but she had never watched a man shave while sitting directly opposite him—she was so close that her knees almost brushed his. She was surprised that she didn't feel shy. Perhaps it was because Néstor kept his eyes on his reflection as he worked in short, confident strokes over his jaw. The angle of his jaw was no different from Casimiro's, but she could not help but be struck by how his face was so much sharper. Perhaps it was the cut of his cheekbone, the proud way it and the corner of his dark eyes drew toward his temple. Perhaps it was how refined his features were. If other men were charcoal sketches, he was drawn in fine ink.

The bare razor blade winked up at Nena. She blinked, then made the fatal error of glancing at Néstor's eyes just as he looked at her.

She looked down quickly, suddenly flustered. She had been staring at him.

"What do you think—should I grow a mustache?" he asked quietly.

This startled a bark of laughter from her.

"Absolutely not," she said. "You'd look so old."

His smile widened, the glint of sunlight on water in his tanned face. It was a relief to see genuine pleasure on a face that had been set with pain all morning. A small blossom of relief unfurled in her chest. Perhaps the terror of seeing him flung to the ground by the vampire would never dissipate, but he would heal.

As he cleaned off the razor in the bowl of water, Nena flipped the mirror around and looked at her own complexion in its rippled surface. She had been in the hot May sun without a hat for far longer than she usually was. No one, not even Mamá, could escape the sun for long on the rancho—Los Ojuelos women worked outdoors and would never be as pale as the wives of wealthy hacendados, the mothers of the men that Papá wished her to marry. But that did not change how Mamá insisted on hat wearing once the girls were past a certain age. The reflection was nowhere near clear enough for Nena to tell what damage had been done over the last two weeks.

She flipped the mirror back to face Néstor as he resumed shaving his other cheek. In response to an inquisitive look, she said: "Mamá will say I've gotten darker, I'm sure of it."

"Hm." He wiped suds off his freshly shaven cheek with a rag, then put a light hand on her forearm to lower the mirror. He leaned closer, examining her face.

He smelled like soap and sunshine and warm skin. Not for the first time, she was acutely aware of how he was not wearing a shirt, how yes, she had seen many shirtless men working on the rancho.

She had even taken off Néstor's shirt the night before to wrench his arm back into place. This should not bother her.

But it *did*.

A thought darted through her head, fast as a fish through clear water: if she were to lean forward, it would be easy to close the space between them and press her mouth to his.

So easy.

Madre Santa, why would she think that? She should banish the thought from her mind as quickly as she could—

Slowly, he raised a hand and pointed at the bridge of her nose with his smallest finger.

"At least three freckles," he said. What was it about his voice that awoke an ache in her sternum, like a thumb pressed against an old bruise? It hurt, it was tender, but there was a sweetness in it that made her wish he would never stop. "My, my," he continued. "However will your father marry you off now?"

The mention of Papá shattered the moment like a stone through a glass window. Why would Néstor bring that up now, when he was close enough to kiss her? Why was she even *thinking* about that?

She exhaled sharply through her nose, a dismissive sound, and lifted the mirror up again. It alone could not form a barrier between her and Néstor—she had to rely on her sharp tongue for that.

"I have no doubt he'll find someone," she said brusquely.

Néstor leaned back slowly, almost lazily, and resumed shaving. He had dropped his eyes to his reflection, but she could feel him measuring her. Watching her.

"What makes you say that?" he asked innocently.

"Nothing stands between Papá and doing what's best for the rancho." It was true. Papá loved Los Ojuelos more than he loved anything, more than her or Javiera or Félix, more than even Mamá. She knew it in the way he oversaw its workings tirelessly, in the way he spoke about it to other rancheros over dinner. The land was home. The land was purpose. It was one thing, Papá sometimes said, to work hard in life to be allowed through the gates of Heaven. It was another to be born on Heaven's soil and sacrifice to earn the bounty that it gave so freely.

The worst part was that he was sacrificing her. He would rather send her away to a stranger's home than let Los Ojuelos face cattle rustlers and land thieves alone.

The worst part was that she loved Los Ojuelos so much that she understood why he would do it. That she would let him do it.

"It's security he wants," she said. "Allying with a larger rancho will provide more protection from Yanquis. He wants a man with power and money. He'll get one, and I'll marry him."

Néstor hissed softly. His hand had slipped; perhaps he nicked himself. "*Shit*," he cursed in English.

The night before, he spoke English to the Rinche. Or, what they *thought* was a Rinche. She thrust the image from her mind. She focused on watching Néstor's blade.

"Since when do you speak English?"

"Beto taught me," he said, grimacing slightly as his hand moved quickly over his upper lip—he was almost done shaving. Good. She should move back from him. Such close proximity was making her want to jump out of her skin. "It's useful for trading with Yanquis. And eavesdropping on them."

"You traded with them?" Nena said, letting disgust curl over the words. "You're not supposed to do that."

"It was on behalf of Rancho Buenavista," he said.

Buenavista. Doña Celeste Romero, the widow of Rancho Buenavista, was one of the most sought-after women in society— she was young, well-liked, and universally admired for both her looks and the enormous herds she inherited from her deceased husband.

Did that mean that Casimiro's gossip about wealthy widows was true?

"My apologies," she said, tasting acid seep into her voice. "I misunderstood. I didn't realize you broke trade regulations and sacrificed principles on behalf of someone you were sleeping with. That casts your decisions in a far more forgiving light."

"I traded with them because it was a job I was being paid to do," he said carefully, keeping his eyes on his reflection as he brought the razor in quick, final strokes across the soft flesh beneath his chin.

He was not denying her accusation.

He was all the vaqueros gossiped about: a womanizer, a drinker, a gambler. She did not know which she hated more: the idea that he had slept with Doña Celeste Romero or that he had left her and proceeded to live a life so blissfully, infuriatingly free of responsibility.

"Not all of us were born with land and money," he continued. "Some of us need to sacrifice our principles in order to eat. Some of us," he added, with a measure of his own acid, "need to actually work."

Defensiveness sprang up hot in her chest. How dare he insinuate that she did not work, after all she had done today? She was weary to her bones. "Everyone works on the rancho," she said hotly.

"But some work harder, and others keep the profit," Néstor said, a stoniness that she did not recognize creeping into his voice. "Haven't you ever thought about that? Why my uncle works until he breaks but lives in a jacal instead of being able to build his own house of stone? I guess you would never have to. Not when the patrón goes on and on about the nobility of life on Los Ojuelos." His voice dripped with sarcasm. "How we should be *grateful* for him."

"Life on Los Ojuelos *is* good," Nena shot back. "Only an arrogant man would turn up his nose at it."

"What if I don't want a good life, if it comes with the way the patrón treats us?" He snapped the razor shut and set it down firmly in the dirt. "What if I want to chase silver and widows and sleep easy at the end of the night knowing that my money stays in my own pocket and not his?"

"You want that? Then go." Nena gestured with a sarcastic flourish at the trail that led away from their camp. "See if I care."

His shoulders tensed; his mouth resettled in a grim line, one corner twisted deep. "I'm sorry."

"I'm sick of hearing sorry," she spat. "Sometimes I wish you never came back."

His eyes flicked up at her, their expression wounded. Good. She didn't care that the words weren't true. She wanted him to feel what she had felt when he left: aching, hollowed out. Abandoned. Cast carelessly aside.

"And what could have become of me if I stayed?" he challenged. His voice was soft at first, but frustration hardened it as he continued: "What future was there for me here?"

"What future?" she repeated, incredulous. A future with her. A future where she wasn't alone. "*Our* future."

The words fell from her lips before she thought to stop them.

But it was the truth. The wound that festered deepest wasn't that of loneliness. She could stomach being alone. She could build calluses against it and grow strong.

It was that by leaving, he had robbed her of *him*. She was left without the one person who listened to her, the one person who made her feel like the heavens spun around no other point but her.

"Like hell we had a future," he said sharply. "You made that perfectly clear last night."

Shame flushed through Nena's chest. It was a cruel thing to say. Even if it was true.

"What was I supposed to do?" he said, color rising dark in his cheeks. "Be happy to be indebted to your father all my life? Be grateful that I got what little time I had with you? Then stand by and watch as he married you off to whichever wealthy ranchero he chose?"

Nena narrowed her eyes at him. He struck her, but she knew how to strike back. She could brawl just as well as he could.

"Isn't that going to happen anyway?" she shot back.

For a heartbeat, he said nothing, his mouth hung slightly open. She had drawn blood.

"That's *it.*" He thrust himself to his feet, hissing with pain as he did so. He seized the water he had used to shave and turned on his heel toward the river. "I am *done* trying to talk to you."

But the taste of a fight only left her wanting more.

"Don't walk away from me," she said, casting his mirror aside as she stood. "I'm not finished."

"I take orders from no one," he said hotly, casting the words haughtily over his shoulder. "You should try it sometime, if you ever grow the spine."

The words hung on the air as he walked away. She watched his retreating back, how it gleamed brown and muscular in the sunlight.

There was nothing but her opponent's turned back and the molten desire to prove him wrong. That he was wrong to turn his back on her.

She followed him. She lengthened her strides to catch up with him, then seized the wrist of his good arm.

"Don't you dare walk away from me," she said hotly. She dug in her heels and yanked him to a stop.

He whirled to face her, thunder on his brow. He opened his mouth to speak—angry words, no doubt—but she never gave him the chance.

She slipped her right hand up the back of his neck, brought his face roughly down to hers, and kissed him.

Néstor inhaled sharply through his nose; Nena felt his surprise brush against her skin. For half a heartbeat, she wondered if she had made a terrible mistake—then, with a bright, metallic clatter, the bowl and razor fell to the ground.

He took her face in his good hand and kissed her back, his urgency stealing a gasp from her. Any kisses she had received from suitors over the years were prim and chaste, cold as an empty bed. Never what she imagined a kiss *should* feel like. This thought was fleeting as mist burned away by summer's heat. No inkling of anything else could survive when her world had narrowed to *this*: Néstor's skin warm under her palms, Néstor's voice murmuring *Nena, mi nena, mi nena*, as his teeth raked gently against her neck. Néstor's mouth on hers again, so hard she was sure it would bruise, yet somehow not hard enough. Néstor's strong hand on her waist, backing her up into the shade and pressing her hips tightly against him. So tightly that she felt every lean, muscled curve of him, felt the hardness of him against her thigh. She was bare embers roaring to life, heat sweeping through her body, fanned by his touch.

There was a part of her that had always wanted this, ever since he returned, from the moment she saw him enter the courtyard of la casa mayor dressed in black and gleaming like polished silver. How could she not? He walked back into her life like a man who knew who he was, shoulders square and chin held at a haughty angle. It was as if he had stepped out of a dream: her first kiss, the first boy she loved so much she felt as if her chest was caving in on itself when he left. He was back. He was more than back: he was running his good hand over her back and waist and lower, grabbing her and pulling her roughly against him.

A soft groan escaped her throat; it broke against his lips.

Néstor pulled away suddenly and rested his forehead against hers. His chest rose and fell sharply, driven by ragged breathing.

His eyes were the one part of his face that was unchanged by time and maturity: their color was warm, so dark they were almost black. In the past, when he looked at her like this, his eyes brimmed with adoration, with a trust so whole and perfect she felt she could walk on water if she tried.

Now, there was a reserve. He was retreating. No—that was the last thing she wanted. She stole a light kiss from his lips, her smile inviting him to steal it back. To go back to what they were doing before.

He didn't.

"Nena, stop," he murmured.

"Why?" she asked, noticing for the first time that her breathing was just as uneven as his. Enough with the talking. She rubbed her nose playfully against his. His eyes fluttered shut.

Though his forehead was still pressed tenderly against hers, though he still held her close, a sinking feeling had opened in her stomach. A fear that if they kept speaking, something bad might happen.

"What are you doing?" he asked, voice low and husky.

The question caught her off guard. Wasn't this what he wanted? She was certain it was. She wore Néstor's regard like a raiment from the moment he returned—if she was present, she knew he was aware of it. She knew he snuck glances at her every opportunity he could. She was sure he tried to be discreet, but he was imperfect. How could he not be? Something fierce and alive bound them, taut as ropes, so palpable Nena felt as if she could reach out and hold it.

What did he think she was doing? She was giving in. She was tightening that rope between them, drawing him close. But how could she put that into so many words?

"Showing some spine," she said. Teasing was easy. It came naturally. It always had, with him.

But no smile tugged at his mouth.

"Nena," he said softly. "I won't be used to prove a point." He loosened his arm and took a half step back. His hand trembled slightly as he pushed strands of hair out of her face, his touch featherlight. "What do you want?"

She wanted the world to disappear around them. No war, no Papá, no marriage to a stranger waiting for her at the end of their journey. Because this was *right*. Because even when they were children, when they spent long, lazy afternoons watching the sheep, they knew they grew from the same roots. Their branches tangled through each other's as they reached toward the sky, and forever would.

But the world crept in. It curled over her shoulder like a nosy tía, prodding at her softest, most exposed parts. What would Mamá or Papá say, if they knew she had behaved this way? The brush of a suitor's lips over her knuckles was one thing; this was another situation entirely. Néstor Duarte had a reputation of his own.

And he was a vaquero.

Once the chorus rose, she could not drown out its cacophony. She could no longer hear herself think, much less speak.

Something akin to grief flickered over Néstor's face. He brushed a thumb gently over her cheek.

"I thought not," he murmured, his voice so low it was almost as if he spoke to himself. Its rough edge struck her in that tender spot, deep in her sternum, right where she was the most bruised.

He dropped his hand. Cleared his throat as he took a full step back from her. He turned and picked up the bowl and razor he had dropped, then walked down the path to the riverbank.

Nena watched his retreating back. This time, she did not follow. She stood, silent and unmoving, watching him go. It took all of her willpower to catch her breath when each inhale threatened to slip into a sob.

She had not been thinking when she kissed him. She rode impulse like a half-broken horse until it threw her to the dirt. Now she lay there, curled into a ball, the flood of competing emotions washing over her honing into a single current, a single note. A single truth:

It was not supposed to end like this.

22

NENA

THEY DID NOT speak to each other as Nena saddled the horses and they set off northwest. She shielded her eyes from the brutal evening sun and did not look at Néstor as they rode. The only sounds that broke their silence were the rhythm of hoofbeats and the swing of the machete as Néstor cleared a path through the chaparral when necessary. After three hours, hunger began to gnaw at her ribs, souring her mood further.

If Néstor commented on a rare bird or what the sunset told him about tomorrow's weather, she gave one-word answers. As they put miles at their back, warring pieces of her hammered themselves into a conclusion.

He had rejected her, plain and simple.

It stung like a rope burn along her palms—every movement, even an innocent breeze, irritated what was raw and red. Reminded her why she often acted the way she did, bending over backward to please people: to avoid this.

"Nena, look." This time, when Néstor spoke Nena lifted her chin at his urgency. He pointed south.

Over the silhouettes of cacti and maguey, four plumes of smoke curled toward the reddening sky, spaced out from one another in an orderly fashion.

There were people there. A group large enough for four fires.

Néstor shifted his weight in his saddle and slowed his mare to a halt. Nena followed in suit, her legs aching from the effort. All she longed for was a hot meal and the feeling of sinking into her own bed. Despite making good time, riding hard from dawn until it grew too hot and, after the siesta, long into the night, Néstor estimated that they were still two nights away from Los Ojuelos. Their stores of food were low. With Néstor's arm injured, Nena bore the burden of trying to find food from the chaparral. It was a heavy responsibility, and one that she never wanted to bear again.

Where there were other people, there would be food. There might even be enough food that the people would consider bargaining it away, for the right price.

Provided they were friendly.

"Who do you think they are?" Nena asked, squinting against the sun at the smoke.

"Do you see those shapes against the hill? Between those low huisaches?" Néstor pointed at shadowy smudges that nearly blended into the slope of the land. Had he not pointed them out, Nena might not have noticed them. They were rectangular, almost like . . .

"Are those carts?"

Néstor rested his hand on the pommel of his saddle and nodded once. "Carreteros," he said.

"Will they have food?" Nena asked.

"Certainly," Néstor said. "The question is what we can give them for it."

They had already pillaged the saddlebags of the horse Néstor had ridden away from the battle. Aside from the machete, ropes, and gunpowder, there was a spare shirt, saddle soap. Bullets. Essentials that would be difficult to part with mid-journey.

Nena lifted a hand to her neck. She pulled out her golden scapular, its thin chain delicate between her fingertips.

"Does this help?" Nena asked.

Néstor's eyes widened when the small golden pendant caught the deep evening sunlight. Perhaps he recognized it.

"It does," Néstor said. "But . . . but that's yours. You've always had that."

The wind shifted. The smell of smoke coiled downhill toward them, and with it came the smell of cooking meat.

Nena's stomach growled.

"I can get another," she said. "I'll tell Mamá I lost it in the battle."

"I'll replace it," Néstor said firmly. "I promise."

The breeze brought another whiff of cooking meat their way. Was that . . . cabrito? It had to be. Nena's mood lifted. Soon, they would be eating.

"Golden scapular, red dress," she listed, flashing him an amused smile. "That's quite the list to take into town. Where do you plan on getting the money for that?"

Néstor gave her a sharp look. He did not reply. He shoved his hat lower over his eyes and turned his mare away from Nena and walked on, toward the carreteros, effectively turning his back on her.

Nena stared at him, mouth slightly open.

She had been teasing him. Clearly he had not taken it as a joke. Not at all.

Awkward silence swept between them, as itchy and thick as if it had never left. It lingered between them, broken only by the clop of the horses' hooves over stones, until they drew close enough to the group of carreteros that Nena could clearly make out the shapes of carts loaded with supplies from the capital. They would have china, cotton, and silver. Dangerous cargo to be carrying through land crawling with Yanquis.

"I think they'll be skittish toward strangers," Néstor said as he dismounted, as if he had heard Nena's thoughts. "We need a story. We don't want them to think that we'll lead Yanquis right to them."

Nena dismounted and brought the reins down over her horse's head. "We're deserters," she said. "That's good enough, isn't it?"

Néstor chewed his lip and did not answer. Evidently not.

"We'll tell them that you're my wife," he said slowly.

Nena's reaction was as sharp as a reflex: "You will do *no* such thing."

"They can't know we're traveling unmarried," Néstor said. "Do you know how bad that would look for me?"

Nena folded her arms over her chest. "I don't believe there's a need for explanations."

Néstor mimed walking up to her as if she were a stranger with an exaggerated tip of the hat. "Buenas tardes, señor," he said, voice falsely bright. "I am a poor vaquero with a sordid history, and this beautiful woman is the daughter of some rancho's patrón. What's that, you ask? Why are we alone in the chaparral, looking very much worse for the wear and clearly running from something? Well, for that I have a perfectly reasonable answer. Vampires, señor. We are running from vampires."

When she narrowed her eyes at him, his false smile dropped. "I have a point," he said flatly. "Admit it."

He was right. She was being unnecessarily stubborn. Was it because she didn't want to find herself in a situation where she was forced to feign intimacy with him? After this afternoon, it would be excruciating. It would be like pouring salt on the wound.

"They won't know I'm your patrón's daughter," she said.

"First of all, he is *not* my patrón," Néstor said sharply.

His tone stung like the bite of a whip. It took her aback. "I don't work for him any more than I work for you. Second of all, the moment you open your mouth, they'll know you come from a land grant family. Carreteros have no interest in being caught up in business that will threaten their relationships with rancheros. A vaquero and a girl of noble breeding, alone in the chaparral?" He clicked his tongue. "Even you are not so sheltered that you don't know how bad that looks. They'll think I kidnapped you."

Nena said nothing. Yes, she was sheltered, but not so ignorant that she couldn't see the wisdom in Néstor's point. That didn't mean she was willing to admit defeat aloud. She rested her mare's reins over the horse's neck and reached up to undo her scapular. When she was done, she handed the necklace to Néstor. The golden pendant swung between them like a pendulum.

"Say what you must," she said. "I'll follow."

Néstor took the scapular, his mouth in a firm line. "I understand that the idea of even pretending to be married to a vaquero must be repulsive to you, but I wouldn't suggest it if I didn't think it was necessary. All right?" he finished briskly. "Now let's go."

Nena followed several paces behind his mare, watching Néstor's turned back, his determined stride.

Frustrated tears pricked her eyes as they walked, hot and wet and unexpected. Twice she had insulted him without intending to. The space between them was now pocked with dangerous crevices, thick and tangled with thorns. She wanted to reach to the other side, to bring him close, but she was too tired to face what crossing that space took. Too hungry to feel anything but stinging hurt at how coldly he had shut her out. At how he had rejected her that afternoon.

Perhaps he was right to. Perhaps he, unlike Nena, had some foresight. Was it not true that anything that happened between them would only end abruptly when they returned to Los Ojuelos? They would leave this in-between, this lawless journey where survival superseded all the rules of polite society, and reenter the world they were born into. The world where vaqueros do not speak to the daughters of la casa mayor, where Mamá and honor and appropriate behavior were the law. The world where Nena's bargain with Papá spelled the end of her freedom.

Perhaps it was right. But it wasn't what she wanted.

What do you want?

She wanted to hold his hand in the night, as if he were a talisman against the darkness. He *was* a talisman. He was rich with magic she couldn't understand, a key to a part of herself that had been dead for a long, long time. To her, he was worth more than he knew. He wasn't a vaquero. He was Néstor. He was *hers*. It was folly for either of them to pretend otherwise.

Yet here they were. Approaching the men who circled the fire and rose warily at Néstor's approach, hands shifting to the rifles at their sides. Pretending they were not each other's, and at the same time, pretending that they were.

"Buenas tardes, señores," Néstor said to the group, taking off his hat respectfully. "My wife and I are traveling to see her family in Laredo. We lost most of our provisions to Yanqui bandits several days ago and I was injured. May we share your meal? Perhaps barter for some supplies?"

He held out Nena's scapular. It glinted in the light of the setting sun.

One man came forward from the rest. He was in his mid-fifties, his face deeply weathered from a life spent on the road, and was built like Tío Macario, the shepherd she and Néstor used to help when they were children: sloped shoulders, stout chest, firm short legs. He squinted up at Néstor.

"I think I recognize you," the man said. "You work for Rancho Buenavista, do you not?"

"I have in the past," Néstor said, smooth as could be. "I've moved between ranchos and have news of many of them. I'd be happy to share that over the fire."

"It's news of Matamoros we want, if you have it," the older man said. "And we have plenty to share in return, especially with travelers hard done by. Come, señora," he said, turning to Nena. He took in her appearance but seemed to find nothing notable in her wearing men's clothing. "I am called Diego. You both look very tired."

"My name is Néstor and this is my wife, María," Néstor said quickly. "And we are exhausted."

Nena followed Néstor to take their horses to where others were tethered, then returned and took a seat by the fire. Even after the relentless heat of the day, Nena welcomed its warmth on her face. Especially because there was an enormous pot of what smelled like caldo sitting in the coals and giving off long white plumes of steam.

Nena's mouth watered. She wet it with a sip from her water flask and listened as Néstor exchanged news with Diego, who appeared to be the de facto leader of this group of carreteros. The carreteros' journey had been disrupted by the outbreak of hostilities in Matamoros; they turned west to avoid the armies and bandits from either side who might see them as a tempting target. Néstor relayed news of the battle, being careful not to make it sound like they were deserters. As Diego instructed caldo to be ladled into jícara bowls for Nena and Néstor, he reported that the carreteros had heard from fleeing soldiers that the battle was lost by the Mexicans.

Nena's heart dropped. She stared down at the hot soup in her hands. The steam warmed her face, but she was numb to it, numb even to its enticing smell and hunks of cabrito floating in the glistening broth.

They had lost.

What had happened to Félix? To Papá? Were they well? Were they safe?

According to Diego, the Yanqui army continued to plow south from Matamoros.

"What of the auxiliary squadron that fought with the cavalry? The group from las Villas del Norte?" Néstor asked. "My cousin rode with them. Have you heard of them?"

"Ah yes," Diego said. "I heard some of them are riding south to continue to harass the Yanquis."

"And the others?" Néstor asked.

Diego shrugged. "That's all I heard." He handed Néstor a bowl of soup. "So what's your story, vaquero? Where are you coming from?"

Néstor began to speak, a story falling from his lips fully formed, detailed and as well-worn as an old pair of boots. He and Nena—that is, "María"—were married three months ago on his father's rancho south of Río Bravo, not far from Matamoros. He named at least six of the twenty cousins from the surrounding area who had attended the wedding, including Beto's name. It jarred the memory that Beto said his mother was from near Matamoros—perhaps all of these details had come from things Néstor heard from his friend.

It was good that Néstor was doing the talking. It was all she could do to keep up with his smooth falsehoods as a listener, much less as a participant. All she could hope that Diego did not ask her any follow-up questions. She was certainly too tired to provide any inventive answers. But Diego was polite: because she was another man's wife, he did not ask questions directly of her, speaking instead to Néstor. As the men's conversation shifted to the weather, she focused on her soup. The goat meat was tender and melted in her mouth; the broth was rich and well seasoned. Nothing had ever tasted so good.

Though they sat side by side, so close their shoulders were nearly touching, Néstor barely looked at her all evening. Nena caught none of his stolen glances trailing over her face and body. She had become accustomed to their presence; she felt their lack like the cold-ness of a turned back.

She stared down at her empty bowl as the men spoke, hot tears springing anew to her eyes. Her throat tightened as if seized by a fist. She blinked the tears away quickly.

She was tired. That was why she was upset. That was it. She was tired, and grateful for the fact that her belly was full of soup and she was not facing another mostly sleepless night.

One of the carreteros was wrapping up a tall tale about Pedro de Urdemañas, then turned to Néstor and urged him to tell a story.

Néstor sipped his soup, taking a moment before he replied.

"I think I might know of one," he said. He cast a glance sideways at Nena. It caught her by surprise—he had barely said a word to her nor looked at her all evening. Then he cleared his throat and raised his voice. "I once heard that on a ranchito near Mier, there were two children, a boy and a girl. They grew up together even though the girl's father was wealthy and the boy's was not. The boy was so in love with the girl that he couldn't see straight half the time, you know?" He gave a low whistle and gestured at his head to indicate *loco*. This drew soft laughter from some of the men. "It made him a little crazy. He was always trying to impress her. One night, he saw a strange light in the night, yellow as gold, and knew it had to mean there was hidden treasure. He and the girl grabbed shovels and ran into the night, convinced they were going to dig and find the buried silver of an old Spanish count. There was no moon. They were alone. And when they reached the place where the strange light shone, it winked out. Something came out of the darkness and attacked them."

The men around the fire had grown so quiet Nena could hear their cattle grazing. Hear the crackle of burning branches and the soft stamp of a horse's hoof. The hum of crickets rose around them like a veil between them and the deepening night. She felt as if she were caught in a dream as Néstor told the story of what had happened to them as children.

"It was a beast, as tall as a man, hairless and wretched, with long arms and a goat's cloven hooves. Its teeth were as long as a rattler's fangs, and its claws were like machetes as they reached toward the girl," Néstor continued. "It was El Cuco, hungry for children. The boy fought as hard as he could, but he was no match for the monster. The girl was severely wounded. The boy carried her back to the ranchito, to her family, but when they reached the house, the girl was dead. Her father shouted that it was all the boy's fault, and so the boy ran. He ran and he ran until his legs gave out, until his heart broke. Then he ran more. He mourned every day of his life until, one day, he had to return to the ranchito.

"When he arrived, he discovered that the girl was alive."

Murmurs shifted through the listening carreteros.

"A curandera, blessed with the gift of healing, had brought the girl back from the dead," Néstor said. "She was a woman, grown and beautiful, and to the boy's grief, she was engaged to a rich hacendado. The boy had nothing, you see. One night he took a shovel and he retraced his steps into the chaparral, looking for the light above the dead Spaniard's buried treasure. If only he were rich, maybe the girl he loved would marry him, he thought. So into the night he went. But the night was black and silent, and though he didn't know it, the darkness began to follow him . . ."

Nena listened, spellbound, as Néstor took their story and wove it into a vaquero tall tale. It rose like mist, slipping from ear to ear among the carreteros. With them, it would travel across El Norte, from town to town, landing on strangers' ears, moving through strangers' lips, morphing and changing until the long-ago night that had driven her and Néstor asunder became as much a part of this land as the sound of the chicharras in the hot afternoons or the rumble of cattle moving through the low, rolling hills by the river.

"Where did you hear that story?" Diego asked Néstor when he was finished.

"From a vaquero I drove with, many years ago," Néstor said. A stock answer. Another tall tale.

Diego ran a hand over his unshaven face. "There's truth in every story," he said slowly. "Out here, there are rumors of dangerous beasts. We've seen them before, near San Luis Potosí. You should be careful."

"We're trying to be," Néstor said. He lifted his wounded arm for emphasis. "The last thing I need after the Yanquis is for El Cuco to try to snatch my woman away."

His attempt at humor was met with a scatter of nervous laughter. Both threats were too close to home.

"Why don't you spend the night by our fire," Diego said. "There's always safety in numbers."

Néstor looked at Nena, his raised brow seeking her opinion. The thought of leaving this circle of people among whom she felt safe, of leaving the golden glow of the fire and going into the night, was deeply unappealing. She nodded.

Together they rose and walked to the horses, where Néstor's old blanket was rolled and attached to Luna's saddle. When Néstor struggled to untie it with his one good hand, Nena reached over his arm and did it herself.

"What did you think of the story?" he asked. He met her gaze as she took the blanket in her arms. Heat rushed to her cheeks. It suddenly felt too intimate, standing there and looking into his eyes. She dropped her gaze.

"It was a bit sad," she said softly, turning to walk back to the fire. He fell into step beside her. "I didn't like how it ended."

Néstor was silent for a moment. Sandy earth crunched beneath the soles of their boots.

"You know," he said in a low voice, "you can change the ending. If you want."

He did not meet Nena's eyes when she studied his face, his profile silhouetted by the orange light of the fire. Change the ending of which story—the story he told, or theirs?

But there was no opportunity to ask. There were carreteros all around, preparing to sleep. No words that she could find to ask him what he meant.

Nena lay out the blanket a slight distance away from the fire and lay down on her back. Néstor took off his hat and lay down next to her, shifting onto his right side to protect his wounded shoulder.

She closed her eyes and listened to the soft rumbles of the camp settling around them. To Néstor's steady breathing.

"Are you all right?" His voice was soft against her ear, soft as it sank into her body. She nodded.

A carretero, perhaps someone on watch, began to sing a low melody. It mixed with the crackle of the fire, with her heartbeat, with her breathing. Sleep had been hovering just over her shoulder all evening; now, it sank over her like a heavy blanket. Her belly was full. Others stood on watch. Néstor was at her side.

Tonight, she could actually sleep.

"I don't think it's repulsive," she said, softly enough that the only person who could hear her was the one who lay to her left.

"What?"

She turned her head to him and opened her eyes, fighting the heaviness of sleep. Her head blocked the light from the fire, casting his face in shadow. They were so close that the tips of their noses brushed.

"Being married to a vaquero," she whispered. "I've never thought that. Not if he's the right one."

His eyes were dark and liquid as he gazed at her. Even in shadows, his beauty caught her in a trancelike kind of stillness, as if the world beyond them had ceased to exist.

If only he hadn't pulled away from their kiss. If only things weren't strained between them. All she longed for was for it to be easy with him, the way it used to be. This felt easy: lying next to each other under heavens that swung low and velvet and heavy with stars. If she reached up, she might be able to touch one, to singe her fingertips on its glow. If she reached to him, she knew they would never be apart again. Nothing had ever felt easier.

It was everything else that was difficult.

"Not everyone thinks that," Néstor said softly.

He was right. Not Mamá, certainly not Papá. Not their allies on the surrounding ranchos who believed that families like theirs were above such things. She knew what her parents feared: that if the Serranos were not held in high esteem by their neighbors, if they faced an attack, they would be left to face it alone. And they might not survive.

Nena turned her face back up to the stars and closed her eyes. Sleep crept up quickly. It softened the world around her, blanketing the sounds of the camp.

"I know," she whispered. "But sometimes, I don't care."

23

⟨∾⟩

NÉSTOR

WHEN NÉSTOR WOKE, the camp was still. The sky was gray with dawn yet to break; birds were only just beginning to sing. The air was crisp with the smells of cold and smoke.

He also smelled Nena. In sleep, she had curled onto her side and moved closer to him. Or he had moved closer to her. Either way, they curled against each other, her hips flush against his, her back pressed to his stomach. The hand of his injured left arm rested on her hip. Holding her close.

He did not know what she would say if she woke to find them in this position.

He lifted his hand. Waited to see if her breathing changed. She slept on.

Pain did not immediately radiate through his shoulder at the movement. That was a good sign. He slowly sat up and tried moving his arm forward, then shrugging the shoulder. Achy, and certainly sore, but far less painful than it had been following the vampire attack.

Perhaps it was how long and deeply he slept last night that did the trick. Beto must be onto something about a good night's sleep.

A glance around the camp showed other men rising, stretching. One stoked the embers of last night's fire and placed a pot for coffee in their midst.

Soon, they would be on the move. So, too, would he and Nena. The air clung to a bite of spring cold, but it would not last: the sky overhead was cloudless and pale. By noon, the heat would be blistering. They had to cover much ground before then.

Néstor checked Nena's boots—abandoned by her side as she slept—for scorpions. Then, satisfied, he put a hand on Nena's shoulder to wake her. She was warm with sleep. Part of him wished he could let her dream for as long as she wanted.

"Nena," he whispered. "Time to go."

Her eyes fluttered open. She sat up, casting a groggy look at their surroundings. Carreteros were passing around tin cups of coffee and warming tortillas. He helped Nena to her feet, and while she rolled and stowed the blanket on Luna's saddle, he spoke to Diego about supplies. Soon he had a cloth sack full of food— tortillas and carne seca and some fruits—to keep them fed for the rest of their time on the road. He brought this over to Nena and the horses, and the two of them set to packing the supplies across their two saddles.

"One more thing." Diego appeared over Néstor's shoulder. When he turned, the older man handed him a small bag that fit into his palm. It felt as if it was full of sand.

Nena peered at the leather bag and brushed a few white crumbs off it.

"Salt," she said.

Néstor searched Diego's face. This man knew that what prowled the night were not simply beasts.

He knew.

"Be careful out there," he said, then turned on his heel and walked away.

Néstor wanted to pull him back, to ask him a thousand questions. But the man was whistling to his people and preparing them to break camp before the sun was fully risen. He exchanged a look with Nena, who looked just as surprised as him. He handed her the salt to put with the supplies attached to her saddle.

After a few more minutes of tightening girths and saddlebags, they were settling into their saddles. He lifted his hand in farewell to the carreteros, then he and Nena took off at a trot into the gray dawn.

THEY RISKED TAKING the main road for several hours and covered a good deal of ground, keeping near the portion of the river that passed Camargo. At noon, they let the horses drink at the riverbank. It was silent but for the click of metal horseshoes on stones, the sound of the horses drinking in long, greedy drafts. Néstor scanned the riverbank opposite them as he refilled their water flasks. No dark forms. No glinting bayonets. The day had been quiet.

Too quiet.

No chachalacas cried at the cloudless sky. No chicharras hummed around them. When she was finished drinking, Luna tossed her head, ears flat against her skull.

A rustling in the undergrowth lit his anxiety. He froze, hand hovering over his gun.

A sharp squeal; Nena yelped at the sound. His gun was in his hand, his heart in the hollow of his throat.

A skittering of hooves over pebbly earth. A group of six javelinas burst through the bushes, bolting away from the riverbank as if the Devil himself were on their heels. He lowered the gun.

soft laugh from Nena. "There goes dinner," she said dryly as
ust left by the fleeing javelinas settled.

ut unease slipped over his shoulders like a fever's chill, slicing
igh the heat and driving down to bone.

omething was watching them. Whatever had spooked the ja-
as lingered nearby, and he did not want to find out what it was.
le gestured to Nena, and they moved on quickly.

SIESTA, THE horses were spent. Néstor found a thick
i of trees where they could rest in the shade, close enough to
ver that they might get the occasional respite of a breeze. Heat
d over the chaparral, wreathing him in the kind of sweat he
ould never dry in this humidity. Even the shade provided little
as they watered and unsaddled the horses.

ingerly, he removed his sling and tested his arm, swinging it
ird and back. It was sore, but functional enough to groom
. He paused as he curried Luna's back to watch as Nena walked
i to the riverbank to refill their water flasks. Noon dripped
ier silhouette; the harsh glitter of sun on the river beyond sur-
led her like the halo of a saint.

er comments yesterday about the scapular and the red dress
ed under his skin, irritating as burrs. God knew he had saved
aved and fully intended to fulfill both promises. The thing
rked him was that she had teased him based on the assump-
hat he *couldn't*. For he was a vaquero, was he not? A man
st who lived in debt to his patrón for the privilege of working
ch man's land? A man who saw no reward for his labor until
iy he died? He wanted her to know that he was a free man. He
d her to know that he had the means to buy land and be a man
iy of asking for the hand of Don Feliciano's eldest daughter.
rhaps that was why he overreacted at her balking to pretend

to be his wife before a group of carreteros. Because he wanted it with an ache as sharp and as present as the pain in his shoulder.

And when he had asked her what she wanted?

Her silence was like a mule's kick to the chest.

He knew exactly what he wanted. He meant to marry her. To build a house for her and make a home with her. To fall asleep smelling wildflower soap in her hair every night for the rest of his life, whatever Don Feliciano and Doña Mercedes thought be damned.

But if he said so much out loud?

Even at a time like yesterday, when she kissed him with a need he thought was only possible in his filthiest dreams, it would have stopped her in her tracks. It might have shattered everything they had built so carefully between them.

Not if he's the right one, she had whispered last night. Nose to nose, their breath mingling.

In another place, that would have spelled the end of this dance. If they had been alone, if they hadn't been in the midst of a dozen strangers, he would have confessed everything: every coin he had saved and what he meant to do with them. How, ever since he had returned to Los Ojuelos and discovered her alive, he spent each night staring at the stars choosing which words to ask her to marry him. Praying she might one day listen.

Perhaps she might. When the time was right. They had come far from her seething proclamation that *vaqueros may call me señorita, or better yet, say nothing to me at all.* Still, he was cautious. Saying too much too soon could ruin everything. Saying too little, as he had yesterday, might be just as damaging. He walked a delicate balance, caution keeping him centered when he feasted on sights like the one before him now: the vision of her striding toward him up the riverbank, their filled water flasks in hand. She handed him his flask, closing her eyes and drinking from her own as she stood next to him. Water dripped on the front of her shirt. He followed

f her chin down her throat and found each damp spot on
t. They drew his eye to the curve of the shirt over her
which naturally led to him thinking about what lay under-
e fabric.

ion kept him centered. Barely.

it together, *Duarte*, he told himself sternly.

tepped back from her and lowered his eyes. They caught on
l and holster at her hip.

you want to learn how to use that?" he asked when she was
drinking. To answer her curious look, he pointed at the

at use is it against vampires?" Nena asked flatly.

was a fair point. "We have Rinches to worry about too, you
e said.

walked slightly away from the horses and the hum of
as toward the river. He took the pistol and, as he unloaded
ed to different parts and named them for her.

he handed it back to her. Their fingertips brushed as she

w aim at that tree and show me how you think you should
he said.

a cast him a suspicious look, then did as he said. She squared
the tree and held the gun in a stiff pose with both hands,
ased with concentration. A surprised laugh cracked out

t bad," he lied. "You're pointing at the thing you want to
vhich is the most important part. Let's fix the rest."

tepped close to her and placed his hands on her shoulders,
them away from the tree she aimed at.

kept her face turned from him, focused on her target. The
er jaw was sharp as it bent toward her ear. It belied how soft
o kiss, how easily she offered her throat to him.

He steadied himself. *Keep it together.*

"Remember that, in most cases, someone is shooting back at you," he said. "Angle your body away so that you give them as little a target as possible."

He stepped behind her to adjust her hold on the pistol. He placed his hand over hers as he gently adjusted her fingers.

"Loosen your grip," he murmured. "Be firm, but gentle."

It was her hand over his when she taught him how to hold a pencil, how to write her name in the dirt behind the schoolhouse. Now, it was his hand over hers, him standing just behind her, close enough that he was speaking in her ear. Close enough that her back was nearly against his chest, as it had been when they woke up that morning.

"After you shoot, the barrel will be hot to the touch," he said. He would not be distracted by how her skin smelled like sunshine. Nor by wondering how warm her cheek would be beneath his lips. Nor by remembering the taste of her mouth on his yesterday. "You've only got three shots before it's too hot to reload. Do you know how to aim?"

"Point at the target?" Nena suggested. Her voice was a bit breathless. It was because she was focused, he told himself. Not because of their proximity.

"This up here is the sight," he said, releasing her hand and pointing to a small notch on the top of the gun. "Line that up with the target, all right?"

He glanced down. Her chest rose and fell irregularly as she nodded. There was no denying it: being this close to him had an effect on her.

A cocky part of him believed that of course this was the case. He knew his way around women. He knew he was good-looking and he knew how to use that fact to his advantage.

The rest of him vibrated with exaltation at this discovery. This was *Nena*, the woman who had slammed the door in his face, who he feared would never look at him again. The woman who could drive him mad with nothing but a few brief touches and her words.

Two could play that game, could they not?

"As you shoot, the gun will kick back with force," he said. "Like this." He moved his right hand to the barrel of the gun and jerked it upward.

"Oh," she gasped, stumbling back half a step and colliding with him.

"See?" he said as she stepped forward, color rising to her cheeks. "Let's try again. Keep your arm loose, but be ready. Brace."

"How am I supposed to be loose and brace at the same time?" Nena muttered, narrowing her eyes over the sight of the pistol. "That makes no sense."

"Arm loose, but brace from here," Néstor said. He slipped his left arm around her waist and placed his palm flat against her stomach, so low that two of his fingers rested over her makeshift rope belt.

This time, he felt her sharp intake of breath as well as heard it.

Two could play this game indeed.

"Make sure your weight is centered over your feet," he murmured as he took his hand slowly away from her stomach. Perhaps he let his fingers drag more slowly than he ought to have over her waist. Perhaps he should have taken a step away. Instead, he lingered so that he spoke in her ear. "Breathe steadily. The trick is to pull the trigger when you exhale."

"All right." Her voice was barely above a whisper.

"Inhale, then aim," he said. "Exhale and shoot."

She took a deep inhale through her nose, narrowing her eyes as she focused.

"Steady," he murmured.

She exhaled and pulled the trigger. A soft click, then silence.

"Bam," he whispered. "You hit the center of the tree. Well done."

She looked over her shoulder at him, a smile tugging the corner of her mouth as she lowered the gun. He wanted to cradle her face in his hands and count the handful of freckles across her nose. Wanted to give in to her as he did yesterday. She had tasted of salt, of warmth, and when her tongue swept into his mouth, it was hungry and searching.

God, all he wanted was to give in to temptation. But he needed to tell her what he intended first. That he wanted her now and he wanted her for forever. It was a conversation that needed to take place. Even if it meant denying himself in this moment, when he could tell from the hitch of her breath and the color in her cheeks that resisting was agony for them both.

Maybe he could give in for a brief moment. Nothing more than a brief, sinful taste.

He brought his right hand to her chin and took it in his thumb and forefinger, lifting her face to his.

"Remember, don't grip too tightly," he said. "Hold it gently, but firmly."

Their eyes met. He forgot where they were. He forgot his name.

"Néstor," she breathed.

He was baptized anew by her voice. He drew his thumb roughly over her lips; then, when she caught it between her teeth, a wicked gleam in her eye, his breath hitched sharply.

Fuck his inhibitions. Conversations could wait.

He—

A shout sounded from the direction of the riverbank.

Néstor wrenched his head up. Dropped his hand from Nena's face. He listened intently, focusing past the pounding of his pulse in his ears.

There were voices—three, if not more, talking over one another. Speaking in English.

Nena's eyes were wide with apprehension, her stance tense and alert as she handed him the pistol. He took it and gestured for her to get behind him. As silently as he could, he moved closer to the trees they had been using as Nena's target, then dropped to a crouch in the undergrowth. Three soft footsteps; Nena squatted at his side.

He fumbled in his pocket for bullets and loaded one with shaking hands.

The voices grew closer.

Plans streaked through Néstor's mind, shrieking past like bats. They were separated from the horses. If they moved, they would be found before they could flee. There were too many voices to even imagine fighting. If they stayed, they would surely be found. But where were the voices going? He strained his ears. Were they creeping closer to the riverbank? Would they come up into this thicket, where he and Nena were utterly exposed?

A clink of heavy chains snaked through the undergrowth. The low of cattle pulling something with great effort.

And a scream that was unlike anything Néstor had ever heard.

24

NENA

NENA CLAPPED HER hands over her ears with a hissing intake of breath. The sound felt like knives being driven into her skull. It was like stone scraping along stone; it felt louder than anything she had ever heard but a crash of thunder. Unlike thunder, it had no crescendo and fall; it stayed at a pitch that only a bat could reach for long, agonizing seconds.

It cut off.

Her eyes watered as she lowered her hands.

Néstor exhaled softly to her right. His brow was furrowed as he peered through the undergrowth, searching for answers.

The sounds of metal chains clanging against one another and more voices rose from the riverbank. They were agitated. Brassy, in the way only English was. Demanding.

Closer.

The sound of at least half a dozen people moving through the undergrowth grew louder. Surely there were too many to fight. They had to flee.

She leaned toward Néstor. "Do we run?" she asked, her voice barely a whisper. Barely above the sound of her heart pounding. She felt poised like a hare in the path of a predator, every inch of her trembling and ready to run at a moment's notice.

He shook his head slowly.

"Wait," he breathed. Then he was still, head cocked like a dog listening to a distant whistle, finger already on the trigger of the pistol in his right hand.

Wait for what? For the strangers to be upon them? For that scream to rend the afternoon in two again? They had to get out of there. She shifted her weight, anxiously preparing for God knew what.

A twig cracked beneath her boot.

Néstor took her hand. Squeezed it. Held it fast. He met her eyes.

Wait, he mouthed.

She had to trust him. Trust that whatever he was planning landed them on the right side of life and death. Visions flashed through her mind: the blaze of bullets through the air; Néstor with a red wound in his chest, falling to his knees. A thousand hands seizing her, tearing her hair, ripping at her shirt.

He squeezed her hand tighter.

Another scream tore through the heat. A gasp seized her breath; she bit down on her lip to keep the sound in. Hard. She shut her eyes, as if that could help.

What in God's name *was* that?

Néstor squeezed her hand again, then tugged it. When she opened her eyes and looked up at him, he gestured with his chin in the direction of the riverbank.

If she squinted through the undergrowth, she could see figures on the bank. A flat-bottomed barge was being poled across the river by men in blue uniforms; it was difficult to distinguish anything about them through the glare of the late-afternoon sunlight.

But the uniforms of the men on the riverbank made it abundantly clear that they were Rinches. There were half a dozen or so: one tossed a rope to the men on the barge, another joined him in pulling the barge to shore.

But when the other men came forward into the view the undergrowth afforded, the breath died in Nena's throat.

Four of them gripped chains in their hands. They pulled something forward into the blinding light, leaning into the act, cursing and digging their heels into the pebbly riverbank.

The four chains were attached to a single metal collar. It was as thick as a yoke and glinted in the sun.

That collar was fastened around the neck of a vampire.

It writhed as the Rinches dragged it forward, its long, spindly arms spasming in the sunlight, its head thrown back in agony. It let loose another scream.

Another man stepped forward with a rifle and struck its head with the butt of the weapon.

Nena jumped. Néstor loosed a low, sympathetic hiss as the beast fell. As the Rinches yanked it bodily onto the deck of the barge. It was nothing but a tangle of limbs, a wide-ribbed heap of gray flesh in the sun. Flies buzzed around its mouth and the wounds on its back in a macabre halo. Metallic clicks sounded as the Rinches used hooks on the barge to secure its chains, pinning it down like an animal for slaughter.

Then the men returned to shore, wiping sweat from their brows and calling to one another as they moved out of the line of Nena's sight.

Her heartbeat roared in her ears. She could barely understand the sight unfolding before her, even as the grotesque act repeated itself with a second vampire. The Rinches dragged it forward. It shrank from the punishing sunlight of the riverbank and howled in agony, its voice rending the afternoon and setting Nena's teeth on edge. She could not tear her eyes from the scene. She could not.

Not even as the first vampire lifted its head as much as it could, despite being chained to the deck of the barge.

It had no eyes. In the sunlight, this was grotesquely apparent: thin skin stretched over sockets in its humanlike face. Its nostrils flared as it turned its face toward the riverbank.

Toward Nena.

A sudden chill swept over her back. The sweat that sheathed her all afternoon went clammy. Cold drilled down through muscle to bone, down to the bottom of her belly.

A prickling sensation swept under the scar on her neck, hot as stinging nettles.

That pain always occurred when they were near. Was it because they were watching her? Because they scented the presence of someone once bitten, of a meal left unfinished?

A fierce need to run rushed through her. Her muscles tensed. She could stay still no longer, not as the vampire flared its nostrils again, scenting the air. Not as the second followed suit, even as it was being fastened to the deck with more chains than the first.

"It sees me," she breathed to Néstor. "*It sees me.*"

The Rinches were occupied with keeping the vampires down on the deck—a task that was proving more and more difficult as they writhed and raised their heads, sucking air through their bat-like noses. The men shouted to one another; tossed one another ropes. They were distracted. If she and Néstor fled now, they had a chance to escape undetected.

"We'll go silently," Néstor breathed. "Make for the main road and gallop."

Nena nodded, unable to tear her eyes away from the sight before her. Unable to shake the feeling that she made direct eye contact with the first vampire. She knew that—eyeless though it was—it *saw* her, just as she saw it.

"Now," Néstor breathed.

She backed slowly out of the undergrowth, Néstor at her side. Twigs snapped as they went; each one piqued Nena's fear, struck a higher and higher note in the shrill need to flee that bored through her head.

Then they turned and bolted, pumping their arms, gasping for breath.

When they reached the horses, they tightened girths with sweat-slick, shaking hands. The food was still attached to Néstor's saddle and the salt to Nena's; they had barely unpacked anything in the scant time they rested in this place.

They mounted their horses and trotted out of the thickest of the growth; then, a cry of alarm rose from the riverbank.

"Go!" Néstor cried.

Nena leaned her weight forward and spurred her mount into a canter. Branches stung her face; her mare stumbled, then righted herself, on the rocky path. To the main road. Once they reached the main road, they could truly flee.

They broke through the chaparral to the road, which was barely wide enough for two horses to ride abreast.

But it was clear.

"Gallop!" Néstor roared. A quick glance cast over her shoulder revealed he was just behind her mare's rump, a pistol in one hand.

She needed no further urging. She sank her heels down, leaned low over the mane, and flew.

THEY GALLOPED UNTIL the horses were slick with sweat and wheezing to catch their breath, until Néstor was convinced they were not being followed. Then they moved off the main road into the chaparral. Néstor led the way, cutting a path for them through the thickest parts. He said he no longer felt safe riding by the clearer area of the riverbank; he felt equally exposed on the road.

They were exhausted. The horses were spent, their withers and girths frothy with sweat. Still they walked through the heat of the evening, until staying off the main road proved worth its weight in gold: low hills sloped up south of the road, speckled with prickly pears and maguey. Farther up the largest of these such hills, exposed rock stood solemn and black.

"There," Néstor said, pointing to where the rock curved inward into a shallow cave. "Home sweet home."

They rode slowly up the hill and found a clearing by the mouth of the cave. The cave itself was barely deeper than a patio—being able to see clear to the back of it meant no predators of any kind lurked in its darkness, but its shade and thick walls provided cool respite from the setting sun. The high location meant that Néstor could scan the surrounding countryside like a bird of prey; as they unsaddled the horses, he kept one eye on the river, searching its shining, winding hide for any sign of Rinches with barges.

There were none.

Her heartbeat slowed. Exhaustion prohibited her from moving too quickly; as the horses were finally groomed and grazing nearby, she and Néstor collapsed in the mouth of the cave.

"No fire tonight," he said. "Might draw attention. Too dangerous."

But having no fire was also dangerous. A trail of gooseflesh tripped down Nena's spine at the memory of the first vampire holding her gaze, its long, oval nostrils flaring as it scented the air.

She forced herself up on aching thighs and stumbled toward her saddlebag. She withdrew the salt that the carreteros had given them that morning.

Better to be safe than sorry.

She used it to draw a thin arc around the mouth of the cave, wide enough to leave space for the horses after sunset. Instead of putting it back in the saddlebag, when she let herself fall to the ground beside Néstor, she set it at her side.

They sat in silence, watching the sun's steady crawl toward the western horizon. Watching the silver, snakelike belly of the river warm to gold, then red. Usually, they would still be riding at this hour, taking advantage of the light and the lessening heat. But the horses were spent from galloping hard through the hottest part of the day.

"What do you think that was?" Nena asked at last.

Néstor cursed softly, then leaned back and lay on the ground, his hat abandoned at his side. He interlaced his hands behind his head and let out a long, defeated exhale. "I don't know," he said. A long moment passed, silent but for the calls of evening birds and the wind in the grasses. "Do you think . . . do you think the Rinches are trying to get rid of the vampires?"

Nena twirled a long blade of grass between her fingers, worrying it as she gazed down at the river. This thought had occurred to her as they rode; she mulled it over, then dismissed it. There were easier ways to destroy the monsters than what the Rinches were doing. They had captured the vampires. They were taking them somewhere, an undertaking that clearly took an enormous amount of effort and time.

It reminded her of watching men haul cannons across the soft earth at Palo Alto, their boots sinking into the muck, their faces red and cords popping out from their necks from the strain.

It was the memory of cannons that brought the notion of weapons to mind.

"No," she said softly. "I wonder . . . I wonder if they're using them to get rid of *us*."

Néstor propped himself up on his elbows to look up at her. "What?"

"Think about it," Nena said. She didn't meet his eyes, for fear that seeing an incredulous reaction would take her idea out at the knees. "What if they get sent before the army to weaken us? They only attacked men on Los Ojuelos, which weakened our defenses. There were rumors among the Mexican army that they were being attacked too. And I know for a fact that they had cases of susto. It's almost as if . . . they're targeting the men meant to defend us. Leaving the ranchos weak against attacks."

"No," Néstor said, letting the syllable drawl long with his disbelief. "Nena, you can't possibly think that."

"So what about the chains?" she cried. "The collars around their necks? They were captives. They were . . ." She thought of the Rinche using the butt of a rifle to knock one of the vampires to the ground. It made her want to flinch. "It made me feel bad for them."

This prompted a sound of sheer disbelief from Néstor. He gestured at the scar on her neck, then his shoulder, which he had only taken out of the sling that afternoon.

"Maybe not very bad," she amended. "But what if . . . what if they are wild creatures, like wolves or vultures, creatures that cannot help but be what they are, and they are being used against us?"

"But *how*?" he challenged. "Breaking a horse is one thing. Breaking one of those . . ."

"Can't any animal be broken, if you hurt it enough?" Nena said. "Besides, Félix always says that Anglos have never met anything they couldn't turn into a means to take what they want."

Néstor sat up and ran a hand through his hair, his brows furrowed as he thought. "I don't like this idea."

"Why?" Nena asked.

He exhaled heavily. "Because it means they're smarter than we thought, and more powerful, and . . ." He let this trail off.

Nena waited. After nine years apart, she still knew the rhythm of his speaking. She knew he had more to say, that he was searching for words or untangling a difficult thought. He was one of the few men she knew who spent time with his thoughts before speaking, even in the midst of an argument or excitement. It was one of the reasons she loved him.

"It makes me feel afraid," he said at last, gazing out into the night. "It makes me think of Dos Cruces."

She pulled her knees close to her chest. Rumors of murder and land theft licked through las Villas del Norte like wildfire. The events that brought Néstor and his family to Los Ojuelos from Rancho Dos Cruces in San Antonio de Béxar many years ago were being repeated again, and again, each time creeping closer and closer. Was it only a matter of time until they were at the gates of the Serranos' rancho?

"That's the whole point of this war, isn't it?" he said flatly. "They claimed the land all the way from the Nueces to Río Bravo. Will they stop there? They'll take, and take, and then what?" His voice was raw with emotion. "What will become of us? Who will we be without the land we grew up on? Without our home?"

Nena curled her arms tight around her knees. As if that could protect her from the fear of what she would become, when Papá gave her to another rancho. She would leave Los Ojuelos behind. Her whole heart was buried beneath the anacahuita grove behind la casa mayor, tucked between the pebbles of the stream bank. It rested every morning under the eaves of the chapel her grandfather had built, waiting for the swallows to sing to the rising sun. Without it, she would be nothing but a husk.

"It's about more than the land," she said. "It's the people too."

"But when they take the land, the people scatter," Néstor said passionately. "I know."

For that was exactly what had happened to his family.

"And then it doesn't matter where you are," he added, grief softening his voice. "There is no home anymore, when the people you love are gone."

When she lifted her head, he was watching her. There was a dreamy look in his eye—she would think he was caught in some fond, distant memory, if it were not for the fact that his gaze was fixed on her, that he was present. That his breath was held as he gauged her reaction.

Was he speaking about her? He was. He had wandered for years, far from home, because as far as he knew, she was dead. She was gone.

How would he feel when she was married and left the rancho? Her throat tightened a measure at the thought. She could not think of that now, not when purple twilight softened his sharp edges, when he looked at her like this, in a way that made her face feel pleasantly warm, that made her feel as if she were the only other person on this earth.

And yet it was the only thing she could think of when he looked at her like that.

"But when I came back, and I saw you, I knew," he said softly. "My home is with you. It always will be."

It was all she wanted to hear. It was what she dreaded hearing. She would only disappoint him. She would only hurt him, and she cared for him too deeply to wound him. She might not be strong enough to prevent herself from hurting him. She had to be honest with him.

"What if I can't be with you?" Her voice was in tatters. Her cheeks were suddenly slick.

He put a hand on her knee and squeezed it gently. There were scars on his knuckles, calluses on his thumb. She imagined that hand flat against the plane of her stomach, or running over her body when they were kissing. She wanted that again. She wanted to feel the heat his fingertips left in their wake. She wanted to be held so tightly she bruised, kissed until she could not breathe.

He had said on the road that afternoon that they would arrive at Los Ojuelos by siesta tomorrow. Reaching the rancho meant they would reenter the world in which she did not spend her days alone with him. Where divisions spoken and unspoken created barriers between them. Where her mother would be shocked to even hear Néstor address her with such familiarity.

In that world, she and Néstor were impossible. They always had been.

"If you want me, I will make it happen," he said softly. "I will move heaven and earth. Nena . . ." He paused to brush tears from her cheeks with tender fingertips. Salty tears dripped onto her lips anyway. His face was so calm, so sure, it made her want to shatter. "I have spent the last nine years saving money to buy land. To build a house. I have enough, Nenita. I will build it for us."

It was what he had dreamed of when they were children: his own rancho, his own house. Them, together.

But to Papá, Néstor would always be a vaquero. He would never be good enough. Papá would never allow it. She had said as much, cruelly, that night they spent in the jacal. She could not say it again. She could not tell him he was delusional, for was she not as well? Did she not envision a small house all their own on Los Ojuelos land or near it, her rising with the sun to make coffee for him in their own kitchen?

It felt so real, yet it remained just out of reach.

"Nena," he murmured, his voice low and husky. "Look at me."

She sniffed and turned her face to him. He touched his nose to hers, gentle and tender. His forehead leaned against hers. His hand rose to the back of her neck and rested there, warm, solid.

Tomorrow, the reality of returning to Los Ojuelos would crash around them. It would destroy them. Even if she were not to marry and stayed on Los Ojuelos, it was impossible to imagine being near him and not feeling this way. Not wanting to be with him every moment of the day. Not wanting to kiss him whenever she saw him.

"I swear I will make it happen," he breathed. "If you will have me, I will make it happen."

A sob caught in her throat. He believed so passionately that it was possible, and it simply *wasn't*. "But what if you can't?" she said.

"Do you trust me?" he asked, brushing away tears and tucking loose locks of hair behind her ears. His fingertips light and loving, his eyes never leaving hers as their foreheads touched.

She nodded once. "I do."

Hope lit his features from within. "Then don't cry, mi nena. We're together, and we'll always be," he said. "That alone is a miracle. You are my miracle."

When he brought his lips to hers, their touch was a promise. An oath sealed.

She closed her eyes and kissed him back, pliant in his arms as he drew her close to the warmth of his body. His chin was rough with stubble, grazing her skin. His hands were firm on her back, on her hips, on her breasts. His touch always awakened a part of her that wanted him everywhere at once.

There were a hundred ways this could go wrong, a hundred paths that led to both of them being hurt. A hundred reasons to resist, to pull away, to say again that it could never be and they should cut their losses now. That she had been wrong to kiss him when she did. That he was right to pull away. That even though she wanted him in ways she had no words for, even though there was no man she could love the way she had loved him—innocently, fiercely, angrily—it could not be.

But how could she, with his hands tangled in her hair? With warmth unspooling low in her belly as he explored her body? As his reverent kisses moved down her throat to her collarbone? She did not want to resist. She did not want anything but to be present in this moment, to take it, to take him as the world around them fell away.

Nothing mattered but this: reaching for his shirt and pulling it gently over his head, drawing her hands down his warm chest, relishing the unexpected softness of his skin. Helping him with the buttons of her own shirt.

"Your hands are shaking," she said. Her voice was more breathless than she anticipated.

His smile was shy, almost bashful, as he kissed her again. He pushed away the fabric of the shirt, slipping it off her shoulders and exposing her skin to the deepening twilight.

He pressed a kiss to the base of her throat, then another lower, and lower, rolling her body gently down to meet the ground, shifting his weight so that he was above her, his knees on either side of her hips. Then he returned to her lips with a breathless, bruising kiss.

"Nena," he crooned against her mouth. "I am yours. Command me."

No matter what happened when they returned to Los Ojuelos, she would always have this night. She wanted to always have a part of him.

She reached for his hips and pulled him hard against her. His groan sent a trill of pleasure through her.

"I want all of you," she said.

25

NÉSTOR

NÉSTOR TOOK THE first watch. The moon was but a sliver; its light was pale compared to the brilliance of the stars. He gazed up at the dark sweep of the sky, his body relaxed, his mind blissfully quiet.

Nena slept to his right. She was curled up on one side, her knees pulled into her chest. Her clothes had been haphazardly put back on. Even in exhausted sleep, even smudged with dirt and sweat from days on the road, she was more lovely than any woman he had ever seen. He wanted nothing more than to hold her close and fall asleep with her against him, his face burrowed in her hair. There would be other times for that. Other nights where they could be consumed by each other, where he would stroke her until she whimpered with pleasure, again and again. A lifetime of nights.

But tonight, he stayed alert. He wasn't sure he could bear to wake her to take her turn on watch, not when she slept so peacefully.

Luna stamped a hoof, startling him to attention. After Nena had fallen asleep, he pulled his boots and clothes back on and brought the mares into the circle of salt. Now Luna raised her head, her ears flat against her skull.

A chill fell over him, as if he had been caught in a cold breeze. A shiver seized his shoulders; an ache twinged in his healing shoulder.

Only there was no breeze.

The night was still. Until moments ago, it was warm, filled with the rhythmic chirrup of crickets. Now, it was silent.

Too silent.

Néstor rose, every hair on his body standing on end. He reached for his holster—swiftly abandoned when Nena had reached for his trousers—then decided against it. He reached over Nena's sleeping body to the small bag of salt. He held it tight in one fist as he stood over her, as he scanned the night around them for any sign of movement.

Something shifted to the left of their small campsite. Out of the corner of his eye, he caught a glimpse of long, muscular limbs, pacing like a wolf on all fours, then vanishing into the darkness.

His heart tumbled over itself.

To the right, another body moved. When he turned his head and stared into the darkness, willing it to reveal its secrets, there was nothing. His pulse galloped in the hollow of his throat. He swore he had seen something. He swore that in the starlight, it had looked gray.

Was it his mind playing tricks on him? Was it merely panic silencing the sounds of the night, or was there something to fear? He wanted to reach for his guns, to feel their weight in his hands, but in his gut he knew they were useless. He had shot a vampire, once, twice, three times, and still it continued attacking him. He had nothing but the salt in his hand and a prayer that what he saw was a trick of the night on his eyes.

That prayer died a swift death.

For there the form was again. Closer. Doubt fled his heart: it was there, a gray torso with ribs protruding like a starved animal. Another. A third. The glint of metal as starlight caught on the collars around their necks.

They were watching him.

He knew this with the certainty of the hunted. His pulse was the only sound in the utter, complete silence.

The predators circled. They paced back and forth, one to the left, the other to the right. Circling. Patient as vultures around a dying bull.

But they remained several paces back from the salt boundary. They did not move forward closer to it.

But neither did they move back.

Nena murmured in her sleep and shifted, oblivious to the danger that stalked mere meters away from them.

He would not let them get closer to her. Never again.

Blood pounding, Néstor stepped forward. Pebbles crunched beneath the soles of his boots as he loosened the drawstring of the bag of salt with clammy, trembling fingers.

Every sinew of his body screamed for him to turn and flee. But still he stepped closer. He crept up to the fragile barrier, crouched, and poured more salt onto the ground.

The vampires drew back into the shadows. One released a long, venomous hiss, like that of a vengeful rattler. Néstor's heart leaped to his throat. But he set his jaw and thickened the salt barrier. With each step he took around the perimeter of the white arc, he added more salt, until it gleamed in the starlight like a vein of spring frost.

He retreated to Nena's side, heart drumming against his ribs.

The vampires paced. They watched him, assessing him, and paced, languid and watchful—but farther back from the salt than before.

Then, between one step and the next, they vanished. They melted into the night, as if crossing through a doorway from one room to the next. As if they had been a part of the shadows all along.

A single cricket's voice rose in the night. Soon, it was joined by others. The heat and humidity of the night draped over Néstor's skin, familiar and uncomfortably close, as if it had never been disturbed.

Still his heart raced.

He crouched, and drew another circle of salt, this time directly around Nena's sleeping form. He stood inside it, over her, his arms folded over his chest, the bag of salt clutched in one hand.

There he stayed until dawn grayed the eastern horizon.

IT WAS NEARLY time for the siesta when they turned off the main road onto a familiar, well-trod path. Soon, the line of the roof of the comisaria came into view. Beyond it rose the high wooden fence surrounding the central heart of Los Ojuelos.

"We did it." Nena's voice cracked—with exhaustion, with emotion, or both. "We made it."

Néstor lifted a hand to his lips and whistled. Two high notes, to catch the attention of the men who guarded the gate into the rancho and assure them that the two strange riders were Los Ojuelos people.

He and Nena rode through the gates, side by side. How different it was, returning to Los Ojuelos this time. No dread weighed in his bones, no anxiety tightened its claws around his throat. All he felt was relief as they drew close to the houses and dismounted. He put Luna's reins in his left hand so that he could walk next to Nena as they approached la casa mayor.

But as his eye fell on la casa mayor, on the older woman who stood on the patio, her hands on her hips, watching them, a profound weariness swept over him. He still had battles left to fight. These might prove the most difficult yet.

"Nena? Nena!" A slim figure tore away from the kitchen of la casa mayor, chickens scattering and squawking in her path. A small yellow dog followed at her heels.

Javiera, Nena's younger sister, barreled into Nena and threw her arms around her.

"Nena, we thought you were *dead*," Javiera cried, her voice muffled from where she buried her face in Nena's shoulder. Nena swayed backward from the force of Javiera's embrace; instinctively, Néstor's right hand rose to her back to balance her.

When he looked up, Doña Mercedes had stepped off the patio and crossed most of the space to him and Nena. She narrowed her eyes at Néstor's hand on Nena's back and shot him a severe look.

So this was how it would begin: immediately, without respite from the road or a chance to explain anything.

He dropped his hand, but he did not drop Doña Mercedes's stare. Instead, he touched the brim of his hat and dipped his chin politely.

"Papá wrote saying you couldn't be found!" Javiera's voice pitched sharp. "What were we supposed to think?"

"I never meant to upset you," Nena said, releasing her younger sister. "We had to run."

"And . . . and . . ." Javiera looked up at Néstor, suddenly shy. "Félix said *he* was missing"—here she nodded her head at Néstor—"and he hoped that meant you were together somewhere, but that did not please Mamá—"

"Magdalena!"

Néstor took a step back as Doña Mercedes swept forward and took her daughter into her arms. "Thank God," she said. "Thank la Virgen that you're safe." She released Nena, holding her by the shoulders. Her eyes shone with tears.

His heart twinged on Doña Mercedes's behalf. Of course her family assumed Nena was harmed, or captured, or dead. He should have found a way to send a message, somehow.

"How could you do this to me?" Doña Mercedes said. "How could you let us fear the worst?"

"We ran," Nena said. "We had to. There was no time for messages. We came back as fast as we could, because—"

"And just look at you. What is this?" Doña Mercedes said, sweeping a critical look over Nena, from sweat-stained shirt to trousered legs. Both of them were filthy and spent, covered in dust and ravaged by mosquito bites—he could not deny that he had brought Nena home looking decidedly worse for the wear. "Never mind. You need to bathe and rest. News from your father came this morning."

"He's safe?" Nena cried. Her whole body was at once alight, alert, as if someone had splashed cold water over her. "He's well? What happened? What about Félix?"

Doña Mercedes explained that after the battle was lost, Don Feliciano and Félix had retreated across the river. Félix was wounded, but he could still ride. The squadron split: some continued to ride south to carry on fighting, others retreated home. Don Feliciano and Félix rode to Los Ojuelos and would arrive within a day or so with the surviving Los Ojuelos vaqueros.

"And what of Casimiro Duarte? Is there news of him?"

Doña Mercedes gave Néstor a cold look, as if he had intruded on a private conversation.

It stung like a scorpion.

He could not be afraid of her. If he was going to marry Nena, he had to prove to her parents that he was their equal. That meant no skirting around them, head down, like another peón. It meant discomfort, and he had to push through it. He looked Doña Mercedes in the eye and waited for her to reply.

She tilted her chin haughtily. "The patrón did not convey news of the vaqueros," she said, her tone frosty.

"Thank you, doña," Néstor said.

That was enough ground won for the day. He was staring down the barrel of a long, hard battle, and he needed to be strategic. He should not fight when he was half dead from a sleepless night and a long day's ride in the heat.

"I'll take the horses," he said to Nena.

"No, you're still hurt," she said, moving her hand—and the reins—out of his reach. "You could barely lift the saddle this morning. You need to go to Abuela and have her look at your shoulder."

Before Néstor could reply, she took Luna's reins from him.

When Doña Mercedes's gaze snapped to Néstor, for a moment, he saw what she saw: the untouchable daughter of the patrón taking the reins from a lowly peón. From a vaquero. He could see how it would shatter the order of her world, how it would make her want to snatch Nena back protectively.

Instinct pushed him to take the reins back. To placate Doña Mercedes, to shy away from her and become as invisible as he was when he was just another child on the rancho.

He stood his ground.

"Let the vaqueros tend to the horses," Doña Mercedes said coldly. To Nena, she said: "Come inside. Now."

"Mamá, I said that he is injured." Nena did not release the reins. "I'll take them."

Javiera glanced from one woman to the other, then to Néstor, her eyes wide with apprehension.

The battle of wills was mercifully cut short when Ignacio—one of the vaqueros who had not joined the squadron because he was recovering from susto—approached.

"Señorita Magdalena. Duarte!" he said. "Thank God you returned safely."

He took the reins from Nena and tipped his hat to Doña Mercedes. "Buenas tardes, doña."

"Don't let him work," Nena said, pointing at Néstor. "He's wounded and exhausted."

Ignacio nodded to the women in farewell. "Of course, señorita."

He retreated with the horses, resuming his invisibility to the doña of la casa mayor, just as every good peón and vaquero should.

It cast Néstor's own behavior in sharp relief.

Doña Mercedes gave Néstor a final stony look that he couldn't perfectly parse and took Nena by the elbow. As the three Serrano women went back to the house, Javiera's yellow dog following at their heels, Nena cast a look over her shoulder at him.

Vespers, she mouthed.

Then she jerked her head in the direction of the anacahuita grove.

Though the women left him standing in their wake, unmoored and exhausted and wounded from that first encounter with Doña Mercedes, this lifted his heart. After evening prayers, they would meet at the grove where they had retreated so many times as children.

In the meantime, he could rest at last.

He turned away from la casa mayor toward his family's jacal.

He was embraced fiercely by Abuela and fussed over, then his belly was stuffed with food.

Later, he lay on his stomach in the quiet darkness of the jacal, surrounded by Abuela's smells of rosemary and lavender and incense, as she applied a poultice to his left shoulder to ease its irritated swelling. The poultice was cool against his skin and brought immense relief.

Abuela was the one who first put salt in his saddlebags before they left. He felt no qualms in spilling the whole tale of the last week to her. From the vampires on the battlefield to that first night, when his arm was ripped out of its socket, and every day since.

"She did well in acting quickly," Abuela said thoughtfully, applying more poultice to his shoulder.

"I know," Néstor said dreamily. His exhausted mind drifted to that night and the way that Nena distracted him as she prepared to thrust his arm back into place. *I like being alone with you. It gives me ideas.* "She's perfect."

Though his eyes were closed, he could practically hear Abuela's skeptical look.

"I take it she hasn't slammed any doors in your face recently," she said dryly.

Néstor laughed. "No," he said. "No, quite the opposite. Abuela, I'm going to marry her."

Abuela did not speak for a long moment. "Mijo," she said, a gentleness in her voice that made him open his eyes and look up at her. "I'm happy to see you healing. To see you hopeful like this. But what of Don Feliciano?"

What of Don Feliciano indeed.

Facing Doña Mercedes was merely the first fence to clear. He would rather face a dozen angry bulls than the patrón.

But for Nena?

For Nena he could. *With* Nena he could. Couldn't he?

"Together, Nena and I can face anything," he said. "Didn't we fight off El Cuco? Don Feliciano is child's play in comparison."

Abuela patted his shoulder. Perhaps a shade of pity flickered behind her eyes; perhaps it was a trick of his imagination. "I hope you're right, mijito. Now rest."

Néstor closed his eyes. Lulled by the sounds of his grandmother singing to herself as she moved about the jacal, he soon fell into a deep, dreamless sleep.

26

NENA

WHEN NENA, MAMÁ, and Javiera entered the house, Nena's cousins Didi and Alejandra descended with heated buckets of water from the kitchen in which to bathe. Javiera followed a half step behind, whatever chores she had for the afternoon forgotten, the gentle click of Pollo's claws on the floors announcing her and the dog's presence.

Didi and Alejandra helped Nena wash the sweat and dust from her hair and combed out tangles, bickering gaily over which of them would inform their mother, Nena's aunt, that Nena had appeared wearing a man's clothes. Neither of them mentioned Néstor. There was no doubt that they knew with whom Nena had traveled; the rancho held secrets like a cracked cup held water. Everyone who saw them ride through the gates and dismount together would tell everyone they knew, and soon the whole rancho would know that they had returned from Matamoros together, just the two of them.

The prospect of becoming the subject of gossip made her want to cringe with her whole body. Néstor was a private thing, suddenly exposed. She felt naked and vulnerable.

But even her chismosa cousins carved looping paths around the subject of Néstor. They avoided asking her about Matamoros as well, choosing instead to fill the room with all that had happened on the rancho in Nena's absence. Perhaps they had taken one look at Mamá ushering Nena into the house with a storm cloud on her brow and decided, out of a sense of self-preservation, that the topic was too dangerous to approach. Javiera had certainly concluded the same.

When Nena retreated to their bedroom to sleep for the rest of the siesta, Javiera followed in silence. Instead of climbing onto her own bed, she followed onto Nena's and curled up against her like she had when she was a baby. Guilt seeped through her tired body when she thought of how tightly Javiera had tackled her when they arrived and the teary sheen in Mamá's eyes. But she was back, and now that she was, she could keep Javiera and the rest of the rancho safe.

NENA DID NOT wake for merienda; she slept until her cousins woke her for dinner and ushered her to the patio, depositing her in front of a steaming plate of rice, tortillas, peppers, and fragrant cabrito. Nena nodded or shook her head to different questions that her tías peppered her with as she ate.

"And which vaquero was it who brought you back?" one asked delicately, as if the subject were an insect or a bat trampled by a horse in the training corral. Something to be stepped around. Something unsavory.

Shame flushed Nena's cheeks with warmth.

When she saw Nena's mouth was full, Didi supplied the answer eagerly, eyes agleam. "Néstor Duarte."

Evidently, she did not have a sense of self-preservation after all.

Mamá gave Didi an arch look. She said nothing, but the shift in her shoulders was a clear indication that Didi should stop talking. Nena swallowed and jumped in to speak before Didi could further irritate Mamá.

"It was good I was not alone," Nena said. "We were pursued for much of the journey."

"By Yanquis? Rinches?" another aunt asked.

"No," Nena began slowly, choosing her words carefully. "By strange beasts."

"What do you mean?" Didi asked.

Javiera stared at her with eyes like an owl's, tense and watchful as she waited for Nena's answer.

Nena tore a tortilla into smaller and smaller pieces, praying for the right words to come to her lips.

"Predators of some kind," she said at last. "Not wolves, nor pumas, but . . . hairless beasts, with many teeth."

Silence fell over the table like a shroud.

"As I said, it was good I was not alone," Nena offered, voice falsely bright, hoping to close the topic and cast a positive light on the company she had returned to the rancho with.

But Didi could always smell a good story.

"Oh?" Her round face was instantly alight. "What happened? Did he save your life from Rinches? He did, didn't he?" she asked, leaning over the table toward Nena.

Mamá stood abruptly. "There will be no more talk of how Magdalena returned to the rancho," she announced, her crisp tone effectively shuttering the subject. "It's time for vespers, and time for us to offer prayers in gratitude that she has come back to us."

The women of the family rose and cleared the table, then began moving to the courtyard of la casa mayor for prayers. As Nena followed, she stopped in her tracks as Mamá took her by the elbow.

"I don't know what story you're spinning," she said. "But there will be no more talk of strange beasts in my house. No more talk of how you rode alone with a peón for days." Nena felt a reflexive lick of defensiveness. Néstor was *not* a peón. He was his own. But she bit her tongue as Mamá continued. "Your honor is the family's, Magdalena. If we have any hope of sweeping this under the table, everyone must keep silent about the matter. Do you understand?"

Hadn't she known this moment would come? That when she returned to the rancho at Néstor's side, Mamá would come down with all the force she had once used to keep Nena in line as a child? She had not used this tone with Nena in years.

And, to her shame, her response was to make herself as small as possible. To speak softly. To placate.

"Yes, Mamá," she said. "I'm sorry."

IN PAPÁ'S ABSENCE, Mamá led the rancho in evening prayers. In addition to the midday meal, it was one of two times a day everyone on the rancho gathered in the courtyard of la casa mayor.

Néstor was there with his grandmother and Bernabé. Her breath caught in her throat when she saw him step slowly into the courtyard, Abuela on his arm. Like her, he had had a chance to bathe and change; he was clean-shaven again, his black hair combed away from his face, his dark eyes shining when they caught hers.

To her right, she heard Mamá clear her throat.

Nena dropped her eyes quickly. Folded her hands demurely before her.

If Mamá was already acting as she was, what would Papá say when he returned? It required little imagination to know that it was as bad an omen as the appearance of an owl. As voices droned through the evening prayers, dread pooled in her stomach, slow and sticky as blood.

Whatever happened, Néstor was going to be hurt. The mess she had created was like a runaway steer that she could not stop from crashing into fragile things.

Prayers seemed interminable. When they finally ended, when the people of the rancho began to disperse for evening chores, she slipped out from under Mamá's watchful eye as subtly as she could. It was as if she were ten years old again as she sneaked around the corner of the kitchen, dodging an aunt or two. She lingered in the herb garden behind the kitchen, sinking to her knees in the soil and pretending to be looking for something.

She rubbed sprigs of rosemary between her thumb and forefinger as she waited, inhaling deeply the soothing smell.

Then, out of the corner of her eye, she saw a figure stride to the anacahuita grove and vanish behind the trunks.

Her heartbeat quickened. She should be calm, but her traitorous body was eager to be near him. It was nervous and jumpy with the flush of childhood infatuation.

She waited a few more minutes, pulse in her ears. Then, with a quick look over her shoulder to make sure no one in the kitchen was watching her, she rose and walked as casually as she could toward the trees.

The hum of chicharras pulsed overhead, rhythmic and soothing in the evening heat. Loud enough that she prayed no one could hear her gasp of surprise when Néstor took her firmly by the waist and pulled her close to place a firm kiss on her temple.

"Néstor!" She made his name a hiss of chastisement. She pushed against his chest; he released her immediately. "If anyone saw, that would be the end of me." She stepped back, flustered, and made a vain attempt to collect herself. Smoothed her skirt, tucked a lock of hair away. It fell back out again at once, tickling her cheek. "We have to be careful."

Néstor slipped the errant lock of hair behind her ear with gentle fingertips. The softness of his touch made her heart fold over itself. "Soon we won't have to be."

She cleared her throat and took a half step back. "Papá returns tomorrow," she said awkwardly.

"I know," he said. He slid his hands into his pockets and leaned back against a tree trunk, a picture of unassuming ease. "I'm ready."

But he wasn't. Neither was she. She bit the inside of her cheek and folded her arms over her chest.

"Mamá is already cross," she said. "I . . ." She knew precisely why Mamá was displeased with her, but she could not bring herself to say it aloud. She should tell him about the bargain she had made with Papá. Its stipulations. She wanted to say that she had made it before Néstor ever reappeared and that she regretted it now. That part of her wanted to throw everything away and be with him, but she couldn't. Not after seeing what the Yanquis were capable of. The Rinches. The rancho was vulnerable, and she had to protect it in any way she knew how—even if that way was Mamá and Papá's way.

But how could she put that into words, when he looked at her the way he did now, with the steady, calm confidence of someone looking at the one missing piece of their life?

She couldn't.

She swiftly changed the subject. "I tried to bring up the vampires at dinner. Javiera's been having nightmares, and I don't want to sleep without salt at the door. But she wouldn't listen."

Néstor's demeanor shifted with the change of topic.

"Abuela said they had two more attacks while we were gone," he said, his expression growing grim. "Only one survived."

Cold slipped over Nena. "Who didn't?" she whispered.

"Tío Macario's third son, Jesús," Néstor said, sadness deepening the lines on either side of his mouth. "Two days ago. He was eighteen."

Nena crossed herself. She should have been here. Instead, she had flung herself headlong into an ill-fated, selfish gamble. This was the price the rancho paid. "Dios mío," she murmured.

Could she have saved him? She would never know.

She should have never left.

But if she hadn't, there was so much she would not have discovered about the vampires. How beheading destroyed them. The use of salt for protection. The Rinches with their chains.

"Javiera told me that Félix sent a letter," she said. "He says they're being followed, but there was something in his wording that made me wonder. I wonder *what* is following them."

"Salt," Néstor said flatly. "Everyone needs to be putting salt at their thresholds."

"And windowsills," Nena added, thinking of the night before she left with the squadron. Of the otherwise silent dog Pollo barking incessantly at the open window. "I doubt that Mamá will listen to me, but Javiera and my cousins will. We have to let everyone know before nightfall."

Vespers happened at twilight; now, the sky was streaked with deepening purples. They did not have much time.

"Ignacio and Elena are already at our house talking to Abuela," Néstor said, straightening. "They could help spread the word."

"You need to go talk to them," she said. For a fleeting moment, it felt as if they were on the road together again, relying on each other to survive. Their lives would never be like that again. "Tell everyone. I have to go back and get salt from the kitchen without making Mamá suspicious."

"May I walk you back to the house?" Néstor asked.

"No," Nena said quickly. Absolutely not. That would only incite Mamá further. "I'll go alone."

A shadow of hurt crossed over Néstor's face.

"It's what's best, for now," she added quickly.

"I understand," he said, but the somber tone of his voice made Nena want to take his hand.

She didn't.

"I'll see you tomorrow," Nena said. "After Papá returns."

She turned to go back to the house.

"Nena," he said.

Was he going to ask her why she was acting so differently? A bolt of terror shot through her at the thought of answering. But when she looked back at him, he shook his head.

"I . . . Never mind," he said. "I'll talk to you tomorrow. Good night."

"Good night," she said.

Her skirts swished as she almost ran through the grass; she entered the house from the kitchen, hoping Mamá did not see her. She grabbed a small jícara bowl and scooped salt into it from the kitchen store, then peeked into the great room of the house.

It was empty. Mamá was either on the patio or preparing for bed.

She darted to her room and shut the door quietly behind her. She turned and nearly collided with Didi.

"Oh!" Didi gasped in surprise. She looked down at the bowl of salt. "What's that for?"

Didi, Alejandra, Javiera, and the dog Pollo all looked up at Nena, their dark eyes glittering inquisitively in the candlelight.

"For protection," Nena said. She crouched and poured a line across the doorway. "Don't tell Mamá."

She stood and went to the window. She closed it, locked it, and poured a thick line of salt across the shallow sill.

Please let that be enough. Somehow, she felt more exposed in this room than she had last night, sleeping on the ground beneath the stars next to Néstor.

She thrust the thought from her mind and turned away from the window quickly. She set the bowl of salt by the head of her bed, then undressed and put on her nightgown. Didi and Alejandra whispered to each other as she blew out the candles and slipped under the blankets of her own bed.

"Protection from what?" Javiera asked quietly. Her eyes and the dog's glinted at Nena through the dark, wide and fearful. Explaining now would cause nothing but a sleepless night full of nightmares.

"From bad luck," Nena said. "Now go to sleep. All of you."

Sleep found the others quickly. Soon the room was filled with their soft snoring.

Though her bed and the weight of its blankets was something she had fantasized about after many nights of sleeping on the ground, though exhaustion weighed heavy in her legs after long days in the saddle, sleep evaded her.

She thought of the shadow of hurt passing over Néstor's face. Of the cold, condescending way Mamá spoke to him.

She was a coward. All day she had twisted and writhed in her shame, in her attempts not to hurt him, but what good did it do? What did it change? The damage was done. It was as if she had already pulled the trigger and stood there, watching the bullet fly toward him, too frozen to save him.

HEAT ITCHED OVER Nena's skin and kept sleep far from her side during siesta the next day; she rose and occupied herself with Javiera's pile of mending on the patio, narrowing her world to tiny, even stitches. Chicharras hummed in the oaks; the crickets' song thickened the heat of the afternoon. The aroma of jasmine rose from the bushes next to the patio. A horse's whinny, thin and curious, rose from far away, perhaps in the direction of the main road.

If someone were to see her, sitting in the shade of the patio counting stitches, it would appear as if the last two weeks had not happened. As if returning to Los Ojuelos had jerked the reins of her life and yanked it rudely back to the beginning. Before the squadron, before the journey. Back to before Néstor had returned.

But there were the saddle sores on the insides of her shins. The ache in her lower back and seat bones from days spent in a too-large saddle had yet to lessen. Deep between her ribs, something had reoriented itself to a new north, not giving a damn what her mind knew was impossible. It hummed, drawing her attention up and out of the corner of her eye, to the Duarte jacal.

So much had changed. So much would continue to change. She was overcome by the sensation that she stood on the lip of a cliff, a broad arroyo dividing what came before and what came next. Against her will, and without warning, something would push her. A sweep of vertigo would rush through her ears; the stomach-flip of a sudden fall. And that would be it. The rest of her life would unspool before her. There would be no going back to how it was before.

The bell of the chapel rang. Once, twice. A third time.

Her needle stilled midway through the cloth.

With the whole rancho waiting with bated breath, that could only mean one thing.

She threw the sewing down on the table and stood. Hitched her skirts and galloped off the patio in three faltering strides, shading her eyes as she rounded the corner of the house and turned to the back entrance of the rancho.

A line of horses was already tethered at the corral.

Papá and Félix were back.

She bolted for the corral.

She arrived out of breath, cursing skirts for existing and yearning for the ease of running in trousers. She wove among the horses and men, nodding and greeting familiar faces. She kept a silent tally of numbers as she went. Were there more coming, on the road behind this first group? Or were these riders all that remained of Los Ojuelos's contribution to the doomed squadron? She swallowed thickly, then turned and spotted a familiar face.

"Beto!" she cried, running forward to greet him.

"Señorita!" He lifted his hat to her, a flash of delight brightening his pale eyes. "Aren't you a sight for sore eyes! Was Duarte with you? Is he here?"

Nena gestured behind her at the jacales. "We returned yesterday."

Beto lifted his hands, palms upturned to the heavens. "Thank God," he said. "Thank God."

"What of Casimiro?" Nena asked.

"Wounded, but with us," Beto said. He nodded to the gates, where more horses were filing in from the road. "Bringing up the rear. We could have used you after the battle, señorita. There were many wounded, and too many infections. And susto," he added, lowering his voice. "My God. I have never seen anything like it."

He shuddered as if an uncomfortable sensation had just run through his body.

"Do you feel it too?" Nena asked abruptly.

Beto frowned. "I don't follow, señorita."

Nena tugged the neckline of her dress to the side, revealing her scar.

"Here," she said, pressing her fingertips to the ripples of the scar. "When they are near. When they are . . . watching."

Beto's eyes widened. "I thought I was going loco," he said, voice low. "Señorita, I fear . . . they have been following us. They have been waiting. I swear it, but no one would believe me if I said anything."

Gooseflesh swept over Nena's arms, sending each hair standing on end.

"I believe you," she whispered. The sun beat down on their heads now, but when nightfall spread its greedy fingers across the rancho, they would all be in danger.

"Go to Néstor's abuela and speak to her as soon as you can. Tell all the other vaqueros what she tells you about salt," she said quickly. "If they don't believe you, just tell them it's my orders and they *must* follow them. That will—"

"Nena!"

Her growing dread made her startle easily; she jerked her head up at the sound of her name.

She gasped at the sight of Félix dismounting his white stallion outside the corral. A bloody bandage was wound around one of his arms.

"Go," Beto said. "I'll do as you say. Be careful, señorita."

"You too," she said.

Then she turned on her heel and slung herself through the wooden rungs of the fence, not caring if Mamá would call it inappropriate, not caring who saw her acting like a child. The faster she could get to her brother, the better.

She threw her arms around his chest and embraced him tightly. He smelled metallic: like blood, like gunpowder. He smelled exhausted and sick. She could tell even before she pulled back and looked up at the gray wash of his unshaven face, the beads of sweat glistening on his brow beneath the band of his hat. She pointed at his arm.

"That is infected," she said flatly. "Come with me to the house." She waved to a vaquero, took the reins from Félix's hand and passed them off with a gracious thank-you. "Now."

"Glad to see you too," he said, wry humor untouched by whatever injury he had sustained. He fell into step with her as they turned to la casa mayor. "You're unharmed?"

"As you see," she said. She paused. What if she tested the waters with him now? To see how ready he would be to calm Mamá—and likely Papá—about the way she returned home? "Señor Duarte escorted me home safely."

"Ah," Félix said. "I suspected." He fell silent for a few steps. "You and a vaquero, alone on the road," he said. Nena flinched at his tone: it was grave. Unamused. "Rumors cannot spread about this. Your honor is that of the family, and if word gets out—"

"I know. That is what Mamá said. But Félix, you must talk sense to her." Please, let her desperation not be too obvious. She needed a voice of reason. The only voice Mamá and Papá listened to. "All he did was protect me. There were Rinches, and worse, and if it had not been for him—"

"Nena! Félix!"

Mamá was on the patio of la casa mayor, gesturing to both of them.

Papá sat at the table, slumped with exhaustion. At the sight of Nena, he stood with great effort and, removing his hat, held his arms open to her.

"Papá!" she cried. "Are you well?"

"Mija," he said. His face was creased with relief as Nena stepped into the shade of the patio and embraced him, resting her cheek on his barrel chest. He smelled of the road. He smelled exhausted. "I am so sorry I did not keep you safe, mija," he said. His voice rumbled from deep in his chest, but when it reached her ears, it sounded reedy. Tired. "I should have never let you come. It was too dangerous. It is a miracle you're home safe."

"Not a scratch on me," she began as she pulled away from him. "Thanks to—"

"But the state she returned in," Mamá cut in. Nena turned her head to Mamá sharply, surprised by how her voice was tight with anger. Félix raised his brows as he slumped into a seat at the table and removed his hat. "Wearing barely any clothes. It was just her and the Duarte boy. He has crossed *boundaries*, Feliciano," Mamá added, voice shaking. She felt trapped as Mamá's voice pitched higher, as she grew flustered and upset. As she watched a storm build in Papá's face, a quiet, detached part of her mind observed that Mamá was doing this to get her way with Papá. It was not so unlike the way Nena begged Félix to speak for her, was it not? Instead of voicing her displeasure for herself, instead of speaking directly to Nena, Mamá stirred the anger of the bull with a hot poker. "The way he speaks to her, the way he touches her? It would be better if she had not returned at all."

Ashamed heat flushed to Nena's cheeks; her throat closed tight with emotion. Mamá's words struck like a slap across the face.

"Whoa," Félix said weakly. His face was paler than it had been before, as if dismounting and stepping out of the sun had sapped the last of his energy. "Calm down, Mamá. Nena is home safe and that is what matters."

Mamá ignored him.

"I told you it was hard to keep them apart as children, but you did not listen to me. You never listen to me. Now the worst has happened," she cried. "This is your fault for taking her with the squadron when I told you she would lose her reputation. Everyone saw them return. Everyone *saw*. Her honor will be called into question by every decent family from here to Laredo. We will never be able to show her in polite society again."

Both Papá and Félix stared at Nena, stunned by Mamá's swift attack. She hid her face with her hands. She had been so fixated on Néstor's feelings about her bargain with Papá that she had not anticipated this. She was struck down, fast and hard, as dizzy as if she had physically hit the ground.

"That's not true," she said. She had to regroup. She had to somehow get Mamá to calm down. There was nothing to be gained from this conversation but more trouble. She dropped her hands and pulled her shoulders back. "You are overreacting, Mamá. Nothing happened and no one will think anything of it. Félix, tell her she's overreacting."

Félix looked from Nena to Mamá to Papá like a drowning man. He was ill. He was exhausted. It was unfair for her to drag him into this battle, but what other choice did she have? She needed his backup. She needed to convince her parents that nothing would happen to their plans.

"*Félix*," she hissed.

"Enough, Nena," Mamá cut her off sharply. "Neither of you know how people talk. This ruins all of our plans, Feliciano," she said, turning her vitriol on Papá. "This is all your fault."

"Then I will solve it," Papá thundered. Nena jumped as he turned on her, towering over her, his chest and shoulders seeming to grow to twice their width. "We had a bargain. I trusted you. You betrayed that trust."

Papá turned on his heel and stormed into the sunlight.

Toward the Duarte jacal.

It was as if the conversation spun like a top, winding tighter and tighter until it was knocked off-kilter. It looped wildly out of her control.

She had to bring Papá back. She and Félix could talk sense into him, but not with Mamá poking him with a hot brand.

Nena turned to follow him. She needed to get Papá away from Mamá, away from Néstor, away from anything that might further inflame his temper. She needed to calm him down. To assure him that their bargain was still whole.

But Mamá seized her by the elbow and yanked her backward.

"You stay here," she said forcefully. "If we have any hope of marrying you to Don Hortensio's son, the boy must be made an example of."

An example. She had put Néstor in harm's way. That was inexcusable. She had to fix it.

Nena whirled on her mother. "What if I don't want that?" she cried, restraint snapping.

Mamá looked as if Nena had slapped her. "Do you not love the rancho?" she said. "This land has been in your family for generations, entrusted to your great-grandfather by the king of Spain. It is our inheritance. It is our *lives*. Would you throw it away like that?" She narrowed her eyes. "Did I raise you to be so selfish?"

"No, Mamá," Nena said. "I want what's best for the rancho just as much as you do."

"Then you will see that we are weak, Magdalena," Mamá snapped. "We have no choice."

"But what if the strength of the rancho is not about alliances?" Nena said. "What if it is the people who are already here? What if I want to stay here, and keep us strong that way? Let me speak to Papá." She wrenched her arm away from her mother.

Mamá scoffed. "At your age, I had a husband and a son and a whole rancho relying on me. You are still a child. Go ahead, speak to your father. But you are still a child if you believe he will listen to you."

Nena curled her hands into fists and turned her back on the patio. On her mother. She stepped into the piercing afternoon heat and raced after Papá.

27

NÉSTOR

"*GET UP! NÉSTOR*, wake up!"

He didn't want to. Every bone in his body still ached from the hard, fast ride back to the rancho. He had been on longer rides, of course, but rarely that hard, and never with such high stakes. What dreams lifted the depth of his sleep were full of monsters ripping themselves free of Rinche corpses, of clawed hands reaching for Nena through the shadows. Of looking up at her from the ground, knowing that he was dying, knowing that he had been killed, and that he could not protect her from the vampire that loomed over her.

He clambered out of sleep groggily. Abuela's ivory braids swung over him; she shook him, looking over her shoulder at the door.

"Mijo, the patrón is here," she hissed. Anxiety rippled off her like heat, slipping under Néstor's skin. "He's angry. Get *up*."

Néstor lurched up from his sleeping mat. Judging from the afternoon sunlight that poured into the communal bedroom of his family's jacal, the siesta was not over yet. His throat was dry, but he had no time to get water. He threw a shirt over his head and followed Abuela to the patio, lifting up an arm to shade his face from the sun as his vision adjusted.

Don Feliciano was on the patio, looking as out of place as a foreigner. Néstor could not remember ever having seen the patrón so near his family's house; it struck him then, through the dense clouds of sleep that still thickened his thinking, that something was very, very wrong.

Don Feliciano was already crossing the patio in three strides, spurs jingling, and seized him by the collar of his shirt.

"How dare you disobey me," Don Feliciano thundered. The patrón's face was lined and tired; but he was lit from within by rage that flushed his tanned face dark. His gray mustache was inches from Néstor's face, quivering with anger. He still smelled of the dust and sweat of the road, the mix of exhaustion and anger making him seem feral.

Sharp, long-buried memories ripped to the surface. Don Feliciano with a belt, standing over Casimiro, whipping him for having allegedly flirted with a visiting ranchero's daughter. Don Feliciano pointing at him in the candlelight the night Nena died.

"I don't believe I disobeyed any of your orders, señor," he said, treading very carefully, keeping his voice low and level.

"You deserted the squadron," Don Feliciano spat.

"I was protecting Señorita Magdalena, as were my orders," Néstor said.

"Don't be glib with me. My orders were for you to keep Magdalena safe with the squadron," Don Feliciano spat. "*You kidnapped my daughter.* I ought to have you whipped."

Néstor inhaled through his nose to steady himself. He had to be calm in the face of Don Feliciano's building storm, as if he were facing an irritated bull in a corral: no sudden movements, no flashes of his own anger, or he might be gored.

"When she was in danger, I delivered her from the battle," he said, speaking slowly and clearly. "She wanted to return to Los Ojuelos and it was dangerous for her to do so alone, and so I—"

"Do you think that excuses your behavior?" Don Feliciano thundered. "You are a stain on her honor. She has a future ahead of her, a marriage, and I will not have rumors about some peón standing in the way of that."

Anger rose like a rattlesnake in Néstor's chest, fangs bared. He tore Don Feliciano's hand from his shirt.

"I am *not* your peón," he spat. "I do not work for you. I owe you no money. I am an independent man and I demand that you speak to me like an equal, for I am your equal."

For a second, Don Feliciano stared at him, as if surprised that Néstor was capable of speech.

Then he tossed his head back. His laughter echoed across the rancho, brassy and mocking.

Over Don Feliciano's shoulder, he glimpsed a female figure running toward his family's jacal from la casa mayor.

Nena.

Néstor curled his hands into fists and clenched them. He had to rein in his temper. It was time for the conversation he had rehearsed a hundred times while riding back to the rancho, whether he was ready or not.

"I am buying a porción near Los Ojuelos," he said, fighting to keep his voice even. "When I have done so, I am going to marry Magdalena. She and I have already spoken about this."

This struck Don Feliciano's mirth a killing blow. His brows drew together, his face a dark mask of surprise.

Not a good sign. Néstor dug in his heels for a long battle.

"Papá!" Nena cried, breathless as she approached. Thank God. His reinforcements had arrived at last, her forehead and cheeks glistening with sweat from the sprint across the rancho. "Papá, listen to me. I needed protection on the road home. You know that. Leave him be."

Don Feliciano turned to her abruptly. "Are you engaged to this man?"

Nena's brows rose; her mouth dropped open. "What?" she said. The question had taken her by surprise. "No, Papá. Come, I need to speak to you alone."

Néstor's stomach dropped out beneath him.

If you want me, he had said to her. *If you will have me.*

A low ringing filled his ears.

She had never answered.

What do you want? Another question that she never replied to.

He said, *Do you trust me?* She said that she did. That was all she said.

But he should not have trusted her.

He should never have believed that she would stand up to her parents so easily.

"Nena," he said, mouth dry. His voice sounded foreign to his own ears, hollow and thin. "Tell him."

Nena ignored this. She didn't even look at him. It bit like the lash of a whip. "Papá, come with me," she said. "I need to speak with you. *Alone.*"

She shot Néstor a look that he could tell was supposed to be meaningful, but he could not parse it. His pulse throbbed in his temple.

"Nena—"

"Silence!" Don Feliciano roared.

If Don Feliciano's face had been dark with anger before, it was now consumed with a wicked sort of delight at this turn of the battle. He lurched forward at Néstor; for a moment, he thought the patrón was going to strike him, and he dodged to avoid it. Instead, the patrón seized him by his shirt collar again. Néstor was slow to catch his balance, too slow to stop when Don Feliciano thrust him forward and threw him on the ground.

He hit the solid tipichil floor with the flat of his back; his skull snapped back and met the packed earth and stone with a *thunk* that sent his teeth clashing against one another.

Abuela cried out; Nena was shouting for Don Feliciano to stop. Néstor's ears rang. He coughed and rolled onto his side, fighting to catch the breath that had been knocked out of him.

Don Feliciano stepped forward. His hand was on his pistol in its holster.

"You're right, you're not my peón. You have no right to be on my property. I banish you," he said. "If I ever see you on my land again, I will shoot you."

Behind Don Feliciano, Abuela's hands flew to her mouth. Nena was at her elbow, her face stricken, her mouth open in surprise.

There was nothing Abuela could do. But Nena could stand up to her father. Nena could step forward and intervene. If Nena were being treated this way, Néstor would have thrown himself in front of a charging bull. He had dismounted and put her on his own horse in the middle of a battle to make sure she was safe. He had faced a monster against whom guns were useless, placed himself between Nena and its machete-like claws.

But she hung back.

She stayed behind her father, her shoulders curled in. She said nothing to defend him. Nothing to confront Don Feliciano.

Néstor's heart folded in on itself. Perhaps Nena meant it when she said she wanted him to stay. She cared for him, he knew she did—he could taste it in the tears he kissed away from her cheeks. He could feel it in the way her mouth met his, in the way she clung to him.

But whatever she felt, it was not enough to speak now. Not enough to stand up to her father.

Not enough.

He had been stupid to believe otherwise. He had been blinded by the brilliance of her miraculous return to his life. By how desperately he wanted her love. How much he yearned for her to stand next to him on the patio of his dreams.

He was foolish, and now he would pay the price.

Don Feliciano stepped back from Néstor, breathing heavily.

"Get off my land," he barked. "Now."

Heart pounding, Néstor rose. His hands shook, but he kept his face stony and hard. He did not meet Abuela's eyes—he couldn't, not when her half-muffled sobs were all that filled the silence. He did not so much as look at Nena as he turned his back on them.

He turned his back on the patrón, on Nena, and on all of Los Ojuelos.

He strode to the corral.

28

NENA

WHEN THE PEOPLE of the rancho gathered for vespers that night, the whispers that ran through them like breezes in the tall grass were not about Papá. Not about the humiliating defeat that the Mexican forces had suffered in Matamoros, though that had been all the Serrano family could talk about throughout the long, stifling afternoon.

Néstor's name slipped through the gathered peones like a half-forgotten guest. It was passed from hand to hand, leaving a bitter taste in its wake. It slinked around Nena's ankles like a snake. *This is your fault*, it hissed.

All Nena could see as Papá led evening prayers were the suspicious looks the peones cast at him. They should be looking at her. Néstor did, when he rose from the ground slowly and deliberately. He had adjusted his shirt with an aggressive, dismissive gesture, his sharp jaw set, his eyes burning.

He turned his back on her.

She should have spoken. She should have done something more

to fix the situation, to diffuse the aggression between Papá and Néstor.

But when Papá shoved Néstor to the ground, her limbs turned to stone. Her body was practiced in the ways of avoiding Papá's anger: be still, be silent, and the storm will pass on. It was a protective impulse, like a hare going still. It was the right impulse, wasn't it?

Now she saw clearly. She watched the scene unfold in her mind, looping from the end back to the beginning like a colt circling the training corral. Coming upon Papá shouting.

Are you engaged to this man?

What? No, Papá.

Surprise spoke, not her wit. It didn't matter that there wasn't a formal understanding between them, words exchanged, rings promised. Papá was attacking Néstor and she should have done something to stop him.

Néstor was right. She was spineless.

And this was the result.

Casimiro and Beto stood at Bernabé's side, both rigid as soldiers. They left a conspicuous space between them, wide enough for a man. Abuela's absence gouged another wound among the people gathered.

Casimiro bore a long red cut down one side of his face that deepened his glower. His lips were unmoved by either prayer or celebratory response to Papá's impromptu return speech that thanked la Virgen for keeping the people of Los Ojuelos safe.

Casimiro was not alone. Surly defiance wove through the shoulders of even the eldest and quietest among the vaqueros. Their prodigal son had returned, grown and handsome and with a thousand colorful stories trailing after him like a peacock's tail.

And Papá had banished him.

Papá did not notice this sentiment among the men. Or if he did, he thought it beneath him to acknowledge it.

But some work harder, and others keep the profit. Papá was speaking, but Néstor's voice rang in her ears. If Néstor had harbored anger like that, who was to say it hadn't buried itself in the other vaqueros of Los Ojuelos?

Nena kept her head lowered in a show of piety, but snuck a quick look up at Papá. Weariness was evident in the lines of his face as he led prayers. In that moment, she saw not her father, but the patrón of the rancho. The man who kept a strict difference between his family and the peones. All the people gathered here: the vaqueros and the shepherds, the farriers, the farmers, their wives and children. Papá kept them under his thumb, in his debt, manipulating their wages like toys on a string. He kept them beholden to him. Beholden to the land that they could never call their own because it belonged to the patrón.

It was wrong.

And yet.

This was the way the world turned: the peones dispersed to the dusk and their tired jacales, the Serrano family retreated into their house of stone.

NENA AND FÉLIX sat next to each other at the table on the patio. Crickets filled the night with song as she unwound the bandages on Félix's wounded arm and placed a fresh poultice where the bullet had clipped him.

"It's a miracle it didn't hit your chest," Nena murmured as she put the cool, fragrant paste on his too-warm skin.

What if it had? What if Félix had not come home at all? The thought turned her mouth sour with dread. The Mexican generals had fled, leaving half their belongings in their wake. It was a humiliation, Papá said. But at least Félix had returned.

"I'm glad you're back," she said softly.

"It was doomed from the start," Félix said, his voice low. He stared off into the evening. A candle was lit on the table before them; it highlighted how like Mamá he looked from the side, with somber, hooded eyes and a pensive mouth. "The vast majority of soldiers were too poorly paid or trained to do anything but desert," he said. "Our government will be its own downfall for not looking after them the way it should. For not looking after us. It takes and takes but never offers us anything in return, not even protection." He hissed as Nena lifted his arm and began to wrap a clean bandage tightly around it. "We should be left to govern ourselves," he added through gritted teeth.

Nena raised her brows. "Now you sound like Antonio Canales." She had overheard many conversations among the more radical rancheros to this effect on the road to Matamoros.

"I sound like a lot of men." Félix's voice was always serious, but now it was fervent, though he kept it low enough that it could not be heard from inside the house. "This is our home. I want it to be safe. I want it to thrive. I want . . ." He sighed deeply. "I want it to be ours, forever."

But the prospect of separating from México meant more men she knew sent to fight and die, be it trampled by enemies' horses or shot or drowned while crossing rivers.

"I do too," Nena said. "But I don't want any more war. Or death."

"Papá shouldn't have allowed you to come," Félix said.

Perhaps not. But if she had not gone, how could she have discovered the cause of susto? Would she ever have allowed Néstor to speak to her?

Perhaps that, too, would have been for the better. The thought tasted bitter, drawing her mood low.

"I was doing my part to defend our home," she said softly. "Now I will do my part to defend it here."

"So you're going to marry Don Hortensio's son after all?" Félix wondered.

Nena avoided his eyes, focusing on tying off the bandage around his arm. Beyond her bargain with Papá, she had agreed to nothing. Mamá had not so much as even broached the subject since her return. She had seemed too angry to. But it could not be long before she did.

Félix tested his arm, raising and lowering it. He winced, a low hiss of discomfort slinking through his teeth.

"Convenient of you to be interested in marrying now, after the way you returned home," he said.

Nena snapped her head up, her mouth dropping open in surprise. That barb could have been plucked straight from Mamá's mouth. But coming from Félix? How it *stung*.

"If you're going to accuse me of something, come out and say it," she snapped.

"I would never accuse my sister on hearsay," Félix said, looking taken aback by her vitriol. "But . . . look, it was a dishonorable thing to do, traveling alone with a vaquero. You know that."

"Would you prefer I had done the journey alone and died?" Her voice shook as she fought to keep it down. There were still voices murmuring in la sala just on the other side of the door; the last thing she needed was a tía or one of her cousins to overhear this conversation. "Or stayed on the battlefield, and died at the hands of Rinches? He saved my life."

"And I am glad he did," Félix said. He took her hands; she snatched them back as if they had been burnt. "I am so grateful you are home and safe. But, Nena, this is the truth: the way you returned home casts doubt on your honor. On the family's honor. You'll have to marry very quickly before rumors start to spread to the neighbors, or . . ." He let the thought trail off as he rose, as if the damnation he implied was self-evident. "I have to speak to Papá about this banishment. We cannot have Bernabé and Casimiro angry with him like this. We cannot afford to lose them, not in times like these. But if he comes back, Nena . . . you must stay away from him. Think of what's best for the rancho."

He stood. Nena stared straight ahead, jaw set so hard it began to ache, as his footsteps crossed the patio. As the door creaked open and shut with a decisive click.

If Félix had yanked her from the back of a galloping horse, it would have hurt less to strike the ground. He had always taken her side in arguments with their parents. Had always spoken for her when she needed him to.

Now, she had no breath in her lungs as she stared at the closed door. No thoughts but this: she was alone. Whatever damage she had wrought by being unaccompanied with Néstor, she would not have Félix's voice on her side to fight for her.

THAT NIGHT SHE lay in bed, staring at the ceiling in the dark, her limbs as numb as if she had soaked in a cold spring for hours.

But her mind was a hive of angry bees.

How dare Félix say it was *convenient* that she was open to the prospect of marrying now. It wasn't convenient; it was that she didn't have a choice. Not only had she gambled with Papá and lost, she was now intimately acquainted with the dangers that the rancho faced. She knew those dangers even better than Félix and Mamá and Papá did: she poured salt at the doorway and windowsill before bed again, hushing Didi, Alejandra, and Javiera's questions. She rubbed her hand over her scar. She had thought so much about the prickling sensation in her skin and what it meant that she could no longer tell if she was imagining it or not.

They have been following us, Beto had said. *They have been waiting.*

And Néstor was alone in the dark somewhere, far from home. Did he have salt? Did he have enough of it?

It was her fault that he was alone in the darkness.

She had known every step of the journey back from Matamoros what waited at the gates of Los Ojuelos.

So why didn't she tell Néstor? She should have warned him. She should have behaved appropriately and enforced boundaries between them.

But she didn't. Instead, she leaned into his touch as if it were the only thing sustaining her. Being apart from him now was like nursing a splintered rib: every breath hurt.

What do you want?

She could already see her whole future unspooling before her: as a daughter-in-law in a new house, she would be thrust low in the pecking order. She would chafe every day at the commands coming from on high—instead of Mamá and the tías, it would be some faceless mother-in-law and a dozen women she had never met. Years, if not decades, would pass until she took up the mantle of being the master of her own household—and even then, there would be her husband's will to grapple with. Would she ever be the master of her own fate?

In that life? Never.

She had taken the ease of partnership with Néstor on the road for granted. She helped him saddle his mare when his arm was injured; every morning she woke to him checking her boots for scorpions. They hunted together, gathered nopal together, cooked together, rode together. She had been terrified and exhausted, but she felt present. She felt listened to. As if she were as important to the survival of their small party as he was. As if she were valuable.

Whereas the future that lay before her was already stifling. It had not yet even begun, but its pieces were already in motion. There was no choosing Néstor, because Néstor was gone. Because she had chosen not to speak up when Papá raged.

She *chose* this.

She turned roughly onto her stomach and shoved her face into her pillow, smothering her sharpening breathing. Beneath the pillow, she had hidden Néstor's pistol when Mamá ordered her to change back into decent clothing. It was hard against her cheek, even through the fabric. A vaquero alone in the chaparral was already low on defenses, but he had given it to her. He had trusted her with it because he trusted that she would watch his back as he did hers.

A sob rose in her throat, hot with shame.

She had made a choice. She had turned her back on him. She wouldn't get another chance to fix what she had done, to choose differently.

Even if Néstor could one day forgive her—and, judging from the hurt that burned in his eyes, that could be a long time away yet—he was gone. He wouldn't come back. Just as she said, he didn't have a steadfast bone in his body.

And neither did she.

Amid the talk of Yanquis and honor and her parents bearing down on her, she had caved. She was spineless. She was weak. And this was her reward: she would be trapped like a rodent in the ground all her life, kept from the air, kept from the light, voiceless and suffocating.

SHE MUST HAVE fallen into a restless sleep at some point in the night, for she woke with a start. All the candles she had left burning before bed were extinguished. Her sister and cousins slept on.

But when she saw the reason she woke, she knew they would not be asleep for long.

Pollo stood at the foot of Javiera's bed. His thin tail was raised, his hackles bristling in the moonlight from the window.

He barked ceaselessly.

A warning.

Nena stripped off her blankets.

Gunshots cracked in the distance.

She ducked out of instinct, hands flying up to her ears. Shouts rose across the rancho. Didi, Alejandra, and Javiera jerked upright with startled cries. Footsteps hammered through la casa mayor as other family members woke.

"It's Yanquis!" someone cried.

More gunshots split the night.

The dog kept barking. Snarling at the open window.

There might be Yanquis attacking the rancho. But Nena knew from the pain in her scar, prickling like a thousand needles, that there was also something much, much worse.

29

❧

NÉSTOR

NÉSTOR RODE HARD and rode west. The setting sun struck him with piercing rays; he lowered the brim of his hat, but did not stop. He had not stopped since he turned his back on Don Feliciano and Nena. His body moved as if commanded by another force, by the brute power of his anger. His hurt.

Nena had not spoken.

It was worse than a betrayal. Betrayal was a woman with whom he thought he had an understanding flirting with or pursuing another man. That had happened to him, and it had stung like horseflies. But he could sweep the feeling away like a horse swept away flies; with alcohol or work or another woman, it did not matter.

This was *Nena*.

Don Feliciano could say all he wanted about her marrying someone else, but for as long as Néstor lived, as long as he had breath in his body, he belonged to her. He thought of siestas in the shade beneath the huisaches, listening to her breathe in time with him as they fell asleep. Every one of her secrets whispered against his ear in the firelight at Nochebuena. The way she took him by the hand and led him into the chapel for school, defying her aunts and her mother.

He had relied on that defiance. It was as much a part of his image of her as her gestures or the dimple to the right of her mouth. But in the years he had been gone, that part of Nena died. Whatever flickers of it he had seen on the road were weak echoes of how she used to be.

For when he had held his hand out for help, for her to grasp him and pull him to his feet as he would her, she let him fall.

This was more profound than a simple betrayal. To her, he was not worth the effort of standing up to her father. He did not need her to declare her undying love for him on the spot and forfeit her family, no—all he wanted was for her to say something. *Anything.*

But she said nothing.

The message was resoundingly clear. He was not worth anything. He brought her home and she discarded him like a used rag.

Before he returned to Rancho Los Ojuelos and saw Nena, alive and breathing, he had never let his dream of the future into the light, never spoke a word of it. After losing his world on Rancho Dos Cruces and then Nena, he even feared looking at it himself. What if it bent and crumbled under the weight of his own regard, as if the reality of reflecting on it were too much for such a fragile thing to bear?

Then he saw her. It was as if someone had thrown the windows open and let in blinding morning sunlight. His dream, once stale and empty, was suddenly flush with movement and laughter. He knew who would stand on the patio waiting for him to return from the chaparral, whose hand he would take as he stepped into the shade.

Nena took that dream and crushed it beneath the heel of her boot. She could not stand up to Don Feliciano. If she cared for him, if she loved him as she had when they were children, it was not enough.

His vision blurred. His hand rose of its own accord from the reins to his face to rub his eyes, brush wetness from his cheeks. Luna, feeling the shift of his weight, slowed. The setting sun stabbed his vision; he grimaced.

He was riding west, alone.

He had once walked, alone.

He left.

Shame flushed through him like a blast of heat from the farrier's forge.

He halted Luna. His chest quickened as it rose and fell, each breath sharper, each more painful.

He left.

When he was a boy, he fled because he was afraid of Don Feliciano. He turned his back on Nena and ran because the patrón pointed at him and bellowed. If he had stayed . . . everything would have been different. If they had been side by side, perhaps Nena would have had the strength to learn to say no to her father. To stand up to the demands of her parents.

But he ran.

And he had run again.

You are a stain on her honor. If I ever see you on my land again, I will shoot you.

It was different this time—it was a voiced threat, explicit and spoken with a hand on the holster. But instead of keeping to his promise, he ran. Just as he had when he was a boy.

He left Nena.

She was Don Feliciano's daughter; his thunderous anger struck a primal chord in her as well. She had always been afraid of him as a girl. She was still afraid of him now.

When they faced the vampire in the jacal, she stayed at his back.

When he was paralyzed by fear, she handed him his pistol and curled his fingers around its handle. When he was flung to the ground, she defended him.

She was a brave woman. She could stand up to Don Feliciano, if he stood by her side.

They had survived thus far because they stayed together. They faced the demon head-on.

When faced with Don Feliciano, Néstor ran.

He had made the same mistake she had.

He lifted his eyes to the reddening sun.

He had once thought what they had was a fragile, perfect thing. It was neither. It was imperfect, yes. If a path to the future lay at their feet, it was pocked and marred with difficulties. But he could withstand it. If he bit down on his fear, if he fought hard enough for it, perhaps they both could withstand it.

For nine years, he had lived his life thinking Nena was dead. Now that he knew she was not, how could he let their mistakes divide them?

He clicked his tongue to Luna. Lifted his reins against her neck.

He put the sun to his back.

AND LATER, AS twilight grew dense, when he came across the corpse of a puma and Luna shied from its desiccated body—sucked dry as if by drought—he gathered his reins.

He bent toward Luna's neck and rode hard for Los Ojuelos.

30

NENA

CANDLES AND TORCHES filled the house beyond the girls' room with frantic, leaping light as Nena yanked on boots and snatched a sarape to throw over her nightdress. She grabbed Néstor's gun from beneath her pillow and strapped the holster over her hips. She prayed she did not have to use it as she strode into la sala with Javiera and the cousins, but it was a thin prayer at best. A weak, faithless thing that dissipated on the fear of the night like smoke.

If she had to, she would. She had to act as she had on the road with Néstor: she could not wait for orders from Mamá and Papá. If they did command her to do something, she might have to ignore them. She alone knew what the burning in her scar meant, and she knew what would have to be done to protect her family and the rancho.

La sala was a flurry of shirts and vests being pulled overhead as Papá, Félix, and the tíos threw on clothes and seized rifles. The sulfuric scent of gunpowder and shouts filled the air; a thunder of bootheels as they ran outside to join the other men of the rancho. Mamá and the tías were left gathered in la sala like a cluster of frightened hens.

"We should barricade the door with furniture," Nena said. Like water dropped in a hot pan of oil, they scattered across the room, the task filling them with purpose.

Nena walked directly to the kitchen.

"Where are you going?" Javiera followed hot on her heels.

The dog kept barking. He circled fruitlessly through Javiera's ankles, pointing his nose to any open window or door and snarling.

Nena went straight to where the knives were kept in the open-air kitchen. Cool night air shocked her skin. The fire was kept to embers overnight; they shone dully in the corner of her eye. Perhaps a fire would help keep the monsters at bay. But first: she had to arm herself and her family. She reached for the largest carving knives, the ones used for butchering pigs and beheading wild turkeys.

She took one knife and handed it to Javiera, handle first.

"I have a bad feeling," she said, raising her voice to be heard over Pollo's barking. And by feeling, she meant literally: the prickling sensation beneath her scar itched and burned like a rash. They were near. They had to be.

Javiera took the knife, a solemn determination settling in her slim shoulders. Didi and Alejandra hung in the doorway of the kitchen, watching Nena with alarmed expressions as she selected knives and handed them to her cousins. Next was the bag of salt. She grabbed it and began to drag it to the doorway.

"Didi, take this," she barked. "Make a line of it around the doorway like I did last night and then *stay back*."

Didi immediately followed her orders; Alejandra was her shadow in doing so.

Mamá appeared behind them, the ghostly white of her nightgown broken only by the long rope of her gray hair, still plaited for sleep.

"Girls, what are you—"

Then her eyes skipped past Nena to where the kitchen opened into the night. Her eyes bulged; her jaw dropped in shock.

Javiera's shriek split Nena's ears. She pointed into the night, beyond the kitchen fire.

So it began.

Nena inhaled deeply to steel herself and turned on her heel, jaw set, to face the vampire she knew waited beyond the kitchen.

A dark figure loomed in the night, rising from all fours to two legs.

She knew it would be there, yet seeing it juxtaposed with the familiar shadows of the kitchen sparked a fierce, protective anger in her chest. It flared bright, burning away any hesitation, any sensation of cool air or fear that raised the hairs on her arms.

It would *not* harm her home. It would not harm her sister.

Slowly, she reached to the table and took a knife, her eyes never leaving the vampire.

"Nena!" Javiera cried. "Get back!"

Motion whipped past her legs. A blur of yellow fur in the dark; a flash of white teeth. A horrific hiss as Pollo sank his teeth into the monster's leg.

The vampire raised its arm to swipe at the dog with its dark, gore-stained claws.

Nena surged forward, sweat-slicked hands gripping the butcher knife.

This vampire was smaller in stature than the one that had attacked her and Néstor in the jacal. Moreover, its attention was directed down, at the dog that ripped into its leg. It looked up at Nena—a flash of teeth, a burst of its hot, carrion-heavy breath— only in the final moment before she swung the knife.

She brought the cleaver down with all her strength. Metal met flesh and ground against bone.

Then Nena stumbled forward. She caught herself before she tripped, still clutching the knife.

Ash fell around her onto the ground. On Pollo, who looked around in confusion. His snout was splattered with blood; flecks of ash stuck to the dark liquid. All that remained of the vampire.

"Nena!"

Nena turned, heart pounding, toward Mamá. Mamá's eyes were platter wide, her nostrils flaring like a spooked horse as she made the sign of the cross. Didi, Alejandra, and Javiera hung by her side, their faces wan and shocked. The knives in their pale-knuckled grips shook.

"What in God's name was that?" Mamá breathed.

What was the quickest way to explain?

"El Cuco," Nena said, gasping for air as she readjusted her grip on the knife. "Or one of them, rather. Salt!" she barked at Didi.

"*One of?*" Didi yelped as she passed a jícara cup of salt to Nena, her voice pitching toward panic. She grabbed another cup and began following Nena's example in making a thick band of salt around the perimeter of the kitchen, enclosing the fire and where the knives were stored. In the distance, gunfire cracked. Nena shied away from the sound, her teeth clashing against one another painfully.

"You mean there are more?" Javiera asked.

"*Are* there more?" Mamá asked, her voice laying over Javiera's with authority, even as it trembled from shock.

Pollo began to bark, snarling from somewhere around the vicinity of Nena's ankles.

"There!" Javiera shrieked, pointing again.

The scar on her neck erupted with the crawling legs of a thousand insects. Nena turned. Beyond the kitchen fire, a gray form prowled on four legs. It paced back and forth, watching her. The vampire crept forward, briefly like a deer in its timidity, and examined the barrier of salt.

It drew back with a start, lifted its head to Nena, and released a virulent hiss.

Nena clutched the handle of the knife, its worn curves digging into her palm. She was angry too. Yanquis were attacking her home. And, if her theory was correct, Yanquis had whipped this creature into a frenzy and released it on her home with a singular intent: to kill. To sweep through the rancho like a plague, draining it of life. Clearing it for the taking.

She thought of the vampires in chains by the river, how agonizing their shrieks were.

A beast could not change its nature. Coyotes were born to scavenge. Pumas would stalk and kill the youngest and weakest of a herd, for they had to eat. Vultures would always circle, not caring if they fed on man or beast.

This creature, whether it was made by God's hand or the Devil's, whether it was born of its own foul will in the shadows of the chaparral, would feed as it had been born to feed.

That alone did not make it evil.

The vampire rose onto its hind legs, baring its long, curved teeth. Dark flecks of rotting flesh wedged between incisors. Nena locked her eyes on its skull, on the delicate flesh where eyes should be. Her scar burned with the searing intensity of the vampire's attention.

She bared her teeth back.

"I don't want to hurt you," she said. Her voice shook violently, but she meant it. The screech of the chained vampires by the river had cut to her marrow. "But I *will* defend myself. I will defend my family." She raised the knife for emphasis. "Leave my land, and I will not hurt you."

She kept her gaze level at the monster, never blinking, firm and aggressive. It stared back for a long moment. A distinct sensation slipped under her skin: it was weighing her as a threat, as a predator of equal might.

It dropped to all fours, turned its back on the kitchen, and loped into the darkness.

It had . . . *listened* to her.

Was it intelligent enough to comprehend her speech? Did it register the defensive stance of her body, the salt and the raised weapon, and decide that attacking was not worth the trouble?

Or was there something in the burning scar that linked them, that revealed her intent? She knew when their attention was on her; did they, too, sense the force of her will back?

She lowered the knife. Her hands shook.

Whatever the truth was, it had worked. Relief flushed her body like a bucket of cold water.

She turned to Mamá. "Put salt at every entrance into this house," she said. Her mouth was dry; her voice cracked. "If there is enough, surround the patio with it. It drives them back."

"Like the stories," Javiera breathed.

Abuela's stories. Nena's attention snapped to the Duarte jacal.

A soft orange glow brightened the night. Someone's jacal had been lit on fire. Beto was on the patio of the Duarte jacal, pistol in hand. Horse whinnies pierced the night; gunfire and the spark of gunpowder echoed close to the jacales. Too close. Abuela would not be safe there.

"Beto!" Nena cried. She whistled, then waved her hand at him, staying behind the salt barrier. "Bring Abuela here!"

He saluted her, then disappeared into the jacal. He emerged with Abuela on his back, clinging to his neck as if she were a child, and began to sprint toward la casa mayor.

Nena ducked as gunfire pocked the night. Tías inside the house shrieked at the sound.

Beto stumbled into the kitchen, taking care to step over the protective line of salt. Abuela slipped from his back into Didi's waiting arms.

"What's happening?" Nena asked Beto as Didi and Alejandra brought Abuela inside la casa mayor's thick stone walls.

"It could be worse," he said, his breathing labored. Sweat shone on his face and darkened his shirt. "There are some thirty Yanquis, about half of them Rinches. Even with our wounded from Matamoros, it's about an even match. But . . ." He took a swift draft from the flask at his hip, then shook his head fiercely. Nena crinkled her nose at the harsh scent of aguardiente. "But Casimiro said there's a group of them by the tree line," he said. "About twelve. In chains. Just . . . waiting."

"Those aren't Yanquis," Nena said.

They were weapons.

A plan began to fall into place in her head. With tormented vampires waiting to be unleashed, the people of Los Ojuelos were grotesquely outnumbered.

But without them?

They stood a chance.

"Beto, I need you to listen closely." She pulled her sarape from around her shoulders and handed it to Javiera. She needed to be able to run unimpeded, and it was too heavy, too unwieldy. "I think . . . You know how your scar hurts when they are watching? I think because of that, they are able to understand us."

Someone had lit candles in the house behind her. Light revealed when Beto's brows raised toward his hairline in disbelief.

"I know it sounds crazy," she said, bending to tighten the laces on her boots. "When one came up to the salt, I told it that I did not want to hurt it, but that if it did not leave, I would. And it *left*."

He watched her as she moved quickly about the kitchen, a tempest of activity. Bullets were loaded into her pistol. Gunpowder spilled over the toes of her boots as she loaded the gun with shaking hands. She filled a small bag with salt and fastened it to her holster by its drawstrings. Finally, she took a knife from the wall and handed it to Beto.

"You need to look them in the eye when you say it, all right?" she said. "Well, where the eyes should be."

Beto stared back at her, apprehension drawing his brows together. He had realized that she was leaving him to guard la casa mayor, and judging from the upward tilt of his chin in understanding, he was not happy about it.

"And where do you think you're going?" he accused.

"Trust me," she said. "Be careful. And if you ever see Néstor again . . ." She steeled herself. "Tell him I love him."

Beto's eyes widened; his mouth dropped open. He held out his hands, as if to say *whoa* and steady a spooked horse and keep it from bolting. To keep *her* from bolting.

"No," he said flatly. "No way, kid. If it's that dangerous, you should stay, and I—"

She turned on her heel and leaped over the line of salt. She set her sights on the tree line and ran.

31

NENA

NENA PEELED THROUGH the night, Néstor's gun bouncing in its holster against her hip with each step. For a moment, she heard nothing but her own harsh breathing. The song of crickets thickening the night.

Then, as she turned around the other side of la casa mayor, there were cries and the clash of metal on metal; a horse's panicked whinny. Shouting in Spanish and in English. Saltpeter stung her nose as gun smoke thickened the air.

Every time she heard a gunshot, she ducked, fists clamped over her ears. Visions of dead men from the battlefield flitted behind her eyelids, spilling dread into her belly. Papá and Félix had escaped the battle mostly unscathed, but only tragedy could come of fighting at such close quarters in the dark.

She swallowed hard and kept running. Some men ran past her, from the jacales toward where the fight was thickest, brandishing machetes and the occasional rifle.

A figure on horseback loped near them, brandishing a broad machete for clearing chaparral.

Her heart leaped to her mouth. It couldn't be. She slowed her run, squinting through the night, praying it was who she thought and not a trick of the darkness.

After a week of riding behind that very figure, she knew exactly who it was.

"Go for the neck!" Néstor cried to the men around him. Then he turned, and spurred his mare into a gallop toward a monster that had a limp vaquero in its arms. A lasso appeared in his left hand, looping as fast as a whip as he bore down on the monster.

He flung the lasso; it sang through the air like a bullet, landing squarely over the head and narrow shoulders of the vampire. Néstor sat back in the saddle and yanked the rope tight.

The vampire reared back on its hind legs with a shrill, surprised cry, dropping the man it held. It pawed at the rope with its claws, but Néstor was already upon it, machete in hand.

He leaned out of the saddle and beheaded the monster in one swift stroke, as if it were no more difficult than clearing a path for cattle in the chaparral.

The vampire turned to ash, dissipating in the night like smoke.

"See?" Néstor roared over his shoulder, turning his mare sharply to avoid trampling the vampire's victim. "Someone get this man to safety!"

Then he galloped off into the fray, toward where the danger was most immediate. Where he was most likely to be injured, or worse.

The sooner she carried out her plan, the sooner this would all be over.

She inhaled deeply and took off at a run again, dodging the men who headed toward the battle, her breath coming in ragged gasps.

There was a torch lit where Casimiro said he had seen a group of what he thought were men waiting, by the darkness of the tree line. Near the path that led to the springs.

From afar, moving at speed, a quick glance did make it seem as if those forms were men crouched on the ground, waiting for something.

But as she drew closer, as she caught winks of torchlight glinting off metal, she knew she had found her quarry.

She moved off the main path, onto the rocky ground behind a small cluster of old oaks, and considered her strategy.

One Rinche guarded the shackled beasts. His eyes were fixed on the fray, even as he patrolled around the monsters.

Behind them were the trees that shrouded the springs from view. If she went into the trees and came upon the vampires from behind, she could evade him. It would take longer than coming at the vampires head-on. If she wanted speed, she could charge forward from where she was.

Secrecy would cost her time, and she did not know how long her plan would take. But if she charged the vampires head-on, the Rinche could easily see and shoot her.

She flexed her fingers, loosening her grip on the knife. Her heart throbbed against the bones of her chest, rebelling against the idea of approaching the vampires on purpose. She hoped the knife would be enough. That the small bag of salt on her hip was enough. She had to go. Time was wasting.

On the count of three, she would change direction and sprint for the tree line for a more sheltered approach.

One.

The Rinche guarding the vampires started forward toward the fray. He lifted his pistol and aimed.

She traced the line of his sight. His pistol was pointed directly at a vaquero wielding a lasso and a machete on a black mare.

Two.

She passed the knife to her left hand and reached for the pistol at her hip. She hesitated. Was it too far to try and shoot? What if she missed? Néstor was not far—what if her bullet swung wide and harmed him instead?

The Rinche cocked his gun. The click resonated in her bones.

Three.

She seized a rock from near her feet and bolted forward from the oaks. Her skirts swished, her legs pumped as she devoured the distance between her and the man.

"¡Oye, Rinche!" she screamed, so loud it ripped her throat. "¡Cara de chinche!"

The man's gun lowered a hair.

Nena dug her heels in, took aim, and flung the rock at him as hard as she could.

It hit his shoulder. He shuddered in surprise, then whirled, gun glinting in the torchlight, searching for who had thrown it. Nena was already on the move. She dived toward the vampires, thighs burning, lungs aching for air.

Her scar flushed with prickling pain as their attention swung toward her. Now she knew why something in their profiles had seemed off, making it look as if they had noses: they were muzzled. Their ankles were tied together with thick ropes; their necks bore the heavy metal collars, locked with padlocks.

That presented a problem.

But it also presented a solution.

With the vampires muzzled, Nena did not hesitate to rush up to the side of the group and duck behind their arched backs and long, lowered necks, using them as a barrier between her and the Rinche.

She heard her own breath. Her pulse in her ears.

The metallic curl of claws into rocky soil. The flutter of thin, batlike ears. The musty smell of skin, of wild beasts. Their soft, wheezing breathing.

If she were to close her eyes, she imagined their breathing would not seem so different from a horse's.

But she kept her eyes peeled. For she heard solid footsteps coming toward her, accompanied by a metallic jingle.

Did the Rinche have keys? If he was the one in charge of releasing the vampires, his keys would unlock all of their collars, would they not?

The footsteps stopped.

Nena's fear spiked.

She dared to lean her head forward slightly, to gaze through the long, muscular gray legs and heavy chains.

Torchlight gleamed on the round belly of the gun in the Rinche's hand.

Over dinner on the road to Matamoros, Félix had told her to avoid the Rinches at all costs: in addition to grudges and an unusually high tolerance for cruelty, he said that they carried pistols with six bullets in their chambers, new inventions called *revolvers*.

This Rinche had one.

Nena had Néstor's pistol. It was loaded, but he had the rest of the bullets.

She had one shot.

The metallic ring of keys. A shadow passed over Nena.

She looked up.

The Rinche looked down the barrel of his pistol at her.

He had straw-colored hair and a mustache that matched. It caught her attention; held it, even as her pulse thrummed in her ears, even as every muscle in her body shrieked in panic.

He was aiming directly at her forehead.

She flung herself sideways. A bullet whizzed behind her. A

strangled, shrill cry seared the night: the bullet had clipped or struck one of the vampires.

She was on her feet, Néstor's pistol in her hand, Néstor's voice soft against her ear. *Angle your body away.* She cocked the pistol. *Inhale, then aim. Exhale and—*

The kickback of the gun wrenched her arm and flung her backward.

A man's scream echoed through her skull as she collided with soft skin, with a bony shoulder. She yelped and shied away from it, disgust metallic in her mouth at the velvety sensation of the vampire's flesh. When she righted herself, she searched the night for the man.

He was down.

She needed those keys. She needed them *now.*

She darted around the front of the group of vampires, ignoring how the prickling of interest in her scar filled her with the sick, helpless feeling of being prey.

Torchlight illuminated the straw-haired Rinche: his hip was wet and dark. He could not rise. He was shouting, screaming at her; it was as incomprehensible to her as the shrieks of the vampires.

She scanned his body for keys. Found them at his waist, attached to a belt that went over his blue uniform. They were splattered with blood.

She set the knife and Néstor's now-useless pistol down and crept toward the Rinche.

He writhed as she walked toward him, as she bent and reached for where the keys were attached to his belt. His pain was obvious, palpable.

She did this.

She, who wanted to become like Abuela, someone who healed wounds and did not cause them. *She* caused him this pain.

Nausea flashed up her throat. Her fingers faltered.

A flash of a hand; her head snapped backward. Pain shot up the back of her neck, searing her scalp.

"¡Puta, tú!" the Rinche screamed in broken Spanish as he pulled her back by the hair. "¡Puta!"

Quietly, barely audible above the man's screaming that bludgeoned her skull, a voice in her mind calmly concluded that if she survived this, she wanted to cut off her damn hair.

Then she reached for the pouch of salt at her hip, tied next to her holster.

She seized a fistful and flung it in his eyes.

He released her hair, screaming anew as he pawed at his face.

Salt worked against all monsters, it seemed.

She seized the keys from his belt and then flung herself back from his reaching hands.

Her boot collided with the revolver, which had fallen to the grass when she shot him.

She picked it up, latched the safety, and put it in her holster. Then she retrieved the knife, shut her ears to the Rinche's shouting. It would surely bring others running. She had only minutes.

She inhaled deeply to steady herself and turned to the vampires, her scar throbbing dully.

They watched her intently, still as only predators could be. The air buzzed with their interest, as if she were standing next to an agitated wasp nest.

Casimiro's numbers were off: there were only six of them, but that alone was enough to ravage a rancho the size of Los Ojuelos. They shifted their weight from foot to foot as she walked toward them, her heartbeat thick in her throat. Their breathing was so much like that of horses: as they inhaled, their ribs popped out like the guts of an accordion.

They were starving. Their hunger would drive them to attack.

Would this work?

She had no choice but to try.

She approached one at the front of the group. This close, it looked remarkably like a bat. Its nostrils were long and slender and lined with delicate, petallike folds; its ears of paper-thin flesh were shot through with narrow purple veins.

Its skull had eye sockets; where eyes might be, thin gray skin, lined with delicate veins, stretched precariously over the hollows.

"I don't want to hurt you," she said.

Her scar pulsed with fresh pain. She inhaled sharply.

Was it listening? It *had* to be listening.

"If I let you go," she said. "You leave." She pointed at the tree line. "Leave my home."

Her heart pounded against her throat, hard and fleshy and panicked to be so near the vampire. This could be the most foolhardy thing she had ever done. This could be suicide.

The vampire lowered its head. A hum reverberated through Nena's chest, so strong she felt it drumming against her bones. So strong she could almost hear it.

Madre Santa, let that be a yes. Please let that be agreement.

Palms slick with sweat, she took the knife and crouched down to the monster's ankles. She sawed through the ropes binding all four of its legs, then yanked the loose rope away.

She lurched backward, out of the range of its claws.

The vampire did not move to grab her. It simply watched.

It waited.

It waited for her to draw near again, watching as she shifted the metal circle of keys to her right hand and the knife to her left. Waited for her to fumble with clammy fingers for the correct key.

She stepped close and slid the key into the heavy metal padlock that locked the collar. Close enough to the vampire's head that when its ear twitched, it brushed her cheek, soft as a moth's wing.

She turned the key. The padlock slipped open.

Beneath the collar, the vampire's pulse fluttered rapidly against its throat.

Was it afraid too?

She slid the padlock away from the collar. With a soft click, the collar came undone and fell on the monster's shoulders. It was heavy; she would need both hands to remove it. Taking a steeling breath, she tossed the knife next to her feet, close enough that she could snatch it out of the grass if she needed it, and lifted the metal collar from the vampire's neck.

She flung it aside. It fell to the ground with a resounding clank.

The vampire was still muzzled. It could run, it could bolt, but it waited.

It lowered its head before her as if it were bowing, low enough that it was level with her stomach.

The muzzle was fastened with a buckle on the back of its skull. This was what kept it from killing the Rinches who had brought it here. The thin, delicate skin of the beast's head was scabbed and blackened; beneath the leather strap, open sores wept in the torchlight.

With gentle hands, she reached for the buckle.

Santa Madre, protect me, she prayed. *If you know anything about these monsters, protect me.* This was the moment she would learn if her plan would work or if she would never see another sunrise.

"I'm not going to hurt you," she repeated. "Please, do not hurt me."

Fingers trembling, she undid the buckle. Took a strap in each hand and lifted the muzzle off the vampire's face.

She took a step back, muzzle in hand.

The vampire raised its head. Two fangs, long as a panther's incisors, extended over its lower lip. These caught the torchlight, bright as silver, as it lifted its head and sniffed the air.

Then it turned its attention toward Nena.

For a long moment, nothing happened. Her heart pounded; her scar throbbed.

A series of high-pitched clicking noises came forth from the vampire's skull, so sharp Nena wanted to cover her ears. The others raised their heads and echoed the first vampire's call.

The first vampire shook out its shoulders, stepped around Nena, and took off at a gentle lope.

It turned toward the dark line of trees and vanished into the night.

It was gone.

And when she turned to look at the remaining five vampires, when she saw their agitation, the way they watched the tree line with expressions she thought might have been hopeful, she picked up her knife.

They would follow the first. She felt it in her gut.

She made quick work of releasing the next four. They were still and patient as she sawed rope and fumbled the keys, as she tossed collars and muzzles to the ground. One even gave her a gentle, almost affectionate shove of its shoulder before it loped away into the night.

The final vampire shifted its weight from foot to foot, making agitated clicking noises.

"I know, I know," she muttered as she fumbled with the keys. Her palms were sore and blistering from sawing through thick rope with a swiftly dulling kitchen knife; her eyes strained in the low light, stinging from the gun smoke on the air and the dying torch. "Almost."

She was so absorbed in her work that she did not hear footsteps approaching behind her. Not as she heaved the last collar off the vampire and tossed it to the side with aching arms.

Not as she reached up and fumbled with the buckle of the last muzzle.

This time, when the final vampire shook its head, at last free of the muzzle, something was different.

It retreated quickly, its movements sharp and aggressive. Fear spiked in the back of her head, where her spine met her skull, as the vampire rose onto its hind legs and flung its arms out wide.

Her knife. Where was her knife? She had grown lazy in tossing it aside; she had not thought to mark where it landed. She could not drop and paw around for it now, not when the vampire hissed and bared its too-many teeth.

She reached to her side for the salt. She fumbled on the drawstrings with shaking hands.

The vampire lifted one arm and brought it down in a long, fierce swipe.

It struck Nena.

It flung her to the side as if she weighed no more than a rag doll.

The heavens spun around her. Breath cracked out of her lungs as she struck the ground.

32

﹏﹏

NÉSTOR

"*THERE WERE MORE* by the trees," Casimiro shouted, gathering his reins. Both he and his horse were out of breath, their ribs heaving. "We should run them off too."

Néstor turned Luna to the east, toward the path that led to the springs, searching the night for Yanquis.

One figure rose, shook its head vigorously from side to side, and dropped to all fours before loping toward the trees.

Those were not men at the tree line.

There was another figure, smaller than the first, with a white skirt and two swinging dark braids.

His world stilled.

It had been full night when he returned to Los Ojuelos. The orange burn of torches from the road sent his heart to his throat and his spurs into Luna's sides—every one of his nightmares about the burning of Dos Cruces began this way, with flames and smoke on the horizon. And this was how the nightmare of an attack on

Los Ojuelos began: his breath coming short as he cantered down a shortcut to the central rancho, branches stinging his face. But he was not a child. He had a gun at his hip and a machete and heels to dig into the dirt as he faced down the land thieves. He had the ability to warn the others so they would not be taken unawares, not how his father and the Dos Cruces vaqueros had been. As soon as he passed the first of the workers' jacales, he began shouting to rouse the sleeping rancho.

"Yanquis!" he cried, lifting a hand to his lips to whistle, signaling that they were in danger.

Then he made straight for la casa mayor. Gunshots pocked the air already; shouting rose from the edges of the rancho. He slowed Luna to a trot—should he check on Nena or join the shouting vaqueros who cut off the Yanquis at the main road? From a distance, he saw figures in la casa mayor's kitchen: a group of young women in white nightgowns, one of whom was laying a boundary of salt around the entrances.

Nena.

She would be safe behind that boundary. Safe within the confines of the house, which would certainly be the focus of the men's protective efforts.

Or so he had thought.

That figure in the white skirt had to be Nena.

He gathered his reins and spurred Luna to a gallop, leaning low over her mane. They devoured the distance between him and Nena. Through Luna's ears, as he squinted against the darkness, shapes began to move.

A Rinche stood where he had not seen one before, a long knife held in one hand. He limped toward Nena's turned back.

A vampire rose on its hind legs before Nena, long teeth bared.

A threat before her, a threat at her back.

He had not reloaded his pistol, but he had the machete in one hand. That was all he needed. He needed to get between Nena and what faced her. He needed to be at her side to defend her.

"Come on," he urged Luna through gritted teeth, even as she lowered her head and galloped as hard as her tired legs could carry her, sweat frothing on her neck and withers. Her hoofbeats thundered in pace with his heart.

His breath caught as the vampire raised one long, clawed hand before Nena. She was backing up . . . directly into the path of the Rinche with the knife.

"Nena!" he cried. "Behind!"

But he was too late.

The vampire brought its arm down with swift, fatal accuracy, knocking Nena off her feet. She went flying and collapsed in the dirt.

She did not stir.

No. *No.*

The vampire ignored her fallen form and lurched forward, claws outstretched. A strangled scream split the night as it seized the Rinche, lifting the man's body into the air and sinking its teeth into his neck.

He was close enough now to see a dark veil of blood spray the vampire's face, to see the creature's ribs contract and expand with gluttonous abandon as it sucked the life from its prey.

He looked away, mouth souring with nausea. He was nearly at Nena. He sat back in the saddle to slow Luna and lifted a hand to his lips to whistle to the others: three sharp notes that to anyone on Los Ojuelos were an unambiguous cry for help.

He threw himself from the saddle, searching for Nena in the grass.

White skirts, their hem filthy.

A limp hand among the rocks.

Nena.

He collapsed to his knees at her side.

Her face was peaceful, her eyes closed as if she were sleeping.

"Nena." His voice cracked. *"Nena."*

She did not move.

A thump to his left. He leaped to his feet, positioning himself between Nena and the vampire, machete at the ready. His eyes peeled wide and searching in the night. His heart thrashed against his ribs, waiting for the vampire to turn to him, waiting for it to bare its teeth and—

The vampire had dropped its prey in the dirt. Without so much as a glance at Néstor, it fell to all fours and ran to the tree line.

It took several breaths for him to realize it was gone. To realize the arms that held the machete at the ready shook violently. To realize that his mare had bolted, and that he was utterly alone.

He dropped the machete and turned to Nena, falling to his knees. He put two fingers to the soft skin of her throat, searching for a pulse. His hands shook too hard. He could not find it. He lay his head on her chest, listening past the pulse throbbing in his skull for Nena's heartbeat.

A soft beat echoed in her chest. Followed by another.

Relief stung his eyes, sudden and hot and wet.

He straightened. Tried to whistle for help a second time. But his breath came in ragged gasps; a sob broke against his fingers instead.

He inhaled deeply. Fighting and failing to steady himself.

"Stay with me," he whispered. He slipped one arm under her torso, the other beneath her knees, and lifted, grunting from the effort.

Pain seared his left shoulder. It fanned through him, burning dully as he stumbled forward. His bad knee ached when he caught himself and shifted Nena's dead weight in his arms.

Her head lolled back.

"Stay with me," he forced through gritted teeth.

He stepped forward.

He carried Nena down the same path he had walked when he was thirteen, toward the smudge of light in the distance that was la casa mayor.

The last scattered gunshots of the battle faded behind him. Night erased years; memories bled between each faltering footstep, each crunch of pebbly dirt beneath his boots.

Nena bleeding from the neck, slumped against him. Her head lolling into his; her cheek cold to the touch.

Nena now, limp in his arms as a dead calf. Her eyes closed, her lips slightly parted. Her braids swinging with each step.

His heart throbbed from the effort of carrying her. His lungs were desperate for air, more air, for he could not draw enough in.

His left shoulder throbbed. His legs burned. His breathing pulled irregular and sharp.

He could not lose her again. He would not survive it.

"Stay with me." It was a prayer, a litany, the one plea that kept him breathing. Kept him moving forward. He would never again leave her. Never again run when he was afraid. She was his home.

The lights of la casa mayor grew brighter; torches streaked the night with flame. They slid across his vision, bleeding into the night like oil. He stumbled forward. Another step, another.

Voices carried toward him. His name, then Nena's. A high-pitched voice calling for his abuela.

A figure appeared at his shoulder.

"Madre Santa," Beto breathed. "Let me help you."

Néstor shook his head, unable to form words. Beto hovered at his side, a half step behind, as he stepped onto the patio. Into the blazing light of torches.

There were people on the patio; their faces blurred as he made for the doorway of la casa mayor.

Doña Mercedes filled it. A hand rose to her lips; she stepped to the side and beckoned to Néstor, inviting him into the house.

For the first time in his life, Néstor stepped through the doorway of la casa mayor, angling Nena carefully so as to protect her head. His legs shook as he lowered her to the floor of la sala; they gave out, and he fell to his knees, cradling Nena's head to protect it as he lay her on the rug.

When his hand came away, it was bright with blood.

One of her arms was scored with claw marks; the sleeve of her nightgown shredded and soaked with blood. It gleamed mockingly up at him in the candlelight.

He was thirteen, staring at Nena, covered in blood, lying on the floor of this very room.

No. He had watched from the doorway, paralyzed by fear. Now he was here at her side, taking a cloth someone pushed into his hands and pressing it against the bleeding to staunch it. Even as his hands trembled. Even as it continued to be difficult to draw breath; his chest hitched, his vision blurred. Distantly, he was aware that people hovered around them, smelling of blood and gun smoke and kitchen fire. He didn't care. His eyes were on Nena.

She lay still.

"Everyone back away." Abuela knelt at his side and put a hand on his arm. "You too, mijo. Enough to let me see."

Néstor released the bloodied rag he held to Nena's wounds; Abuela clicked her tongue.

"Keep the pressure on," she said, and began to check Nena's pulse.

Nena's sister, Javiera, broke through the blur of people. Falling to her knees across from Néstor and Abuela. Her cheeks were flushed; her chest rose and fell as if she had been running. She held out a small bag to Abuela, who took it.

Everything Abuela did was even and measured; her calm diffused through the room like incense smoke. The scent of rosemary steadied him as Abuela pulled herbs from the bag and began to murmur prayers over Nena.

"Call her back," Abuela said to him.

Néstor looked up at her, confused. She had never once asked him to help heal someone. This had to be a mistake. His job was to fetch things or send for people and then back away, to stand in the corner silently, out of sight and out of her way.

"You heard me," Abuela said. "Call for her."

He looked down at Nena. At the scatter of freckles that stood stark on her nose and cheeks drained of color. At her slim brows, her dark lashes. The mouth that relaxed as if she were sleeping. He wanted to see it smile again, for the dimple that hid to its right to wink at him. For her voice to call for him. To chide him or insult him or say sweet things to him, it didn't matter—he wanted it all.

"Come back to me, Nena," he whispered. "Come back."

33

NENA

VOICES SWIRLED OVERHEAD, looping and diving like bats swooping through the black. The darkness thinned.

She was aware she lay on her back. She was aware, somehow, that she was no longer outside—perhaps it was the smell of the kitchen, the rustle of clothing around her.

She shifted. Pain laced through her skull, bright as a bolt of lightning.

Oh, how she longed for oblivion to wash over her again.

"Come back to me, Nena."

Her heart stumbled in surprise at the voice.

Her eyes snapped open. She searched for him; found him immediately. He knelt at her left side. His hat was gone, his hair sweaty and pushed away from his face. Tears cut tracks down his dirt-streaked cheeks, fresh and wet. He was crying, even as relief broke across his features like a sunrise.

She wanted to hold him. To cradle his face and comfort him, to croon that it would all be all right. To bury her face in his chest and let oblivion sweep over her again.

She tried to sit up.

A sharp scolding noise halted her. Abuela sat beside Néstor, a bundle of rosemary in one hand, a stern expression on her face.

"Be still, Nenita," Néstor said softly. "You're bleeding."

"Her head is what I'm worried about," Abuela said. "Thank la Virgen she didn't strike her temple."

"You left," Nena said to Néstor. Words flowed from her mind to her lips like water from a jug. There was no stopping them. No barrier of hesitation between thinking and speaking.

"I'm sorry," he said, voice low. "I shouldn't have. I should have been braver."

"No, I said all the wrong things," she said. "I didn't say enough. It's my fault."

She sat up, pushing with her right arm. Stars erupted across her vision, sharp as gunshots.

"Magdalena!" Abuela scolded. "Lie back down."

She ignored her. She slipped her arm over Néstor's shoulder and buried her face in his neck. He smelled like sweat and gunpowder, but beneath it all, she smelled him. The only other person's scent she knew like that of her own skin. For a moment he was stiff, as if unsure of how to respond; then he relaxed. The palm of his left hand rested on her back, holding her close.

You must find a way to heal yourself from it, Abuela had once said when she declared that Nena's aura was wounded. *Can't you sense how it confines you?*

Néstor's disappearance had planted the seeds of fears that grew feral and wild through her ribs. Fears that if she was not obedient or perfect enough, those she loved would vanish with their love or snatch it away, leaving her empty and aching. For years, they had trapped her.

She had hoped against hope that she could have a second chance to choose him. Now here he was. And if she said the right words, perhaps he would stay.

His right hand still pressed against her arm. It ached. Something was wrong with it. She couldn't bring herself to care.

"I'm so sorry," she murmured. "I love you."

He held her tighter. Spoke into her hair. "You know I love you."

"So marry me," she murmured.

A breathy, surprised laugh brushed against her ear. "Is that a proposal?"

"It is if you say yes."

"Of course." His voice cracked. He rubbed her back gently. "Of course."

She never wanted to open her eyes. She wanted to lay in the crook of his shoulder forever, listening to his heartbeat.

"Madre de Dios, there's a cut on the back of your head too," Abuela said, clicking her tongue again with displeasure. "At least elevate her arm, Néstor."

It was as if Abuela's voice shattered the barrier of quiet between them and the rest of the room. Rustling voices rose in a hum around them, rhythmic and gossipy as chicharras.

Then they stopped.

In the silence, Papá's boots rang against the floor.

Nena stiffened. She released Néstor and, as Néstor raised her wounded arm as instructed, she turned to look up at Papá. Mamá stood just behind him.

He stood over them, glowering down at Néstor.

"What did I tell you?" he said to Néstor.

"Not another word," Nena snapped, shifting so she sat between Néstor and Papá. "He stays."

"He will not," Papá said.

"Then I won't either," Nena snapped.

Mamá's hand flew to her mouth, her expression stricken.

A tremor of surprise rippled swiftly through the room. It ended in Nena. Its touch was like that of freezing water: it sank into her skin, down to her belly.

Los Ojuelos was the land that raised her, that cradled her in its streams and shadows, that grew with her through seasons of drought and seasons of plenty.

She would give it up.

For *home* was this person behind her. The one who pressed on her wounded arm to stop the bleeding. Who had returned despite her father's anger and her mother's disapproval. Who had shown her time and time again that he loved her. He spirited her out of danger on the battlefield. He snuck to la casa mayor in the middle of the night when they were children to leave gifts and notes on her windowsill. He teased laughter from her even when the night closed dark and threatening around them.

He came back.

If she let him leave again, if she failed him again, she would never feel whole. It was that simple.

"If he leaves, I go with him," Nena said, raising her voice so that everyone could hear. Her voice rang with something that sounded like confidence; it belied the tremor in her hands. The way each intake of breath shook. "If he stays, then I stay."

"But Magdalena," Mamá said. Her voice was sharp, close to cracking, but her expression betrayed sincere concern. Blood was smeared on the skirts of her dress, as if she had been binding wounds. She looked close to shattering from the events of the night. "What will people say?"

"I don't know," Nena said. "Maybe they will care. Maybe they won't. But if you want this rancho to be strong, then keep us. Keep us all together." She inhaled deeply, looking around the room at her sister and brother, her cousins and her tías. Their nightclothes were covered in dirt and splattered with blood. Her heart ached at the thought of leaving them. "We don't stand a chance against our enemies if we are separated. The only way to defend this rancho is to stay together."

She looked at her parents, her heart beating like a trapped bird's. Staring them down was worse than looking in the face of the first vampire, wondering what might happen when she loosened its muzzle and bared its teeth to the night.

But this time, she was not alone.

Néstor rested his free hand against the small of her back.

When Papá opened his mouth to speak, Nena cut him off.

"I know, Papá. I know rich allies could help," she said. "But there will be other ways to win them. Can't you see we are already strong? Don't alienate the strength that is already here, with the people who are already here. Don't drive them away. Don't drive me away."

"Magdalena," Papá said, his face falling.

"I've made my choice," Nena said, holding firm. "Now you make yours."

34

⮜⮞

NENA

Diciembre 1846

THE NIGHT OF the Los Ojuelos Nochebuena celebration, Nena sat on the sidelines of the dancing by her parents, watching as Didi and Alejandra were spun around the dance floor by different young men, faces shining with laughter in the light of the bonfires.

She relished their joy. Lately, the shoulders of everyone on Los Ojuelos had been heavy with worry. Matamoros fell. The Yanqui army fought on; Anglo settlers and cattle rustlers crept south, closer and closer to Río Bravo. The Mexican government did nothing to stop them. Canales and other politicians—Félix included—began strategizing about independence from México, for how could las Villas del Norte defend themselves if they continued to be ruled by a government that did not care if they were overrun by Anglos?

Rancheros and politicians argued; the war raged on.

Didi and Alejandra shouted at each other over the music, carefree as mesteñas galloping across a plain. Tonight, her cousins would collapse in the girls' bedroom with curls fighting to be free of their careful hairstyles and wispy hairs stuck to their sweaty faces, grinning and gossiping and keeping Javiera awake well into the night. Nena felt a prick of longing in her breast—she actually missed having to shush Didi and Alejandra as they all went to bed and how crabby Javiera was the next morning. She slept elsewhere these days.

The song stopped; applause rippled through the dancers. As the chief violinist struck the first notes of the next song, a young man approached Nena. He greeted her parents with a broad smile, shaking Papá's hand and nodding politely to Mamá.

It was a sight that Nena used to think she would never see.

When one of the itinerant priests of las Villas del Norte appeared on Los Ojuelos in the midst of summer, people packed into the chapel that very evening, still in their work clothes: Abuela, Bernabé, Casimiro. Beto, who had elected to stay and help Néstor build a jacal and a corral on his newly purchased land. Every other vaquero who was not in the chaparral. Félix and Javiera, Didi and Alejandra.

When Nena and Néstor said their vows, her parents were not there.

The only sign Don Feliciano was thawing was the gift, several months later, of a portion of Los Ojuelos land that adjoined Néstor's land. The gift included part of a quarry. The same quarry from which Nena's ancestors had taken the stones to build la casa mayor of Los Ojuelos.

Mamá had braced for gossip from other rancheros' wives; with bitter relief, she reported that war and loss dominated conversations among the notables of las Villas del Norte. The marriage of Don Feliciano's daughter to a vaquero was rarely mentioned.

Day by day, step by step, bridges mended. Hands of peace were extended, and accepted.

Nena rose to greet Néstor, smoothing her skirt. The fabric was redder than fruta guadalupana—it was a deep, scandalous red.

One of the tías had raised her eyebrows disapprovingly and whispered behind a hand that it was too reminiscent of blood.

"May I have this dance?"

He was dressed as he had been when he returned to Los Ojuelos and turned her world on its head: in his Sunday best, polished like a silver coin. His smile was sharp; it gleamed in the light of the bonfire, its angle playful. Perhaps a little wicked.

"I suppose so," she said, taking Néstor's hand and allowing herself to be swept away. Soon she was laughing as loudly as Didi or Alejandra as he spun her through the dancers. His hands were warm and firm; though she wore no shawl, she did not feel cold. Winter air could not touch them; nothing in the world could touch them here.

A FEW DAYS after Nochebuena, Nena left her and Néstor's jacal at dawn. Cold crystallized her breath into gray mist; she drew her sarape tight around her shoulders against the damp as she walked down the path to the stream for water. She had noticed a patch of yarrow near the stream bank; a cloth bag bounced against her hip as she walked, empty and waiting to be filled.

She hummed to herself as she walked; when she turned the last bend, her tune slowed, then died.

A telltale tremor rippled under the scar on her neck. She paused at the edge of the stream, pulse quickening.

Across the rushing water, a vampire rose on its hind legs, disturbing ribbons of mist. Its skin was so like the gray of the morning that it could have been a ghost. Around its neck was a rough scar, as if a rope had burned its skin with friction, or metal had blistered the flesh in the sun.

They gazed silently at each other for a long moment.

The vampire's nostrils flared.

Then it dropped to all fours, turned, and vanished into the mist. Nena stared after it, her heart pounding.

Had it recognized her?

She retraced her steps quickly to the jacal. Voices rose from the corral; they grew louder as she approached, rising in greeting. They had come to their ranchito for the promise of good wages and never being beholden to unfair debts. Some brought women with them, and one, a child too. They were the first of the people who would make this land—Rancho Las Flores, a name chosen by Nena for its abundance of wildflowers—a home.

Néstor was saddling Luna. Alongside him were about eight other men: some were from Los Ojuelos, others were strangers to Nena, acquaintances of Néstor's from his days on the road.

Néstor turned, took her by the waist, and gave her a lingering kiss. His lips were warm against the December chill.

They ignored Casimiro's suggestive whistle and Beto's call for them to hurry up.

"I saw one, at the stream," Nena said when they drew apart. "Be careful."

"Always." He gave her one last swift kiss, then mounted. "I'll be back at noon."

At noon, they would ride together to Los Ojuelos. Abuela had sent word that one of the vaqueros' wives was due to deliver any day now, and she needed Nena on hand.

She watched the men disappear into the mist, tightening her sarape around her shoulders.

The war continued in the south. Danger prowled around their home, persistent and hungry.

But every night, she and Néstor laid salt at the threshold. They had protected their home once, and would do so again.

Beyond the corral, beyond her house, the world slumbered. In time, winter would lessen its grip. Ice would melt from the springs that gave Los Ojuelos its name. Néstor would carve stones from the quarry for their casa de sillar; Nena would sink her hands into new soil behind the kitchen, planting seeds from Abuela's herb garden.

And when the earth thawed, they would stand with shovels in hand on the land that he had bought. Together, they would break ground on the foundation of what would become their own house.

Perhaps, if they dug deep enough, they might find Spanish silver.

AUTHOR'S NOTE

Flocks of vampires, in the guise of men, came and scattered themselves in the settlements . . . Many of you have been robbed of your property, incarcerated, chased, murdered, and hunted like wild beasts, because your labor was fruitful, and because your industry excited the wild avarice which led them.

—Juan Nepomuceno "Cheno" Cortina (1824–1894)

In the summer of 2021, I sat at my mother's dining room table, leafing through the books she had used to write her master's thesis. I had been fiddling with a novel idea involving vampires in nineteenth-century México, but I was dissatisfied. I fretted that the supernatural element felt shoehorned in. Then I came across this November 1859 proclamation by Juan Nepomuceno Cortina to the Mexican inhabitants of the state of Texas.

It reached up from the page and seized me by the throat.

Vampires. I was dumbstruck. 1859 was decades before the publications of *Carmilla* and *Dracula* took Europe by storm. Decades before Friedrich Engels wrote of the "vampire property-holding class" or Karl Marx's repeated images of capital as a vampire. Decades and thousands of miles away.

And yet.

Vampires.

It burrowed under my skin. *Vampires* was what Cortina had chosen to call the Anglo settlers who stole the land, cattle, and even the lives of Mexicans living in what is now South Texas.

Why vampires?

VAMPIRES OF EL NORTE used to be a very different book. I was initially inspired by tales of tlahuelpuchis, or bloodsucking witches, but I began to wander toward an incarnation of the vampire that was more monstrous. More beastly. At the encouragement of my editor, the idea wound its way to South Texas, where my mother's family has had roots for generations.

There, it bolted away from me.

Second books notoriously resist domestication. Editing *Vampires of El Norte* took its tithe of blood, sweat, and tears. Brainstorming and first drafting, however, was a wholly different experience: it felt like being swept away by a galloping horse. The characters chattered loudly in my head, their voices crisp and bright and effortless to pin to paper. The setting unfolded beneath my fingertips, settling into shape like a well-worn map. There were times I reflected that it felt like writing fan fiction. Times where I felt as if I were channeling a force beyond myself as I chased the colors of a Texas sunset or the smell of my grandparents' backyard in the spring.

I think this is because I wrote this book for my family. For every time one of us has been asked variations of the question *when did your family come to this country?*

As a young person, I struggled to answer. My grandfather came to Texas in the 1940s, and my grandmother's mother during the Mexican Revolution, but the rest of my grandmother's family? The Rio Grande Valley is a pocket of the world where the border has moved more often than the people living there.

I have realized that the answer is, in fact, a question itself. A question that became the heart of this book.

When did this country come to *us?*

IN THE MIDDLE of revising *Vampires of El Norte*, I successfully defended my PhD dissertation. Seven years spent in the ivory tower means that I will always write with an historian's eye, but I happily acknowledge that I now use history as the servant of story. I admit that elements of South Texas's tumultuous 1830s and 1840s have had their edges buffed or reflections altered to best support a tale of romance and monsters that lurk in the dark.

That said, half the fun of historical fiction is weaving in the true details that make a place feel lived in. My mother and aunt helped plant the trees around Rancho Los Ojuelos. They darkened the skies with storms and filled the air with the sounds of cicadas and chachalacas and javelinas in the bush. But what about the clothes that people wore in the 1840s? What kind of food did they eat?

Texts that aided me greatly in this undertaking include "A Trip to Texas in 1828" by José María Sánchez, translated by Carlos E. Castañeda; *Tejano Empire: Life on the South Texas Ranchos* by Andrés Tijerina, *Their Lives, Their Wills: Women in the Borderlands, 1750–1846* by Amy M. Porter; and *De León, a Tejano Family History* by Ana Carolina Castillo Crimm. I often referred to discussions of susto and recovering from traumatic events in *Woman Who Glows in the Dark: A Curandera Reveals Traditional Aztec Secrets of Physical and Spiritual Health* by Elena Avila and *Curanderismo Soul Retrieval: Ancient Shamanic Wisdom to Restore the Sacred Energy of the Soul* by Erika Buenaflor. I encourage readers to seek out these and other texts written by Chicano and Tejano historians, curanderos, and folklorists.

I owe an incredible debt to the work of Jovita González, the oft overlooked Tejana folklorist. She is the author of *Dew on the Thorn, Life Along the Border: A Landmark Tejana Thesis* and the posthumously published *Caballero*, a monumental work of historical fiction that was deeply influential on early drafts of *Vampires of El Norte*. González's *The Woman Who Lost Her Soul and Other Stories* is also where I first encountered tales of buried Spanish treasure and the trickster hero Pedro de Urdemañas.

Folklore and oral history played an important role in nineteenth- and early twentieth-century vaquero culture, and thus in *Vampires of El Norte*, but also in my own family. I will forever cherish the hours I have spent at my grandparents' kitchen table, listening to them share stories of their childhoods and relatives. Because of them, my work is full of family legends and ghosts, the cadences of their jokes, and their musings on the past.

Their voices breathe between every sentence of this book. There will come a time when I no longer get to hear those voices, but it is my hope that they will echo forever in the imaginations and hearts of my readers.

ACKNOWLEDGMENTS

I wrote this book in New York City; Victoria, B.C.; Austin; Chicago; Paris; London; and while tucked away in the peaceful woods of Seabeck, Washington. I wrote it on planes and trains and ferries. I wrote it in between chapters of my PhD dissertation. I wrote it exhausted. I wrote it while sick. I wrote it while crying with frustration. On my aunt's couch. On my mom's couch. At my grandparents' kitchen table. In my in-laws' dining room. This book carried me from one chapter of my life into another, both of us kicking and screaming the whole way. I extend my most sincere and tearful thanks to the village who believed in this book long before I ever did.

First and foremost, Kari Sutherland: the best advocate of my writing and career that I could ever ask for. And Jen Monroe, whose sharp eye saw the shape of this book from afar and helped shepherd it into existence. What would I do without you two?

I thank the indomitable marketing and publicity teams at Berkley for their passion, diligence, and excitement for both *The Hacienda* and *Vampires of El Norte*, especially Lauren Burnstein, Tina

Joell, Craig Burke, and the incomparable Jessica Mangicaro. I also thank the publishing team, especially Claire Zion and Jeanne-Marie Hudson, for their support and enthusiasm for my writing. I must also raise a glass to the art team and cover designers for their gorgeous work—it never fails to thrill and delight me how silly sketches of mine become gorgeous map graphics and how beautifully typeset pages and stunning covers alike can bring me to tears. Your work means the world to me.

I surely would have lost my mind while writing this book without my Clarion West 2018 classmates B. Pladek, N. Theodoridou, and Ewen Ma; the sidesplittingly hilarious Berkley debut group (aka the Berkletes); and the writers I have had the immense fortune of becoming friends with and receiving support and advice from on this bumpy publishing ride, especially Hannah Whitten, Tanvi Berwah, and Shannon Chakraborty. Thank you all so much for your wisdom and brilliant, inspirational spirits.

To my University of Chicago support system, without whom I would have never made it out alive with a doctorate clutched in one white-knuckled fist: Sam, Annie, Kyle, Mohsin, Betül, and Sarah L., but especially my adviser, Hakan Karateke, whose patience and encouragement as I drafted this book in between writing chapters of my dissertation I never took for granted. Teşekkür ederim, hocam.

I am deeply indebted to Jeanne Cavelos for being so flexible as tight publishing deadlines and unexpected life hiccups interrupted my time at the Odyssey Writing Workshop, but also for feedback and wisdom that made this book better and fills me with confidence and joy as I face down future books (and the challenges they may bring). I am a changed writer (and pre-writer, and reviser, and reader) thanks to you and to Odyssey. I also thank Scott H. Andrews for thorough feedback and sharp insight on the opening of this novel.

I thank my friends for cheering me on as I wrote, but especially

Kara, Debbie, Christine, and Liam for early reads and enthusiasm. You mean the world to me.

This was the most difficult book I have ever written, yet at the same time, the characters and setting came to me with an ease and clarity that left me slightly suspicious. But then I remember that I wrote it because of my family, for my family, and could not have written it without my family. I thank Aunt Rori for providing space in her home to write, for descriptions of weather and flora in the Valley, and for delicious food and chats over top-shelf zinfandel. I thank my mom, not just for discussions of the Valley, for her history books, and for allowing me to read her thesis, "Un Lugar Intermedio: A Place In Between" (MA Dartmouth College, 2014), but for wisdom and endless support. I thank my grandparents, Elvira Cañas and Arnulfo Flores, for telling me stories about their pasts and their families while I sat at their kitchen table, drinking it all in. I thank the rest of my loud, beloved, outrageously funny family for not just their support, but for being a constant source of storytelling inspiration. I would do anything to make y'all laugh (and squeal with fear!) while reading my books.

I thank my in-laws Mary, Michael, and Alison for cheering me through fast-drafting and exhausting revisions and for reminding me to celebrate every milestone. You are shelter when the going gets rough. I love you all.

Thank you, Honore, my dear violence adviser, for dislocating Néstor's shoulder. Thank you, Aurora, for teaching Nena how to aim a gun. (I promise the next book will be less scary. I might be crossing my fingers.) Thank you, Javi, for lending your name and for starring alongside Pollo. You all keep me humble and enrich my soul.

And finally, Rob—my story doctor, my pillar, my rock. You are the reason I could tackle one more chapter each night and are the heart of every story I write. I could not do this without you.